KU-167-934

PALE HORSE
RIDING

Chris Petit has written a trio of acclaimed "beyond black" political thrillers covering a serial killer operating in sectarian Northern Ireland (*The Psalm Killer*); dirty money in World War II (*The Human Pool*); and terror, arms trading and the bombing of a civilian aircraft (*The Passenger*); as well as *The Butchers of Berlin* which also features the characters Schlegel and Morgen. He is an internationally renowned filmmaker.

PALE HORSE RIDING

CHRIS PETIT

SIMON &
SCHUSTER

London · New York · Sydney · Toronto · New Delhi

A CBS COMPANY

First published in Great Britain by Simon & Schuster UK Ltd, 2017
A CBS COMPANY

Copyright © Chris Petit, 2017

This book is copyright under the Berne Convention.
No reproduction without permission.
® and © 1997 Simon & Schuster, Inc. All rights reserved.

The right of Chris Petit to be identified as author of this work
has been asserted in accordance with sections 77 and 78 of
the Copyright, Designs and Patents Act, 1988.

1 3 5 7 9 10 8 6 4 2

Simon & Schuster UK Ltd
1st Floor
222 Gray's Inn Road
London WC1X 8HB

www.simonandschuster.co.uk

Simon & Schuster Australia, Sydney
Simon & Schuster India, New Delhi

A CIP catalogue record for this book
is available from the British Library

Hardback ISBN: 978-1-4711-4344-1
Trade Paperback ISBN: 978-1-4711-4345-8
eBook ISBN: 978-1-4711-4846-0

This book is a work of fiction. Names, characters, places and
incidents are either a product of the author's imagination or are
used fictitiously. Any resemblance to actual people living or
dead, events or locales is entirely coincidental.

Printed and bound by CPI Group (UK) Ltd, Croydon, CR0 4YY

MIX
Paper from
responsible sources
FSC
www.fsc.org   FSC® C020471

Simon & Schuster UK Ltd are committed to sourcing paper
that is made from wood grown in sustainable forests and support the Forest
Stewardship Council, the leading international forest certification organisation.
Our books displaying the FSC logo are printed on FSC certified paper.

And I looked, and behold, a pale horse! And its rider's name was Death, and Hades followed him.

(Book of Revelation, 6:8)

When life arises and flows along artificial channels rather than normal ones, and when its growth depends not so much on natural and economic conditions as on the theories and arbitrary behaviour of individuals, then it is forced to accept these circumstances as essential and inevitable, and these circumstances acting on an artificial life assume the aspects of laws.

(Anton Chekhov,
The Island of Sakhalin)

Whatever Germans build turns into barracks.

(Erich Kästner, *Going to the Dogs:
The Story of a Moralist*)

I

The commandant rode the white mare drunk. These dawn rides happened most days, hanging on for dear life, still plastered from the night before.

The endless paperwork taken home took until past midnight, drinking all the while, followed by more drink, smoking and the gramophone, in the futile hope of relaxing. Most nights he collapsed on the couch or the floor.

He showered before riding and changed into a fresh uniform; standards to maintain. He left through the garden gate in the wall that led directly into the garrison. That morning he staggered more than usual on his way up the main street to the stables. The clean smell of the stalls, dry hay and the compact aroma of horse manure never failed to reassure, compared to the general stink.

The mare stood patiently as he clumsily saddled her. He could have got someone else, except he didn't want to see anyone and didn't wish to be seen in an unfit state.

The mare's shoes sparked on the cobbles as he rode out into the last of the night. Usually their ring was a first sign to sober up, prelude to the gallop to come, close to 50kph, shaking the drink out of him. Some days he was too drunk to saddle up and rode bareback. Lately he had taken to using the western saddle, with its long stirrup and exquisitely tooled leatherwork, given as a birthday gift so he could think of himself as riding the range. That morning the western had been too heavy to lift and he took the ordinary saddle.

At the gate the guard raised the barrier. The commandant didn't return the salute and kicked the mare into a trot. After the river, he spurred her and rode fast through misted countryside, close to the mare's neck, anticipating the transition from drunkenness to clarity. It was the reason to drink, but too often now he experienced none of the pleasure of the blur of animal grace, the magnificence of the beast beneath him, pounding speed, sky, weather and landscape. Instead everything he had been drinking to forget came crashing down.

Once, half-blinded by a hailstorm, he had achieved a glimpse of what he considered the equivalent to sainted revelation. His anointed task took on a sense of divine mission – as others more elevated than he must see it – rather than the usual endless, uphill struggle.

He spurred the mare on, leaning forward, using the whip, mesmerised by the ground rush beneath, mud kicked up. Racing through shallow water, it splashed his face. Let the mare decide their course. She fancied to have a mind of her own that morning and they could have ridden on forever, away and away. As she raced like a beast possessed, his stomach rebelled at the previous night's drink and he turned his head and spewed, watching silver spittle and vomit taken off in the slipstream. Done now, catharsis achieved. For a delicious moment he thought of nothing. Forgot about his wife, her coldness, and his hopeless infatuation for her seamstress that ran through him like a dark river. Forgot about the colossal difficulties of the job, the endless feuding, the cretins he had to carry out his orders, dross that mocked any notion of elite, the daily mountains of paperwork, impossible logistics, disease, squalor, and an unsympathetic superior command that issued no helpful or clear instructions, interpreting only in terms of what he could not have, what was not available, answering every complaint by telling him it was his to solve as he saw fit. Nine days a week would not be enough to accomplish half what needed to be done. He had never dreamed he would preside over something of which he was so secretly ashamed.

He had no mind to go back, but duty called. He slowed to a trot, became aware of the bedewed morning and cloudless sky above the mist.

He saw himself from a heavenly standpoint, a creature lost.

He recalled hair-raising bareback rides and how such moments of solitary risk, in which he entrusted his safety to the mare, provided the only pleasure in life. First light. Every day a brand-new morning. Wildness of thought drove him where others saw only the obtuse bureaucrat. The sun pierced the horizon. He must have had a skinful. Usually one stiff gallop was enough to clear the head. He breathed deep and surveyed the land: paradise lost, his bitter thought. Not his fault it had turned out that way. His kingdom still; vanity perhaps to think of it as that but he had forged it with his bare hands, through the power of his will. Did anyone thank him now for managing the arsehole of the world?

He wept at his dedication, reduced to the administrative equivalent of janitorial duties.

The bell-jar of intrigue. His world on the point of penetration. The constant threat of outside interference. Unthinkable!

He stared at the rising sun, returned its merciless gaze. In the white inferno a darker shape appeared to hover, he could not make out what, but it spooked the mare, causing her to rear. Her frenzy spun him and the world spun too.

She gave a bellow of fright, more human than animal. As he felt himself start to fall, he saw the shape was familiar, not something he ever expected to see in his lifetime even with all the terrible things he had witnessed.

He lay spread on the ground, arms outstretched. His brain felt loose in its pan. His body shook, the mare's terror transmitted; she, docile now, grazing to one side.

He staggered up, shaken, and stumbled to the mare. Already he doubted what he had seen, but his visions in drink had hitherto revealed nothing like that. He feared he might be spiritual after all, however bitterly he fought against it, feared too the priests were right, saying give them the child for its first seven years and it was theirs for life. For all his fanatical dedication, he remained susceptible to the lapsed state.

Blinded by the light, he told himself. If he was so afraid of what he had seen why did he not look back to have his fear confirmed?

The commandant watched the garrison doctor with his medical bag and shiny boots crossing the lawn. He had told him to take the short cut through the garden. Just a quick check nothing was broken. A tall man, he thought sourly, a careerist, seduced by the elegance of the uniform, who likened membership to that of a good club. The commandant's patience was tested by this new breed of soft-soapers that hesitated before knocking.

He answered the door himself, in shirtsleeves, braces hanging. He took the doctor through to his study. The doctor rubbed his hands as though it were chilly.

Arms raised, fingers and toes waggled, head turned from side to side, collarbones checked, a stethoscope produced,

4

blood pressure taken. The doctor's hands were clammy and the commandant understood why he had rubbed them.

No mention of what he had seen, or thought he had seen. *Delirium tremens*; would the doctor tell him that? No mention either of the black spots that still danced before his eyes. He wished he could confess he was on the verge of nervous collapse, however unthinkable. He'd had to go right to the top to get his medical history removed from the military record. His greatest fear was that *they* – for all his friends in high places – would stop at nothing to get rid of him. It was his camp; he its creator, however foul and broken-backed, the ugly child he was bound to love. He knew himself well enough to say: I may not be clever but I am smart enough to know this place would be nothing without me and I nothing without it.

The doctor lectured the commandant on high blood pressure, correct diet, alcohol intake and lack of exercise.

The commandant protested he had just fallen off his horse. What was riding if not exercise? As for drinking, they all drank like fish and smoked like chimneys, except no one said that any more. Three cigarettes smoked during the consultation, stubbed out in the wrought-iron ashtray made for him by prisoners, as had the rest of the furniture, including the huge desk, in whose locked drawer he kept his schnapps. He thought better of offering the doctor one, knowing he didn't drink, as an excuse to help himself.

The doctor told him to rest as much as he could.

'With my workload!'

The house sounded busy. Sometimes the commandant felt he could barely move for girls sewing away, in the attic and downstairs too, maids running around, cooks, nannies, gardeners, shoe cleaners, not to mention the regular service orderly. His wife employed beyond the point of generosity. He asked the doctor if he wanted a cup of anything, thinking the answer would be indicative of whether the visit had an ulterior motive. The doctor asked for tea. The commandant, on guard, rang the bell on his desk and a skivvy hurried in with an awkward bob and a curtsey.

While they waited to be served the doctor made a show of admiring the furniture, particularly the desk whose entire surface was covered with family photographs, held in place by a sheet of Plexiglass whose size alone was a statement of his powers of acquisition.

The commandant suspected the doctor was fishing. He was having his house done and no furniture was available in store. Everything that could be confiscated had been. To have it made you needed connections the doctor could only dream of.

'I could get you an appointment with Erich Groenke.'

The doctor had heard stories about the man's legendary capabilities. He suspected the offer was a bribe, disguised as a favour.

The commandant said, 'Big Erich has access to designers with swatches of material, from which garrison wives choose their curtains.'

At home the doctor had a single camp bed, a wooden chair and an improvised table. His architect had taken months to come up with the piping for the plumbing, and the promised taps, due weeks ago, were still in mysterious transit; and the place was supposed to be nearly ready for his wife and children to move in.

The maid returned.

'This is good tea!' exclaimed the commandant, as though it was an exception to be served the best. He had taken off his shirt for the doctor's inspection and not put it back on.

He slurped his tea, holding the saucer under the cup. A cigarette burned in the ashtray.

They were interrupted by the commandant's wife. The doctor stood, took her hand and made to kiss it but restricted himself to a bow. She smelled overpoweringly of violets.

The commandant suspected she fancied the doctor for his gentleman's manners.

Strange woman, the doctor thought. Her main expression with him was a fixed grin. Stately in manner if not appearance, she dressed down in styles too young for her, including white ankle socks. Such dowdiness was at variance with her main interest, which he knew was fashion. She made a point of false modesty and charitable works, was keen on culture, which her husband was not. She was off that evening to Kattowice to see the Vienna State Opera perform with Elisabeth Höngen.

The commandant continued to sit in his vest, dragging on another cigarette. The doctor counted six in the ashtray. The commandant said to his wife, 'The doctor is having trouble finding furniture. I suggest he talks to Big Erich.'

They discussed the matter until the commandant asked his wife, 'Shall you be staying in Kattowice?'

'It gets late otherwise. There's talk of dinner with Höngen and Böhm.' Böhm was conducting. The doctor considered her far more socially assured than her husband.

'Talking of furnishing,' she said, and went to the door and called upstairs, then told her husband to put his shirt on.

They were joined by a young woman, who stood on the threshold, eyes downcast, demeanour modest. For all that, there was no denying her beauty. The commandant was staring.

'The most exquisite seamstress,' announced his wife. 'She

has already made the most wonderful tapestry. You must commission one for when your wife comes.'

The commandant continued to gawp. His wife told the young woman to fetch a sample.

They waited in silence. The sound of a vacuum cleaner came from the next room.

The commandant's wife eventually said to the doctor, 'Next time we have a social you must come.'

She turned away before he could answer and announced the young woman's return. The tapestry was of a mill.

'It's called "Autumn Landscape".'

The doctor made polite noises. It was ghastly and he was a long way from needing anything like it. Compared to his standard of living, the commandant's was luxurious, frivolous even, if his wife could employ people to produce such inessentials.

The commandant looked on proudly. 'Exquisite,' he said, which earned him a look from his wife.

The doctor addressed the young woman. 'Yes, I should like you to make us something once I have the house in a more presentable state for such fine craftsmanship as yours.'

How awkward he sounded. The seamstress bowed her head. The doctor was aware of the commandant glaring with what he was astonished to realise was jealousy.

The women left together. The vacuum cleaner was in the hall now. The doctor smelled furniture polish, a relief after the cloying perfume. He wondered whether the woman was having an affair. Nearly everyone was. The commandant was clearly smitten by the seamstress, and the doctor wondered if that could be used against him somehow, except he was not one to whom intrigue came naturally. Nor was the commandant, he suspected, but he had swum in murky waters for so long.

Before leaving, the doctor drew himself to his full height and formally restated his case.

'May I bring to your attention again that the garrison security police's opposition to my reforms involves criminal acts. I officially request – again – that an outside judicial commission come in to review and end these despicable practices.'

'Yes, yes,' the commandant said testily.

'A prosecuting judge has gone into a garrison near Weimar—'

'Enough!' said the commandant. 'You have just told me to get plenty of rest.' He smirked. 'Go and see Erich,' he said, picking up the telephone.

Erich Groenke did not look like a convicted rapist, though the garrison doctor had no idea what one should look like. Don't let him bore you, the commandant had said. 'He likes to go on but get him on your side and he will do anything for you.'

The leather factory, which Groenke ran, stood between the garrison and the station, in a restricted area, a mixture of staff quarters and commercial buildings, including the dairy and garrison abattoir, and the grocery store which the doctor had never been inside because his Polish skiv fetched what little he needed.

Groenke wore a corduroy jacket with lots of pockets, a leather waistcoat and fine boots which he pointed out he had made himself. He was considered one of the camp's success stories, the reformed lag, one of the original gang of thirty – tough jailbirds hand-selected by the commandant to come from home to crack Polish heads and get the place on its feet.

9

'Not easy when you are bottom of everyone's list. The Old Man was always complaining they would give a refugee camp more.'

The doctor could see he was expected to ask what methods existed for advancing work on his house. Groenke implied that access to the pharmacy was a potential point of discussion, but the doctor refused to be drawn. He wasn't entirely naïve.

He left empty-handed; almost. Everyone had a dog, Groenke said; man's best friend and that. The doctor's children would not be able to resist. The dam was a Belgian shepherd and the doctor would get first pick of the litter. The cost struck him as exorbitant and he said he was hard up. Groenke dropped his price and the doctor realised it was more a test of his negotiating skills, and he probably hadn't heard the last of the pharmacy.

Perhaps a dog would not be so bad. He missed the lack of affection. Garrison men made themselves out to be tough. Social occasions were brittle. The women were as bad as the men when it came to drink. No one seemed much interested in their children. He had heard of parties where couples paired up and went off together.

He constantly reminded his wife in his letters that her love and support were of inestimable value. He tried to keep the tone breezy – he wrote most days – but it was hard to find cheerful news. He knew she read the letters to the children and had to find coded ways of expressing his physical longing. He took an optimistic view on the progress on the house. He made no mention of the ghastly stench and wondered how she would cope. At least she would never have to see the state of the prisoner infirmaries or conditions in the new camp.

That morning the Polish girl produced a plate of bread

with chopped egg and gherkin and stood waiting to see what he made of it. He was in the middle of writing but too polite to refuse. 'Good,' he said, making a show of appreciation.

She was a plain, bold creature. He had given her some cream for her acne and it seemed to make no difference to her skin or their awkward relationship. He knew he gave her too little to do. She cleaned his boots and shoes, not well enough for him not to have to do them again, and did shopping and housework and took his laundry and dry-cleaning to the outlet in the garrison, which meant she didn't have to wash or iron.

He continued to write while eating. 'Still I remain in good spirits, as do we all. The job we have is not easy as I keep telling you, my angel. We try and perform a humane task but half of it is trying to educate everyone into keeping proper records. Seeing themselves as pioneers, living on "the wild frontier", they are impatient of what they call bumph, and see the likes of me as fusspots. I sit in our new house picturing our future, you sitting here (and lying with me upstairs) and the children running around (or asleep!). As for anyone who tried to take away my house, my happiness or my beloved, I would bash in his skull!'

She had written back more than once sensing he was under great strain. Wanting to avoid misunderstanding, he added, 'I am not serious, of course, but you know what I mean. There is much to be done in teaching people about eliminating disease. For all the attention they pay, I might as well be up the Limpopo River 150 years ago! But I reserve my greatest frustration for your absence and count the days.'

He signed off, adding all his love ('and more') and looked at his desperately unfinished surroundings. The novelty of camping had long worn off and he was tired of the hotel where he kept a room to retain a degree of personal hygiene.

Yet most of the rest lived in acceptable accommodation, some little short of luxurious. He could try the housing office, he supposed, and insist on being put at the top of the list, or make a proper effort with Groenke, who probably had private access to furnished apartments more than suitable for his needs. Or they could camp out and make an adventure of it, doing the place up bit by bit.

Something the doctor had managed to scrounge was a stove. Winter was coming. The house had no chimney, being designed for central heating – yet to be installed, of course – but he thought it would be possible to put a flue in to take away the fumes even if he had to smash the hole in the wall himself.

After an irritable, restless morning, the commandant returned home for lunch; his every passage through the garden gate an entry into a different world where the doting father lavished affection on his children, in contrast to the stone mask he had to wear for work. He went in through the kitchen where the staff ate lunches prepared by his wife with her own hands. Why, he couldn't understand. He had told her they had servants for that.

The seamstress wasn't eating with the rest that day; he could hardly ask where she was. He recited to himself: 'Thy neck is like the tower of David builded for an armoury, whereon there hang a thousand bucklers, all shields of mighty men. Thy two breasts are like two young roes that are twins, which feed among the lilies. Until the day break, and the shadows flee away, I will get me to the mountain of myrrh, and to the hill of frankincense. Thou art all fair, my love; there is no spot in thee.'

He felt compelled to cut his lunch short and ride out again. He hurried to the stables and took the western saddle.

He and Groenke, who sometimes rode with him, were Karl May fans. Oh, to be cowboys, they lamented, eating around the campfire and sleeping under the stars.

He saw a distant work gang walking down the railway line in direct contravention of the bulletin his office had issued the previous week. The only other movement was a blur, half a kilometre away, which he supposed was the garrison psychiatrist on his fancy racing bike.

A garrison shrink! What were things coming to? The way it had always worked with anyone on the wobble was a couple of stiff drinks and being told to act like a man. Never had he thought that his world would include a shrink on a bike! Getting paid to worm his way inside people's heads was not a proper job. No one was sure even why he was there.

The commandant didn't like the way the man held his eye, as if to say, 'I know what shadows lurk inside.' Shadows lurked within them all; the commandant knew that as well as anyone. A soldier's job was to manage his own mind rather than run bleating to a brainbox who made a point of not getting his hands dirty. As for himself, of course he would like to rest his head on the bosom of the seamstress and fiddle with her twat and not have a care in the world, but he wouldn't because if he didn't set an example who would?

He rode out in dread of what he had seen that morning existing only in his head, a vision, a portent or ill-omen, with dire personal meaning.

He went back the way he thought he had ridden. Like an Indian scout he attempted to read the ground from his earlier trail, but the prints could have been from any old ride. He dismounted to examine the turf for the freshness of its broken surface and hadn't a clue what it was telling him.

He hadn't realised there were so many telegraph poles. He saw guards, tiny specks in the outer watchtowers. Flat fields. He remembered splashing through water. It was all like that, miles and miles of it. The river boundary, with what little water there was, sluggish. He could not remember. Nothing there. Oh, dread vision! He had found no mention of any such incident in the endless arse paper that had crossed his desk that morning, when he would have expected to be informed: *Does anyone know who attached a crucified body to telegraph pole number such-and-such and to what purpose and on whose authority?*

His days were like that: to what purpose and on whose authority?

The garrison psychiatrist often saw the commandant out riding. They shared the same preference for being up before the rest of the world. He thought nothing of doing fifty kilometres before his first appointment, pushing pedal, clearing the mind, then going out again for the midday break. Whenever they passed, the commandant was too busy talking to himself to notice.

Once, he had followed and watched the commandant dismount in a glade. He did so again that afternoon. All his actions were as before: he continued talking to himself while he removed his jacket, shirt and vest, tore branches from a sapling and thrashed his naked back, babbling on even when he pulled out his tool and vigorously masturbated while standing, and afterwards wiped his hand on the grass, watched by his mare.

The commandant stripped to his shirtsleeves and mucked out the stables. After that he went to Groenke's and they chewed the fat and drank tea from Japan, which he supposed came via its Berlin embassy. Several dozen tins of

Seville oranges stood on a table, earmarked for his wife. They sipped plum brandy with the tea as the afternoon sun moved across the skylight.

The commandant went home to find his wife about to leave for the opera. She was standing in the kitchen, wearing a magnificent fur-collared evening coat, issuing instructions to staff.

'When I come back we'll all make jam, which will be fun!' she promised.

The commandant was rewarded with a brief glimpse of the seamstress passing through the hall. He failed to catch her eye.

He did what he could to turn his confusion into safe, concrete gestures. What nerve it took on his part to raise the subject with his wife, about how they could improve the young woman's conditions, by taking it upon themselves perhaps to help furnish her room.

'Do you think she would be allowed her own things?'

His wife was sure they could dig out something. 'There's that rug with moth I haven't had the heart to throw out.'

The commandant was pleased, for himself, and for his wife, pretending that what pleased her made him happy too, contenting himself with the surreptitious relish of his innocent obsession.

His wife proffered her cheek. She had no right to be taking the car. Oh, let it go. He wasn't prepared to berate her in front of staff. The time would come when he would delight in her humiliation. He recalled his Corinthians: 'For the man is not of the woman; but the woman of the man. Neither was the man created for the woman; but the woman for the man.'

*

Transported, thought the commandant's wife. The heartbreak of the story! The misunderstandings that were still possible between two so in love. Orfeo must not look back and Euridice takes this as a sign he no longer loves her.

The auditorium was full, a throwback to another era, with everyone dressed up, the civilised rapture of the audience, the elegance of the uniforms, the women in evening dress. The commandant's wife had a box. She considered it good that people still appreciated culture in straitened times. She was very jealous of the woman sharing with her, the wife of a local general. The woman's full-fur coat was the most beautiful the commandant's wife had ever seen, making her feel dowdy by comparison. The woman had travelled, to France, even North Africa, and she had been nowhere.

Events reached their climax as Orfeo's forbidden look caused Euridice to die. You could have heard a pin drop, thought the commandant's wife. A tragedy for their times! To have a love like that, she sighed, even if it were lost. Love was, the Bible said, the great mystery. Nothing written or uttered since had provided an answer. But where was love?

The commandant thought: Strange that he had not thought of the seamstress during his purge in the woods. He wondered where she was now.

Several drinks and smokes later he was assailed by the terrible image of his wife crawling naked on the floor, proffering her ample rear to some faceless stud. Or worse, could the crowbar tool be Erich's? The man was a committed rapist, perhaps unable to control himself, a perpetual offender for all his reformed air, and his wife was no oil painting. Only too clearly could the commandant picture

Groenke taking proprietorial delight in his wife's stolen, gasping pleasure. Over a year now since she had shared it with him; and it wasn't as though it had all been going swimmingly before.

The doorbell rang. The housekeeper answered. The commandant adjusted his dress in time to be standing to greet the garrison doctor. The man was such a transparent fellow, obviously there to press his cause under the guise of a follow-up to check on his health and give him another earful about what he considered his moral duty. Yes, the good doctor had arrested the march of disease, but that was not the point.

Teaching the facts of life was normally done by man-to-man chats over stiff drinks, except the bloody doctor didn't drink. The commandant listened to him bleat on about how the security police were guilty of irregularities. Of course they were! It was called initiative. There was no point in banging on about regulations. If they waited for Berlin everything would have been swamped years ago. The compounds were riddled with informers, spy networks and double agents.

What the commandant did not volunteer was that he secretly shared the doctor's shame at the state of the place. It was the real reason for him to block anyone coming in.

What a nightmare, thought the doctor, and always that split – between the uniform and his oath of loyalty versus his Hippocratic duty and individual conscience. As for his wife, what a relief it would be to write honestly that his mind was assailed by dark and troubled thoughts about the hopelessness of it all, really.

Corruption was a cancer eating away at them, there from the start, with the place being so neglected, but what came after was beyond all imagination. The shrink had observed something interesting. From what he could tell, no one there dreamed any more.

The shrink preferred to eat alone, so that evening the doctor was surprised to be invited to share his table, even though the man had finished.

Like many, the doctor suspected the shrink had been sent there for underhand reasons.

He was as good-looking as a film star, which set him apart, and was further distanced by a solitary manner. The natural nucleus of the garrison was small tables of urgent, drunken groups, caught between boisterous and conspiratorial talk.

The doctor ordered duck and red cabbage and wondered how much he was being manipulated when the shrink announced that he knew about the doctor's difficulties in trying to open up the garrison. This was not something the doctor had talked about to anyone than the commandant.

'The commandant and his boss in Berlin are tight,' the shrink said. 'The boss is still smarting from having another of his camps turned upside down by a pushy investigative prosecutor named Morgen, who has a history of rocking the boat. The business in Weimar was an embarrassment – people on the home front lining their pockets while our lads take a pasting; not good publicity. So the commandant will have been told to repel all boarders. However, there may be a way to get Morgen in.'

He looked enigmatic and wondered how the commandant's wife was getting on at the opera.

'She is rather smitten by you, as it happens.'

'How do you know?' the doctor asked in astonishment.

'She told me.'

If garrison men weren't keen on consulting him, their

wives were and the commandant's had led by example in what became a fashion.

'Not much treatment involved. Most of it is hard gossip. She considers you a gentleman, out of her league.'

The doctor said stiffly such information was confidential and he shouldn't be told.

'Confidential between us now. Let's say I am seeking a second medical opinion. Now, let's be serious. As I understand it, you, as garrison doctor, believe this place should be properly run in terms of hygiene and labour. It should more resemble a functioning work camp than a penal colony. In a nutshell?'

The doctor could not tell whether the man was to be trusted.

'There may be a way of opening the place up but it won't be done by your complaining,' the shrink said.

'What do you propose?'

II

It had been a difficult summer for August Schlegel. There was his long mend after nearly getting himself blown up at the end of a murder case which he should not have been on as his job was financial crime not homicide. He was back on duty part time, left to sit on his hands and unable to decide if he was in purdah. There were no congratulations or commendations when the butchers case went to trial. He was required only to provide a written statement, which spared him the ordeal of confronting a gang that thought nothing of flaying their victims alive and feeding them into the food chain. Schlegel sensed the case was an embarrassment – it remained unreported – and was being swept under the carpet and he with it.

When he stopped bothering to go in to work most of the time no one complained. As for Morgen, his irksome, errant partner, he remained conspicuous by his absence, off elsewhere, doing what no one knew.

Why Morgen had been transferred to Schlegel's department in the first place still no one was sure, unless it was to rattle their cage. Despite an up-and-down career, including six months' penal detention and another six fighting on the Russian front, Morgen – to his own professed astonishment, as much as anyone's – remained a prosecuting investigator, one of those shadowy, feared inquisitors who could be after anyone, including Schlegel and his colleagues. It was accepted that everyone spied on everyone but intrigue in the past months had become an even thicker stew. The question of where anyone's real loyalty lay was hardly worth asking. On the night of the butchers, Schlegel had seen Morgen sitting in the back of Himmler's car.

Schlegel thought: The spy spies on the spy spying on the spies, into infinity; life as a hall of unreflecting mirrors in the land of the undead.

It was, the cynics were saying, inevitable, a controlled fury directed inwards now there was nothing left to shout about. No one could pretend the news was good. An almost visible depression hung over the city, rain or shine. It was only a matter of time before Berlin became the relentless target for enemy night bombers. Hamburg had burned like an inferno. Refugees poured in, putting a huge strain on the stations and causing confusion and panic with horror stories of pavements turned to rivers of fire.

People were starting to leave in anticipation of what was to come, with children and women not in defence work evacuated.

The raids started at the end of August, resulting in the shortest journeys taking hours as entire streets collapsed, with buildings around the Kurfürstendamm and Lietzenburgerstrasse burned out. Blank spaces appeared, like missing teeth.

In all of this, Schlegel found his attention distracted to where he least expected, starting with discovering his indomitable mother standing in her kitchen, of all places, holding a potato, of all things, saying she could not remember what it was.

He had tried to make light of it by saying she had servants to take care of that, but he noticed the moments became more frequent, until she said, 'I forget things and then I can't remember what it is that I have forgotten.'

He put it down to the wider distraction, refusing to accept her mind was starting to go.

Schlegel saw his mother and stepfather more that summer, often staying over. His leg still hurt and he had trouble managing the long climb to his little apartment in Auguststrasse.

And there was the excuse to see Sybil.

Sybil was the anomaly.

Why his mother should risk everything to harbour Sybil was something to which Schlegel had given much thought without being convinced by any of the answers. Widely known as the bitch imperious, she and his stepfather lived close to the heart of the beast, which made her decision the more astonishing.

Sybil had by default been an extension of his mother's social circle: Jewish and until the big February roundup protected from deportation by her tailoring for a company with a high export rating. Her reputation for craftsmanship preceded her and Schlegel's mother treated her as a protégé, introducing her to many senior wives, to her private amusement, as few had the figures or élan to carry off their incessant demands for copies of French couture.

Following the roundup – a clean sweep of the city's remaining Jews – Sybil had gone underground with her female lover until arrested by the Gestapo. Sybil had survived. As with everything now, the situation was not black and white, Schlegel had come to realise, but infinitely shaded. If a moral compass still existed its direction was no longer readable.

Schlegel supposed his mother's Englishness, which made her an outsider too, played a part in protecting Sybil. It probably came down to bloody-mindedness and her dislike of overbearing German correctness. Although conventionally anti-Semitic, just as she was critical of any of the darker races – even the French were suspect – she seemed not to regard Sybil through the prism of her wider prejudices.

Schlegel hadn't been looking to fall in love. It was hopeless, really. Even as he was aware of her casting her shadow over his soul he blamed his weakened state, treating his love for her as part of his sickness.

He took to reading in the summerhouse where Sybil worked. She slept in the attic upstairs. It was as safe as anywhere. The house lay in an expensive westerly suburb, shielded from the road, with a large garden screened from other houses.

He took to watching her surreptitiously as he pretended to read. Sometimes he played records on an old wind-up gramophone. She said she liked working to music. Her favourite was 'You Shall Be the Emperor of My Soul', with its line 'in the free land of my heart'.

They didn't talk much but she seemed to find his presence reassuring. There wasn't much to say. Sybil was still mourning for her lover, killed in the most brutal way by the Gestapo.

In the time he and Sybil had together, Schlegel entertained the fantasy of creating an island of his mother's summerhouse, they its castaways; a precarious dream he knew could not last. Each time he left with the greatest reluctance, just as his step was lighter with every approach.

He kept his true feelings hidden, often from himself, most of all from her. He rarely admitted that he found her unreadable, and therein lay the heart of the attraction. He suspected her enigma, the state of not knowing, and the impossibility of love and her hiddenness made her the ideal projection for his confusion. Not that it mattered because whatever was between them would remain unresolved. She would be shocked, he was sure, were he even to hint at what he came to think of as the troubled calm of her company.

He talked instead of his mother's memory lapses and confessed the condition unnerved him. He told her he sometimes experienced a lurch of panic between seeing a commonplace object and the relief of naming it. This led to its own form of lunacy, wondering why a table was called a table, rather than a fountain pen or an armadillo.

For the first time in as long as he could remember he saw the trace of her smile. Perhaps he never had seen it. Such fleeting moments sustained him for days.

Where his mother's mind was starting to go, his stepfather, always the most contained of men, was losing physical control. One day Schlegel had found him stalled in his study, standing but unable to walk. Schlegel was told to put his foot in front of his stepfather's.

'Like a hurdle.'

Schlegel did and his stepfather's stuck foot moved effortlessly over it and he carried on walking as though nothing had happened. Schlegel asked how long it had been going on. About three months, his stepfather said. Had he seen the doctor? His stepfather appeared quite uninterested by the interrogation and said instead, 'I am more worried about your mother.'

So over that summer domestic preoccupations came to dominate Schlegel's mind and the bigger conflict recede. He wanted to buy Sybil something, a token or keepsake that she could keep innocently, without knowing it was a declaration of his love. Nothing obvious. He couldn't decide.

Then the hammer blow.

Schlegel put in an appearance at work. Even though going in was a waste of time, they could just as easily throw the book at him for absenteeism. He suspected he was damned either way. His secretary had been transferred. He had no casework. His superiors ignored him, all the way up to

Nebe, the boss, who was a friend of his mother and stepfather. His mother said it was happening more, panic at the top and everyone wandering around like ostriches, with their heads buried.

'I have no trouble remembering a word like ostrich,' she said.

He was surprised when his stepfather telephoned that morning, telling him to come immediately. Such a call or summons was unprecedented. He was an enigmatic man, probably of high influence, who never said, any more than he indicated, what he did.

Schlegel found him weeping in his study. At first he thought him upset about his illness.

His stepfather was unable to speak but could walk unimpeded. Never one for physical contact, he took Schlegel's arm. It was strange being touched by such remoteness. They went out through the French windows of his study to the summerhouse where the mess told its own story. Stuff kicked over. A record or two smashed. Casual violence. Sybil gone. Schlegel asked if his mother had been taken too. His stepfather nodded.

Gestapo.

Enquiries revealed nothing of their whereabouts. Schlegel's sense of persecution grew. He feared they would come for him or his stepfather next. The shock of the arrests was compounded by his stepfather's failure to intervene, despite his influence – or maybe he too was a victim of some latest power play. Schlegel was sure the telephone lines in the house were being listened in to. He took to sleeping in Sybil's room in the attic of the summerhouse, almost inviting them to come and take him away. His stepfather grew more withdrawn. His mother's social circle greeted the news of her arrest with schadenfreude and astonishment at the removal of such a permanent social fixture.

Schlegel got nowhere with the Gestapo. He didn't expect to as the butchers case had exposed one of their rising stars as corrupt and homicidal.

He took the matter to Nebe but Nebe was a fastidious washer of hands and master of the hanging silence.

It was as though they had never existed, even his mother, the nexus of a whole social network.

The last conversation with her, where she had irritated him by not minding her own business, became increasingly poignant.

She asked point blank, 'Are you in love with the Jewish girl?'

Thrown by such a direct question, he said it was complicated.

'That wasn't what I asked.'

'I suppose,' he said, feeling ticked off.

'Put her out of your mind. No good can come of it.'

'I don't know,' he said lamely.

'You make a habit of wanting what you can't have because it's safer.'

He supposed. The image in his head of Sybil was a distant, idealised portrait of passive repose: the lowered gaze, the circular motion of the sewing hand. Thinking about her brought him the only peace of mind he had, regardless of how inappropriate that love was. She could do nothing with it. He could give nothing to sustain her. Love declared would add nothing to her life. There were too many obstacles. Let alone all the rest . . . race, history, war, persecution.

'So the daisy chain goes,' were his mother's last enigmatic words to him.

That same afternoon he remembered being asked by his stepfather to fetch his pills from his dressing room. There in a half-open drawer he came across magazines showing bound, naked oriental women in positions of brutal submission.

The veil of secrecy covered everything.

After a silence of weeks, Morgen called. His telephone manner dispensed with any preamble and he said only, 'I need you to come with me to Horcher's. At least you will get a decent lunch.'

Schlegel's only instruction was to ask for table seven.

Table seven was an exclusive booth, a sign of their mysterious host's standing. Schlegel was first to arrive. He had no idea who they were meeting. Schlegel doubted it would mean anything to know his name. In the higher echelons, it was up to juniors to interpret according to rank. The cardinal rule was to avoid such encounters in the first place.

For all the belt-tightening, a crowd was in. The place had closed at the start of the big austerity drive six months before, later circumvented by Göring doing a deal with Goebbels for it to reopen as a private dining club.

Horcher's was dull and stuffy, in the baronial style, with wood panels and what looked like a job lot of Italian oils. The one above Schlegel featured a corpulent cherub. He knew it from sombre birthday treats with his stepfather and not his mother, who preferred livelier joints. Schlegel had decided not to tell Morgen about his mother and Sybil, for the question remained whether Morgen was a hypocrite or a man of conscience. Was his nihilism a variant of the regime's and he its watchdog? Was the maverick stance to provoke others into betraying themselves, or a reflection of a properly subversive nature: for instance, declaring the Germans bureaucrats of desire, being too theatrical and too philosophical, and the Austrians even worse, resulting in a lethal combination of wild dreamers and pettifogging clerks.

One fact Schlegel could say: superiors tired easily of Morgen.

Morgen strolled in twenty minutes late to find their host had trumped him by being even later.

He sat without any greeting and automatically lit up. He wore a new suit to replace the one the moths had got. The criminal police was plain-clothes. Out of uniform Morgen looked like a resting actor.

He broke the first rule of the house by snapping his fingers at a waiter, who looked like he might keel over from the breach of etiquette. Morgen ordered a beer and for Schlegel too, after he said he didn't want one.

Schlegel was annoyed by Morgen's lateness. Morgen ignored his obvious mood. Schlegel, apprehensive, looked around.

'Don't worry,' said Morgen. 'Given the venue, I would say we're not going to be taken out and shot.'

'Why are we here?'

'I haven't the faintest idea, honestly.'

Schlegel asked where he had been.

'Shovelling shit.'

Morgen was in the process of explaining how people were in the end answerable for their actions when they were interrupted by the arrival of their host.

Schlegel found himself subjected to intense inspection by a tall, lean man with a lopsided grin and eyes full of hard amusement. Schlegel couldn't tell who he worked for because he also wore a suit, better than either of theirs. A man young enough to be dynamic, old enough to be senior. Schlegel's impression was of authority at ease with power.

The man turned to Morgen. 'You're the troublemaker.'

Morgen said nothing.

'Two wise monkeys, perhaps.'

He showed good teeth, in contrast to the usual abysmal dentistry, and held Schlegel's eye with a stare that had nothing funny about it.

The menu was waved aside and the waiter told to decide.

He did not volunteer who or what he was. Whatever was going to be discussed was going to have to wait until after eating. Guinea fowl as it turned out, with preserved cherries and cabbage.

The man treated food as an interruption barely to be tolerated. Morgen excused himself to go to the washroom. Schlegel thought: Why not just summon us to an office and get on with what we need to be told? Unless of course the man didn't want them to know who he was. So much ran on intrigue these days.

The man surprised him by asking if he rode. 'Your stepfather owns racehorses.'

Schlegel, disconcerted at finding him so informed, said he had but didn't much.

Morgen sauntered back and was asked if he rode too.

Only a couple of times, he said. 'Too far off the ground.'

Their host showed his teeth.

'I trained at the Fegelein riding academy before the war.'

He stared at Morgen, who remained poker-faced, and Schlegel sensed the stakes had just got higher.

'You investigated Fegelein, I believe.'

'Nothing came of it.' Morgen, sounding casual, looked tense.

'Let's hear it from the horse's mouth. Bad joke. Go, go.'

The case had come to his attention two years before in 1941, Morgen said. Fegelein had been posted east, in charge of a cavalry unit on active duty behind the lines. The investigation was into Fegelein's theft of Jewish furs from a confiscated company in Warsaw, which he had taken over.

'I was ordered to desist. The Führer's mistress was indirectly implicated. Fegelein had protection in high places.'

Schlegel supposed Fegelein was a friend of their host. Morgen's next remark, calculated to produce a reaction, was that in some quarters he was known as *Flegelein* – little lout.

The man treated them to the same dark look.

'Tell me about Buchenwald. You created quite a stink.'

Morgen sighed, as if expecting it would come to this.

'A few months ago the Kassel police sought my cooperation because a known embezzler had escaped them by attaching himself to an SS camp, which lies outside their jurisdiction. As a prosecuting judge, however, I could gain entrance.'

The other man cut him short. 'How did you get into the camp?'

'By presenting myself.'

'Turning up at the guardroom?'

'Exactly.'

'And made yourself extremely unpopular.'

'Be that as it may, I encountered witnesses murdered as they tried to cover up their corruption.'

'You made big trouble for the man in charge here in Berlin.'

'Pohl. He made that clear to me, in no uncertain terms.'

'How is it left between you and Pohl?'

'All his camps have orders to refuse me admission, however much the subject warrants investigation. In Buchenwald the corruption was so blatant that the commandant and his wife were moved on before I turned up.'

'Your conclusion?'

'It reflects badly on Pohl; either way.'

'If he doesn't know what is going on he is incompetent.'

'Yes, and if he does then he deliberately covered it up.'

'There is an anti-corruption crusade, of which Pohl is bound to take note.'

'Not to the extent of permitting external examiners into his camps.'

'He has several commandants under review, which suggests he is attempting some housekeeping.'

'The camps are a sequestered world. Anything could be going on.'

Schlegel wondered about their host.

'What do you want from us?' Morgen asked.

'I want you to go back.'

'To Buchenwald?'

'Auschwitz.'

'We won't get past the gate!'

All Schlegel knew was it was one of those vague names connected with terror, somewhere in the General Government.

The man steepled his hands and told them it had come to his attention, through the army post office, that a staff dentist was using its services to smuggle gold declared as food parcels.

'Gold?' echoed Morgen.

'The post office will pass on its authority, allowing you in under its aegis.'

'You mean we go in undercover?'

'To get you in.'

'And we have a roving brief until we get thrown out?'

'Fair summary.'

'Pohl's men will arrest us on any old charge once we set foot inside. I doubt anyone will send in the cavalry.'

'Look at what you achieved in Buchenwald. You brought down the commandant.'

'Luck.'

'What if lightning struck twice?'

'New broom?' asked Morgen cautiously.

Their host showed his palms. 'We have reached the stage of cure and incentive.'

Morgen asked what was the point of Schlegel being there; he hadn't gone to Buchenwald.

'There's a financial angle. The fact of the post office's involvement.'

'And if we need to reach you?' Morgen asked carefully.

'I will contact you.'

'How do we contact you?'

'You don't. This is the last you will see of me.'

'Your name, at least?'

'Irrelevant.'

'On our own, you say?'

'An entrée. Talk to Horn, who runs the garrison post office. He will point you in the right direction.'

Schlegel spoke up at last, telling Morgen, 'We don't have to do this.'

The man turned to Morgen. 'Your faint-hearted colleague is correct, you are within your rights to refuse. The matter vexes me because I cannot strictly order you.' He addressed Schlegel. 'But we both know when Morgen's blood is up he is unstoppable. Besides, as a sweetener for you, someone you know is there.'

With that he was gone.

After the lunch a silent, brooding Morgen did his disappearing trick until late one morning he called to check Schlegel was in the office and said he was coming in. Their office was a dingy hole where the sun only ever appeared as a crack on the wall opposite, which Schlegel had grown to accept as a metaphor for life.

He had learned that where they were supposed to be going had a telephone number with an area code that could be dialled direct from Berlin. A switchboard had answered, like anywhere. The operator put him through to general enquiries. The first few times no one answered. When a brusque-sounding man eventually did and Schlegel said he was criminal police and needed to check on two women he was told the place wasn't a publicity company, and that was that.

Morgen turned up distracted and sat at his desk opposite. Schlegel couldn't remember the last time he had used it.

'What do you know of our destination?' Morgen asked.

'Only that it's one of those places no one talks about.'

'Yea, the black hole into which countless disappear. Do you have any desire to make the trip?'

'None.' Unless it was for Sybil, which Schlegel didn't add. He was surprised Morgen hadn't picked up on their host's final remark.

'Me neither. We are a couple of gunsels.'

The term was unfamiliar.

'A little man carrying a gun. US slang. That's us, two gunsels.'

Schlegel could only agree. He was no hero. He didn't understand the world, beyond it being a miserable place that happened to coincide with his existence.

On top of that, always the troubling question of where Morgen's true loyalties lay.

'We can only be prepared,' Morgen went on.

Schlegel couldn't see how when everything was secret.

Morgen agreed. 'No one knows how the SS works, probably not even Heini Himmler, our glorious leader and supreme bureaucrat. How much do you understand about how we are governed?'

It was ubiquitous and amorphous, that much Schlegel knew.

'Exactly!' said Morgen, patronising. 'With the potential for a well-oiled, efficient machine, all parts working independently and synchronised, and, at the same time, a blueprint for total dysfunction. Nowhere is that model more evident than in the case of our employers.'

'Is this about our host?'

'His name is Dr Kammler.'

'How do you know?'

'His name was in Horcher's reservations book. I looked.'

The name meant nothing.

Morgen looked glum. 'I suspect Dr Kammler is using us like divers in a bathysphere, testing how deep we can go before the plates start to buckle. Actually, that flatters us, we're more bit parts in a bad play being sent into the underworld. Bring your coins to pay the ferryman.'

All Morgen's old amphetamine energy was gone. Even his smoking lacked enthusiasm.

'No map I can find of this place, apart from a pre-war street one of the town, with Polish names. I believe the camp is huge and everyone is employed – I use the word loosely as I doubt they get paid – to build a petrochemical plant.' Morgen threw up his hands. 'There must be a weight of paperwork but I can't get near it. Stuff from a couple of years ago you can find – squabbles about who is supposed to pay for maintenance work, the SS or the army, from which it leases its barracks. Lists of quartermasters' supplies. The number of vehicles owned by the garrison, and even their service records, down to changes of oil and the number of tyres used. But nothing after the end of 1941, which coincides with the big reshuffle that put Pohl at the top. Oh, and it's a family posting, with schools and kindergartens.'

'In a maximum-security area?'

'It is, but information still available from the SS education office lists the books supplied to the adult and children's libraries, and the prisoner library too.'

Morgen said he had taken the precaution of coming up with a doctored warrant of investigation, assigning them on behalf of the post office, validated by the criminal police, with an array of impressive official stamps.

As for personal passes, he had thought of that too: standard-issue identity cards, with their names replaced by a couple so anonymous they were laughable.

'Where does Kammler fit in this?' asked Schlegel.

'What's your instinct?'

'Propaganda or Speer's man.'

Morgen shook his head. 'Trained as a civil engineer. For several years fairly junior in Berlin's city administration. Came to the attention of the SS when he was involved in the creation and design of its garden village in Krume Lanke.'

Schlegel knew it slightly. Gingerbread cottages and grassy paths; beyond Zehlendorf.

'Then employed by the Luftwaffe to construct airfields in northern France, before being headhunted by the SS, as one of a new breed of super-technocrats.'

The world was increasingly full of such men with careers based on terrifying efficiency.

'But why employ us to expose a corrupt dentist?'

'Not clear, but two very interesting facts about Dr Kammler.'

'Either good?'

'The man has done well. He is now in charge of all SS construction.'

Schlegel thought with the war effort construction was on hold.

'Head of construction is somewhat misleading. Dr Kammler has a huge work pool at his disposal, perhaps running to hundreds of thousands. Dr Kammler is in command of all forced labour.'

'The man we met!'

'A pharaoh, lord of all slaves.'

Schlegel found the information difficult to process.

'More to the point, Dr Kammler is Oswald Pohl's number two.'

The inference was obvious. 'You mean Kammler is setting us up on behalf of Pohl?'

'An interpretation we ignore at our peril.'

'And where does Pohl stand?'

'He runs the WVHA, known to those that work there as We're Very Harmless Actually. Economics and Administration is the harmless interpretation, but a huge section is unaccountable – the secret organisation within the larger secret state.'

'The camps.'

'And God knows how many of those there actually are. They are the core of Pohl's empire.'

'And the man himself?'

'Ex-navy, around for years. Good organiser now considered a bit passé. Keen on hiring and firing. Mood swings. Don't mess with. A bit of a thug, but also a collector and environmentally friendly. Supports bio-dynamic farming. That he has acquired landed estates may have something to do with it.'

'Why does Pohl hate you so much?'

'Politics. He's protecting himself. If corruption is endemic in Pohl's empire – and obscured from Heini – how better to scotch trouble than by inviting the idiots investigating into the lion's den.'

'What about the time I saw you sitting in the back of Heini's car?'

Morgen sighed. 'Heini, for all his fearsome reputation, is a vacillating man. He frets that temptation is corrupting his elite, but he remains faint-hearted because he dislikes bad news. Heini's real anxiety, I suspect, is that Pohl governs an empire inaccessible even to him, which is why for the moment our activities are unofficially condoned.'

'Are you thinking Kammler might be Heini's go-between rather than Pohl's?'

'Certainly Kammler and Heini know each other, but I think Dr K is too ambitious to confine himself to the role of intermediary. Even if he is acting as envoy, he will have his own agenda.'

Schlegel said it looked like they were being used as bait.

Morgen agreed.

'What about us, what do we do?'

Morgen shrugged. 'We have anonymity on our side. Klein and Richter.'

Their train turned up five hours late. Morgen took such delays for granted; Schlegel's punctuality was shown to be increasingly pointless.

Morgen arrived after four hours without cigarettes. The prospect of a smokeless journey was unbearable. He patted empty pockets and said, 'I will have to throw myself off the train.'

Schlegel told him to look after his bag. Morgen asked why was he standing on the crowded platform when there was an officers' waiting room. Schlegel feared their assignment would reduce them to bickering.

The arcade where the racketeers loitered included a little old fellow, bow-legged as an ex-jockey. He was suspicious when Schlegel asked, knowing he was police. Schlegel said he was going away so it didn't matter. Ten minutes later the man returned and charged the going rate. Schlegel paid, thinking it would be amusing for a patrol to turn up now.

Morgen was in the officers' waiting room, which was nothing like as busy as outside. Schlegel gave him the cartouche of cigarettes. Morgen lit up with shaky hands. He had the most punishing hangover, he said.

'The whites of my eyes are yellow.'

The train at last backed into the station, hissing and blowing grey smoke over the platform. The crowd steadied itself for the onslaught of embarkation. Morgen looked unbothered. He had a disability card.

'Fake.'

A small riot ensued as everyone shoved to get on. Morgen's mood deteriorated when it became apparent that the train was a mongrel of carriages from different countries, with no first class.

He announced himself to the guard, who looked unimpressed until he saw Morgen's papers, grew obsequious and marched off, officious. He came back and led them to a French second-class carriage where they had to shove their way down a corridor full of grumbling, standing passengers. There in a compartment two empty window seats waited.

Morgen, too hungover to be grateful, asked what had happened to first class.

The seats were upholstered but threadbare. Morgen prodded his before sitting down. The compartment was like an aquarium, with resentful faces in the corridor glaring through the glass. Schlegel wondered who had been turfed out and if they were among those staring in.

The compartment offered the usual mixed bag: by the door, two junior officers in uniform, passed out, as hungover as Morgen, who immediately fell asleep, as if bewitched; next to Schlegel an overlarge boy, who smelled of urine; his chaperone, a sour crone in widow's weeds, who clicked false teeth; opposite her a stick-like man in civilian clothes, with a toothbrush moustache, looking too ill for military service. The only interesting one sat next to Morgen, a young woman with attractive knees and a watchful air.

After a final slamming of carriage doors the departure whistle at last sounded. The train crawled forward to the airport where they waited forty minutes. Then the outer suburbs of Mariendorf and Marienfeld slid by, like a diorama, leaving Schlegel to wonder if it was really the landscape moving while the carriage remained stationary. The unfolding picture showed everything shabbier.

The long journey east continued in fits and starts, marked by flat horizons, dreary villages and towns, and fields after harvest. They entered a land beyond boredom, briefly enlivened by the sound of a scuffle down the corridor, which stopped as suddenly as it started, presumably because there wasn't space for a fight.

While the rest of the carriage fidgeted or snored the young woman remained composed. She was tidily dressed in what Schlegel presumed was an old suit because nothing was new any more.

The sense of leaving was palpable as they crossed the old border. With that came a sense of the past receding and an unwelcome future. No one stuck their heads out of carriage windows and grinned, as they once had for propaganda shots; not any more.

Morgen slept on. The boy smelling of urine squirmed. The careful eyes of the young woman suggested she wouldn't stand for much nonsense. Hair fair, between blonde and brown. A sharp, angular face. In defiance of the habit now for women not to use make-up, she wore lipstick. She crossed her legs and patted her skirt. Their eyes met. She held Schlegel's gaze, neither curious nor inviting. He looked away and decided she seemed sad or at least reluctant. His attention kept returning. What was it about her? Something hidden and mysterious, perhaps. He wasn't conventionally attracted. He thought she might consider herself rather plain and too thin for popular taste. Her case on the rack above was a tatty leatherette, its luggage tag too far away to read, with no stickers to tell him anything of her story.

The train rattled its excruciating way across countryside duller than before and not worth the view.

They stopped again. At first it seemed like another delay. They had wasted hours stuck in different sidings waiting for more urgent transport to pass. Morgen woke and asked what was going on. When the guard passed down the corridor he went and asked. The guard, white-faced, said a young soldier had shut himself in the toilet at the other end of their carriage and slit his throat with a bayonet. Blood coming under the door had caused someone to pull the emergency cord.

When they showed no sign of moving, people started to get down to stretch their legs. Schlegel and Morgen did too. Morgen offered his hand to the young woman, helping her down, while Schlegel was stuck with assisting the crone and her smelly ward.

They were halted in a sandy gully with tall pines. Schlegel looked at the sky and wished he could jump ahead to the return journey. The mood became one of growing irritation at another delay, laced with morbid curiosity. Someone said the dead man was just a kid and hadn't wanted to go back to the front after being dumped by his girlfriend.

The guard conferred with the driver and his stoker, then peeped his whistle and asked if anyone was police. Morgen sighed and stepped forward. Schlegel watched them confer, aware of the young woman standing silent among the general grumbling. He wondered if it gave him reason to go over.

Morgen told the guard the local police would have to hold the carriage and write a report.

'Otherwise straightforward, as the death was unwitnessed and self-inflicted. We're not talking about a locked-room mystery.'

The guard looked uncertain. 'What about those in the carriage?'

'Either they find space in the rest of the train or wait for the next one available.'

The guard said that would be in the morning, when the night train came through.

They all got back on and after half an hour came out of the trees, started crossing an empty plain and eventually came to a small settlement with a siding, and a primitive inn opposite the station halt and a water tower.

The young woman in their carriage surprised Schlegel by saying she was in no obvious hurry. Nor he. Her voice was easy and attractive. The old woman with the teeth and her ward annoyed Schlegel by deciding to stay too. He went to the inn to ask about rooms. A youngish woman with a scarred lip and a rural accent told him she had ten and all but one vacant. Not many passed through these days. Schlegel asked if there was food. Not much, she said.

The view from the window of Schlegel's sparse room was primitive. He wondered where he was, actually – in the middle of nowhere, obviously – and in his passage through life. Would he die young like most of the rest of the men on the train? He found their destination impossible to envisage. The size of a town. Abandon all hope, he thought. Faust? He supposed it lay somewhere between the meanest slums and the dread forests of childhood imagination.

Morgen corrected him later. Not Faust. When Dante and Virgil reach the gates of hell.

He gave Schlegel a light look. 'Don't be too melodramatic.' He studied his dusty shoes and changed his mind. 'You are probably right. We enter the realm of superstition.'

Her name was Elizabeth Schulze. When Morgen and Schlegel entered the dining room she was sitting alone.

'What's in a name?' Schlegel asked irreverently, without meaning to, when Schulze introduced herself. Morgen, more gallant, asked if she wanted company, as they were already travelling companions; it was up to her. Please do, she said, she was half-dead from boredom.

They sorted out where they all came from. She had been born in the Ruhr and had lived near Hamburg. Morgen was from Frankfurt. Schlegel had always lived in Berlin but had been born in Shanghai.

'How exotic,' said Schulze.

Schlegel was unsettled by the woman, as though they were fated to meet in that realm of superstition mentioned by Morgen; which made no sense.

They were served a cabbage and potato soup, which they agreed was more than passable, followed by cauliflower cheese.

'What about you?' Morgen asked Schulze.

She avoided answering directly, saying she was coming back from a course in administration in Berlin. Schlegel saw she faced a dilemma. It was always dangerous to volunteer any personal view, especially to two men in suits carrying sidearms. Morgen's was visible on his belt, where his jacket had slid.

Caution made everyday conversation increasingly elaborate and meaningless. Schlegel didn't feel much like talking and lobbed her a couple of easy questions. She obliged, looking relieved, telling them about her time in the girls' league, sent to Stettin, to help ethnic Germans coming back from all over to their spiritual homeland to serve the cause.

Morgen said he remembered the newsreels, like big biblical processions, horses and carts piled high with worldly possessions. Schulze said she had appeared in one as part of a greeting for these homecoming pioneers. She added brightly, 'Many came to learn modern farming practices before being sent to the new territories.' Right where they were now, she added unnecessarily, looking out of the window.

Schlegel wondered if she might be ironic or just dull. He wanted to ask directly: Why am I interested in you? He thought she must be more interesting than she let on. He wasn't so sure when she told them her specialities were physical training and domestic science.

Schlegel looked at Morgen and said, 'I think it is all right to tell her we are not secret police.'

'Just ordinary criminal police,' added Morgen. He turned to her and said, 'You were saying?'

She recovered quickly. 'I was boring you with my story. I can't really talk about now.'

'Quite so,' said Morgen. 'The past is safe. Things were still glorious, so one can't be held accountable. However, we can safely say this cauliflower is not bad. Go on. I am not bored. What next?'

'I left the league and did a stenographer's course in Berlin.'

'What made you leave the other job?'

'They wanted me to move into children's education, which I didn't want.'

'So you became a stenographer. What made you decide?' Morgen sounded curious.

Schulze said she had come across an advertisement in a magazine.

'At the orphanage.'

'Orphanage?' echoed Morgen.

'A man I knew in Stettin had gone there, and I was young and foolish and invited myself to visit when it was obvious he was having an affair with the woman running the orphanage, who had also been in Stettin, so more fool me.'

'What did they do at this orphanage?' Morgen asked.

'Select children suitable for adoption to be sent home to be educated. I only did the dormitory patrols and I was supposed to be on holiday. A few times Dr Krick let me help with his measurement tests.'

'Excuse me,' said Schlegel in surprise. 'Dr who?'

'Krick. Do you know him?'

Schlegel shook his head, saying he had misheard, thinking, fuck, Krick.

'Strangely enough, he turned up last year where I am now.'

'Was that awkward?' asked Morgen.

'At first. Talk about a small world. But I am over him.'

Schlegel wondered what were the chances of stumbling across his name.

Krick was an unwelcome reminder of the time Schlegel had done his hardest to forget. Morgen knew of it, having read his file, but they had passed over the matter quickly and Schlegel had not mentioned Krick.

Two summers before, criminal police from all over,

44

including Berlin, had been assigned to the new eastern territories for anti-partisan duties. Schlegel had been responsible for processing operation reports and it wasn't until he had gone into the field as an observer that he learned that such duties were a euphemism for the roundup and elimination of whole villages. Once he had ended up in a ditch, knee-deep in bodies, administering the *coup de grace* to the poor devils whose shooting had been botched.

Spending all day shooting civilians proved more psychologically arduous than anyone anticipated and suddenly no one was pretending the job was easy. A tier of management was quickly brought in to rationalise, including Krick. Schlegel recalled a handsome man, of composed manner, who said the big task they faced was how to normalise the process. He thought the days of firing squads were numbered. 'In the meantime, don't discriminate against those who say they have no stomach for the job. Plenty will.'

'Lost your appetite?' asked Morgen.

Schlegel looked at his unfinished plate. It had gone cold. He chewed disconsolately, struggling to get the now-slimy mixture down his throat.

Morgen had them on slivovitz after dinner. They learned a little more about their companion. Where she was now stationed had been in quarantine for almost a year and it had only just been lifted. She coloured attractively and said she probably shouldn't be telling.

Morgen waved the matter aside and asked about her recent course in Berlin. It was out in Steglitz, she said, where she had done her stenographer's training.

'The first time was great fun. Everything is more serious now.'

Schlegel could not get over her knowing Krick. Lovers, by the sound of it; he was sure despite her saying she was over him. Krick had the air of a ladies' man, who seemed to take for granted he could go to bed with any woman he wanted. Even in the field, with none available, there had been his seductive cologne and charm.

'Have you been where you are long?' Morgen asked.

Since the beginning of 1941, she said.

So over two years. Schlegel noted that wistful expression again. Morgen continued to probe, but she would only say hers was a garrison posting and she worked in a construction office.

'As in building things?' asked Morgen.

She laughed at his obviousness. 'As in building things.'

'Construction?' repeated Morgen. 'Are you by any chance familiar with Kammler?'

She produced a sound that Schlegel could interpret only as a suppressed squeal of surprise.

She whispered, 'The man is a god.' She stared and asked if they knew him.

'Not as such,' said Morgen. 'It was when you mentioned construction. Do you?'

He leaned forward, interested.

She had met him, she said, some months after her arrival. There had been a major reshuffle over that summer. The old local construction office was disbanded and Dr Kammler came from Berlin for several inspections. It had fallen to her to show him where everything was.

'Why you?' asked Morgen. 'Wouldn't he have been assigned an adjutant?'

Schlegel could see it was difficult for her to say more. He supposed assigning someone so lowly had been intended as a garrison snub to Dr Kammler.

Schlegel thought, first Krick now Kammler. Perhaps she was much more interesting than she let on.

*

He wondered that again when he woke, or dreamed he woke, in the night to discover her at the end of his bed. His first thought was she must be sleepwalking, then saw she was still dressed.

Blue moonlight shone through the thin curtain. He asked what she wanted. She asked the reason for his hair being white. He didn't know why he didn't resort to his usual excuses and admitted he had once shot a lot of people in a ditch. He couldn't prove it but he thought one was a result of the other. He asked if there was anything she wanted. She shook her head and he saw her face was bathed in tears. Outside rain started to fall, driven by the wind against the window.

Schlegel thought he hadn't slept, yet he must have because when he woke she was gone.

He could make no sense of why she had come to him. He supposed her neurotic or lonely.

Perhaps she hadn't been there at all and it was a dreamlike projection of an obscure desire. He was not one that others sought out, yet from the start he had been aware of her looking at him.

She was not in the dining room for breakfast. Morgen was already down. There was bread and jam and a watery concoction pretending to be coffee. Was she avoiding him? Schlegel wondered. Maybe she was annoyed he hadn't made a move; a woman turning up in a man's room at night . . .

Should he have told her about knowing Krick? No one had mentioned Auschwitz, but it was obvious that was where she worked.

Now Krick was with her; and soon they would be there too.

III

Darkness was falling as they reached their destination. They arrived parched and foul-tempered after another day wasted in sidings, making way for troop and munitions convoys, then crawling forward into an unseasonably stifling heatwave.

The night train had come through after only an hour's delay. On the platform the widow and the kid were the only faces Schlegel recognised. No sign of Schulze. A big crowd gathered, locals going to market, including cattle. Schlegel thought he glimpsed Schulze up ahead as they embarked. The train was even more crammed than before. Morgen bribed the guard with cigarettes to let them travel in the goods' van where they at least could spread out but had to share with the cows and their copious ordure.

Through the ventilation slit Schlegel stood watching an endless eastward procession of young men in uniform and contemplated the bonds of indissoluble comradeship, forged in a storm of steel. That was the theory; not for him, all that laying down one's life for country and blood and earth.

Until the war he had always supposed his life would be spent slacking around, chasing women (a mystery), sitting in night clubs listening to risqué music, as much as that was possible, and drinking in bars. He had no plan, to the exasperation of his mother, for whom position mattered. His stepfather was easier-going and suggested the racing world, which would have been perfect, being louche, except he disliked horses. Did he have principles? Coveting other men's wives was inevitable, he supposed. Thou shalt not kill; he was in agreement with that, a rather unfashionable stance. Any thoughts of equality were laughed at by his mother. 'Come on, darling. There's always a pecking order, even among equals.' Thou shalt not steal; yes, except he had in his youth, shoplifting, more for dare and amusement than gain, and got caught. He suspected his mother had been secretly proud, being impatient of sticklers. Most of the time he was aware of his own insignificance in the greater scheme. He was one of the meek and, regardless of the Sermon on the Mount, he would not inherit the earth, or even get close. At least he didn't subscribe to what Morgen called the raving nihilism going on all around them. It wasn't that people didn't believe in anything, Morgen said, in an unguarded moment, they believed too much, in all the wrong things, as though history could be stage-managed in a phantasmagoria of wishful thinking and willed destiny, fuelled by too many dangerous dreams.

'For the Yanks it was a land grab, none of this dressing up in historical fulfilment.'

Schlegel suspected Morgen knew too much and wasn't telling.

They stood in the booking hall, stunned by the anticlimax of arrival. Considering the lateness of the hour, the station remained crowded, its smells like anywhere, except worse – coal, tobacco, sweat and dirty toilets.

Men hung around hoping to pick up nonexistent girls, standing at a refreshments stand and beer stall, sucking on bottles and noisily talking a strange language.

A tinny loudspeaker announced a delay of the night train to Vienna.

Morgen put his bag down and lit a cigarette. His tiny holdall suggested he had no plans to stay long. Schlegel had overpacked.

The stickiness brought on by the crushing heat left everyone's shirt and jacket stained with sweat.

Morgen suggested a beer. One of the drinkers, nondescript and sallow, sidled over and in fractured German attempted to scrounge a cigarette. Morgen said, 'Fuck off, son.'

The man continued to stand smiling and uncomprehending, his hand stuck out.

'Oh, for God's sake,' said Morgen, flipping him one. 'Now fuck off.'

The man backed away, bowing.

'Hungarian, at a guess,' said Morgen. 'Christ, it's hot.'

Outside the full heat of the night hit them and Schlegel thought he saw Schulze walk away in the velvet dusk. Two cabs in a taxi rank waited in white-painted boxes, under a sign. A huge flag hung off a large formal building on the far side of an empty square.

Morgen had a row with his taxi driver, who said he was close enough to walk. Typical of Morgen to pick a fight, Schlegel thought.

His impression was of a dirty old town, smoke and factories. The square in front of the station with its dusty horse chestnuts was an open expanse no one had got around to paving. The grand building opposite, draped with its flag, looked like the architect had only half-remembered how to copy the French style.

The taxi driver told Morgen it was his hotel, all of two minutes' walk and not worth the meter. Schlegel thought the episode ridiculous until deftly solved by Morgen offering a fare upfront and ordering the man to drive around the square until the money was used up.

Morgen invited Schlegel to join him. Schlegel preferred to walk and drink the rest of his beer. Benches stood in the middle of the square. On one sat a kissing couple, the lad with his hand up the back of the girl's blouse. She caught Schlegel's eye and gave him a brassy stare. Schlegel sat down away from them and watched the absurd round of Morgen's taxi. He stared at the baked ground and thought of summer downpours that started with a few heavy splashes of rain. The girl had smelled of sweat and something more pungent.

He thought about Sybil and about Schulze.

Morgen's taxi had the square to itself. A few couples strolled arm in arm, looking like melting ice creams. Mosquitos were starting to come out. Schlegel slapped his neck and saw the kissing couple were gone. He picked up his case and walked over to the hotel as the gathering darkness sucked the colour out of the day.

Schlegel's tiny room in the eaves reminded him of his little rooftop box in Auguststrasse. The view was of the square and the station, and in the last of the light he made out a goods yard and factory buildings. A big moon hung in the sky. In contrast to Berlin, lights were on. No blackout. He found it hard to convey to himself the utter strangeness and remote beauty of it, even in that shitty town.

A fly spray came with the room. He gave a couple of desultory squirts and watched them dissolve. The smell was toxic.

The thought of being able to stroll through lit streets led Schlegel back outside. Left took him to a checkpoint and a squat sentry box bathed in sticky yellow light. The station stood revealed as a long, low affair, impressive in scale and sardonic in tone, as though the town's sole point of attraction was departure.

He walked the other way towards the town, passing non-descript buildings in search of an identity, the more superior a job-lot in the neo-classical style, the less-favoured little more than huts. No one was around. An empty bus rattled past, lit up, and again he stared. Shops looked shut for good, streets were in poor repair, with horse droppings and rotten drains. Schlegel supposed all the action was at the hotel. A town with lights on and nowhere to go!

The hotel toilets were scrawled with graffiti. Schlegel sat in his stall listening to the drunken traffic using the urinals, accompanied by copious splashing. Someone vomited and said: 'That's better.' Graffiti danced in front of his eyes. A *vagina dentens*, labelled Jew cunt. Scribbled exhortations to fuck my cock bitch. Recommendations for the best givers of fellatio. Bragging and aggression of the dreariest kind, apart from one fanatically neat inscription, chilling by comparison, which rocked Schlegel.

Make friends with the beast.

Morgen was waiting in the dining room, at a table in the corner. He waved a mimeographed sheet. 'Look, a choice of dishes and nothing crossed out.'

Apart from the serving orderly, no one paid them any attention but Schlegel was aware of surreptitious inspection.

The place seemed principally for the use of officers, uni-formed bucks, who noisily fancied themselves, sitting and standing drinking, not eating. Women were in too. Schlegel guessed most were garrison staff, though they were surprisingly dolled up. The tone was superior, even if most were in the process of getting roaring drunk.

Morgen said, 'Cushy billet.'

Schlegel wondered if Schulze drank there, and dressed up. He looked around to see if Krick was in. Morgen said nothing. The room grew raucous, with women staggering and whooping, steadied by equally drunk men sweating booze who felt them up. Morgen struck Schlegel as not at all himself, as if the journey had robbed him. He complained that even his cigarettes tasted foul.

Eventually he said, 'Remember in those American westerns, how before the ambush someone always said it was too quiet.'

'You can't say that of here.'

'Too noisy but I suspect the same. Tomorrow we find out if we are being set up.'

Schlegel slept badly. During the night he was woken by a fistfight outside, a woman's shrieked climax and mosquito attacks.

He lay feeling like a stranger in his own life.

The next morning's sullen progression of checkpoints was in no hurry to process them. It was going to be another unseasonably, stinking-hot day. The guards scraped their heels as they slouched. There wasn't much soldierly about the place. 'Is this the cream?' wondered Morgen.

Inside the garrison, it was hard to see what all the palaver of getting in was about. It all looked desperately ordinary, not a fortress or a citadel or anything resembling a prison particularly. They emerged into a commercial sector, with industrial sheds, some brick, and temporary wooden huts crammed wherever. They passed a row of working stables. Morgen asked one of the grooms where the post office was. Nobody seemed to know. A horse kicked a stable door, making Schlegel jump. They walked on. More sheds. A water tower. A tall chimney. Schlegel had already sweated through his jacket.

He blinked at the dome of pitiless sky; on the horizon a billowing stain of smoke.

They wordlessly removed their jackets. Everything aspired to dull military regulation, kerbs marked by stones painted white, with link chains. Even the scrapyard next to the motor pool appeared pointlessly tidy.

They passed out of the working area into the garrison proper. A wide, long avenue ran down to the main gate, with red-bricked barracks, grass verges and flowerbeds. Two women in uniform walked out of a building, laughing and carrying files. One wore becoming dark glasses.

They ignored them and carried on laughing.

The post office was in the block next to the big staff hospital, opposite the tall chimney, which stood behind a high grassy bank, planted with wilting silver birch. The entrance to the block was in the middle, up a short path and a couple of steps. Scorched grass watered by feeble sprinklers made tiny rainbows and sprayed their feet. Schlegel wanted only to lie down and get soaked.

Inside, everything was arrowed. Construction department, first floor to the right. Post office, ground floor left. Laundry and dry cleaning, left. The wide central corridor had fire extinguishers and its waxed floors gleamed in the muted light.

The post office was a large room with a counter and a wired-off section, with boxed shelving full of parcels and letters, presided over by a tiny man no taller than a child.

Morgen said they were there to see Horn. The tiny man looked surprised, as though no one had asked before. When he was gone Morgen said there used to be a minimum height requirement.

The man returned, lifted the counter and told them to follow, complaining that someone had stolen his electric fan.

An airless corridor of shelves smelling of hot dust led into a back room where a corpulent man with an enormous waist sat in shirt and braces behind a makeshift plywood desk. He was surrounded by a mess whose lack of organisation said nothing for the efficiency of the postal service.

The tiny man departed, still grumbling about his fan. The fat man offered a wet handshake.

'It's like a fucking sauna in here. My fan has been stolen too.'

Horn looked exhausted, with huge bags under his eyes, one of which had a weeping stye. His hair lay plastered like dried seaweed over a pink scalp.

Morgen produced his pass.

'Ah, yes,' said Horn, inspecting it. 'Herr Richter.'

He didn't sound particularly convinced but turned out to be more efficient than he looked. He reached down and picked a parcelled box out of the mess. Though still wrapped and loosely held by string, it had been opened. Horn rummaged inside and produced two large gold nuggets. They gleamed less than Schlegel was expecting, and were much bigger, the size of a child's fist.

'His name is Bock. We call him Dr Gold, ha-ha. A dentist working here. As regular as clockwork with his postings, Wednesdays and Fridays, sent to a sister in Freiburg, labelled food parcel.' He peered at the label. 'Dry goods, it says, in brackets.'

He produced a large hardback register, with ruled vertical columns, listing all packages and parcels posted, with stated contents.

'For insurance purposes. In case they get lost.'

The record confirmed previous transactions to the same address.

Morgen picked up one of the nuggets and asked if the dentist was stealing gold from his own clinic.

Horn said undoubtedly.

'Nevertheless, a lot of gold.'

'There is something of a surplus.'

Morgen looked at him sharply. 'On whose authority did you open the parcel?'

'My own.'

'Reason?'

'Tip-off.'

'Anonymous?'

'Of course.'

'Why of course?'

'How things work here.'

'No idea where this anonymous tip-off came from?'

Horn sighed mightily. 'Prisoners. Jealous colleague. A rival in another department.' He added with a mirthless laugh, 'Everyone hates everybody here.'

'And who did you inform?'

'What do you mean?'

'Aren't you why we're here?'

'I see what you mean. I informed my superior in Berlin. He said someone would come and here you are!'

Morgen asked why he was laughing and Horn said he never expected anyone to turn up.

'Tell us about Bock.'

'Average. Nondescript. He'll be in again two-thirty tomorrow, if the register is right; catch him red-handed.'

Schlegel thought Bock must be brazen or stupid to use the army post office. Maybe nobody cared.

'This amount of gold in a dental practice?' Morgen asked.

'Quite so. I am looking forward to seeing his face.' Horn paused, thoughtful, pointed at the gold. 'Why don't you help yourself? Everyone else does.'

Morgen looked at Schlegel. The words – 'everyone else does' – hung in the air.

'Actually, it's policy now,' said Horn, offering them a

mint. 'The garrison healthcare and dental programme is excellent, by the way. Really first rate.'

'What is policy?' asked Morgen.

It was one of those conversations neither looked like he wanted to continue.

Horn, sucking his mint, asked, 'What do you know about here?'

'Little more than we have discussed,' said Morgen.

'Have you looked around?'

'We came straight from the hotel.'

'Has anyone said about the epidemic?'

'Only in passing,' Schlegel said. Schulze had mentioned a quarantine lasting almost a year.

Horn looked at Schlegel. 'So you do talk. This place has been in lockdown for as long as anyone can remember. Typhus. Figures off the scale. I lost two members of staff. Everyone stuck here, going out of their minds from boredom. There's a private holiday centre in the hills where people go. There are only so many clubs one can join. I don't sing and I am too old for exercise. But I digress.'

'What policy?'

'This place is a huge recycling and sorting centre. Nothing wasted.'

'Policy?' insisted Morgen.

'Maybe not actual policy, but what I heard. With so many dying and nothing allowed to go to waste, someone had the bright idea of recycling the gold from the teeth of those taken by the typhus.'

Schlegel looked at the nuggets, and thought: From the mouths of the dead.

Horn added, 'Gold being not infectious.'

Morgen said, 'That is a lot of epidemic.'

'The smoke?' Schlegel offered.

Horn nodded. 'Smoke is the epidemic. Belching smoke, ashes, day after day. That nasty stink is cremation. Typhus has ravaged this place, killed God knows how many. Dog shit and geraniums are all here is good for.'

'Is it true about the gold?' asked Schlegel, as they emerged, staggering under the weight of the sun.

'The idea has been around for years. Victor Scholz.'

'Who is Scholz?'

'I have no idea now. Then he was a student and his doctoral thesis at the University of Breslau was entitled *Possibility of Recycling Gold from the Mouths of the Dead*. Published in 1940.'

Schlegel always feared one day he would become contaminated by Morgen's secrets.

'How do you know this?'

'I read about it in a legal magazine, discussed as a point of law, not long after publication.'

Schlegel shivered in spite of the heat.

Morgen didn't want to wait for Bock and said they should pick him up now.

They wasted a couple of hours trying to locate his clinic where they were told he wasn't available, being away on a course that day, which Schlegel supposed was an excuse for bunking off.

With nothing else to do, they went back to the hotel and agreed to eat early.

Schlegel sat in his room and wrote a tired letter to his stepfather. He had to use a blunt pencil, borrowed from the desk downstairs, because his pen was already missing. The soft lead made the letter look like a product of psychiatric care. The content made him appear backward. For security reasons, he was unable to say where he was or what he was doing, other than being away and he hoped everyone was as well as could be expected, and so on. The act of writing depressed him even more than the lazier alternative, which was not to.

They ate in silence. Tench with potatoes, cucumber and dill salad. Already by six the room was noisy with drinkers in for the long evening.

Morgen's mood did not improve when they heard his name being called. Schlegel turned to see a lean man of upright bearing, impeccably suited, with soft, spoiling good looks, bearing down on them.

'Morgen! Fegelein,' he announced.

He insisted on shaking Morgen by the hand, then Schlegel, who mumbled he was Klein, thinking their cover was already blown.

'Morgen!' Fegelein repeated. 'Here of all places!'

He turned to Schlegel. 'Morgen and I are old adversaries.'

Morgen said, 'Can you please stop using my name.'

'Oh, I see, ha-ha!' Fegelein said it with a little shuffle, to show he was quick on his feet. He winked at Schlegel. 'Here to snoop, are we?' He clapped Morgen on the shoulder. 'Our friend here failed to get the better of me a couple of years ago, and he was the one who ended up in penal detention, not me!'

Schlegel felt obliged to loathe the man. Kammler and Morgen had talked of him – the equestrian involved in a fur scandal, which Morgen was warned off.

Fegelein clicked his heels. 'Now I am the Reichsführer's personal staff liaison to the Chancellery. And you?'

Schlegel wondered if his presence had something to do with them being there but Morgen seemed to regard him as no more than a consummate brown-noser.

'What brings you?' Morgen asked, ignoring the question.

Fegelein looked around and clapped his hands.

'A bit of official, a bit of unofficial. Hence the mufti. Actually, I am here for horse experiments to find a breed able to survive the Russian winter.'

'Bit late for that.'

'Defeatist talk. I could have you shot, ha-ha! I must say, dear Heini admits to being quite bamboozled by you. I follow your career with interest.' He tapped his nose. 'Not a word to anyone.'

He touched his lips as if sealing them. 'I'm here a few days. We must reacquaint. Smoke the pipe of peace and all that.'

He gave a breezy wave before strolling off, leaving Morgen shaking his head.

'One of the most unsavoury arseholes in the whole of the Reich. Consider our cover officially blown. We may as well get drunk.'

They were still trying and failing to, despite enormous quantities of liquor downed, when they were accosted by the commandant's adjutant who said they were to follow him. For the second time that evening someone seemed to know who they were.

He told them they were in breach of etiquette for failing to pay their respects to the commandant.

'Juppe,' he said. 'I will drive you.'

Juppe was blond, supercilious, china-blue eyes, cheek-bones, aquiline nose; everything correct except reduced height and a prominent Adam's apple that was impossible not to stare at.

They made a point of sitting in the back of the car, reducing Juppe to the role of chauffeur. No one spoke. They took a ring road around the prison, which was walled, lit up and manned with watchtowers. It looked huge compared to the adjacent garrison where they were waved through the main gate.

The adjutant parked outside the first block and led them across the road to a door in a high wall.

What lay beyond was a shock: an abundant private garden in late bloom, lawn and roses, ferns and exotic shrubs, bathed in the glow of street lamps behind. Within the garden stood a further walled space, revealing a secret enclave, with a gazebo and summerhouse of whitewashed brick, with verandah and murals, trellises, a large formal pond and a children's sandpit.

A dark object on the mown lawn, Schlegel realised, as he nearly trod on it, was a tortoise.

A man stood on the patio in braces and shirtsleeves, smoking a cigar. He tersely announced himself as Hoess, commandant, and dismissed Juppe.

He inspected them slowly, with a gaze of considerable power. At the same time, Schlegel couldn't help thinking he looked like a clerk or schoolteacher. The obvious thugs were at least predictable.

'State your business.'

The high voice further undermined the image strived for by the razored bullet head, the jut of the chin and mirrored shine of the boots. Schlegel suspected any suspicion of being laughed at would release wild rage.

'A case of gold smuggling,' said Morgen.

'Show your authority.'

They produced their false papers. The commandant held them disdainfully at arm's-length and squinted. 'The post office! Richter and Klein? Is this a comic turn? Really?'

'We are investigating on behalf of the post office.'

'Why wasn't I told? We have our own discipline, Richter. Or are you Klein?' The voice dripped with sarcasm.

Schlegel was sure the commandant already knew because of Fegelein.

Morgen said, 'The post office is bound to investigate violations of its service.'

Smoke wreathed the commandant's head. Schlegel realised the man was stinking drunk. The roses shone deep pink in the night.

They were joined by a woman in silhouette, stepping out of the summerhouse.

'Why are you talking to these men?'

The commandant grunted. 'My wife.'

Schlegel had the impression they had interrupted a row, not one of the shouting ones. The woman looked more the type for silent invective. He couldn't see her properly because she remained in the shadows.

Morgen said, 'You have a beautiful garden.'

The commandant relented somewhat and said it was his wife's work.

'The pride and joy of the whole family,' she added.

Schlegel read hatred on his part, contempt on hers, so obvious they could have put up a hoarding. In Berlin he found people altogether harder to read. Here they seemed like comic-strip characters with thought bubbles. The one coming from the commandant's head might be saying: *Here am I, a god in my own land and yet . . .*

The wife's appearance brought an impasse but with it an almost imperceptible change, like the slightest shift in wind direction, warning of storms to come.

She posed statuesquely while the commandant inspected the last of his cigar. The atmosphere grew electric. Schlegel found the commandant and his wife like figures in a provincial drama, dressed up for no reason, in a place less real. He had a dim inkling that someone like him had once stood in Roman Mesopotamia or Jerusalem watching such a scene. Maybe the same few limited scenarios of love and hate played themselves out, like a repeating film, and their story was already decided, only they were in the dark because unlike actors they had not been shown the script.

The commandant asked Schlegel, 'Do you ride?'

Schlegel was thrown by the question because it had been Kammler's too. The commandant asked Morgen the same.

'Once or twice and badly.'

'First we ride, then we have a little shooting party. Six o'clock at the stables.'

Back at the hotel, the bar was hellbent in pursuit of oblivion, more cranked up, on the turn, with a prospect of fistfights.

Was there still a plan, asked Schlegel, standing in the squash.

Morgen said, 'I fear we will be reduced to terrible improvisations.'

They stayed up drinking.

Schlegel talked to a man with owlish spectacles, less drunk than he was. The man puffed contently on his pipe and told him the region was a secret crisis area and the trains that came were split between incoming workers and hospital transports for the sick, which were confined in vast quarantine pens.

Schlegel, interested, asked if the man had seen the area.

'Strictly off limits, but people who have were issued masks to prevent infection.'

He was a food expert, he said, working on synthetic rations and mineral supplements. He had it on good authority that the sick were from the epidemic raging throughout Europe and the eastern territories. 'None of it reported, of course, and it will kill far more than the war, like the Spanish influenza of 1918. It's nature's way of saying who is in control.'

He spoke as one who knew. Later, standing on the fringe

of a noisy drinking crowd, Schlegel pointed out the man to the woman next to him, and told her about his food research. She looked at him in astonishment. 'Gunther?' Schlegel already felt a fool. Gunther was a clerk in the paymaster's office.

'You're late,' snapped the commandant.

He wore riding jodhpurs, complete with spurs and a whip. His mount carried an elaborately tooled cowboy-style saddle.

The breath of the waiting horses mingled with the thick mist that had fallen over the garrison, reducing visibility to soft outlines.

Morgen said they had got lost because of the fog.

They were badly hungover. Schlegel stood unsteadily on the mounting stone. When he put his food in the stirrup the saddle slipped.

'The girth is loose!' screamed the commandant.

Two grooms emerged, little more than boys. The commandant asked which had saddled up. The two stood rooted, incapable of speech, until one lad pointed to the other, shifting the blame.

The commandant said, 'Since he is incompetent, show him how.'

He waited, whacking his leg with his whip while the saddle was fixed.

Schlegel remounted and was trying to get his loose foot in the other stirrup when the commandant slashed the groom at fault across the face with his whip. The groom remained at attention, bleeding from the cut under his eye. The commandant turned away as though nothing had happened. Morgen remained inscrutable. The commandant mounted and waved the grooms away. He stared glassy-eyed as Morgen viewed his horse, a stallion, with suspicion. When he tried to mount it skittered sideways, hooves ringing. When he tried again the horse repeated the move, with a hostile glare. Schlegel suspected it read Morgen's nervousness. To spare him further embarrassment, Schlegel got down and told Morgen to take his horse, which seemed more docile. He formed a stirrup of his hands and told Morgen to use it. Morgen managed to haul himself up, with the help of the pommel. He sat aloft, looking down uncertainly, while the commandant glared unamused. Schlegel calmed the stallion. The horse repeated its move and he was left hanging on with insufficient leverage to haul himself up. It crossed his mind that the choice of a difficult horse was deliberate on the part of the commandant.

The commandant scoffed at their display. 'Fall off and break your necks for all I care.'

Morgen rolled uncomfortably as they rode out, past huge shapes looming in the mist. Schlegel thought how ridiculous they must look, two men in suits on horseback, accompanying this martinet in full fig. He found keeping his eyes shut lessened the hangover's vertigo. Gunsels indeed.

They crossed the unseen river into white, misted countryside. It was at least still cool, which was the best Schlegel could come up with in the way of anything positive. His brain felt corroded, his blood as sluggish as sump oil. The commandant would insist on at least a canter, probably in the hope that one or both of them would fall off. He told Morgen to keep his reins short if he wanted to pull up. Morgen growled, 'I know what a short rein is.'

The mist half-lifted, leaving everything below their waists shrouded, making them like ships on a white sea. A line of trees appeared on the horizon; above them what looked like towering pillars of cloud. The commandant halted. 'See how beautiful,' he said with a sweep of his arm. 'As for your business, you have twenty-four hours to complete it. One minute over and I have you thrown out – with or without your wretched little man – or arrested, whichever I decide. You're not worth the paper you're written on. Has either of you served a term before?'

Morgen said six months in detention. The commandant asked what for.

'Insubordination,' said Morgen.

'Then you know what to expect. We certainly taught those Polish fuckers the meaning of work.'

The commandant leaned forward, stroking the neck of his mare. Despite the early coolness, he was sweating. He said, 'I saw my first action in Baghdad at the age of fifteen. At seventeen I was the youngest sergeant in the army in the fourteen–eighteen war.'

Schlegel didn't know whether to believe him.

'After that we were nobodies. Hard times. You're too young to remember. Someone had to keep order, after what we had fought for. The treasurer of my free corps unit was Martin Bormann, and look where he is now. Secretary to the Führer.'

The commandant looked pleased on behalf of his old colleague. Fuck, thought Schlegel. Never would he have guessed the man had such connections.

The commandant was also a big moaner, going on about how hard it had been setting up the garrison, reduced to driving around the countryside in person, helping equip the place, down to pots and pans.

'Barbed-wire fencing, what a nightmare to find that! But we did and made something we could be proud of.'

Morgen looked comic, smoking on a horse.

The commandant again asked sarcastically if he was Klein or Richter.

A strange man, Schlegel thought; stranger than he had seemed the night before. He flinched at the memory of the casual and incisive use of the whip on the groom.

'Did you go to college?' the commandant asked.

Schlegel said he had done compulsory labour instead. For the first time the commandant looked interested.

'Tell.'

A troubled youth, he said, caught shoplifting.

'Shoplifting where?'

In the big department store KaDeWe. Schlegel didn't add that his stepfather had fixed for him not to go to prison.

The commandant was amused. 'At least you were robbing from the rich. That shows some class. What kind of labour?'

Building an autobahn, he said. The commandant's eyes gleamed. 'Yes, it is good to work with the hands! You understand what I mean. Hope for you yet.'

Schlegel didn't say he had been given the easy job of the surveyor's chain boy, which had required little more than hold the surveyor's theodolite and sit in a hut.

The man showed no sign of letting up. At least it stopped them riding. Morgen looked tense at the prospect. What speed was a canter? Twenty-five, 30kph? Schlegel thought he could probably manage, but Morgen? And if either lost their seat would their foot get caught in a stirrup so they ended up being dragged by the horse? It didn't bear thinking about.

The mist was lifting. Schlegel saw patches of countryside.

The commandant told them his own background lay in communal farming. It was how he had met the Reichsführer. Fuck, thought Schlegel, another huge name dropped. Farming was how he had met his wife, the commandant went on. Schlegel struggled to picture her scratching around in the dirt, feeding the chickens. Heini, of course, had been a chicken farmer. In irreverent moments, people made clucking noises at mention of his name.

The commandant said, 'Once there was a future to this place. Now it is little more than a refugee camp. I say this with no side, gentlemen; they are the facts. Now let's ride.'

He wheeled his mare and was off, racing away and back, a man exhilarated, circling them, urging them on, telling them not to be girls.

Schlegel caught Morgen's look of resolve as he punched his heels into his mount's side and set off at a brisk trot, barely in control. The commandant continued to circle, shouting encouragement.

Schlegel sensed his horse neither liked nor trusted him. He reached a canter and shut his eyes, feeling the air on his face, hearing the heavy pound of hooves. He opened his eyes, felt briefly better. The ground raced. Morgen was off to his left, ahead. The commandant had split away and was riding hard towards the trees.

The mist remained in patches, making holes of the land-scape. Far away strange insubstantial shapes hovered. They looked huge – the size of aircraft hangars – rendered almost invisible by their transparency.

He splashed through marshier ground. Reeds and a lake came into view. Watchtowers rose in the distance and a line of telegraph poles counted its way along the horizon. The commandant disappeared into white.

Schlegel's horse had a way of twisting his neck at speed, testing his limited skill. There was disobedience and mis-behaviour too. At one point the brute veered off to rampage through the shallows of the lake. Schlegel tried to pull up but they careered on. He struggled to take control, which the horse resented, and went into a spin, splashing and twirling, bucking in an effort to unseat him. When he realised the horse was enjoying itself at his expense, he stopped fighting it. Whereupon the stallion grew deceptively docile, only to charge off again, across country in the direction of the commandant.

His horse insisted on running himself out. The horizon jumped and blurred. Morgen charged out of a patch of mist, being thrown around in the saddle, the most inelegant show of horsemanship Schlegel had ever witnessed. Worse, Morgen was holding on one-handed, using his free arm to make windmills, and laughing like an idiot.

From the other direction came the distant whinny of the commandant's horse, a cry of alarm sensed by Schlegel's horse. Schlegel saw the commandant's mare rise on her hind legs and the man lift one arm in what looked like a valediction. With the remaining mist and speed of the gallop it was hard to make out. There was no time to think because Morgen's horse was charging towards him, riderless.

Schlegel followed the direction it had come from. He called and got no reply.

He followed the hoofprints, angry scars in the boggy ground. Morgen eventually answered. Schlegel found him on his back, blowing smoke.

'Soft landing,' Morgen said.

'What happened?'

'The nag and I were getting on. I fancied a smoke at speed.'

'Didn't you think to stop first?'

'It was lighting the smoke at speed I fancied, but I had to use both hands, which was where it went wrong and I slipped in the saddle. Dropped my lighter. It was quite a good one.'

Schlegel's stallion was breathing hard, flanks working like bellows, obedient at last.

Morgen clambered to his feet. 'No bones broken. Look, here he comes.'

The commandant emerged out of the start of the day's heat haze, walking his mare and leading Morgen's horse.

Looking like he had seen a ghost, thought Schlegel.

The commandant made no acknowledgement as he approached, so preoccupied he gave no sign of seeing them. He wordlessly handed Morgen his horse, showed no concern as to how he was, then pointed away from the direction he had come and said, 'We take the bridle path back.'

He led the way with Schlegel following. Morgen took up the rear. Schlegel watched the hypnotic rise and fall of the man's back. A gurgling brook ran beside the path. At one point the commandant halted and held up his arm for them to do the same. A cyclist flashed past on a drop-handlebar bike, wearing a fancy riding kit, like a real racer, and in the blur of his passing Schlegel recognised Krick.

Outside his house the commandant tethered his horse to the fence, told them to do the same and wait in the hall while he changed; Groenke would come shortly to collect them for the shoot. He called out to ask if anyone was around. His wife appeared at the top of the stairs but didn't come down. He shouted up to say the gardener should return the horses. Schlegel noted that the commandant waited for his wife to disappear before going upstairs.

The hall was well appointed, with polished parquet and oriental runners. Morgen inspected an oil painting and grunted. Schlegel, in the grip of his hangover, was grateful for the pause. His head and his legs ached.

A big man in civilians wandered through the front door, announced himself as Groenke and asked if the Old Man was about. Morgen said upstairs. A burst of children's laughter came from above.

Groenke looked at ease. The commandant's wife made her entrance, descending with the light behind her, coming from the long window which made a feature of the stairs. She seemed to make a point of appearing plain, when she wasn't, and modest, which Schlegel suspected she wasn't either.

She greeted Groenke and ignored them. She briefly left and returned with samples of materials and said, 'That's the one I want. That would look best.' She looked at Schlegel and Morgen and asked, 'What do you two think?'

They could only approve. Having come to her attention, she said they must sign the visitors' book on the hall table, which everyone who came to the house had to, however high or humble.

She showed them where the Reichsführer had signed on different occasions. 'And there is Hanns Johst, the poet laureate, who came on one occasion with the Reichsführer.'

She flicked the pages. 'Oswald Pohl. Pohl again.'

So the commandant's boss was a houseguest, thought Schlegel. The commandant seemed extraordinarily well connected for such a provincial posting.

Staff were starting to turn up in twos and threes. It all appeared very informal. Some came through the front door without knocking. Others arrived by the kitchen. The commandant's wife made a point of issuing cheerful greetings. She held out a pen for Morgen to sign the book. Schlegel couldn't decide whether he was amused or nervous when Morgen signed himself 'Richter, Post Office'. He gave nothing away as he handed the pen to Schlegel, who saw further up the page Fegelein had written 'Chancellery' next to his name, adding, 'A privilege and pleasure as always.'

The commandant's wife was discussing the order of the day with the servants. Schlegel heard the commandant coming downstairs, calling for Groenke. He turned away from signing as two women came through the door.

Until that moment everything was normal or ordinary, or whatever you wanted to call it, thought Schlegel. Time stood still and in the detonation of a moment everything changed.

The woman on the right was Sybil.

Her hair was shorter and she was dressed plainly but it was unmistakably her.

The world expanded and settled again with the commandant suddenly among them, dressed in a fancy shooting waistcoat full of pouches and pockets in unlikely places, being loud with Groenke and upstaging his wife.

Schlegel, in shock, replayed the moment, and her look of terror as their eyes met. The commandant's wife had greeted her and received a good morning as Sybil split off and ran upstairs.

He was in a mind to follow, regardless of the threat he seemed to pose. He started to go up, asking for the toilet, and was told in no uncertain terms by the commandant's wife that the guest lavatory was down the hall, and she pointed him to it.

Schlegel sat in the toilet, composing himself. He could not tell whether Morgen had seen her. He questioned his judgement. Had he projected her onto someone else? No, it was her voice.

He made a show of flushing the toilet and washing his hands and stepped back into the hall, light-headed. The commandant was grumbling about being kept waiting.

An open wagon was parked outside, the horses gone. The commandant, wearing dark goggles, drove them to the armoury where more men waited. All wore civilian dress and knew their way around guns, especially a loose-limbed blond beast who moved with a hunter's grace.

The commandant broke the barrel of their guns before handing them over, accompanied by a belt of shells.

Hearty shoulder slaps between the men contrasted with the absence of any introduction for them. Fegelein strolled in and clicked his heels. Schlegel's spirits sank. He could not shake the feeling that the man had been sent to watch them.

Groenke sat next to the commandant, who drove, with Schlegel and Morgen in the back, and the others followed in a second car.

'Bitch of a heatwave,' said Groenke, holding his hand out to catch the slipstream.

Schlegel thought back to visits to Sybil in hiding and her threatening his young life with sudden, incomprehensible joy. His hangover came in waves and the exultation of seeing her gave way to a crushing hopelessness.

Two crows rose out of the trees, black wings flapping. Two shots punched out. One continued to rise while the other balled and fell, leaving feathers in its wake. It hit the ground past Schlegel, bounced once, and lay there, wings beating uselessly.

Schlegel was at the end of the line. Next to him was the blond beast, who appeared capable of nailing anything. Groenke and the commandant were fair shots, unlike Schlegel, who aimed to miss because he disliked killing. Fegelein shot as he would have expected, a natural sportsman. Morgen looked bored and barely bothered to raise his gun.

A couple of stray pheasants flew out of the ground, their

panicky, low trajectories barely getting them up before they were brought down in a hail of buckshot.

The blond beast amused himself by drawing a bead on the beaters. The commandant joked that the men were performing a useful task, but Schlegel saw that the two men annoyed each other. The beaters were prisoners, dressed in shabby clothes distinguished by their markings.

The commandant was now sunniness itself, sharing a hip flask with Groenke, wisecracking, toasting and congratulating spectacular shots. The blond beast sometimes fired from the hip, and was rewarded with whistles and cheers; jeers on the rare occasions he missed. He had a soft, almost baby face, and funny eyes. Despite his joker's manner, Schlegel suspected he was a hard man; what Morgen would call a proper specimen.

The shoot was competitive and casual to the point of laziness. Whether out of protocol or deference, the commandant had been allowed to claim the first bird and Schlegel watched the wood pigeon cartwheel down as the commandant removed the cigarette stuck in the corner of his mouth and whooped like an excited schoolboy.

They stopped often for what the commandant called a drinks break. The men all had flasks. Schlegel, the worse for wear, was grateful none offered. The talk was all man-to-man, resting easy with crooked guns.

Fegelein said, 'Nice to think of the little women tucked up safe at home.'

'Who was it who shot a beater after a disappointing bag?' Groenke asked. The question sounded like part of a repertoire saved for every shoot. 'Was it you, Palitsch?'

The blond beast gave a shy smile and said he only did head jobs. The men roared with laughter, except the commandant, who glared. Schlegel suspected the moment had registered with Morgen, despite him giving the appearance of being entranced by the local insect life.

They moved on. A panicky whirr of wings announced the flight of the bird which moved across the line towards Schlegel. The other guns left it. He had the bird in his sights, felt the start of the trigger squeeze and stopped – arrested by the notion that it was a symbol of his and Sybil's fate. He fired low and late. The other guns, which had been tracing the bird's arc, let loose, apart from Palitsch whose gun was aimed at Schlegel's head, in an easy way, like he was admonishing him for his miss. It didn't stop him from firing, close enough for Schlegel to feel the shot pass his head. He turned and watched the bird fly on, then falter.

The dogs couldn't find it, which left him with the stupid hope that it had got away.

When it got too hot they returned to the cars. Fegelein drifted on the edge of the group, a casual sinister presence, tailing Morgen. Schlegel presumed Palitsch was a maniac. How close had he been to shooting him, or was it a garrison joke? Barely nine and Schlegel felt done in. Groenke made a point of escorting him back to the car. He gripped his elbow and said, 'Your friend, whatever his name is, ha-ha, is not popular after what he did in Buchenwald. Don't let him shit in the soup as he did there.' He gave Schlegel's elbow an extra squeeze.

Back at the armoury someone was shooting inside. It was the commandant's adjutant, Juppe, passing the time with target practice.

It was obvious he was waiting for them and equally clear what the commandant intended. Juppe was duly assigned as their escort for the day. They would be given no leeway. It explained why they had been dragged out riding and hunting. The commandant wanted them under watch. Morgen protested.

'The choice is not yours,' the commandant said. 'While you are in the garrison I am responsible for your safety.'

'Does that mean we are not safe?'

'Juppe will be with you at all times.'

The men drifted off, leaving them stuck with Juppe, who remained formal and correct, however hard an impatient Morgen pushed him.

'Why don't we amuse ourselves?'

Juppe repeated his lines. 'The commandant demands you be escorted so you don't get lost.'

They had no choice. It wasn't as though they had anything to do until returning to the post office. Schlegel's hangover refused to budge.

They started with the garrison metal works. Juppe had all the dull statistics, recited at length. He had no small talk and resisted any questioning or being provoked into personal observation. After the metal works it was the dairy and the general concession where the garrison could buy its provisions. A theatre. Library. Sports facilities, including gym and pitches for the local football league. A swimming pool was in the process of being built.

Then it was to the leather factory where they saw Groenke again, down on the shop floor among the workers. He enjoyed shouting encouragement, offering cheery greetings to supervisors, admiringly inspecting an elaborate piece of leather tooling, going around opening windows, saying let's try and get some air in here.

Groenke was asked what they produced. From the way he and Juppe interacted, Schlegel could see that it wasn't the first time this sort of time-wasting had gone on.

'Leather for the military. Boots, panniers, satchels, rifle straps. There was a rush order recently for binocular cases, but we still find time to make furniture. We have designers who do a nice line in leather chairs. If you want one we can arrange to have it shipped. For the commandant's birthday we made him an exceptionally fine saddle in the American style.'

Schlegel supposed Groenke about forty, one of those tough nuts who made a point of an irritating bonhomie, which assumed everyone saw the world as he did. He had changed since the shoot. Everything about his appearance spoke of a certain quality. The high leather boots were both practical and ostentatious, with lacing all the way to the knee, featuring what Schlegel was astonished to note were real silver cleats. The man was a walking advertisement for his work. A kid waistcoat, unnecessary in the heat, looked as soft as chamois. A wide studded belt was obviously hand-made, as was the broad watch strap. On his other wrist he wore an elaborately braided leather bracelet. There were even leather patches on the knees of his trousers!

He gave them his little lecture, telling them proudly how he had qualified as a master shoemaker as part of a prisoner initiative to retrain for civilian life. Schlegel wondered why such a brute wasn't in the army.

The morning went on like that, with Juppe never less than thorough without giving anything away. Morgen wondered aloud if it was his job to point out the obvious. Juppe didn't laugh, even out of politeness.

'What's that strange smell?' Morgen asked.

'Poles,' said Juppe, with a shrill laugh.

The smell was of animals being slaughtered. Schlegel knew it from Berlin and Morgen would too. The garrison had its own slaughterhouse, as it did everything else, and they weren't going to be spared an inspection.

It stood behind a high wall, like in Berlin. Closer to, they could hear the nervous, lowing animals. Inside, an arcade ran down one side of the building with the killing sheds to the right. They saw herded cattle waiting, heard the dry cough of the stun gun.

It was a large professional outfit, though nothing like the scale of Berlin. Men in hats and blood-spattered aprons supervised. The smell of blood, mixed with his hangover, made Schlegel nauseous. Juppe was reciting: how many cattle, sheep and pigs. The garrison abattoir accounted for the excellence of the meat in the officers' mess where they would have lunch. They passed a line of butchered carcasses hanging ready for dispatch.

The arcade led into a large courtyard with several regular workshops unconnected to the slaughterhouse. The air outside was only marginally less foul. Morgen lit up.

The courtyard was a dead end and they had to pass back through the arcade. The butchered carcasses were being added to by a gang with trolleys to carry the animals, which were hauled up using pulleys. Their supervisor was a small man with a long sharp knife, used like a conductor's baton.

The man was depressingly familiar. Morgen had spotted him too.

It was Sepp from the Berlin slaughterhouse. Sepp had once skinned humans for sport.

The biggest shock was that Sepp was still alive. The last Schlegel had heard, execution was on the cards for the lot of them.

Morgen's frustration spilled over.

'I thought you were supposed to be dead.'

Sepp smirked, apparently unsurprised, almost as though he had known they were coming.

'No shortage of death,' he said, 'but a dearth of master butchers, so here we are, on reprieve.'

Sepp lisped to deliberately irritating effect.

'We?' asked Schlegel.

'Say hello to Baumgarten on the way out. He will be delighted to see you. We were talking about you boys only the other day.'

Baumgarten had been the foreman of a gang of Berlin butchers, a man of frightening size and violence.

Juppe wanted to know how they knew each other. Morgen told him to fuck off and marched out.

Schlegel thought: First Sybil; now Sepp and Baumgarten. All once part of the same case.

He walked out with the queasy impression that he had arrived at the place where nightmares relocated.

They wasted the rest of the morning being driven back out into the countryside. Morgen sat in the front and chain-smoked while Schlegel tried to process how the garrison seemed to have a habit of combining moments of sharp shock with an otherwise utter eventlessness. It had started with Fegelein. He wondered who next.

They drove to a nearby garrison village where they saw a crocodile of kindergarten children.

Morgen said he was surprised it was a family posting.

'We're part of the General Government, so of course.'

It was blindingly hot. There was the market garden. The huge transparent buildings Schlegel had seen earlier were industrial-sized greenhouses, cathedrals of glass, designed by a famous Polish prisoner architect. A staff woman wearing a lab coat and sunglasses told them the bulk of the crop was devoted to cultivating a dandelion from central Asia whose sap was being used to produce latex rubber. Morgen yawned. The woman took it for rudeness.

On it went. The new hygiene institute. The weather station. The herb farm, a special project initiated by the Reichsführer-SS.

Where Morgen had previously been sarcastic, he could no longer be bothered. Juppe seemed oblivious to insult.

Schlegel wondered whether to risk approaching the commandant's wife with some excuse to speak to Sybil.

They were shown where marshland had been drained and the river levels regulated to prevent flooding. The big fish farm was closed for stock replenishment, otherwise Juppe would have shown them.

'Now there's a pity,' said Morgen, rallying briefly.

Lunch, which Juppe insisted on calling luncheon, was taken in the officer's mess. It was silver service, elaborate and pointless. Schlegel thought about the futility of colonial enterprise, out on the edge, pretending everything worked the way it did at home. He supposed all pioneers felt like that, with their thin hopes and the battle against homesickness.

Juppe asked how they knew the butcher in the abattoir. Morgen told him, in unsparing detail, how Sepp had been part of a secret counter-insurgency campaign in the east, devoted to bestial and barbaric acts that were blamed on the local population, and how they had brought the killing virus home and used the Berlin slaughterhouse to carry on their work.

With Juppe present, Schlegel and Morgen had little to talk about. They ate in silence until Schlegel said, with a show of false bonhomie, 'Actually, Juppe, there is something useful you can do for us.'

Juppe looked unsure. Morgen's eyebrows shot up.

'We might have to subpoena an employee of the commandant's household and take her back as a witness.'

Juppe looked uncertain, Morgen even more so.

Juppe said, 'I will have to ask the commandant, of course.'

'In the meantime, what can you tell us about her?'

He gave a physical account of Sybil as Morgen tried to work it out.

Juppe recognised his description. He said she hadn't been there long and she was a favourite of the commandant's wife.

'What's her name?' Schlegel asked, curious to know how Juppe would answer.

Juppe was dismissive. He didn't learn prisoner names.

'Is it Sybil?' asked Morgen, having worked it out. The question was addressed more to Schlegel, who nodded, than Juppe, who ignored it.

'But you know who I mean.'

'Yes. The seamstress.'

'Have you met her?'

Juppe contemplated, deciding how to answer, then said, 'Once. The commandant's wife asked me to pass on several items of furniture on their behalf.'

'So she is quite well looked after?'

'She has her own room. Most don't.'

'What's it like?' asked Morgen, who continued to give Schlegel quizzical looks.

'Top-end luxe. VIP stuff.'

'VIP like on the outside?' asked Morgen.

'Yes. We speak the same language here,' said Juppe, with his own attempt at sarcasm.

It sounded like Sybil was protected. Schlegel didn't know whether that depressed him, given the inevitable favours that would be demanded in return.

There was no chance to discuss anything with Morgen. When they adjourned to the washroom they were joined by Juppe, and stood pissing three in a row, with Juppe forced to take the middle.

As Morgen washed his hands, he said, 'I wish to inspect the post office.'

Juppe looked unsure. Morgen said it was up to Juppe whether he came. They were going anyway.

They sat in the post office for an hour, waiting for the dentist. Horn said the fellow was usually as regular as clockwork. Schlegel thought the man must have been been forewarned, as part of the general runaround they were being given. Morgen told Horn to telephone the dentist's surgery. Horn reported that he wasn't in and was on his course.

'So-called,' said Morgen, and Horn admitted coursework and truancy were indistinguishable.

Juppe gave Horn a fussy look that said he was being indiscreet. Horn shrugged. Schlegel recalled Horn saying how they all hated each other.

After an hour and a half Morgen gave up.

He stood outside, smoking, fed up.

Juppe said, 'The commandant is very keen you see the recreational centre in the hills.'

'Do you ever give up?'

'No,' said Juppe, matching Morgen's truculence.

Morgen asked what each garrison building was for. He seemed to be deliberately testing Juppe's patience. Juppe dutifully recited: commandant's office; administration block – which they were standing outside; garrison hospital – which also contained the officer's mess where they had just eaten; and over the road the crematorium and next to it the security police block.

'Why a crematorium?' asked Morgen.

Juppe recited, 'Death certificates are the responsibility of the security police not the civil administration and the Poles bury their dead, so there are no local cremation facilities.'

Morgen was already marching off. Juppe asked where he

was going. Morgen said he wanted to introduce himself to the security police.

The only person in the large unmanned reception was a young man sitting in the waiting area, tootling on an accordion. It was hard to say what he was doing there as he wore civilian clothes, yet he looked quite at home. He was pencil-thin, with dark, lustrous hair and bottle-thick glasses, and the knowing air of one amused by the foibles of the world.

He started by telling them no one bothered saluting officers outside their own departments.

Morgen asked who he was. He said his name was Broad. He was minding the desk until the guard got back.

Morgen asked why he wasn't in uniform.

Broad said it was optional in his department.

Morgen asked his rank. Schlegel was surprised by the answer – junior for a man with such an assuming manner. The accent was one Schlegel couldn't place. He asked.

'They call me the Brazilian.'

Born in Rio to a German mother and English father. He was studying to become an interpreter on account of his languages. He continued to play as he talked.

Morgen asked irritably, 'What's with the squeezebox?'

Schlegel saw he was annoyed by Broad treating them as a captive audience.

'Accordion,' said Broad lightly. He stopped playing and flipped a cigarette from a packet, offering it around.

Morgen accepted.

'Ibar, the Yugoslav choice,' Broad said in a deep voice, like he was advertising the brand. 'My father's definition of a gentleman was a man who can play the accordion but chooses not to.'

He winked at Schlegel. He seemed to know who they were. Who didn't? wondered Schlegel.

Morgen asked Broad the name of his boss.

'Grabner. Everyone calls him Chief.' He added that the chief was busy. 'Court assizes tomorrow. Can I help?'

The casual initiative was the opposite of anything Schlegel had encountered so far, as was the droll manner.

'What do you know about gold smuggling?' asked Morgen.

Broad laughed. 'You mean Bock the dentist.'

It was one of the rare occasions on which Schlegel saw Morgen speechless.

Broad went on. 'He's being held in the punishment block as we speak.'

He said it as though it were the most natural thing in the world.

'On what charges?' asked Morgen, still flabbergasted.

Broad continued to look amused. 'Gold smuggling.'

'We need to talk to him.'

'I told you, court assizes tomorrow. Everyone busy.'

He started playing again, a professional, refined piece. Seeing Schlegel curious, he said it was Bach.

Morgen asked Broad if they were being led a merry dance.

Broad switched to a polka and said, 'We are here to help, we really are, but you can't question your man now as there has to be a member of the security staff available and none is. It's the rule book.' He looked at Juppe. 'He knows.'

'Why don't you sit in with us?' asked Morgen, still friendly.

'Only too happy to, but I am manning the fort here.'

'What about him?' Morgen asked, meaning Juppe.

Juppe said he was the commandant's office, not security.

Schlegel decided the whole thing was a stitch-up. He could tell Morgen thought the same.

Broad played a flourish on his accordion, as though he had just thought of something. 'Come to the punishment barracks tonight. Block eleven, in the far left-hand corner as you go through the side gate opposite here. I am on duty from seven, and will see what I can do.'

'Why was Bock arrested?' Morgen asked.

'A tip-off, I expect.' He stopped playing and stood. 'Tell me one thing.'

'What?' asked Morgen.

'People are worried someone is going to come one day and start taking names. That's not you, is it?'

'What do you mean?'

'The hot story going around is there is a regime change and things are about to get a lot more Soviet.'

Schlegel asked, 'How Soviet?'

'Lining everyone up against the wall.' Broad made a pistol of his finger.

Juppe looked agitated. Schlegel saw that Broad wasn't bothered. He had the feeling Broad was soliciting them somehow and wondered whether he was Kammler's man.

A klaxon sounded. Broad said, 'Another block fumigation, courtesy of Dr Wirths.' He turned to Schlegel. 'Remember to keep my name off your list, as a friend of the revolution.'

Schlegel revised his previous estimation of those in the garrison being easy to read. Broad seemed to make a point of unpredictability.

'What do you think about Bock's arrest?' Morgen asked Broad.

'I am not important enough to think.'

'I am sure you do yourself a disservice.'

Schlegel was inclined to like Broad, though Morgen was not.

'Studying to be an interpreter in what?' asked Morgen.

'English and Portuguese. I have some Russian too.'

'Do we have grounds for such international skills?'

'Not yet but when we rule the world somebody is going to have to tell the *untermensch*.'

'Ha-ha, very good,' said Morgen flatly.

Outside, Morgen said to Juppe, 'Take us to your wretched recreational hideaway; anywhere so long as it is not here.'

It would take about half an hour, said Juppe.

To get out was a relief. Schlegel stared at the passing countryside, rural and peasant-like, with the occasional cart and oxen. Having found Sybil, he was in a funk: if she was protected, crashing in could do more harm than good.

They drove alongside a depleted river, moved into hillier wooded territory.

The retreat was set on a hillside with fine views. Schlegel could see why the spot had been chosen. It looked like home.

Juppe explained it had been built as a staff getaway during the quarantine. There were plans to turn it into a country club.

The location was idyllic in a picture-postcard way, with handsome firs and tumbling streams, the air fresh. A large main building was in a rustic alpine style, with a broad sun deck on which people lounged in deck chairs. Private cabins in the woods gave an impression of an exclusive holiday retreat. Paths took them over little bridges, through glades with naked sunbathers, men and women, taking advantage of the softer late-afternoon light. They were ignored, apart from one lithe young woman, lying alone on her front, who looked up and smiled, catching Schlegel's eye. Her skin was so soft and honeyed he wanted to reach down and touch it.

Broad was waiting for them in the punishment block guardroom.

It was their first time in the prisoner compound. The barracks looked identical to those in the garrison, with little hanging lamps announcing the block number, except it all felt deader and more threatening. Schlegel hadn't realised how big the prison was. A few prisoners hung around outside, the more privileged, he supposed, smoking and wearing their own clothes.

Only the roll-call parade ground, which they crossed, gave any indication of the numbers that must gather there; it was dominated by a long gibbet with hooks.

Juppe's usual running commentary had dried up.

The sun at last had lost its strength. Schlegel was aware of his weak shadow in the dirt.

Unlike other barracks, the space between the punishment block and the next was sealed by a high wall with a large gate. They had to ring a bell to gain entry. A slouching guard eventually answered and showed them to where Broad sat waiting, in uniform now, still tootling on his accordion, with his air of suppressed amusement.

'It seems like your dentist has checked out,' he said laconically.

Morgen glared. Schlegel saw he had been naïve thinking there would be an end to the runaround.

'It seems he didn't like the food,' said Broad.

Seeing Morgen's barely suppressed anger, Broad snapped at a guard to produce Bock's registry details.

The card showed theft as the reason for custody. There was a note in a different hand recording his transfer to Block 10 (medical) after being 'taken ill'. Transfer time was given as 6 p.m., an hour before Broad came on duty.

'Why wasn't he admitted to the staff hospital?' Morgen asked.

'Garrison men taken ill under arrest are always sent here. They have doors with locks.'

'Taken ill?' Morgen repeated sceptically.

'He could order food in. He was staff. He could send out to his mess kitchen. Maybe someone spiked it.' Broad seemed entertained by the idea.

Schlegel wondered if it was always this casual.

Broad said he had to remain on duty and Juppe could take them over. It was only next door. The three of them trooped out, with Morgen muttering.

The entrance to the medical block was not locked but no one was around. Unlike in garrison barracks, there were no signposts. Schlegel saw the vein in Morgen's temple pulse as he turned on Juppe and told him to find someone.

Juppe came back looking not pleased, accompanied by a stout middle-aged woman. Her white coat was badly in need of a wash, her grey hair scraped back in an untidy bun. The reason for Juppe's irritation was the woman was a prisoner doctor and not entitled to deal with staff cases, but she was all he could find.

The woman confirmed no one else was available. The garrison staff had gone home. She spoke with a heavy central European accent.

She took them up to the corridor where police prisoners were kept. Behind an unattended desk hung a board with numbered keys.

The woman said she wasn't entitled to show them the rooms. Morgen told her to wait.

Morgen made Juppe open the doors. The windows were sealed with metal plates, turning each into a claustrophobic space, made more stark by a dim central lightbulb. The rooms were all empty with made-up cots, apart from one with the bed in disarray, but no sign of occupation.

Juppe's look said Morgen should recognise he was beaten. Morgen was about to walk out when he said, 'There's a shoe under the bed.'

He found a uniform hanging on the back of the door, hidden with it open. He went through the pockets until he found an identity card.

'Bock, the dentist,' Morgen said flatly.

The photograph showed a rabbity man, anonymous, as Horn had said.

'Maybe he is in the washroom,' said Juppe unhelpfully.

Morgen went back to the woman and asked what else was in the building.

Medical research blocks, she said, and the prisoner brothel.

Morgen pulled a face to say he had heard everything now and turned away impatiently, saying they could probably discount Bock going off for a girl. He asked the woman what else.

There was only the temporary morgue in the cellar, she said.

Morgen sighed and said, 'Take us down.'

She led the way to a winding staircase, dimly lit. The sharp smell of disinfectant failed to mask the underlying odour of decomposition. At the bottom, Schlegel sensed a dark space stretching ahead. He could make out little more than blocked shapes in the sparse security lamps. Only when the doctor switched on the main lights was the horror revealed.

Under a nauseous green glow lay what Schlegel could think of only as a huge bathroom of corpses.

He didn't know where to begin. Perhaps as many as fifty baths, each filled and containing a body, in the case of children sometimes more. Each corpse was stripped naked.

The woman said, 'It's the only way to keep them from decomposing in this heat.'

Even Juppe looked as though he had no idea such a world

existed. It made a mockery of the dreary positives of his endless tour.

Schlegel tried to make sense of what he was seeing. In some cases the baths were part of long communal corridors where the partitions had been ripped out. Extra baths had been brought in and were positioned willy-nilly.

Morgen showed Bock's picture and told them to start looking. When Juppe hesitated, Morgen snapped, 'Do it, soldier!'

Schlegel walked among the dead. He developed a sideways flick of the eyes, avoiding full inspection, enough to check that a body wasn't Bock. The sense of dead flesh was overwhelming, making it hard to pick out the faces.

Images of corpses in various states of death assaulted him: waxen, blue, livid, and in one case quite black, some bloated, some emaciated, little more than skeletons. He was overwhelmed by the many singular compositions within the shared state of death.

One bath contained four children and there were two further communal sports-type pools with perhaps as many as thirty bodies, some floating, some submerged. Schlegel was wondering how on earth he would find the stomach to look at each one individually when Morgen called out.

A couple of pistol cracks came from the yard upstairs as Morgen matched Bock's picture to the corpse in the bath. Bock lay on his back, his head resting on the rim, in a pose of almost voluptuous surrender.

'End of story,' Morgen said.

Two more shots came from upstairs as they were joined by Juppe and the woman.

Bock's torso was covered with an unseemly pelt of hair, from his neck down to his shrivelled penis. Schlegel felt embarrassed for the man and all the others, once as individual as the four of them standing there, now dead meat.

He said they must be shooting people in the yard next door.

'Small arms. Two shooters,' Morgen confirmed, matter-of-fact.

No one screamed or cried out apart from one who shouted a patriotic cry, followed by a shot.

With the next shot came a scream. 'First one botched,' said Morgen, measuring the pause before the *coup de grace*.

Morgen murmured, 'To err is but human.'

Schlegel counted the shots at intervals of twenty or thirty seconds, a dozen altogether, taking no more than three or four minutes.

The silence from the yard felt more profound than simply the stopping of something, interrupted by a voice behind them demanding to know what the hell they were doing.

The approaching man wore a white tunic with a high collar. Morgen angrily asked who he was. Staff medical orderly. The accent was Polish-German. The man was squat, with a broad neck and a bodybuilder's torso. Muscles bulged under the sleeves of his tunic.

He turned on the woman. 'No prisoner doctors down here without staff in attendance.'

Morgen said, 'Here on my orders.'

Morgen gave his rank and position. The orderly looked unimpressed and insisted the area was off-limits without authorisation.

'I thought you had all gone home,' Morgen said.

'Not me,' the man said unpleasantly.

Morgen asked if he had seen the dead man before.

The orderly shook his head.

'Where's his medical chart?'

'Not my patient, wouldn't know.'

'What do you know?'

'He was admitted complaining of abdominal cramps.'

He told them he had been in reception at the time but hadn't seen who dealt with the case.

'Can you tell me how he died?' Morgen asked the woman. He sounded hopeless.

'Not without an autopsy.'

The orderly said loudly she wasn't allowed to touch the body and the autopsy would reveal natural causes.

It was a farce from what Schlegel could see. Dentist alive one minute, dead the next.

The orderly said, 'The seizure was witnessed. The man grabbed his heart and keeled over, after complaining of feeling dizzy.'

Schlegel caught the prisoner doctor's eye. The orderly started whistling.

Morgen asked the name of the ranking doctor on duty that evening.

The orderly said the man had already left to go on leave.

The woman gestured for Schlegel to move so he blocked the orderly's view. She quickly parted the corpse's chest hair and Schlegel saw the small, bluish puncture mark above the heart.

The moment was broken by a clatter of boots on the stairs. It was Broad and another man in boisterous spirits. Schlegel recognised Palitsch, the sharpshooter from the morning hunt. They had their arms draped around each other and were sharing a schnapps bottle. The sharp tang of cordite cut through the smell of disinfectant and rotting bodies. Broad sniggered.

'Paperwork all in order?'

Morgen gestured up towards the yard. 'The court hearing isn't until tomorrow.'

Broad snapped his fingers and laughed. 'Always a backlog.'

'Riffraff clear out,' said Palitsch.

Broad toasted them and said, 'Today the blood spurted out as if from a beast.' He indicated his bespattered jacket. 'And they make us pay for our own dry-cleaning!'

The doctor stared at the floor.

Schlegel asked Broad if he had known the dentist was dead when he sent them over. Broad did an exaggerated double take.

Palitsch's eyes were bright from killing. He said, 'I need to get laid.'

Broad said, 'My gun is still warm.'

Morgen looked exhausted and disgusted. 'Get your cocks seen to, boys.'

Schlegel followed Morgen's heavy tread as they all trooped upstairs. The orderly made himself scarce. Morgen dismissed the woman. Broad and Palitsch left singing loudly, leaving them with Juppe.

The gates to the execution yard were open and the crop of bodies was being taken away on a cart, watched by a thin bald man wearing running shorts and a tracksuit top.

'What's going on?' he asked when he saw them.

His legs were unnaturally white.

He seemed to know who they were. 'Grabner. Head of security. Call me Chief. Come. I want a word.'

Juppe made to follow. Grabner said, 'Not you. Just them.'

Juppe hesitated.

Morgen said, 'You heard. Dismissed.'

They watched Juppe's departing back with relief. Morgen flashed an obscene gesture and Grabner guffawed.

He took them into the prisoner block and showed them into what he called the courtroom, a fanciful description for such a small, unadorned space, dominated by a portrait of the leader.

Grabner's utter strangeness only became apparent when he spoke at length. A terrible collision of words emerged, often incomprehensible, a wreckage of language whose disconcerting effect was enhanced by a fussy Austrian accent, as comic and sinister as the commandant's yap. When he lost his way in the middle of a sentence he seized on a word or phrase and repeated it, stabbing his finger for emphasis.

Schlegel's summary of the man's linguistic dog's dinner was that Grabner's agents had informed him that he and Morgen weren't safe. In fact, he didn't need informers to tell him because it was obvious to anyone with half an eye.

Something worth saying once bore saying again, and again.

'Anyone with half an eye ...' 'Even if I had half an eye I could tell you ...'

They listened to him go round in circles until Morgen asked, 'Who killed our dentist?'

'Your dentist?' Grabner pouted. 'Your fault he's dead.'

'Ours!'

'We watch the man. Matter of fact, we talk to him and he is prepared whatever to cooperate.'

'He was working for you!'

'Until you tread on my toes.'

'Then who killed him?'

Grabner made an injecting motion.

'So I believe,' said Schlegel.

According to Grabner's towering, shapeless sentences, Bock was one among many medical staff involved in pharmacy and dental gold theft, including a large illegal trade in morphine. After getting caught, he was working as their informer in exchange for immunity, a word Grabner needed help with.

'Set a thief,' Grabner said. 'Now we lose him, thanks to you. Big waste of time. Important operation comes to nothing because of you.'

It was a disconcerting combination, the mixture of fitness fanatic and mangled language, both at odds with the man's rather shy and soulful look of an ascetic monk, in contrast to his reputation as the terror of the garrison.

'My advice is go now before the doctors give you one of their clever shots.'

Morgen said he wanted any autopsy report forwarded.

'You'll be lucky. Did you meet garrison doctor Wirths?'

Morgen said they hadn't had the pleasure.

'Big hero. Cured the epidemic. Maybe he knew about Bock, maybe not. Maybe one of his underlings makes the decision. But Dr Wirths is in the business of morphine trade, guilty as anyone. We watch his house. He has a new stove. Not connected. Why not? For what he can hide up the chimney. Being the good doctor, he uses profits to finance his research, upstairs in the block you came from.'

'What research?' asked Morgen.

'Cancer shit.' Grabner leaned forward. 'I spell it out. Gang of doctors. They help themselves. Anyone who gets in their way they give a little injection. If Bock is informing, they remove him from the face of the picture. I am not happy you are here because it sets me back weeks. Leave us to do our work. You can go now. Go soon. I don't want to investigate your deaths.'

'No, you don't,' said Morgen, with a levity that fell flat.

'I do you a favour. I do me a favour. Wild elements here, close to out of control, we do our best to contain. You should not be here because you are Berlin boys.'

They departed, alone for the first time since joining the commandant for his ride at six that morning.

Morgen said, 'Are you sure it was Sybil?'

Schlegel described what he had seen. He couldn't tell if Morgen believed him.

Morgen said, 'The shootings just now, I am sure they were not authorised.'

'What do you mean?'

'The judge doesn't come until tomorrow. Who authorised those shootings?'

Schlegel supposed Grabner. He was more shocked by the transformation of Broad from sociable, would-be man of the world to blood-spattered executioner.

Morgen flicked the butt of his cigarette away. 'Do we have a friend in this place?' he asked rhetorically.

Waiting at the camp exit was the inevitable Juppe, who could barely contain his delight as he told them to accompany him.

He escorted them the short distance to the commandant's house where Hoess was waiting. Juppe was dismissed. Juppe gave a smart salute. The commandant, with the air of a man sharing a joke, said Juppe had done good work that day. Juppe looked grateful out of all proportion to the casual compliment.

The commandant took them through to his study where papers lay strewn, with a full ashtray and a bottle next to it.

He was appraised of the facts, he said. They had wasted their time.

'You can't prosecute a dead man.'

There were further questions, Morgen said, if the man was murdered.

The commandant rolled his eyes. 'Spare me. I have people here to deal with that. We don't need your interference. We can manage. We get enough people sticking their noses in as it is.'

'The doctors in particular—'

'Enough!' shouted the commandant. 'No more. My job is to make sure this place functions when it is barely capable of doing so. It is a nightmare of improvisation. It doesn't bear inspection, which is why I am ordering you out. Besides, you are here under false pretences. I could have you locked up for impersonating post office officials.'

He gave a whinny of amusement.

Schlegel said, 'I have some questions about a seamstress working for your wife, whom we also wish to question.'

'Too late!' The commandant affected vagueness. 'Which one is that?'

'The one you are taking an interest in.'

'Only on behalf of my wife.'

An awkward silence fell.

'Let's not be naïve,' the commandant went on. 'Spies everywhere, for a start. Prisoner informers, staff informers. This seamstress turns up, an attractive young woman, to be sure, but the first question you ask is why, and who is she working for, exactly? Has she been sent to spy?'

'You furnished her with a room.'

'Only to isolate her and find out what she is really up to.'

The commandant gave a crafty stare.

Schlegel found it no longer possible to tell what was true. Perhaps it didn't matter. Truth didn't exist. There were only degrees of ambiguity.

The commandant said, 'Your business is done. See yourselves out. As of zero-eight-hundred hours tomorrow your passes are no longer valid for the garrison.'

Outside, the heat had barely dropped.

Morgen said, 'We have failed and leave empty-handed.'

Schlegel found himself devoid of will, which he recognised as a side effect of the general moral infection.

'A power struggle, is my guess,' Morgen went on. 'How would you describe the difference between comradeship and camaraderie?'

Schlegel was tired and didn't care. Comradeship was more natural, he supposed. 'Camaraderie is tighter, more to do with the group.'

'It elevates itself over outsiders. It excludes external control.'

'Meaning you don't talk to outsiders.'

'You especially don't talk to us.'

'Yet Grabner is willing to implicate the garrison doctor.'

'Clearly he wished to draw Wirths to our attention.'

'What are you saying?'

'There is a crisis of authority, which Kammler recognises. We are not dealing with a rational bureaucracy.'

The fact of it was they were being chucked out.

Schlegel asked in exasperation, 'What *were* we supposed to do?'

'That's not going to happen now.'

Schlegel thought of Sybil, surrounded by that ghastly other normality, which they had seen only from the reflecting side of the looking glass.

Morgen paused to light up and waved his cigarette. 'All this pedantic bookkeeping, the resistance to external control, the general sickness – let's not forget that – and you have morale in constant decline. It must be hard when they all loathe each other. Arbitrariness becomes proof of obedience, do you see?'

Schlegel wasn't sure he did.

'Obedience allows for plenty of deviance and lenience, providing the transgression is carried out in the spirit of camaraderie.'

'Meaning it stinks from top to bottom.'

'To be literal. Blind obedience is the instrument of terror.

But while the commandant is in overall charge, the security police operates its own fiefdom, and the medical, labour and construction offices are both answerable and unanswerable to the commandant's office. Huge zones of uncertainty exist and this, I suspect, is what concerns Kammler and why he wished us here. Not that it is any clearer which uncertainty in particular interests him.'

'And what if someone were to grow truly arbitrary in such a situation?'

'It doesn't bear thinking about.'

That night, in the uneasy stage of drifting off, Schlegel reflected on the sullen atmosphere, its deadening ordinariness, and the usual quirks and rivalries of institutional life, its gangs and cliques; the unseasonably hot weather where, in contrast to the mood, the sun blazed tropically hot through the smoky haze, beyond which lay clear blue skies, all the way to outer space, he thought, as sleep eluded him. He hadn't imagined anything about the place, certainly not a garrison magazine with details of a football league, and prisoner XIs and spotty photographs of touchline crowds shouting their sides on, and advertisements for concerts. He thought about Schulze and prayed Sybil was safe in the passage of the night.

The commandant rode out the following dawn, through the enchanted mist and deathly quiet, riding bareback, after finding himself incapable of saddling the mare.

That morning she seemed to gallop ahead of herself. His hangover came in pounding waves. Oh, for the arbitrary bullet, spinning its way, to drill his brainpan and end it all. For months now, however much he forced himself to knuckle down, he could see life only in terms of ending.

The mist burned off in patches. He saw the lakes ahead, like glass. He rode to the shoreline and paused in awe. The low cloud left the thinnest visible strip above the mirrored surface, reflected white.

He dismounted and undressed, folding his clothes, and leapt up naked onto his mare, using her withers. He nudged her gently, wishing not to disturb the surface. The water rose, deliciously cool, felt rather than seen because of his head wrapped in the soft bandage of mist. They moved deeper, until they were almost submerged, and in that narrow space above the water he saw the lake stretch ahead like infinity.

Krick was out too, racing his bike. It was now his habit to play the game of watching the commandant. He recognised the area where they were, further out than the commandant usually came.

Krick had lost sight of the commandant, who had ridden like a man more than usually possessed. He paused, taken by what he surveyed, so still it looked like the world had never been disturbed. He was not a romantic man but felt obliged to dismount to admire such dazzling tranquility. He walked towards the water's edge with a sense of the moment being almost over, the strength of the sun about to punch its way through the enveloping shroud.

His attention was drawn to something lying on the shore – the commandant's boots and folded clothes. He supposed he had gone for a swim and was envious he had not thought of it first. He decided to leave him to it as a ripple broke the surface, with no immediate explanation for its cause, then out of the water rose the nag's head and the commandant's, beads spilling off them like silver mercury. Krick had a brief vision of the man utterly drained and contented, eyes shut, with a beatific smile, before disappearing into the mist, leaving only the horse's neck and rising flanks and the man's truncated white flesh.

After his watery submergence, the commandant's vision of himself was of a marbled emperor, riding with his arm aloft, sceptre in hand. His scalp prickled and, dressed again, he felt pleasantly cool and damp, not having bothered to dry himself. It would be a good day; one of the few. He would drink in moderation, the better to manoeuvre his wife – submissive for once in a blue moon – into not being the usual withholding bitch, and offer up her comfortable, bovine rump to him that night.

The commandant had been dimly aware of the sinister figure of the shrink in his spiffy, ridiculous gear that rendered him almost invisible in the pale light of early morning. What he really did was anyone's guess, other than indulge a number of wives – his own included – into believing that what went on between their ears was of the slightest consequence.

The mist had burned off, to reveal the start of another day of remorseless, sullen heat.

Further towards the garrison, he spotted the shrink again, up ahead, in the distance; waiting, not on his bicycle, but standing in the road. Maybe he had a puncture; serve him right.

The shrink held up his arm.

He said nothing until the commandant was alongside. The mare stamped her disapproval, as though sharing his mistrust of the man.

'You should take a look.' He gestured towards the ditch by the road.

IV

Whatever Schlegel had been expecting, it wasn't a dead young woman in a splashy print dress with scratched legs, slide-away eyes and her brains bashed in, lying on a gurney in a large tiled room that resembled a morgue except it was too hot to keep anything cool. The women's feet turned inwards, making her look pigeon-toed. Such was the unreality of the hot morgue that Schlegel started to believe she was sweating even in death. He thought of the cold-bath corpses in the medical block and the dead dentist. Two garrison murders in as many days.

They had got as far as the station and the omens were good, with the train on time, and a dining car. Morgen was calculating that evening's entertainment and didn't care what it was; getting out was enough.

The night sleeper from Berlin drew up on the incoming platform and the station became busy with passengers disembarking.

Schlegel saw Morgen looking over his shoulder.

Juppe was striding towards them. For a second Schlegel thought they had forgotten something but he knew their reprieve was in the process of being undone. Juppe demanded they come on the commandant's orders.

Morgen looked disinclined. Schlegel was in two minds, thinking: Sybil. As they were leaving they were approached by a tall man in uniform, carrying a suitcase, who said he was just off the night train and could he scrounge a lift. He introduced himself as garrison doctor Wirths and when Morgen gave his name he took a step back, visibly unsettled.

Schlegel presumed it could only be because he knew who Morgen was and had something to hide.

Morgen sat in the front. The doctor, as tall as Schlegel, if not taller, folded himself into the back. His long, angled limbs reminded Schlegel of a wading bird. After his moment of alarm, his manner became sociable and friendly. He asked whether they had just arrived too.

'So to speak,' said Morgen.

'What brings you?' asked the doctor.

'No one seems to be able to agree on that,' said Morgen. 'But in a word, corruption.'

Wirths appeared flustered again. He seemed to want to talk to them but not in front of Juppe.

'Are you up to date with your jabs?' he asked.

They were supposed to present their medical cards at the staff infirmary to check their vaccines and booster shots were in order.

'You should do it this morning,' said Wirths. 'I will be there until one o'clock. We can't have you getting ill.'

Was it a summons? Schlegel couldn't tell.

They dropped the doctor off at his house.

The room where the dead woman's body was held was part of the garrison complex with the tall chimney, which stood behind the grassy bank. Juppe was dismissed so they were alone with the commandant.

Schlegel wondered what had made the commandant change his mind about them.

'I had her brought here to show you. A young German woman, murdered, obviously. She will be taken and kept at a more appropriate temperature until an autopsy can be performed. There is a backlog.'

He marched them out and up the main street, where they were joined by a blue-eyed German shepherd that trotted alongside the commandant, obviously familiar, tongue lolling. They crossed into the industrial zone and a complex net of alleyways. Schlegel lost his bearings in the maze of narrow overshadowed runs, where it was at least cooler. The commandant's sweating neck bulged over his collar, razored almost to the rim of his cap. Schlegel saw blackheads, and smelled sweat and cologne.

The commandant led them to a small, low, windowless building surrounded by its own security fence; Schlegel was reminded of an electricity sub-station. The dog was told to wait, rewarded with a treat from the commandant's pocket.

Keys were produced and the security gate and entrance unlocked. They stood waiting inside for the tube lights to flicker on. The single room was bigger than it looked from outside, full of glass display cases and dozens of racks. Some of the walls had photographic enlargements pinned to boards – stark forensic images.

The commandant said, 'This is our black museum.'

He crossed to a table where a handbag lay.

'This was hers.'

He emptied the contents. Nail file. Identity card. Handkerchief. Pretty pathetic, thought Schlegel, in terms of worldly possessions.

The commandant picked up the card. 'She is wearing spectacles in the photograph. Aged twenty-one. Tanner, Ingeborg. Secretary in the motor pool. She was seeing a man or men plural because, according to her dormitory supervisor, she often spent nights away, not so unusual among these women. Fucking for the fatherland!' The commandant gave a shrill laugh and reached for a large envelope. He took out photographs.

'Taken in situ. A rush job.'

They showed Tanner's body from different angles, including a close-up of her caved-in skull, which forced Schlegel to turn away. The commandant appeared trans-fixed by the woman's final expression, which reminded Schlegel of photographs taken at the wrong moment, when the face was not composed as it should be.

Morgen commented on the professional quality of the job. The commandant looked pleased. They had been done by a prisoner who had been a police photographer.

'Rigor mortis hadn't set in by the time she was found.'

'Who found her?'

'The garrison psychiatrist while out on his bicycle.'

The commandant made the image sound risible.

'Is that Krick?' asked Schlegel, surprised.

The commandant sounded surprised in return. 'Yes, I found him with the body. He said he had just come across it.'

Schlegel saw that the photographs on the wall were of women's bodies hanging from fence wire, with more hacked corpses on the ground, blood black as oil. In the glass cases were what looked like crime-scene exhibits, carefully labelled, including billy clubs and knuckledusters.

'Where was the body found?' asked Morgen.

'On the road to Rajsko, within the larger security zone. She could have been visiting. There are garrison quarters there.'

'We are not homicide,' said Schlegel, a line he had used before.

'You are criminal investigators.'

'Financial. You have your own police.'

'Security police, not investigative.'

Schlegel pointed to the pictures on the wall. 'Someone must have investigated that.'

'On the contrary. The security police made arrests but it did not require criminal investigation.'

'Why ask us back when we are *persona non grata*?' asked Morgen. 'What is wrong with your own people?'

The commandant gestured helplessly. 'Can I trust them? What if it is one of them? A killing in a high-security area.'

'Are you asking for our help?' asked Morgen dubiously.

'Work for me in confidence and I can help.'

'Invite me at your peril.'

'Get rid of Grabner.'

Morgen looked doubtful.

'Isn't that why you are really here, man? A clear-out,' insisted the commandant.

Morgen remained slow to react.

'See garrison doctor Wirths,' the commandant urged. 'Don't say I sent you. Ask about Grabner. He will tell you all you need to know.'

'You have resisted tooth and nail to opening the place up.'

'I was trained in Dachau where we were taught to mind our stall.' The commandant drew himself to attention. 'But we can't have German women being murdered.'

'Are you saying this is a garrison murder?' Morgen asked.

'The shrink who found the body breaks it down into the four Ds. Drunkenness. Demoralisation. Dames. And denial.'

'Is he right?'

'Everyone stuck in this place for a year, unable to get out. Someone was bound to snap.'

'Denial?'

'About what a hole this is. Pretending everything is normal.'

'Still, a better life than the prisoners.'

'Except their demoralisation is catching. They not only pass on physical disease, they infect us with their depression.'

'Perhaps the garrison needs a shrink after all.'

'He'll be a spy. They are everywhere. On top of that, he is vain and views the garrison as an experiment for his study.' The commandant paused. 'There is a terrible homicide rate among prisoners. We are constantly told of cases where one prisoner beats another to death for no reason, other than some congenital fault or behaviour problem. The women can be worse than the men. Look at this.'

He crossed to the photographs Schlegel had noticed earlier.

'That was the women's sub-camp at Budy last autumn. I was called out in the middle of the night. A Jewess attacked a German prisoner and all hell broke loose with women being chucked out of windows and cut to pieces. In fact, German female prisoners turned out to be responsible, egged on by the guard, many of which were involved with these women, who were prostitutes. Confronted with such degeneracy, the guard was inevitably corrupted. One must be vigilant at all times. We are not given the elite by way of staff, not even the rank and file. Minimum height used to resemble something passing for normal; now you can be little more than a dwarf. It is what we are reduced to. Our fighting troops get the pick. We were forced to employ anti-Soviet Ukrainian guards, until they had to be transferred. One headache after another, I tell you! There are bound to be rotten apples in such a poor barrel. But now, this!'

'And if we find out who did it?' asked Morgen.

'I would like nothing more than for you to tell me you have discovered a stray Russian prisoner hiding in the zone who is responsible for murdering these women, but what if one of my men has cracked? I am bound to describe them as mine, as their commandant. I know of several who are going off the rails. On the other hand, don't discount some of the prisoners, the ones that have freedom of movement and can drive trucks and so forth. Better it were one of them.'

'You said women, plural, suggesting more than one murder . . .'

The commandant ignored the question and moved on to another set of photographs.

'Come, look.'

Schlegel saw mutilated bodies in rags, half-drowned in mud.

'Russians took to eating each other. That's what we were having to deal with. We prepared ourselves for many things but not that!'

The bodies looked like they had been hacked open with blunt instruments or torn apart with teeth and bare hands. What was the man trying to tell them? Schlegel wondered. That there was only so much of this sort of stuff his men could take?

'They turned up starved after marching for weeks.'

'When was this?' asked Morgen.

'Two years ago, autumn of 1941. Thirty thousand! Three times as many prisoners as we already had. They had to be kept in a field to start with because there were no quarters, and they became animals, howling like dogs. We found half-eaten bodies buried in the mud. Hearts and livers ripped out. Cannibals, like in darkest black Africa.'

'Are they still here?'

'The cannibals?'

'The Russians.'

'Gone, mostly.'

He pointed to another set of photographs. The light was poor, the images grainy. Schlegel took a while to understand they were desiccated bodies.

The commandant said, 'Polish prisoners remain convinced that vampires walked among the Ivans. These two corpses were drained of their blood. They ate their flesh and drank their blood. Is that natural?'

'Did this Russian violence extend beyond themselves?' asked Morgen.

'No, but their coming was the start of everything going wrong.'

'In what way?'

'Terrible overcrowding. Language. Translation.'

Morgen asked if the garrison had come to believe in the vampire stories.

'Of course not, ha-ha!'

But the question nagged and the commandant paced before announcing, 'In some respects, yes, we were bound to. Bloodsuckers. Red corpuscles. The bacillus. We were right to fear them. They brought the typhus. Which was the start. They didn't even have the decency to stay dead.'

He pointed at a group of photographs of decomposed corpses half out of the ground.

Morgen asked, 'What's that?'

'What it looks like! Bodies resurrecting themselves!'

Morgen murmured, 'Next we will be talking of transubstantiation.'

'Not funny,' said the commandant. 'We are not discussing superstition here but facts. Fact – the Russians died like flies. Fact – they didn't adapt. Fact – they weren't given enough to eat. Rations are controlled by Berlin. Fact – few were equipped to survive the winter of 1941/2. Fact – they had to be buried in the woods and – fact – last summer they started pushing themselves up out of the ground.' He surprised Schlegel by giggling. 'Body gas, marshy substrata and extreme heat combined to form a chemical reaction where they appeared to rise from the dead. Fourth of July. What a day! There was a train from Slovakia that morning, a Saturday. The last of Kammler's deal.'

'Kammler?' asked Morgen sharply.

'Yes,' said the commandant irritably. 'A shortage of construction workers, so a deal was done with the Slovak government. I had dead Russians coming out of the ground; the stink was indescribable; hotter than it is now. And the same day the doctors threw up their hands and said an epidemic was unavoidable – unavoidable! – and I had a general inspection on my plate in less than a fortnight.'

'How did that go?'

Morgen reminded Schlegel of a straight man feeding a bad comedian his lines. The commandant appeared dangerously absurd.

'We kept quiet about the epidemic.'

'Why?'

'Political reasons.'

The commandant pointed back to Tanner's bag.

'This woman is the maybe the fourth, perhaps even the fifth in terms of numbers.'

'Murders?'

'Disappearances.'

The commandant crossed to the far wall and pointed to photographs of three women, all young and physically different.

'Are you now telling us this isn't the first?' Morgen looked like a man who suspected he was about to put his foot down on a rotten plank.

'The first time there has been a body.'

'And those?' asked Morgen, pointing to the three.

'Vanished. Disappeared.'

'Reported missing?'

'Not at first. Two were unmarried. One was a switch-board operator, the other worked in the staff pharmacy. It was several days before it was noticed they were gone. We find anyway the younger ones don't stick at it. They're always coming up with excuses. Going off to get married is the usual, when they are not. It was thought these two had bunked off or run away with a man.'

'And the third?'

'She was married. Eventually reported missing by a neighbour.'

'Not her husband?'

'He presumed she had made herself scarce and gone home because he found out she was having an affair.'

'So, while these disappearances were noted nothing was done?' Morgen asked.

'Women are notoriously unreliable. There was no indication of anything untoward.'

'Didn't anyone gossip?

'They do nothing but!'

'No family enquiries?'

'No.' The idea seemed not to have occurred to the commandant before. He considered. 'Life in wartime. A lot of young women come here to get away from home.'

'Now you have this latest body, you wonder if these other women—'

'One is bound to.'

'Where is the missing woman's husband?'

'Transferred months ago.'

'And the man she was having an affair with?'

'Palitsch. He's still around.' The commandant rolled his

eyes. 'You may remember him showing off at the shooting party.'

Palitsch again, thought Schlegel, as Morgen asked, 'Did no one worry for these women?'

The commandant stared at the ceiling. 'The worst anyone thought is they might have been abducted by partisans, but all three had a reputation for flightiness. Women do, frontier life and all that, with a lot of men passing through . . . Women can't be listed as deserters because their job description is voluntary helper. As for the wife, there's no law against her leaving her husband, ha-ha.'

The man's tight laugh died in the room.

'You said there was maybe a fifth.'

The commandant cast around and searched through a stack of folders.

'A hit-and-run. It may have been just that. God knows, there is enough drunk driving.'

He produced photographs showing a fair-haired young woman lying at the side of the road, with her arms thrown up in what looked like surrender. She bore a passing resemblance to Tanner, with the same tall, slender build.

The commandant looked embarrassed. 'The thing is, we still don't know who she is.'

She had been found on the road into town but her papers corresponded to nobody in the garrison. Schlegel presumed not much of a search had gone on. He asked if garrison vehicles had been checked for damage. The commandant didn't know.

'Was anyone in charge of these cases?' asked Morgen.

'I was, in as much as there was time, but it is only now we are seeing them in a possibly different light.'

Morgen looked sceptical. 'Why leave a body this time if he is such a surreptitious killer?

'Perhaps he was disturbed.'

'Then what is the motive? This latest doesn't look like a sex attack.'

'Palitsch would be a suspect in my book.' It was said as if the commandant had just thought of it. 'He was all right until his wife died.'

'Are there any other names you would care to pluck out of the hat?'

Morgen's irony was lost on the commandant.

'Start with Palitsch. You get an instinct for a wrong 'un. Not at first, but he has let himself go, grown coarse and no longer decent. None of this must get out. That would be unthinkable.'

'If no one can know what we are investigating, why would we be asking questions?'

'Ha-ha, of course. Say you are still following up on the dentist, and this Tanner woman is a suspected accomplice and you are trying to locate her. Start with Palitsch.'

'And what is the conclusion of our case, once Palitsch has confessed?'

'Ha-ha, yes, of course. You'll think of something.'

'And if it's not Palitsch?' ventured Morgen.

'No more garrison women killed, full stop. That's your responsibility. Palitsch can go in the clean-up. My wife and I are having a garden party this afternoon. Come at four. Free beer and cigarettes! And food. A barbecue. Palitsch will be there. You can observe him at close quarters.'

Morgen was not impressed.

'Why call us back when he was so desperate to get rid of us, just to waste our time. You heard him. We're not even supposed to be seen to be investigating.'

Schlegel was cheered at the thought of still trying to subpoena Sybil.

Their bags had been dropped at the hotel. Morgen said he was going back to make some calls. Schlegel thought he saw early signs of Morgen's mysteriousness, a period of elusiveness, which prefaced another of his disappearances.

It was a working Saturday morning. Schlegel wasn't sure how to approach Elizabeth Schulze. It turned out to be straightforward: hers was a big office with its own reception where he asked for her. The walls featured large photographs of sturdy industrial buildings.

She came out a couple of minutes later, a little reserved, as if self-conscious of being seen in uniform. Apart from tilting her head in enquiry, she showed no surprise at him being there, as if expecting him sooner or later.

Schlegel said he was trying to locate a prisoner. He didn't know who else to ask as he still didn't know the form.

Schulze said she could spare five minutes.

'We can go to the central prisoner file down the corridor.'

She said there were two registers, one listed by name, a second by profession.

Sybil's name was not in either.

'You say she works in the commandant's house.'

From the tinge of exasperation in her voice, Schlegel feared she took him for a time-waster.

'Yes. A seamstress.'

They checked again in the professional file.

'She has to be here.' Schulze paused. 'Do you know Erich Groenke?'

Schlegel said he had been shooting with him. She looked mildly impressed.

'You do get around.' He couldn't tell if she was mocking.

'Ask him. He acts as an unofficial foreman for the commandant's wife. We could have asked Ilse, too.'

'Ilse?'

Ilse was the works supervisor for staff in the commandant's house.

'She's on leave. Try Monday.'

Schulze's professional manner was brisk, almost as
though they had never met.

He went and sought out Groenke at his factory, which
was in the process of closing for the day.

Groenke, upbeat as usual, took Schlegel up to his office,
perched on a gantry, beyond a tiny room where an ostentatiously pretty secretary sat.

An electric fan blew sweet cool air in a rotating arc.
Groenke addressed the secretary as darling, and ordered
coffees. He added he would have a beer too and asked if
Schlegel wanted one.

Schlegel mumbled that he would stick to coffee, knowing
he would regret it. He waited for the occasional moments of
cool breeze that blew in his direction. The fan had a paper
streamer attached, which fluttered hypnotically.

Groenke said, 'I am not supposed to talk to you.'

'Who says?'

'The Old Man. You make him nervous.'

'That was yesterday. He just invited us back.'

That was news to Groenke.

Schlegel took advantage to say, 'It has been suggested we
talk to a seamstress employed in the commandant's house.'

'Name of?'

'We thought you might be able to help with that. She's a
favourite of the commandant's wife. She apparently leads a
well-off life, with her own room, which they helped furnish.'

Groenke viewed Schlegel with suspicion. 'Why do you ask?'

'I was advised to talk to you. As you say, our presence makes the commandant nervous ... even if we have been invited back.'

Groenke gave a big laugh. 'Of course it does if you sign his wife's fucking visitors' book using a couple of false names! That went down really well!'

He saluted with his beer bottle, which looked enviably cold. Eyes that had seen everything, Schlegel thought, from which no mystery of life had been withheld.

The coffee was a weak substitute, a sign probably of how Groenke regarded him. The man was bound to have bags of the real stuff.

Groenke volunteered, 'I would have vetted this woman for the commandant's wife.'

'How come?'

'It would be unseemly for her to go down to the labour exchange. Anyway, it's too late by then. The best skilled workers get picked off before even getting there. Seamstresses are especially in demand. If you're not quick someone else gets them. Frau Hoess's selection is limited as it is.'

'How so?'

'She won't employ some of the best seamstresses.'

Groenke clearly meant Jews. Schlegel could hardly say he had heard the woman was a Jew.

'Out of tact,' Groenke went on. 'She feels it would compromise her husband as commandant.'

He supposed Sybil's Jewishness had somehow been overlooked but that didn't make sense either; her card would be stamped to say exactly what she was. An accident of bureaucracy? It didn't work like that in Schlegel's experience.

Groenke said, 'You could go through the labour exchange or the woman's block warden or her work supervisor. But they will want a request submitted in writing. On the other hand . . . Here's the thing. The commandant's wife believes you have actually been sent to help her.'

'Excuse me? Help how?'

'She said to me, "I think these are the men who have been sent to help."'

Schlegel didn't know what to make of any of it.

'That was all she said, other than adding she believed it in a biblical sense, as in what had been ordained.'

The garden was full of the fatty smell of sizzling meat. The commandant had changed into a white suit with white shoes.

Schlegel arrived wondering what it meant, the commandant's wife believing they had been sent to help. Morgen was none the wiser, other than to wonder whether the woman, rather than her husband, was behind their recall.

'Welcome to hell,' Morgen said, pointing to the barbecue where a slender figure stood prodding sausages with a fork.

The floppy chef's hat distracted Schlegel from seeing who it was, then, sure enough, slaughterhouse Sepp grinned nastily at him through the paraffin haze.

Morgen grunted. 'We should add him to the list of suspects for Tanner's killer if we can name anyone we want.'

'She was hit from behind,' Schlegel offered; Sepp's preferred method.

Morgen went over and asked Sepp what he was doing.

'Catering,' said Sepp smugly.

Morgen came back shaking his head. 'Does it really surprise you when a convicted killer turns up at the commandant's garden party?'

'Not really, given the strange levels of fraternisation in this place.'

Schlegel looked around. Everyone dressed in civilian best. Sixty or seventy guests going through the motions of social exchange. Everyone knocking it back. Getting drunk seemed to be the point. Behind the bonhomie he sensed glumness, as though the party were a ghost of livelier ones, apart from a buzz around Fegelein, who attracted young women with his indolent, inviting smile.

Palitsch drifted past wearing a nice, short-sleeved, open-neck shirt, looking relaxed and non-homicidal. Schulze came through the garden gate, accompanied by Krick. The swept-back hair had been replaced by a crewcut showing new grey, and a moustache had been added. Krick looked leaner, with long grooves down the sides of his mouth. Schlegel noted his watchfulness. Krick's gaze quickly passed over him, despite a flicker of recognition. Had Schulze told Krick about him? She was gesturing and laughing with another guest. He saw Broad with his perpetual accordion and the tall figure of Dr Wirths, conspicuous for being the only one in uniform and drinking mineral water.

Morgen smoked and said he didn't understand what was going on.

'Kammler sent us. We failed and have been immediately recalled on quite another matter. I can't decide if the two are connected, and whether the commandant's request is genuine, or a decoy, or a countermove against Kammler. By the way, I assume that is the eldest of the commandant's brats in the process of getting the family dog drunk.'

A supercilious boy of thirteen or so, dressed in military khaki, was encouraging a woozy shepherd to drink out of a bowl.

Morgen went on. 'What a charming cameo. There are too many loose ends. Including her.'

Frau Hoess had appeared on the patio, wearing a green

satin cloak with a hood. Schlegel watched her survey the party, pausing to note them.

Morgen said, 'I suspect we're the real loose ends. I am sure there is a logic to everything else, unavailable to us. The depressing thing about history is the way it shows us leading our lives all wrong, so why should it be different now?'

Fegelein had moved on to talk to Groenke, who had swapped his artisan outfit for smart slacks and a silk shirt. Fegelein, wearing an expensive hacking jacket, flicked ash and greeted whatever Groenke said with his most charming smile.

'There's a likely pair,' Morgen said, just as they were accosted by Dr Wirths, telling them in his friendly way that they had forgotten to come and see him. Schlegel suspected Wirths was a buttonholer. Wirths asked who they knew.

Morgen said no one really, apart from the obvious. Wirths pointed to the crowd Schulze was part of, presided over by a burly, beetle-browed man of around fifty, which made him older than most. He said they were the construction team and the man was their boss.

'Nothing they build works.'

Wirths pointed to the tall chimney over the garden wall. 'They spent ages replacing that and almost immediately it had to be closed for repairs and has since been discontinued.'

Schlegel asked, 'Is that why the morgue is hot instead of cool?'

'You know about that? They messed up the heating and the ventilation.'

Schlegel watched the party notch up a gear. A woman gave a couple of whoops. The beetle-browed man said something that caused him to double up with mirth. His cronies joined in. Schlegel was pleased to see Schulze did not. She seemed to note him watching and he supposed the friendly look was meant for him. He couldn't see Krick anywhere.

Dr Wirths continued to list at length the construction department's shortcomings. He blamed overspending and underperforming.

Schlegel stopped listening. He was vaguely aware of the doctor telling them to avoid the new camp. The construction department again was responsible.

'Absurdly grandiose schemes. I reserve my greatest contempt for it, given the shoddiness of the goods delivered. I keep telling anyone who will listen, money gets spent on the wrong things. What I could have done with a fraction of its crematoria budget. I am afraid everyone regards me as a grinding bore, I am sure you do too.'

Schlegel was surprised by such unlikely self-awareness.

'They could have saved a fortune and countless lives, had they looked after the living, instead of just thinking of how to get rid of the dead.'

Morgen asked who was responsible.

'Dr Kammler. They are his follies.'

Wirths stopped like a wound-down gramophone and Morgen and Schlegel extricated themselves without him seeming to notice. He remained smiling politely, watching the party's signs of disarray – the now staggering dog and a woman who sat down hard on her bottom.

Morgen said, 'Perhaps we have underestimated Dr Kammler. A construction pharaoh as well as lord of all slaves.'

Seeing Schulze in the company of Broad, he suggested they go over.

Schlegel was surprised Broad and Schulze knew each other.

'Oh, yes,' said Schulze. 'The security police always has a long litany of complaints to address to the construction department.'

They had the easy manner of people who got on. Broad complained that Schulze had yet to return the last book he had lent her.

'What was that?' asked Schlegel.

'Lermontov,' said Schulze.

'*A Hero of Our Time?*' he asked, surprised.

'Get to know thine enemy,' said Broad.

Morgen said, 'Tell us about Dr Wirths.'

Wirths was now lecturing several wives who were looking around for their escape.

Broad gave a sneaky grin. 'Not popular, which is why he can't get any building supplies or workers for his new home.'

He caught Schulze's eye.

'How come?' asked Morgen in surprise.

Broad said, 'An interesting alliance of my boss, her boss, and . . .'

He pointed to Groenke, still in conversation with Fegelein and a group of adoring young women. 'You have to admit it's funny, the man hasn't a clue. That's how it works.'

Broad pointed to the pond in front of the summerhouse and said, 'Ask Schulze about the pond.'

'Go on, tell us,' said Morgen. 'We are impressed by the quality of your gossip.'

It had happened just after she just arrived, she said, when she found herself being cultivated by the commandant's wife, invited to tea and so forth, then landed with the responsibility of providing her with the pond she so wanted.

'For the kiddies. Off the books and not paid for. Baptism by fire,' said Broad.

'How did you manage?' asked Morgen, intrigued.

'I asked around who the camp's top organisers were.'

She pointed towards Groenke.

'And you didn't even have to sleep with him,' offered Broad.

'I wouldn't have anyway. He was all right. He organised it without a word to her and let me take the credit.'

'Why is the doctor so unpopular?' Morgen asked.

Broad said, 'One of the bleeding hearts, and we sail a leaky boat, thanks to Dr Wirths being so manipulated by the prisoner underground. It causes us a lot of headaches. Big security crackdowns, arrests left, right and centre, a lot of overcrowded cells, and one mighty angry garrison doctor.' He glanced up. 'Look scarce. Here comes the Old Man.'

The commandant was waving his arms, encouraging everyone to circulate.

Schlegel and Morgen gravitated to Groenke and Fegelein, who was saying, 'As a matter of fact, I am dating the sister of Adolf's companion. Monastic, vegetarian, teetotal Adolf. Actually, he's more fun than he lets on.'

The man moved through the gears of social interchange as expertly as any racing driver, and the throwaway manner contrived not to sound like boasting. Groenke lapped it up.

Fegelein turned to Schlegel. 'Actually, we were discussing philately.'

Schlegel's lack of answer was taken for ignorance.

'Stamp collecting,' Fegelein prompted.

'Are you a connoisseur?' Schlegel asked, floundering.

'A bit. Martin is the one who is.'

'Martin?'

'Bormann.'

Of course, who else? thought Schlegel, depressed. Number two in the land.

Morgen said with false joviality, 'You are the most epic name-dropper.'

Fegelein chose to take the remark as a compliment.

'Erich has philatelists on his books.'

'We have a dealer offering one of the Baden 9 Kreuzer error stamps.'

Schlegel did his best to look knowledgeable.

'Imagine the flurry of excitement over that,' Fegelein added, before saying he needed to pay his respects to their hostess.

One of the commandant's children ran past with a wooden rifle and he and Fegelein indulged in a gun battle. The proverbial life and soul of the party, thought Schlegel sourly.

'How much is the stamp worth?' asked Morgen.

'A fortune if genuine,' said Groenke. 'But a lot are Jewish fakes.'

The party was in danger of falling flat, despite everyone getting drunk. The commandant carried out a windup gramophone onto the patio and put on a polonaise to liven the mood. People started to dance. A woman proudly sporting a black eye was telling people she had walked into a doorpost. 'That third gin, darling,' someone said, and laughed.

Frau Hoess summoned them over with a twist of her head. The cloak had been discarded. She wore heels but they were sinking into the lawn, making her appear to subside before their eyes.

She recited, 'If the sun is shining, the music stirs and gladdens one's heart, then this does not seem such a bad place after all.'

She slipped off one shoe, then the other, using Schlegel's arm to steady herself, and stood barefoot. Her feet were surprisingly big.

She jigged in time to the gramophone music and asked, 'Are you familiar with Hörbiger's world ice theory?'

'I am not,' said Schlegel, with what he hoped was a straight face.

Morgen was quick to add, 'It explains how Atlantis was destroyed by a great flood caused by the collision of an ice moon with the earth, and the ancient survivors founded a great civilisation in Central Asia, the capital of which was called Urbe.'

She leaned forward and whispered, 'Tibet. You must stay until the end. I shall be putting on a little show that reflects my love of the legend.'

Schlegel scrutinised his beer bottle, wondering how the hell Morgen knew this nonsense.

Food was announced and everyone stopped to eat. Schlegel didn't fancy Sepp's offerings and carried on drinking, availing himself of passing trays of beer.

He wandered around on his own, not bothering to talk to anyone. The commandant was dancing with a woman on the patio, desperate to keep everything jollied along. Several couples were in the bushes. A man lay on the lawn, asleep or passed out. A voice in Schlegel's ear said, 'The background stink of shit and burning bodies and disease and the pall of smoke and the ashes that fall like the finest snow on the roses in this, the commandant's garden, how does the newcomer get used to that?'

Schlegel looked into the man's dark eyes. Again the mystery of whether he remembered him; Krick was comfortably drunk when many were staggering.

'Quite,' he said, after Schlegel's silence. 'No answer really, except for my jaded explanation that however appalled the novice is it is soon forgotten because everyone gets sick upon arrival, vomiting and shitting until nothing is produced but mucus and water, so by the time you get better all that once looked and smelled horrible now feels almost normal and "almost normal" is everyone's operating mode.'

True, thought Schlegel. Guests making a show of having a good time. Children running around pretending to kill each other. Awkward conversations, even as everyone got smashed. A drunk dog.

'Have you been sick yet?'

'Ingeborg Tanner,' Schlegel ventured in return.

Krick said, 'Too pleasant an afternoon to talk about that. Come and see me. I am told we know each other. I don't remember.'

'My hair wasn't white then.'

'Does that make you albatross or harbinger?'

Krick smiled at his cleverness, and was gone.

Palitsch, drinking alone nearby, raised his bottle and strolled over.

'I am still drunk from yesterday. Or was it the day before?'

He was friendly but Schlegel wasn't sure if Palitsch recognised him. He reeked of sex. His fingers were nicotine-stained. Schlegel mentioned Tanner.

Palitsch looked blank and eventually said, 'I tend to avoid garrison women. Too clingy. Who are you fucking?'

Schlegel, feeling a prude, said he had only just arrived. Palitsch gave him a dig in the ribs.

'Everyone's wiping their dick on someone, don't tell me you're any different. Morphine and Jewish cunt, that's a good combination. Slav cunt best. Gypsy cunt good too. The women are wild and grateful for any chance.'

Palitsch's eyes were puddled, wistful and faraway. Schlegel sensed a floating distance between them and mentioned the name of the wife supposed to have been his lover. Palitsch stared uncomprehending.

Schlegel said, 'She was garrison.'

Palitsch squinted and asked, 'Are you on my case?'

Schlegel said, trying to flatter, 'Women obviously gossip about you.'

The man nodded, briefly sober. 'It's bust at the moment but the Palitsch tool is a friend to many women.'

His donkey laugh filled the garden, coinciding with Frau Hoess clapping her hands.

Krick was gone, as was Schulze. So was Morgen. Schlegel hadn't seen him leave; always expert at the unnoticed departure. Wirths stood near the front, with an ingratiating smile of expectation. The commandant sat on the patio, smoking, knees crossed, his children around him, leading the applause for his wife.

The now very drunk dog wandered around in unsteady circles.

The late afternoon light made everyone look like cutouts of themselves. Frau Hoess addressed the guests from the verandah, proposing for their cultural edification a series of *tableaux vivants* based upon the race of ancient Canarians whose islands formed the only remaining part of the ancient kingdom of Atlantis.

'Until the European settlers came; the conquering of the Canary Islands by the Christian Spaniards remains one of the most appalling examples of the poisonous effects of Jewish-Christianity on the soul of the European people.'

A trio of musicians had taken up positions at the side of the summerhouse. One was Broad, accompanied by a violin and the third with a flute and tambourine. Broad looked casual, smoking as he played, his skills obviously superior to what he had been asked to provide.

Frau Hoess announced each tableau. 'A tribal society of prosperous farmers who painted their bodies green, yellow and red.'

Small groups of what Schlegel supposed were prisoners posed as ancient, noble natives, wearing straw skirts and appropriately daubed.

'Golden locks, rosy cheeks, white skin,' Frau Hoess intoned.

Each display was greeted with a smattering of barely polite applause.

The whole thing was a staging of enormous miscalculation, amateurish and barely competent despite the best efforts of its components. The poses were appropriate, the musicians more than adequate. It was just the last thing the end of a not very successful drunken party needed.

Schlegel watched the commandant enjoy his wife's humiliation, though she was thick-skinned enough not to see it as that.

'They mummified the bodies of their elders. On islands some sixty miles off the coast of northwestern Africa, they had long lived in relative isolation.'

Those posing as islanders were joined by others dressed as conquistadores, who took up aggressive poses.

Frau Hoess ploughed on. 'During the thirteenth century, European navigators began to frequent their ports, carrying news of the islanders back to Europe. Eventually Spanish ships arrived to begin baptising the Canarians by the sword.'

The tableau threatened to get out of hand as the struggle gave way to pushing and shoving.

'The inhabitants fought tooth and nail but they could not long resist European muskets and European germs.'

The sound of Palitsch vomiting by the summerhouse was audible from where Schlegel stood. Palitsch emerged wiping his mouth, hugely pleased, and was studiously ignored by Frau Hoess.

A musical interlude came as a relief. People started to sit

on the lawn. Palitsch lay down and slept. The woman with the black eye winked at Schlegel. Children were shouting in the house. The commandant sat alone on the patio, crouched forward, staring intently at the pond.

When Schlegel next looked he was standing in the water, up to his calves, then bent down to fish something out. No one else appeared to notice. Schlegel couldn't see what it was but the spasm of disgust was unmistakable as the commandant stepped out, the bottom of his soaked trousers clinging to his legs.

Again no one watched as he crossed the lawn. By the far garden wall he stood for a moment, then made an overarm throw.

Schlegel turned to find himself facing Dr Wirths, who was also following the commandant's unsteady progress. Evidence of the abandoned party lay all around – litter and discarded bottles and glasses on the lawn, passed-out bodies and pools of vomit.

'Excessive drunkenness is encouraged as a form of safety valve. I recently had to attend to the commandant after a riding fall and the man was drunk before nine in the morning.'

The commandant marched past, oblivious. Wirths lowered his voice. 'This place is enough to drive anyone to drink but in the case of the commandant I would suggest it impairs his judgement.'

Schlegel excused himself. Manners prevailed in that he chose to thank the commandant's wife for her hospitality.

Before he could speak, Frau Hoess hissed *sotto voce*, 'Did you see what he threw over the wall?'

She swept by, telling him to follow. She took him through the garden door and asked where he thought the commandant had been on the other side of the wall. They were ankle deep in ivy. Frau Hoess now had flat shoes on. She suggested they search.

A trail of ants led them to a severed finger.

'I would rather you got rid of it,' said Frau Hoess with a shudder.

Schlegel dug a depression in the loose soil with his heel, kicked the finger in and covered it.

The woman was there to do her own digging too, he was certain, and sure enough she asked how he found her husband.

The best he managed was that he seemed under a lot of pressure.

Frau Hoess folded her hands demurely and said, 'I wish to be frank on my husband's behalf because he is the last one to speak up for himself.'

Schlegel wondered what levels of intrigue they were embarking on.

'I am in no doubt you and your friend are here to clean the place out and we do want Grabner gone, and Palitsch. On that my husband and I agree but I am in a dilemma.'

Schlegel, drunker than he thought, couldn't see where she was going with this.

'I do worry for him that the pressure of the job is too much. Best all round would be if you could arrange a sabbatical.'

He looked at her in astonishment. 'Who would run the place?'

She snapped, 'The garrison can take care of itself.'

'What would you do?'

'Stay, of course.'

She wouldn't dream of disrupting the children's education. 'My eldest has had difficulties but he is settled now.'

Obviously the monster's problems were not seen to extend to getting the dog drunk.

Frau Hoess looked at him on the verge of tears and said, 'It's not normal to walk into a pond in the middle of a garden party, however drunk.'

'And the finger?'

'It seems to be some terrible twisted way of drawing attention to himself. The more charitable interpretation would be a cry for help.'

'Would it be so bad if he stepped down? He has had a distinguished career. I am sure he would be well looked after.'

'Then I would have to leave too. It would break my heart. I know you have a job to do. I expect it is more dangerous than you imagine. Be that as it may, my husband has a secret project, very close to our hearts, and were we to be posted we would not be able to carry on with it. If he remained it might be detrimental to his health but if he was sent to recuperate for six months while I stayed, then I could still supervise for him. The project is highly confidential but has the backing of very senior figures.'

Schlegel felt he had entered another dimension. Mystified, he asked, 'Can you say what it is?'

'That would be telling. Now can I rely on you?'

He could only say of course, calculating that the woman's influence may yet prove useful with Sybil.

After watching her return to her garden he walked back through the garrison. He hadn't gone far when he became aware of Broad's accordion and spotted him sitting on the grassy bank beneath the chimney. Compared to what he had been asked to produce for Frau Hoess's show, he was playing something complicated.

Schlegel had the feeling Broad was waiting for him. Was it enticement or was he currying favour? Schlegel could not tell.

'Tanner had a reputation as a party girl. The big secret

here is there are only two things people are interested in. Drinking and fucking.'

'Enough to get her killed?'

'She was keen on a gippo prisoner. Maybe even to the extent of going full horizontal. Doubly *verboten*. Not so clever. As an unsullied vessel of German womanhood that counts as racial defilement, whereas if Palitsch fucks Gypsy Vera it doesn't, sort of, but he may yet get his comeuppance.'

Schlegel thought of Palitsch saying everyone was wiping their dicks.

'But Tanner and her Romany lover,' Broad went on, 'totally out of order, crosses the line, and if you have someone super-zealous about these things he might take exception. Tanner was considered too much of a good-time girl anyway, oh-la-la. We've had the commandant banging on about the epidemic of prisoner homosexuality and the epidemic of prisoner lesbianism and now it's the epidemic of garrison promiscuity.'

Schlegel realised gossip was currency, as much as any black market. He wondered what Broad was trying to sell him and about the price.

The next day they experienced the full deadness of a garrison Sunday.

Schlegel told Morgen of his strange encounter with Frau Hoess and her even more unlikely proposal.

'Special project? What can she mean?'

Schlegel had no idea other than it being, according to her, authorised. He passed on what Broad had said about Tanner and garrison promiscuity.

Morgen grunted and said there was a difference between having information and being able to act on it.

Morgen thought a long time before saying, 'I think this is

a place where you consider very carefully what is under your nose and do not look up. Our priorities remain the same. Do what we must to get out in one piece. In the meantime find out what you can about Sybil. We can always try the same trick and subpoena her.'

Morgen expressed an interest in extending their discussion with Wirths to include the dead dentist.

'I suspect the doctor's real quarrel is with cynicism. I got waylaid by him again and he was saying the garrison treats death as a casual thing, barely worth note and meaningless, in that proper records were not only not kept, they were scoffed at. I think for Dr Wirths death is an extremely meaningful and serious business.'

As for the day's other entertainments, various events were advertised on the bulletin board, including a football match, a classical recital in the garrison gymnasium and a visiting variety show with comedians and dancing dogs.

Dr Wirths saved them the business of seeking him out by turning up for lunch and inviting them to join him.

They were politely reprimanded again for not coming to see him. Morgen said all his shots were up to date. Schlegel couldn't remember but nodded.

'Prevention is always better than cure,' Wirths warned. 'The garrison has no history of planning, only of reacting to crises.'

It wasn't that he was unlikeable, Schlegel thought. All his gestures and mannerisms were those of a considerate, decent man – the way he held himself, the thoughtful incline of the head, the considered delivery. Unlike the rest, he seemed not to be trying to tell them anything other than what he was saying, but given a captive audience he was incapable of shutting up. He bombarded them with details of his improved healthcare programme with new prisoner disinfection centres, and his dream of a huge garrison field hospital.

He possessed just enough self-awareness to add, 'Strange to use the word dream in such a context, but unless we teach each other to share a vision of the future then we will be lost.' He looked at them. 'I can see you are not like others. It's important to understand before you become inured. Indifference is the real killer here.'

Morgen, terse, merely asked, 'What is the death rate in this place?'

'Still nothing to write home about.'

'How important are accurate medical statistics?'

'Essential for curbing disease.'

'And accurate postmortem records?'

Schlegel looked around, curious to know if anyone was listening. Most of them were well on the way to being Sunday drunk. No one gave a hoot for the doctor and his sanctimonious lectures. If anything, they were getting the odd look of sympathy.

Wirths said it was of no use if a fall was listed as the cause of death when it was typhus.

'Does that happen?'

'The medical records have been appalling.'

'Whose fault was that?'

'No one's as such. It was more of a culture.'

'That one didn't bother with prisoners?'

Wirths looked depressed. Morgen leaned forward.

'A dentist we were supposed to question was taken mysteriously ill while in custody and has since died.'

Wirths looked shocked.

'Of a seizure.'

Morgen pointed to above his heart.

'What does the death certificate say?' asked Wirths.

'I am sure it won't say lethal injection.'

It was Wirths' turn to look around.

'Phenol,' said Morgen.

Wirths hung his head.

Schlegel asked, 'Phenol?'

'A cheap disinfectant,' Morgen said, 'which causes cardiac arrest. In Buchenwald they used it to get rid of my star witness. I suspect Bock was similarly dispatched.'

Morgen made to leave.

The doctor, aghast, asked, 'Can you do nothing to help?'

Morgen said, 'Give me something to prosecute! Your doctors may be ethically wild, but they can claim they were acting within general guidelines, preventing the spread of disease with emergency measures.'

The doctor wrung his hands, saying his own staff placed him in an impossible position.

'Get rid of them, man!' said Morgen.

'The worst offenders have been transferred but they delegate to orderlies to carry on their work. They come in the middle of the night.'

Schlegel said, 'Take the case of our dentist . . .'

Morgen carried on. 'If the security police has a practice of referring to doctors for lethal injection, on initiative, and unauthorised, we have grounds for prosecution.'

Still the doctor dithered. 'The security police pick off my supervisors. They wreck my cure programme. Yes, they refer on to my staff and there are plenty still willing to do the job. I am not without courage but I am vulnerable and isolated and there are only two of you.'

Morgen struggled to keep his temper. Wirths accompanied them out of the dining room, now nervous and grateful, saying he was glad to feel they were making progress.

Morgen waited until the doctor was gone before venting his spleen.

'Wirths sees himself as a martyr, a tortured soul placed in an impossible situation. He is not a natural intriguer but he is not without intrigue. He will take the principled stand, but he holds himself above it all, which makes him as dangerous as the rest.'

Schlegel spent the late afternoon attending the recital in the gymnasium, featuring a Bach trio sonata. Morgen would not be persuaded and again Schlegel suspected him of making his own plans.

They sat on canvas chairs, with a good turnout, the occasion a bit boring for its provincial nature. The commandant's wife swept in, setting the tone, without her husband.

Careworn prisoners took to the stage in formal dress. Schlegel was quite unprepared for the exquisiteness of the performance. What they created was something else. He was not musical but he saw how they played for themselves, became the embodiment of the music, thus rebuking the rapt audience, which stood at the end to applaud.

They had played for the dead, against the living; Schlegel was sure of that.

Back at the hotel bar, Morgen produced a folded piece of paper from his pocket and flipped it across, saying, 'It was on the noticeboard.'

A mimeographed sheet had been made up to look like a Wild West bandit poster, the image unmistakably of Morgen, and underneath in crude print it read: 'WANTED: DEAD or ALIVE', with a reward of $1000.

Morgen sighed. 'Childish but nasty.'

The bar was starting to fill up. Schlegel spotted the odious Fegelein approaching, sleek in a quasi-uniform of cream double-breasted sharkskin jacket and trousers with a broad red stripe. He held his glass of beer like he was advertising it. He had a bruise on his cheek that he had tried to cover with a cosmetic. Seeing Schlegel stare, he said a horse had struck him with its head. Fegelein showed his teeth, ignoring Morgen, keeping up an easy patter about what a dull city Berlin had become outside of the enclaves in which he moved.

Schlegel could not believe the man's charm fooled anyone. The calculation was so transparent. He was congratulating himself on his insight when Fegelein dropped all pretence and subjected him to a reptilian stare.

'Be aware that you and your friend here are figures in a puppet play, of no consequence.'

Schlegel stared at the floor, thinking: Yes, that's how I feel most of the time.

Fegelein said Morgen didn't understand how things worked, which was why he got into trouble, whereas he did, which was why he was ensconced and they weren't.

Morgen said evenly, 'I could throw my drink over you except it would be a waste of good drink, regardless of your laundry bill. Say what you have to say.'

Fegelein gave his best laugh.

'Martin is keen that—'

'Spare us the chumminess, drop the full name. Bormann is keen what?'

'The commandant is hands off.'

'As in what?'

'Not to be investigated.'

'Why should Bormann care about anything other than guarding his master?'

'Just telling you what you need to know. Tread carefully.'

Fegelein offered a casual salute like an old adversary bidding adieu.

Morgen, speechless, looked angry and, Schlegel realised, he was scared. Chancellery involvement was a cause for great alarm. Nobody knew much about the penumbral Bormann, other than he controlled the inner sanctum. If Bormann had thrown his hat in the ring, their position was truly precarious.

A crummy space was allocated them by the commandant's office, little more than a broom cupboard in a windowless room on the back staircase of the administration block, large enough, just, for three small desks and an empty filing cabinet. Morgen wondered who the third desk was supposed to be for.

He went off to the post office to ask about telephones and came back with the news that none was available and Horn wasn't in; the tiny man didn't know why. Any calls would have to be made from public booths downstairs by the switchboard.

The best Schlegel could manage from the stationery office was a few sheets of paper, a couple of pencils, no sharpener, and a ruler between them. A request for a typewriter was greeted with general hilarity.

Thus did the dead hand of officialdom replace initiative, rendering Tanner a phantom in the machine. Even permission to view her sleeping quarters had to be put in writing.

Krick, the finder of the body, didn't answer his telephone. Groenke had not given, or withheld, the name Sybil was working under. No one in the motor pool was interested in talking about Tanner, beyond saying they thought she was on leave.

Schlegel was struck by the partial nature of information. Broad knew Tanner was dead, and was willing to say so, yet her colleagues acted as though her absence was normal.

Either this blanking was a coping strategy or they weren't willing to discuss it with anyone asking questions.

The labour office told him everyone was in a meeting.

When he went back later and asked to speak to Ilse – the name of the works supervisor given him by Schulze – he was surprised to have her pointed out. It was the first cooperation he had encountered that day.

The office consisted of three interconnecting rooms of ranked desks, many of which had been personalised with kitschy souvenirs.

Schlegel used Schulze's name to introduce himself.

Ilse, suspicious at first, brightened. 'We think of ourselves as sisters though we barely know each other.'

She wore a print dress and sandals. Schlegel supposed her a civilian. From what he could see plenty were seconded to the garrison. A bead of sweat gathered attractively in the hollow of her throat. Her accent was unusual. The colour of her eyes was that of a troubled sea. She reminded him of someone.

He said he didn't have a name for the person he was looking for.

Ilse asked him to describe her, frowned and said, 'Follow me.'

She led the way to a stack room with the air of someone who knew what she was about. As always with such people, Schlegel was a little intimidated. Schulze had the same effect on him. Ilse opened a drawer, flicked through it with rapid fingers and pulled out a card with a photograph.

'Is that her?'

It was.

The photograph showed Sybil. But the name was different and she wasn't listed as Jewish. Her category stated 'social undesirable'.

He was aware of Ilse looking at him.

'Where have I seen you before?'

Schlegel didn't know.

She said, 'I definitely have.'

'In Berlin?' Schlegel ventured.

She laughed. 'Chance would be a fine thing.'

Schlegel proffered the card. 'Is it possible to take a mime-ograph of this, so I can show my boss?'

'What's it about?'

She sounded more curious than suspicious, indicated by a light touch on his sleeve.

Schlegel noted her strange playfulness, an automatic flirting, weirdly attractive for being so mechanical. It made him conscious of the garrison's high level of sexual tension, close to out of control. Now this woman, to whom he didn't think he was in the slightest attracted, yet found he wanted rather badly.

He asked about the commandant's wife. Ilse recited in a calculated bored voice, 'Frau Hoess is a good employer, she hires a lot of people, but she is changeable. Pet one week, out of favour the next. I am not telling tales here. Frau Hoess says the same of herself.'

Schlegel couldn't decide if she was waiting for him to make a pass. He remembered where he had seen her.

Ilse continued in a strange singsong way, 'Paperwork is the only thing that keeps a record of time here. For most of us, one day is the same as another.'

'It must be a good job, working for the commandant's wife.'

The best, she said. Schlegel, incapable of tearing himself away, felt mildly deranged.

'How does the job market work?' he ploughed on. He supposed the conversation had a logic.

'Like anywhere, there are good jobs and bad jobs. Most are bad and those in them devote all their efforts to getting moved.'

'What counts as good?'

'Indoors and the chance to eat well. Staff kitchens, domestic appointments.'

Schlegel pointed to the index card and asked, 'How would she have got her job?'

'The way of the gods is entirely mysterious.'

'Where would she live, for instance?'

'Block five, ground floor, room four. Size of a palace.'

'How do you know?'

'It's my job to be on top of things.'

'What does that mean?'

'I am only indiscreet with people I like.' She gave him an exasperated look. 'You don't get a room like that without favours.'

Schlegel felt as though he was being pleasantly kidnapped by this persistent woman. He supposed any novelty was a distraction. She would be bossy in bed; not necessarily a bad thing.

'Favours?' he repeated.

'Sugar daddy.'

She laughed and licked her lips. Schlegel seemed to have stepped into an emotional quagmire. A woman he was inexplicably lusting after was telling him the woman he loved had been shacked up with some man for her own protection. He was jealous.

'Does the man have a name?'

'No one is saying and wise not to ask.'

She mimeographed a copy of Sybil's card. Schlegel watched her muscles tauten as she worked the machine.

'Is it true there is a shrink here?' he asked.

'You bet. Do you need one?' She laughed. 'A lot of messed-up heads. No, I am joking. The garrison has a full complement of medical therapists, from chiropractors to analysts and orthopaedic surgeons.'

Schlegel suspected her wisecracks disguised loneliness. Perhaps she struggled. He laughed at himself. He was being pompous. Her parting remark seemed to say as much.

'We are going to have to teach you about innuendo. It's what the place runs on.'

He said, 'You look different with your clothes on.'

The naked sunbather who had smiled at him at the hillside resort.

She said, 'I wondered when you would remember.'

Sybil's image had smeared where the machine's ink had clogged. Copying seemed to have stripped it of any meaning. Schlegel could decipher nothing, apart from her being another person with a new identity. He thought back to her moment of horror upon seeing him. At first he supposed her fright was of a woman desperate not to be recognised, but wondered now if it hadn't been shame at the extent of her compromise.

He folded the sheet carefully, thinking to treat it like a talisman.

He had a choice, he thought, and decided on close to the truth.

He boldly marched up to the commandant's house, rang the bell and asked to speak to the commandant's wife.

She emerged a moment later into the hall from the kitchen, with floury hands and wearing an apron.

Assuming a deferential manner, he asked if it might be possible to have a word with her seamstress. He knew the woman from Berlin where she had done couture work for his mother.

He could see Frau Hoess was curious about his mother's social standing. Only the higher echelons could afford such work. He was saying he had a message from his mother for the seamstress when she cut him short.

'I am a great believer in coincidence. What a shame. She no longer works here.'

'But I saw her—'

'Gone. Transferred out.'

Schlegel felt panic's claw.

'Where?'

'I am sure I have no idea.'

'But she was here,' Schlegel repeated helplessly.

'I didn't know then she was in violation of her terms of employment. When it was brought to my attention, I had no choice.' She looked momentarily exasperated. 'What a pity. I wish I had known about her and your mother.'

The news was crushing.

Frau Hoess had no idea of the woman's whereabouts or destination, other than she was due to be shipped out or was gone already. He would have to take that up with the relevant departments.

Schlegel left, walking as stiffly as an automaton.

The relevant departments had no record of any recent transfer or firing from the commandant's household. He was snidely informed by one objectionable clerical lackey that paperwork didn't update itself.

He looked around in desperation for Ilse, who wasn't at her desk.

He went to the transport office and requested to see its prisoner transfer sheets. Put it in writing, he was told.

Morgen was as surprised as he was by the speed of Sybil's transfer. He agreed that the commandant and his wife must have fallen out over her, but was he the sugar daddy?

It was late afternoon before Schlegel found Ilse at her desk again. He was relieved to see her, the only friendly face of the day. Her skin glowed so that he wanted to touch it. He complimented her on her appearance, which was unlike him. Perhaps flirting was an obligatory extension of camaraderie. Perhaps it was to do with trying not to look over his shoulder.

Ilse knew nothing of the dismissal. She seemed taken aback, saying, 'If anyone was safe you would have thought . . .'

Normally with any case of firing from the commandant's household she would have been called upon to handle it. The agency temp who had been filling in for her knew nothing of the matter either.

'Do prisoners have contracts of employment?' Schlegel asked, feeling naïve.

'It's a polite way of saying there are rules and if you break them you lose your job.'

'What happens to the offender?'

'A hearing, followed by a custodial sentence, served in one of the garrison's penal colonies, after which the offender is reintroduced back into the labour market. In this case maybe after four to six weeks.'

'And if she was being transferred?'

'It would take several days to sort the paperwork. That's the transport office and they're not helpful.'

'So she will still be here?'

'She should be.'

'Where would she be now?'

'As an employee of the commandant she should be in the custody of the commandant's office.'

'Not the punishment block?'

'The commandant's office has cells for its own offenders.'

Schlegel asked Ilse if she could check. He supposed he could just as easily fix to see Sybil in her cell.

'Here's the odd thing,' Ilse said, putting down the receiver afterwards.

Apart from Frau Hoess saying, there was no record of Sybil's dismissal or of her being held.

Their next visitor was a surprise.

'Schulze,' she said.

Schlegel feared he was blushing.

'How can we forget?' said Morgen, affable and uncharacteristically flirtatious. 'What brings you to our grim abode?'

'I have been sent to work with you.'

She didn't look happy about it.

'Why, when you have been sent on a course to Berlin?'

'The department isn't ready for me yet. I have been asked to be with you until you find your feet.'

'Asked by whom?'

'My boss is angry with me for going off and doing the course.'

She shrugged to say she didn't know if that was the real reason.

'Are you being promoted?'

'Not if I am being sent here.'

'And what do you see your duties consisting of?' asked Morgen.

'General hand-holding, I suppose, but I won't serve you tea and biscuits, not that there are any.'

'We don't have a kettle. We could do with a telephone too.'

'You'll be lucky. You will be bottom of everyone's list.'

'What else will your duties consist of?'

'Reporting on you, probably, though no one has asked me to yet.'

She seemed diverted by the prospect.

Morgen said, 'As you know the ropes, perhaps you can tell us what is and isn't possible. Telephone?'

She pulled a doubtful face.

'Kettle?'

'One pack of cigarettes.'

'Typewriter?'

Schulze made an equivocal gesture. 'Typewriter not impossible but forget the ribbon. Carbon paper the same. Correction fluid possible, but no point without a typewriter.'

Morgen looked approving. 'And then we were three.'

Schlegel thought on behalf of Schulze: Not by choice.

The next day Morgen had a typewriter and pointed to it happily. Schulze explained it was hers and she had requisitioned it from herself, in triplicate. The ribbons she had been hoarding. Schlegel saw the filing cabinet now had a lock.

'An electric kettle too,' said Morgen. 'A woman of untold ingenuity. Who cares if she is spying on us.'

'But nothing to put in the boiling water.'

'Don't be hard on yourself,' said Morgen, in a rare good mood.

Schulze said the reluctance of anyone to give them a telephone showed how popular they were.

'Now, thanks to you, I am not popular either.'

The most frustrating aspect of the Tanner case remained its existential nature. Presented with a body, what were they investigating, really? Most criminal cases were straightforward: crime committed, telephone calls made, evidence gathered, leads followed and, with luck, a solution reached. Yet Schlegel had the repeated feeling that even if they did find out who killed Tanner they would not necessarily solve the case.

Morgen continued to fret about Kammler. He had said neither who he was nor what he represented and was more sinister for revealing nothing of his hand.

'It is a maze and there will be a way out.'

Schlegel thought Morgen sounded more convinced when he said, 'If we report the truth they will merely shoot the messengers.'

They fell into that state of distraction which was the presiding feature of garrison life – drunken nights and hungover days the polar points by which it steered its course. What chance had they with Tanner or Bock, let alone determining Sybil's whereabouts, when enquiry and investigation were so alien to the nature of the place?

Sybil's whereabouts remained a mystery. Schlegel became aware of seeking Ilse out, as one of the few agreeable souls. They continued to find no record of who had removed Sybil or where she had been taken. Her registry card hadn't been updated, showing her still working at the commandant's house.

Schlegel risked quizzing Groenke, who claimed to be in the dark, then blamed the security police.

That was a new one on Schlegel.

'Don't be naïve, man. Unless the commandant's servants act as informers they lose their jobs.'

'Including the seamstress?'

'I thought she came with high protection, but apparently not.'

'Are you saying she was put there by the security police to spy on the commandant?'

'Maybe more of a Mata Hari thing.'

'Seduce the commandant?' Schlegel could not believe what he was saying.

*

Palitsch strolled into their office unaccompanied. 'I hear you want to speak to me, skip,' he said to Schlegel, and gave Schulze a breezy smile.

Morgen said ponderously to Schulze, 'This is confidential.'

Schlegel watched her make herself scarce with the practised efficiency of one used to being told to clear out for private meetings.

Palitsch asked, 'Can I take a load off?' and sat in Schulze's place without waiting for an answer.

'Confidential,' Morgen repeated.

Palitsch nodded. 'These four walls. It's how ninety-five per cent of conversations start here, no problem. Shoot.'

He listened carefully to Morgen. Schlegel hadn't properly noticed the paleness of the man's eyes, barely blue.

Palitsch looked from one to the other and slowly said, 'You think because I had an affair with one of the missing women it puts me on the list of those to question about Tanner.'

'You know her name?'

'Open secret.' He gave a hoot of laughter. 'Like everything else here.'

'How did you hear?' asked Morgen.

'They sent an ambulance.' He beat out a rhythm on the table top. 'She was a good kid.'

He didn't sound particularly convinced, but surprised them by turning serious.

'Not counting prisoners, the garrison has several thousand living or working here. There were about fifty when I started. Our little planet grew, full of so many dramas. My wife died last year. What can I say? Hands up, I fooled around, everyone does, but no one could doubt my devotion. I don't care about anything now. I drink all the time, but everyone does. In my case, without trying to stoop to self-pity, I believe every drink is a result of her tragedy.'

'How did she die?' asked Morgen.

'Not by my bashing her brains in.' He gave an inappropriate guffaw. 'She died of the sickness.' He stopped, eaten by sadness, and recomposed himself. 'I am loathed. I make a point of it. The prisoners hate me. The commandant hates me. I look like a poster boy and he doesn't, and nor do you, and nor do the prisoners. The wildest story was that prisoners had a plan to contaminate my laundry so I got the sickness, but my wife died instead. I held her in my arms as she passed, wanting only to take her place.'

He looked at them with watery eyes. Schlegel thought Palitsch's description of himself as a poster boy flattered him somewhat.

'We were told Tanner was having an illicit affair with a Gypsy,' he said.

Palitsch laughed in disbelief. 'She was reckless, not foolish.'

'What's your version?' asked Morgen.

'Some women go missing, probably leave for their own reasons. The woman I had a thing with had every cause, given her asshole husband. I may be a bastard but I know how to respect a woman. As for Tanner, the Poles detest us. It's their old homeland, after all, and they're going the way of the Apache and the Sioux. Endangered species. If a partisan cuts the throat of a guard it is an act of terrorism and will lead to roundups, shootings, maybe even their own family. Bash a German woman over the head. Nothing. Easy score. No reprisals.'

'Why not?'

Palitsch laughed. 'Women aren't seen to be worth the candle.'

*

148

Schlegel caught himself surreptitiously inspecting Schulze when she wasn't looking, legs and knees especially. He put it down to boredom, while also being uncomfortably aware of the irony of mirroring the commandant's infatuation. He blamed the garrison's combustible mix of repression and social decorum, fuelled by bouts of drunkenness that were anything but liberating. The unrequited state was bound to prevail, even when combined with open carnality.

He tortured himself with his impossible obsession and guilt at entertaining thoughts of other women. Any true feeling, beyond hysteria and rage, from what he could tell, was impossible. The general mood of desperate sentimentality corresponded to his own state, of which he did not feel he was the real author, as though someone else was writing it for him.

Morgen, with a lighter touch, plied Schulze with questions about the garrison's social habits.

She enlightened them on why people were generally so hard to get hold of. Since the lifting of the quarantine there had been what was jokingly referred to as an epidemic of truancy. Any excuse to get out. Courses were invented. Schlegel asked about Krick and she said she thought in his case it was genuine. He had connections to Swiss psychiatry and travelled to Zurich.

'While I sit at a desk.'

She remembered one strange manifestation during the big confinement: terrible giggling fits among the women; the more inappropriate the setting, the more acute the attack.

'And the men?'

'Raucous, as you would expect.'

Schlegel saw it wouldn't do to condescend to her.

'And what about garrison women as a whole?' Morgen asked.

'The same as anywhere.'

They divided into good-time girls and those that held back, who were treated with a mixture of false respect and contempt.

'Yes, yes,' said Morgen eagerly. 'It's what you get in any encoded society, a mixture of idealism and hypocrisy.'

It seemed a remarkably grown-up conversation, thought Schlegel, to which he was contributing nothing.

Morgen raised an eyebrow before asking, 'Which category do you fall into, if I may be so bold?'

Schulze had the grace to laugh. 'Neither.'

The dormitory where Ingeborg Tanner had slept was immaculate: hospital corners on the beds, no more than three personal items on display, a metal locker and chest of drawers.

The dormitory was at the top end of the camp, in one of the ubiquitous wooden huts that had sprung up in the last years. When Schlegel waved the chit finally giving written permission for an appointment he had to endure the whole tedious routine of sighing and scratching and questioning from the block supervisor, who made it plain with every twitch and grimace that she regarded his request as tantamount to persecution. He listened to the insolent slap of her slippers as he followed her down the corridor. He tried asking about Tanner but she wasn't interested, she minded her own business and didn't care for anyone else's. She unlocked the door and slouched her way back.

Schlegel counted six beds. Tanner's was stripped, the chest of drawers empty and the top cleared. Waste of time, he thought. The locker was locked. He went back to the warden's hutch and asked for the duplicate key. He got the whole eye-rolling act and as she was about to say 'written permission' something in him snapped. She lifted her hands, thinking he was about to hit her, and handed over the key. Fuck it, Schlegel thought. He was not in good shape.

Ingeborg Tanner's locker was in fantastic contrast to its plain surroundings. Two hangers were taken up with frumpy uniforms; otherwise it was a row of colourful dresses. There was even a fur coat and fox stole. French fashion houses. Continental labels. Oslo. Athens. Half a dozen pairs of shoes crammed in the foot of the locker, none practical, mostly heeled and open-toed. Stuffed on top was a bag full of silk underwear and nightdresses, silk stockings, French brassieres, a pessary, lipstick, foundation, powder, eyeliner, mascara, scent with names Schlegel recognised, in all a treasure trove of items that the healthy make-up-free young German woman should not possess. When would Tanner have worn any of this? He had noticed women in the hotel relatively well turned out for evening sessions, but it didn't go beyond a discreet application of frowned-upon lipstick and a smartish dress. He had memories of the immaculate and beautiful friends of his mother wearing such clothes before the war, but had seen nothing like it since.

He stuffed everything back and on the locker floor noticed a green brooch, beautiful and expensive-looking. He pocketed it without thinking.

'What sort of clothes?' Schulze asked carefully when Schlegel told them about the contents of Tanner's locker.

She made a show of no interest. He sensed she was resorting to the garrison's standard blocking technique.

Morgen roused himself from his inertia to ask, 'How many balls in the air? The death of the dentist; the extent of the racket; the mystery of our beloved seamstress; the motives of the commandant's wife, regarding the seamstress's dismissal and the special project she speaks of; the garrison wars; Fegelein and the real reason for him being here; and who killed Tanner?' He turned to Schulze and said, 'Enlighten us on any of these if you can.'

Schulze asked only, 'Beloved seamstress?'

Morgen sighed. 'Not now.'

Schlegel considered his priority Sybil and she was probably lost to him already.

Morgen declared himself sufficiently interested to inspect the contents of Tanner's locker. Schlegel walked with him.

They heard laughter coming from the dormitory and interrupted two giggling young women.

One, standing by her locker in her slip, said, 'Men aren't allowed.'

She showed no self-consciousness about her state of undress. Her companion sat on her bed painting her toe-nails. Both on the right side of attractive, and insolent, Schlegel decided.

Morgen ignored them and inspected Tanner's locker. The one standing by her locker had the door open. Its contents were modest compared to Tanner's.

'Is she allowed to paint her nails?' Morgen asked.

The other woman said, 'Keep your shoes on and nobody knows.'

Morgen held up a pair from Tanner's locker. 'What if you have open-toed ones like these?'

The same one said, 'Then you wouldn't paint your nails.'

Morgen looked amused.

The women claimed to know little about Tanner, apart from her being superior, largely unpleasant and mainly absent.

'Any men?' asked Morgen.

The one on the bed said, 'What else are we going to do?'

'There was a boyfriend,' said the other.

'Several.'

They grew vague. They worked in quite another part of the garrison, they said, and Tanner wasn't around much and often stayed out.

They had no recollection of her wardrobe either. Morgen pointed to the locker and they shrugged.

'Canada,' one said, sounding bored.

'Where's Canada?'

'North America,' said the other.

'Ha-ha,' said the first.

'Why Canada?' asked Morgen.

They didn't understand the question.

'Why is it called Canada?' Morgen asked slowly.

The women started to look sulky.

'Land of plenty,' the one sitting mumbled.

'And what is it?' Morgen insisted.

'A storage depot,' the one standing eventually offered.

'Out of bounds,' confirmed her friend, implying that the state of their lockers meant they weren't helping themselves, unlike Tanner.

Morgen moved from Tanner's locker to her stripped bed. He inspected under her mattress and found nothing. He opened and closed the drawers of her bedside locker and saw they were empty.

'Where is Tanner now?' Morgen asked, becoming exasperated.

'Gone,' said the one painting her nails. They started to get the giggles.

'Gone how?'

Spluttering turned to outright laughter. Schlegel found it contagious and Morgen's stony face made it funnier.

Morgen returned his attention to the drawers, taking them all the way out. His ponderous manner made him look vaguely comic, or maybe it was just the girls giggling.

Schlegel thought back to the days of Stoffel in Berlin – tough old-school cops, aggressive investigation, backup, scene-of-crime tape, forensic outlines, a machine in itself – and how they would have fared in the garrison. Quite easily: Stoffel would have cosied up to the security police, knocked heads, made his mark, arrested the suspect who could be most made to fit the frame, dusted his hands and gone home with a citation. Any rough-house behaviour would be excused by a corresponding instinct for the emotional pattern of any case, akin to feminine intuition, or so it was claimed, which was why Berlin homicide referred to each other as girls. To be called girl was a sign of acceptance. Schlegel never had been.

The young woman standing by the locker eventually managed to compose herself enough say, 'She gave an officer a dose of clap and had to leave in a hurry.'

That set them off again.

The one on the bed steadied her hand enough to apply the finishing touches to her nails, and said, 'Blow on them, dear.'

Schlegel thought: We are being made fools of.

Morgen told the woman with the nails to open her locker. She said to ask her friend. 'I'm not dry yet.'

The other did so, disagreeably. The locker contained a couple of uniforms and ordinary cheap civilian dresses. He asked again about Tanner's wardrobe.

Both shook their heads.

Schlegel supposed they were implicated but had cleared their lockers.

Sensing their seriousness, the one standing said, 'We're not told and we don't ask.'

They left carrying the contents of Tanner's locker, over their arms and stuffed in bags.

Morgen said, 'This was taped to the back of the drawer.'

It was a tiny battered black leather notebook, blank except for two pages of numbers.

Schlegel hadn't seen Morgen find it. He looked at the neat columns, always the same amount of digits; telephone numbers, he supposed. There was nothing to say to whom they belonged, not even initials.

It was obvious Morgen expected him to do the legwork. He also wanted to know whether Tanner's autopsy showed her having gonorrhoea.

'I want to see the report.'

Schlegel spent a sticky, uncomfortable forty minutes sweating in a hot telephone booth, chasing Ingeborg Tanner. He was used to being treated as Morgen's dogsbody. It had less to do with rank than Morgen being nearly a decade older.

The garrison pathology department had no record of holding Tanner's body, or any autopsy. The largely helpful clerk said postmortems were sometimes done on behalf of the medical department by prisoner doctors in a laboratory located in one of the new crematoria. Schlegel found the number and spoke to a doctor with a thick middle-European accent, who drolly informed him he'd had no women with bashed-in skulls.

All this takes the time it takes, he thought, while I sweat like a pig.

He spoke again to the same clerk, who asked with which authority the body was lodged. Apparently that made a difference. Schlegel said the commandant's office. He was told in that case it should be in the morgue next to the old camp crematorium. Schlegel said the one he had been in was more like a sauna.

'Yes, but the room next to it is nearly as cold as a deep freeze. You will need a pass from the commandant's office.'

Schlegel was desperate to get out of the booth. There was no way of jamming the door open, not that it would make any difference; it was just as hot outside. The glass was condensing like in a greenhouse. He was about to leave when he remembered Tanner's black book and sat down again with a sigh.

Upstairs in the office, Morgen was inspecting Tanner's clothes.

Schulze was saying, 'I think it is a famous French fashion house.'

She looked uncomfortable. Schlegel supposed they had all helped themselves.

He mentioned about needing a pass for the morgue.

'Fuck that,' Morgen said, and apologised to Schulze for his language. Schlegel detected a trace of amusement, or perhaps it was relief at being spared further quizzing on Tanner's couture.

The morgue was all of two minutes' walk. It struck Schlegel how close together everything was. There was plenty of outer sprawl – the hotel was a twenty-minute walk – but within the garrison everything involved little more than crossing the street.

Schlegel told Morgen he had tried two numbers in Tanner's book. They were telephone numbers, as they had thought. The first was the general one for the motor pool where Tanner worked and was accessed via the switchboard. The second he had let ring for a long time and was about to hang up when a female answered, young and heavily accented. Schlegel presumed she was one of the Polish housekeeping girls. He spoke slowly and asked which house.

House Palitsch.

Morgen looked doubtful. 'A bit convenient, perhaps, given the commandant's suspicions. Anyone could have put the book there for us to find.'

They arrived at the crematorium complex. The sentry posted was wanting to know on what authority when Morgen grumpily cut him short and said they were there to inspect the mouths of the dead.

There was no answer to that and the sentry waved them past.

Schlegel had noticed how the correct accent, bad temper, an assumption of stupidity on the part of those addressed, and the presumption of limitless authority cut through a lot of bullshit when dealing with the lower levels. Morgen possessed the knack; he didn't.

The complex was smaller than it looked from outside. One sign pointed to the incinerators. A notice issued by the construction department stated them out of order. Down a short corridor was the room where they had first seen Tanner and next to it double doors led into another corridor of delicious Arctic chill, taking them into a space commanded by what looked like a garden shed, in which sat a female orderly, wearing a thick coat and wrapped in blankets, who was playing a complicated-looking game of patience.

Her skin was grey and her lips blue from the cold. Schlegel felt the sweat dry on his back. The woman's proximity to the dead seemed to have reduced her to a colourless, shapeless figure of indeterminate age.

Morgen said he was there for the autopsy report carried out on Tanner.

The woman looked blank, then said, 'Oh, brains in the ditch. No autopsy.'

'What?'

'Not possible.'

'One is being carried out?' Schlegel said. He could not decide if it was a question.

'Up the chimney.'

Morgen asked, 'Are you telling us the body was removed before autopsy?'

The woman nodded.

'Who signed the release?'

'Mr High-and-Mighty himself. Garrison doctor Wirths.'

Morgen asked if Schlegel could think of a single connection between Tanner and what they knew of Wirths. Schlegel couldn't.

Morgen asked the woman, 'Do you have a sheet on Tanner?'

'On whose authority?'

'Oh, fuck the paperwork for once,' said Morgen. He laid two cigarettes on her sill. The hag contorted her face into a horrible attempt at a smile. 'Correct answer. I am only letting you because I haven't got around to filing it.'

'My saviour,' said Morgen, leaving Schlegel thinking how in Berlin flirting was a selective social art rather than endemic.

The report was out with a mess of other papers. Morgen said there was quite a lot she hadn't got around to filing. He kept the mood light, jollying her along until she simpered.

The sheet, finally produced with a flourish, gave Tanner's bare details. Cause of death, fatal blow. The box next to autopsy was ticked.

The woman grimaced. 'Ticked in advance. By me. An autopsy had been scheduled. Booked in. Backlog. Another staff shortage. But his lordship turned up and took the body.'

'Is that something he has done before?'

'Are you kidding? We are way below his level of consideration. It was the first time Dr Wirths has deigned to visit our humble station and I told him so.'

They returned to the empty office where they were joined shortly afterwards by Schulze carrying a large pile of folders.

'Garrison hospital records,' she said.

They were hanging folders, the sort that didn't stack neatly and slithered across the surface of her desk. Morgen leaned forward with surprising alacrity to catch one as it fell to the floor.

'Garrison hospital records?' he asked.

'Since the beginning of last year it seems there have been nine cases of garrison women being admitted to the staff hospital suffering from severe bruising and broken bones, always described as the result of a fall.'

Schlegel remembered the woman at the commandant's party sporting a black eye.

'Are we thinking this connects to Ingeborg Tanner?' asked Morgen.

He was being patronising and Schlegel saw that she could tell.

'I am not the detective,' she answered tartly. 'I am just collating possible evidence for you to consider.'

Morgen held up his hand in apology. Schlegel found it hard to tell whether she was being deliberately cool or just professional.

'How did you know about this?' he asked, trying to sound conciliatory.

'I didn't,' she said, sounding more exasperated than mollified. 'I found this pushed under the door.'

She passed over a narrow sheet. It looked like a strip of

ticker tape, on which was typed a terse message recommending inspection of the garrison medical records of the named women, including the hospital picture library.

'How odd,' Morgen said. 'What are the circumstances of these cases?'

Six of the nine women were married, Schulze said, and living with their husbands.

'Are we talking about private violence?' asked Morgen.

'It would seem so.'

Schulze appeared sufficiently troubled for Morgen to ask what was the matter.

'Such cases aren't usually noted. They are treated and forgotten about.'

'How do you know?'

'I am aware of situations where things got out of hand. Incidents like that do not appear on a woman's medical record even after treatment. I made a date of the incidents – not that there's any pattern.'

Morgen scanned the list. 'They started around eighteen months ago, in January 1942. Two incidents that March, one in April, then nothing until August, with four since – one in September, two over Christmas, with one in the current year on 3 February and nothing apparently in the six months or so since.'

He read the medical notes, noting aloud bruising to upper arms; fractured cheekbones; bruising to buttocks and thighs; broken nose; dislodged molar; one example of cutting, as a result of head hitting a radiator.

'Married?'

'Four were.'

'And their husbands?' Schlegel asked.

'All transferred.'

'As a result of disciplinary action?'

'The personnel office has no record of any.'

'And the wives?' asked Morgen.

'A soldier's file lists his postings and dependents, with no further details on them.'

Morgen tossed the paper on the desk and asked, 'Is this a real lead or another wild distraction?' He looked at Schulze. 'Do any of the cases note rape or sexual assault?'

'They wouldn't.'

She had to explain such matters were considered private between the parties concerned. Her look suggested that Morgen as a man of law should have known that.

'But this is odd,' she said, producing more folders. 'In the five cases since 18 August last year photographs were taken.'

They were unprepared for what they were shown. A set of professional portraits displayed a woman's smashed and bruised face from different angles. One eye was entirely closed. Further shots of her naked body, from front and behind, revealed the extent of livid damage to the torso, legs and arms, and lacerations on the buttocks and upper thighs.

'Always described as a fall, you say. Why document the evidence, then describe it as something it clearly isn't?'

Morgen gestured at Schlegel, who had no answer. Schulze spread other photographs out. The cumulative effect was forensic and intrusive to the point of being pornographic. Schlegel was reminded of his stepfather's pictures of naked women in bondage, which had something of the same shamed staring.

'Did you know this sort of thing went on?' Morgen asked.

'No, but socially things could get pretty wild,' Schulze replied. 'Men consider most women fair game.'

Perhaps sensing Morgen's next question, she added, 'I made sure I was attached. Not very adventurous but easier than spending the whole time being chased.'

'Are things less wild now?'

She didn't answer and said, 'A senior doctor named Hartmann is the referred physician in several cases. I have made an appointment for you to see him.'

Hartmann had more important concerns than garrison women who provoked arguments. 'It's not as though we haven't enough on our plates.'

Hartmann was a dapper ethnic German, with a corresponding accent, pomaded hair and breath that combined a kick of mouthwash, booze and halitosis. The office's main feature was a caged canary. It trilled unpleasantly. The blind was mostly down. Hartmann sat silhouetted behind his desk and left them standing.

He couldn't remember why a decision had been made to keep a visual record of such cases and his manner said nor did he care.

'And the cases themselves?' Schlegel asked.

'They had to be treated.'

'Domestic falls covers a multitude of sins.' Morgen made no effort to make it sound as though he liked or respected the man.

A classic stonewaller, Schlegel thought, as he watched Hartmann move his pen from one side of the desk to the other.

'There used not to be a report at all in such cases. They were patched up and sent home.'

'Did this happen a lot?' Morgen's tone remained unpleasant.

Hartmann matched it, saying, 'I couldn't tell you really. I don't hold surgery.'

Schlegel expected it had; there was an epidemic of everything else.

'Then reports had to be made, as of the beginning of last year. Why the change?'

'A directive probably.'

'From whom?'

'You can't expect me to remember . . . We get a load. The commandant's office, the garrison doctor, Berlin . . .'

'What about the instruction to photograph such cases?'

Hartmann looked blank.

'Did you take the photographs?'

Hartmann snorted.

'Who did?'

'I have no idea.'

'Did you not arrange it?'

'I told an orderly to sort it out.'

Schlegel looked at him expectantly, until Hartmann said, 'He got drafted. If that is all.'

Hartman picked up his fountain pen. He looked far from busy.

As they left, Morgen said, 'Let's go and see if Dr Wirths is holding surgery.'

Wirths had an office in the same building. An outer room was managed by a prisoner secretary. Wirths was working with his door open and, spotting them, he came out, presuming they had come about their shots.

He asked for their medical cards, which they were supposed to carry. Morgen had left his in the hotel. Schlegel's showed he was due a booster shot.

Wirths told him to roll up his sleeve and asked the secretary to prepare a syringe.

Morgen smirked and said he hated needles.

As Wirths was about to inject Schlegel, Morgen, who made a point of watching, said, 'We have some questions about Ingeborg Tanner.'

Wirths paused. Schlegel, who had been looking away, turned and saw Wirths with the syringe poised, looking blank.

The name meant nothing, he said.

'Ingeborg Tanner?' Schlegel prompted.

Wirths stuck the needle in his arm. Whether the man was inept or did it deliberately, the shot hurt like hell. Schlegel felt the depression of the plunger and was very aware of the needle in his arm.

'There will be side effects,' the doctor said. 'Drowsiness almost certainly.'

'How do we know what you are pumping into him?' asked Morgen jovially, more to discomfort him, Schlegel suspected, than the doctor.

Wirths laughed politely and said, 'This name. I am at a complete loss. Help me here.'

'You removed her body in person. We saw your signature.'

Morgen watched Wirths fiddle with the syringe, put it in an enamel bowl and fussily cover it with a towel.

'Oh, her,' he finally said.

Schlegel suspected Wirths, for all his agreeable air, resented any questioning of his authority or integrity.

'Yes. I am sorry. I do remember. What it was, we're always on the lookout for female autopsy cases with gonor-rhoea, in relation to research we are conducting, especially tubo-ovarian abscesses. I am rather red-faced for having forgotten.'

'How did you learn about the case?' asked Morgen, sounding less than persuaded.

Wirths indulged in a bout of concerned nodding. 'It must have been one of my orderlies. They're told to keep a lookout. Yes, that would be it.'

'Tanner was a garrison woman who was murdered.'

Wirths looked at them, from one to the other.

'Didn't you notice half her head was missing?' asked Morgen.

'Oh Lord, I assumed she was a prisoner.'

'Yet you bothered to fetch her yourself.'

Wirths appeared stricken. 'To tell the truth, I was rather excited. It's not often such opportunities fall into our hands. Alas ...' His long face registered disappointment. 'She did not have gonorrhoea or any other form of sexually transmitted disease, so I abandoned the project.'

'And had the body cremated?'

'I had no reason to do otherwise. No one told me. Of course, had I known ... I followed procedure.'

However honest the doctor was or wasn't, Schlegel was sure he was a man of conscience and procedure.

On their way back to the office they passed Broad lounging on the grassy bank, smoking and without his accordion for once, on what he lazily called intelligence-gathering duties.

Sometimes Schlegel wondered if they weren't being surreptitiously followed and in Broad's case perhaps not so surreptitiously.

Schlegel asked if had heard anything about the seamstress. She should have been in the commandant's detention cells following her dismissal but was not.

Broad looked knowing, making the most of his moment. 'Perhaps because she was passed on to us.'

Schlegel was barely surprised, given the levels of serpentine intrigue. 'By whom?'

'One of Groenke's stooges, I suspect, with Groenke acting for either the commandant or his wife, but this is no more than higher intuition.'

'Was passed on?' asked Morgen.

'For a couple of days. We were told she needed to be taken care of.'

'Taken care of!' exclaimed Schlegel.

Broad laughed. 'Not like that. I talked to her once or twice, lent her a book. Interesting woman. She was permitted to read. She was even allowed the block's cat for company, which is a privilege.'

'Did she say what happened?'

'She got caught in a blazing row between the commandant and his wife.'

'According to the wife, she was due to be shipped out.'

Broad laughed nastily. 'I doubt it.'

The implication was obvious. Schlegel tasted his revulsion. He asked if the commandant was her sugar daddy.

Broad said, 'We know she's his crush, but sugar daddy I couldn't say.'

'Are there other men?'

Broad laughed. 'Bees round honey.'

'Are you saying the commandant still has her somewhere?'

'He or someone else. Either way she has been moved on.'

'Then there will be paperwork,' said Morgen, sounding like a man who knew there wouldn't.

'There's an exemption clause known as fuck the bureaucracy,' confirmed Broad.

'Then where is she now?'

'Anywhere. You will discover if you stay with us long enough that we live in an entirely theoretical world. There are other possible explanations. She could be trying to hide herself. A woman who is not a dog is fair game. A jealous supervisor, for instance.'

'Then she may be dead?' asked Schlegel.

'Occupational hazard, old boy. Prisoners are always falling out, and the supervisors are all certifiably crazy.'

The 'old boy' was typical of the informality of the garrison. Broad would have been perfectly aware he was addressing his senior.

'And if she isn't?'

Broad gestured towards the zone.

'Out there. Plenty of space to stash someone, for weeks, months even.'

Schlegel was about to leave but Morgen wasn't finished.

'And what do you know about us?' he asked.

Broad appeared entertained. 'The big question. We know the commandant has a bee in his bonnet over a dead garrison woman, but it wasn't given to us, and you were called back as outsiders to investigate under the table.'

'You're very well informed.'

Broad smirked. 'Courtesy of the commandant's domestic staff.'

'How so?'

'The commandant is old-fashioned in his use of the telephone. He thinks it is necessary to speak up. When he telephoned Berlin and spoke to his boss he was ordered to bring you back, just when he thought he had got rid of you.'

'Why tell his boss?' Morgen asked.

'Panic is the word, and perhaps he wants to keep him sweet because he's nervous about his job.'

'Good information,' said Morgen, and inspected his packet of cigarettes. 'There are five in there. You have them.'

They left Broad happily lighting up.

Schlegel said he wanted to search for Sybil, providing he could find some form of transport. He supposed there were areas to isolate, people to ask. He had Sybil's picture to show around.

'I think you should, and while you are about it check on Horn and Palitsch, who both live in Rajsko.'

'How do you know?'

'Garrison directory.'

Morgen looked smug. The garrison directory was a legendary publication, known to exist, but impossible to get one's hands on. It was bureaucratic madness. The post office held a copy but when Schlegel had requested to see it he was told it was classified. The commandant's office and the security police held copies but again security was cited as the reason for it being unavailable for inspection. The switchboard's copy was guarded with equal zealousness. Recently a couple of operators had been dismissed for showing it.

They were back in the office. Schlegel was astonished to see Morgen produce his own copy. He refused to say where he had got it. Schulze was hugely impressed. She said not even the construction department had one. Morgen continued to look complacent.

'How do you make telephone calls?' Schlegel asked Schulze.

'We have our own directory but no private listings outside of department staff.'

Morgen said, 'Now we no longer have Bock with us, it would be useful to know what else Horn knows, sober or not.'

The tiny man in the post office had made a drinking gesture regarding Horn, who wasn't answering his telephone.

Schlegel guessed Morgen wanted to know if Palitsch's residence showed similar signs of acquisition to Tanner's locker.

Morgen tossed the directory to Schlegel and said, 'Check and see if any of the numbers match those in Tanner's book.'

The number given for Palitsch's address matched the one he had rung.

He looked up all the names he knew. The commandant

wasn't on Tanner's list. Nor was Juppe, nor Dr Wirths, nor security chief Grabner.

But Broad was.

So was Krick.

Schlegel didn't say because Schulze was present.

Instead he asked, 'It's all very well, but how am I supposed to get around?'

Morgen shrugged. 'I am sure you could do a deal with one of the taxis for the day.'

Schulze said no unauthorised civilian vehicles were permitted in the zone.

Morgen asked her where the best place was to hide a prisoner.

Schlegel asked where he could find a map of the area.

Schulze had her own in her drawer. Schlegel could see she was in two minds about lending it. She winced as he unfolded it carelessly. He could see he was meant to apologise.

The map was printed on cloth, stamped 'confidential' and showed the greater secret area. On the page Schlegel thought it rather resembled the outline of a bear, its snout the point where the two rivers split. By the southern boundary the distance between them was considerable.

Morgen asked Schulze where she thought Sybil might be.

She stood next to them, nervously twisting a strand of hair. Babitz, she said, pointing near the top. Plawy. The big fish farm at Harmensee. All had women's camps. The landscape and gardening division at Rajsko, near the garrison village where Palitsch and Horn lived.

Morgen asked if she knew the region well.

She told them one of her first jobs had been with a civil engineer from Breslau, for a report on the potential for livestock and fish breeding. Now there was a poultry and rabbit farm at Harmensee. The rabbits had previously been housed near the garrison stables. She used to go up there some afternoons and missed them when they moved.

She recited these memories in a way that sounded rehearsed.

She told them how the commandant had stopped off to inspect when they were surveying Harmensee, how bitterly cold it was and he encouraged them to contemplate the toughness of their task with the hardness of exile.

She retreated back behind her desk and apropos of nothing said, 'You hear the wildest stories that aren't true. When Dr Wirths told us about the possibility of a new high-frequency delousing machine everyone said afterwards it was us that were going to be zapped.'

'Why?'

'That's how everyone thinks.'

'What else do they say?' asked Morgen.

'There was one about doctors using prisoners as guinea pigs for a hangover cure. Quite a lot of hope was invested in that! There was another about strange trains that stopped in special gassing tunnels somewhere in Russia and no one came out.'

'What do you think?' Schlegel asked.

'What I think is not important. I am not paid to think.'

She avoided his eye. Schlegel felt he had insulted her.

Eventually she said, 'You're new.'

He could see how important it was not to appear gullible, hence the flippancy and cynicism.

'"Who makes this stuff up?" is what you learn to say,' she said.

Schlegel asked if she had a bicycle he could borrow.

She said he would look funny on it even if she had, with his height. Hers had been stolen ages ago.

'No one will lend you a car. You will find a horse easier to come by than a bicycle.'

It was her idea to telephone Juppe and ask him to request permission from the commandant to exercise a horse.

'Horses are his soft spot.'

She volunteered, saying, 'It's easier if I ask.'

Not only did the answer come back positive, Schulze said she had been made to wait only a few minutes before Juppe said the commandant approved.

Schlegel started up in Babitz. Fields full of shapeless, bent-over figures in headscarves. The guards appeared lethally bored. He showed one Sybil's picture, barely looked at before a shake of the head. Schlegel thought he would have more chance with the lottery.

Away in the distance came a wail of sirens, different from the usual.

He became used to riding again and relaxed. Saddle and horse felt substantial beneath him.

Further on, he grew aware of an unusual amount of activity. Vehicles racing back and forth. More sirens. Whistles. A distant armed patrol moved ahead of him through trees. He waited, aware of how isolated he was, anxious in that unspecified way which had become second nature.

The area was more than large enough to get lost in. Whole tracts passed where the fences and watchtowers went unseen, leaving a sun-coshed, tranquil landscape, and he understood something of the commandant's dream. Cultivated arable, dykes and embankments, brooks, lakes, a sea of reeds, a huge sky. He crossed a wooden bascule bridge over a channel and from it could see the railway and a distant cluster of buildings he presumed was Budy. More women worked in fields. His spirits sank. Weeks of searching wouldn't necessarily take him any nearer to finding Sybil.

He rode on for a long time until the fence appeared, marking the southern boundary. He followed its line until he reached an unmade-up road, which led to a small inn and houses where washing was drying in gardens that appeared better tended than the houses. The inn was shut. The road out of the village took him to a point where he could see a manned checkpoint on a bridge over the other river.

He passed through another deserted hamlet with a few dirty whitewashed buildings. None of the places was signed or named.

The peace was broken by the noise of an approaching motorbike and sidecar, trailing dust. He was able to make out two men hunched down, sinister in goggles and helmets, the one in the sidecar with a submachine gun. He moved off the road to let them pass. They drew up short and waved him over. Schlegel shouted for them to turn off their engine because it was frightening the horse. They ignored him so he dismounted, trusting the horse not to go off.

The man in the sidecar kept him covered. He realised what all the fuss was about. There had been an escape. He wondered what it would be like being hunted through such a landscape.

They told him they were clearing the area because the posse was coming.

'Posse?'

'Men on horseback. Hunters with dogs. Stay on the road. No sudden moves if anyone approaches.'

They roared off. The road took him to the camp's sentry line and down a narrow course between the boundary fence and the river.

The horse heard them before he did. It stopped and

pricked up its ears. The sound of galloping hooves seemed to go on for a long time before Schlegel saw them, on the other side of the fence, in tight formation, fifteen to twenty riders, fanning out until they resembled a cavalry charge. Many rode one-handed and brandished rifles. Yelping dogs ran with them.

Schlegel was sure he saw Baumgarten, the foreman of the butchers of Berlin. Perhaps trusted prisoners were permitted to ride with the posse. To a bystander it was an intimidating sight. The pounding receded and the whooping of the men grew thinner, and the only noise left was the irritating buzz of the returning motorbike.

Realising that the posse was sweeping south and there was still time, Schlegel turned back towards Rajsko. It was still light but getting dark.

The women's camp was away from the village, bleak wooden huts, a security fence and the name of the camp spelled out in wrought iron above the gate. The surrounding fields were empty. This turned out to be because everyone had been confined to camp after the escape. Schlegel sent a female guard to fetch the prisoner supervisor. He sat on the step waiting, and stared at the parched bare square of dirt. Its inmates may have worked for the gardening department but no planting extended to their accommodation.

The female guard returned with an older weather-beaten woman. They looked like archetypes from a fable: the round young one with a slung rifle shadowing what could have been a thinner, older version. Schlegel was aware of being noted for his lack of uniform. He could of course be Gestapo, though one look at his face probably told her he wasn't.

He showed Sybil's image. It produced no reaction, not even a shake of the head.

The woman waited to be dismissed. Prisoners didn't volunteer information, especially to strangers asking questions.

How many women worked there? he asked.

She grudgingly admitted about three hundred.

She handed him back the card.

That was that, thought Schlegel. He would repeat the action in all the other sub-camps and be told the same. He imagined everyone moving Sybil around to make sure he never found her and saw how easy it would be to develop a persecution complex. He rode away depressed.

Rajsko's garrison quarters by contrast were nice little houses with pleasant gardens, surrounded by an abundance of what should have been green but struggled in the drought to retain its colour. A man was taking advantage of the late light to tend his garden. Older children still played in the street. Both cautiously greeted Schlegel as he passed. The pronounced homeliness was in such contrast to where he had come from he found it hardly worth noting.

Palitsch lived down a side road at the far end of the village. His house had crossed diagonal wooden fencing like the rest. He was no gardener. Schlegel supposed he was still out as no bike was around. The house was a two-up, two-down, detached, with a steep, pointed roof. It looked like a new build. The general cosiness suggested the sort of place where people didn't need to lock up, despite all the pilfering. Palitsch's door was open, presenting Schlegel with the dilemma of whether to enter. The garden ran round both sides. He went to the back where two apple trees stood with a slung hammock and a stack of empty beer bottles beneath.

Against the rear wall was a windowless lean-to, securely padlocked. Schlegel supposed the house was left open to stop break-ins and any valuables were put in the store. The kitchen door was unlocked. Schlegel pushed it open, calling out, trying to pretend he was behaving naturally.

Always the contrast, he thought, between what lay open and unrevealed.

The house's tidiness he attributed to the housekeeper. He found nothing but essentials and empty bottles crated for return; not even a radio. He was taken aback by children's beds upstairs. He wasn't expecting that. No pictures on the walls, no personal photographs, no trace of a man's life.

The main bed looked slept in since that morning. Schlegel stared at semen-stained sheets and reminded himself that Palitsch shot people for a job.

Schlegel heard someone coming up the path to the house. There was no point in hiding. Anyone could see his horse tethered. He made a show of strolling downstairs, expecting Palitsch. A woman's voice called, 'Gerhard!' then more sharply to ask who he was.

She was natural-looking and attractive.

Schlegel said, 'I thought he might be upstairs asleep.'

She looked suspicious.

'Are you sure you should be here?'

'As sure as I can be about anything,' he said cheerfully as he walked out. She smelled of perfume.

Horn's house stood in an orchard, its trees heavy with apples. It was now nearly dark and the mosquitoes were out. Schlegel left the horse tethered to a tree. No lights were on. He walked through the murmuring dusk, thinking: Beware the house in the woods.

He meant to leave it at that but was curious to know whether the same open-door arrangement applied.

It did.

He called out, waited, and hesitated before stepping

inside. He wanted to know if Horn lived in the same featureless way as Palitsch. His eyes took time to adjust.

Horn clearly had no servant. The state of the place was more like what Schlegel expected from Palitsch: a pile of dirty washing-up in a sink of scummy water; a strong smell of cat and something more putrid; dozens of uncrated empties; some plates lay dirty on the table, covered with what looked like rat shit.

Schlegel again called Horn's name and got nothing back. He asked himself what he was doing when he knew perfectly well. It was called foreboding.

At the back of his mind, he had known since riding out, which was why he had left it to last.

Anticipation played harder on his nerves than the moment, nasty as it was. Schlegel wondered whether mosquitoes fed on dead flesh. Maggots certainly did; he could see silvery traces where they had burrowed under the grey skin.

Horn lay sprawled in an armchair, a man-mountain made no prettier by death. Which the grubbier, thought Schlegel irreverently, the chair or the man. Horn wore a singlet, vomited down, and soiled pyjama bottoms. More than maggots had got to him. He had been chewed. Schlegel wondered about the cat.

From the number of empties lying around, Horn must have drunk himself to death, Schlegel supposed, knowing he hadn't really. It took all his nerve to touch the cold flesh and pull the greasy singlet away, enough to see the telltale puncture mark over the heart.

He could think of no earthly reason to report the death because the knowledge of others would add nothing. Against his better judgement, he picked up the telephone.

He sat outside, waiting in the dark for the ambulance. He

supposed Horn had been killed for the same reason as Bock: for knowing too much and being an inconvenience. It was no longer a matter of hunting individual murderers. Perhaps the same man had killed Bock and Horn, perhaps different men, but they were interchangeable. Horn, like Bock, had been killed by a system, their killers its servants. It wasn't even psychopathic, just a fact of life, a form of tidying.

The ambulance came with Broad, who grumbled about having drawn the short straw, being on standby duty. A doctor came a few minutes later, driving his own car, and wasted no time pronouncing Horn dead. One of the ambulance men doubled as the photographer and the room lit up whenever the flashgun fired. Broad said he only knew Horn as the fat guy in the post office.

'I heard he was a doper and a lush.'

No one seemed much concerned or bothered. Schlegel supposed Broad's report would write itself, with the copiousness of empty bottles cited as evidence of an epic, fatal drinking session.

Schlegel decided not to point out the puncture mark. He doubted if the autopsy – if they even bothered – would either.

Broad organised the death scene with brisk, professional cynicism. They all had to give a hand with the stretcher because of Horn's weight.

'All breathe through your mouths, boys,' said Broad with ghoulish relish. 'One, two, three and lift!'

Horn's weight left them staggering like drunks with the giggles.

'Where's a prisoner detachment when you need one?' said the photographer.

After managing to slide Horn into the ambulance, Broad offered cigarettes and said, 'I'm not going back in there.'

Always jovial, thought Schlegel.

As the ambulance prepared to leave, Schlegel said, 'Your number is in Ingeborg Tanner's book.'

Broad looked at the ground and up at him.

'How come? I didn't know her.' He sounded plausible.

He walked away, unconcerned, calling back, 'I expect my number is in a lot of people's books.'

Later that night Schlegel said the same to Krick.

'Whose book?' asked Krick in apparent innocence.

'The woman whose body you found.'

'Is that her name? I have been away, only just back tonight.'

'Anywhere interesting?'

'Zurich, as a matter of fact. I have to go back.'

Schlegel wondered if Schulze had told Krick she was working for them.

He had run across Krick in the lobby while looking in the bar for Morgen, who wasn't there. On Krick's recommendation they adjourned to what he called the residents' lounge, a quieter room with tables and chairs, about half full.

'Why should I be in this woman's book?' he asked earnestly. 'What can you tell me about her?'

Schlegel said she seemed to have had several lovers. Krick approved. He thought women in the garrison progressive and generally ahead of the times.

'Instead of being shackled to that ghastly monogamy.'

Schlegel said Tanner had a wardrobe of clothes beyond her means.

'Are you thinking I was one of her lovers?'

'Are you telling me you were?'

Krick shook his head and continued to puzzle over being in Tanner's book. After that they sat in silence. Schlegel was trying to decide if it was companionable when Krick said, 'What we have in common is people wonder why we are both here.'

He fiddled easily with his cigarette lighter, and asked, 'Where is your colleague?'

As of that minute, Schlegel didn't know. He said somewhere around.

Krick said, 'I heard he has gone to Lublin.'

'Not as far as I know,' Schlegel said uncertainly.

He supposed it wasn't out of the question and typical of Morgen not to say. Schlegel found Krick disconcerting.

'Why are we all here?' he asked, trying to steer the conversation back.

'People fear we are part of a cleaning agency. Funny how a man such as the commandant, who has as much power as anyone could want, is so insecure.'

'Only because he is worried about having it taken away.'

'Is that what you think?' Krick clicked his fingers and said, 'I remember now.'

Schlegel expected to be reminded of where they had met before.

'I would have to check my records but I think the Tanner woman telephoned my office to speak to me.'

'What about?'

'Her depression.'

'Then you must have met.'

'That's the thing. She failed to turn up for her appointment and it was the last I heard.'

'Why would she not?'

'She must have found some quack to prescribe her antidepressants, or even better signed up as a guinea pig for one of the pharmaceutical testing programmes where they hand out trial pills like sweets.'

*

Already the office kettle had been stolen, despite the room being locked. There was no sign of Schulze. Schlegel sensed an anxious torpor to everything, beset by strange symbols and portents, as though a spell had been cast.

His anxiety over Morgen turned to worry. He had taken the man's absence at breakfast for just that; nothing to worry about; typical even, except Morgen made a point of breakfast. Perhaps he was ill.

He went down to the telephone booth. Morgen wasn't in his room. He hadn't checked out either.

Schlegel returned gloomily upstairs. They hadn't been getting on particularly. He put that down to strain and uncertainty. Morgen had said it was like trying to investigate in a thick fog. Now he wasn't there Schlegel missed him and during the fretful course of another wasted afternoon he started to fear Morgen was in trouble. After Buchenwald he had many enemies, from the top down, starting with the commandant's boss, Pohl, who – according to Broad – was aware of their presence. The wanted poster would have refuelled that animosity. Schlegel asked himself whether there was a persecution campaign and how far it would go.

He considered another alternative, more personal. Given Schulze's absence, Schlegel was left wondering if she and Morgen had something going. Normally, such a thought would not have occurred but given the nature of the place ... However absurd the idea, it kept returning.

He sought out Ilse, ostensibly to ask about Sybil when he knew it was about feeling sorry for himself. They ended up in the canteen where they talked about this and that, inconsequential stuff and pleasant for it. She sensed he was having problems and asked. He spoke of his frustration dealing with the endless red tape and the constant blurring of information and gossip, and how most of what they were told turned out to be not true.

She said for the most part everyone made it up as they went along.

As they parted she said she wasn't sure whether to mention one story she had heard, given what he had just told her, because its source was unreliable.

'Now I am bound to ask,' he said, enjoying her company.

She told him the seamstress was supposed to be in one of the smaller, more remote penal colonies, but comfortably ensconced, which suggested she was still protected.

'Do you want me to see what I can find out?'

Schlegel could see no reason not to, even if it turned out to be a wild-goose chase.

'It will probably cost,' Ilse said.

He hadn't expected anything else.

When the situation duplicated itself with Schulze, Schlegel wondered if he wasn't being steered, perhaps even with the two women working together.

Schulze was back in the office, her return as mysterious as her disappearance. He didn't ask where she had been.

Like Ilse, Schulze suggested the way forward was through purchasing information. One of Tanner's dormitory companions was prepared to talk to her.

'Are you all right with paying?'

Schlegel shrugged. 'If she's worth it.'

He was trying to sound tough and could tell she saw through that.

'Are you all right with her talking to me?'

'Why won't she talk to me?' he asked, knowing the answer.

Schulze confirmed there was an unofficial embargo surrounding Tanner.

In the case of Ilse's lead the price was a wristwatch while Tanner's dormitory companion wanted a bar of French soap.

In retrospect, the narrative attached to the incident of the wristwatch floated away, leaving only a few salient details whose meaning became detached from the episode surrounding it. Schlegel spoke to a rugged, impassive female supervisor, who, in exchange for his watch, left him feeling he was being taken for a ride. What he remembered afterwards was how the woman beckoned for him to hold out his wrist with the watch. He didn't care. It was the cheapest of watches, of no sentimental value. Why he didn't just take it off and hand it over he had no idea. He did as she asked, feeling strangely powerless and in thrall to her dexterous fingers. She held his eye, hers dark pools that reflected nothing living, until he felt transported beyond authority and ritual into a primitive, exposed space. The anxiousness of the occasion lingered long after the rest was forgotten.

A car had come about a week before in the middle of the night, she said, and referred to the female passenger as the commandant's ride, a remark that left Schlegel sagging at the knees. They were warned off touching her. The description of the driver matched no one Schlegel knew. It turned out he was a prisoner, a detail omitted at first. When he expressed surprise at prisoners being allowed to drive around at night he could see he was regarded as a hopeless novice.

A couple of days later the same man came back and took the woman away in the same car. That it was a car not a lorry was significant. A car was equated with privilege. The car was an Opel.

The garrison motor pool turned out to have several Opels, one of which could be driven by a prisoner as it was used by the commandant's household and known as Frau Hoess's shopping car.

The driver in question, hired as a gardener, told Schlegel he hadn't taken the car that night and had no idea who had.

Faced with another dead end, Schlegel's brief elation curdled. He had a proper lead, he kept telling himself; the reality was much more like chasing phantoms.

Schulze said she was willing to get the soap and settle with him afterwards, but Schlegel insisted he went; for the experience, he supposed.

She gave him directions and the name of a man from Canada. First he had to go to the camp bank to withdraw cash.

The man operated not out of the big Canada shed but a small outpost in an obscure part of the garrison, down a cobbled alley. His door was split like a stable's, with the open upper half protected by a wire mesh. Schulze gave Schlegel a numbered ticket like a cloakroom one. The only difference from what she had told him was the price. He was informed there was a 10 per cent handling fee. Schlegel suspected he was being fleeced but was too listless to argue; Dr Wirths' booster shot induced long periods of drowsiness, as promised.

Schlegel gave the soap to Schulze and later that day she related to him what she had been told.

Again he experienced the sensation of being transported into another realm and could not shake the impression it was her own story Schulze was relating, at a remove, as a form of confession. He didn't believe that but it excited him in a shameful way to think of her being part of that world. Was it in fact her secret body parts that would smell of perfumed French soap?

Schulze told him that the year before, in the summer of

1942, there had been a lot of dressing up and wild parties, with Palitsch's given over to orgies. Tanner was supposed to have taken part in these but Schulze wasn't so sure because the woman trailed a lot of stories in her wake. The party scene had lasted only a few weeks, until female prisoners became the next vogue, which meant the garrison women in effect got dumped.

Schulze recited all this in a matter-of-fact way in the plainest language.

The most specific angle on Tanner was that one of the men she was having sex with was a colleague in the motor pool, a mechanic, Fritz, who was two-timing her with a female prisoner he impregnated. Tanner in a fit of pique reported the illegal relationship to the security police, after which Fritz received a punitive transfer.

Schulze said, 'Fritz arranged to have her killed after he left because she had snitched on him.'

Fritz could demand this because he had been a major organiser, widely regarded as performing valuable services.

So, a motive, thought Schlegel. Murder by proxy. Where was Fritz now, was the obvious question.

Fritz turned out to have barely survived Tanner and may even have predeceased her. He was supposed to have been killed in a quarrel over gambling debts.

Another dead end, but Schulze had more. She had found the man who had taken the photographs of the abused women. He was a medical orderly named Haas. He was prepared to talk.

'How did you find him?'

'There's a photographer's studio but no one there knew of any medical pictures. There is a prisoner who takes police photographs as required.'

Schlegel supposed he was the one who had recorded Horn

in all his departing glory. He was reminded of how far off the case he was. He had been so distracted by Horn's death and the fact of Broad being in Tanner's book that he never thought to ask if the photographer knew about the pictures of the beaten-up women.

Schulze had gone to the popular garrison photography club and asked if any members worked for medical departments. Three did. Haas, she said, usually specialised in taking pet animal pictures.

Haas was a nasty shock, being the sinister musclebound man who had turned up in the basement of Block 10 following Bock's death. He gave no show of remembering Schlegel.

Unlike Palitsch, who wore his depravity lightly, Haas displayed elements of the psychopath, in his insistence on shaking hands as a way of intruding on Schlegel's private space and pretending to engage by not quite looking him in the eye.

Haas's office was in one of the medical blocks at the top end of the camp. His work seemed to consist of a desk with nothing on it, a telephone and a coat stand, next to a washbasin. Through an arch Schlegel could see a consulting room, with a table and chairs, a folding screen and a couch.

What was it about the garrison? Everyone had an opinion or a story. Schlegel was reminded of a pageant. Theatrical role-playing, dramatic intrigue and a sense of image were not dissimilar to life there; both were highly artificial, with sexual scheming forming another level.

In normal investigations people were forthcoming, not forthcoming, helpful, ignorant or clued-up, devious and deceptive, but in the garrison, beneath the overarching mood of threat, everyone seemed to have their account ready, more like you would find once a case had gone to trial.

Haas was the same. While he talked, he surreptitiously flexed his muscles and admired them. Any surprise Schlegel had hoped to gain by producing the photographs failed.

Haas looked without picking them up.

Whether it was mental agility or robotic programming, within minutes he was talking about the excellent garrison facilities for adult education and how he had learned his photography through the society, which was then run by the camp ornithologist.

Schlegel presumed ornithology was another hobby, but Haas corrected him; it was a garrison appointment.

'What happened to him?' Schlegel knew he was being distracted; it was almost easier.

The ornithologist was gone, along with most of the birdlife, which had migrated and mysteriously not returned, apart from carrion.

They were interrupted by an orderly assisting a shuffling, stick-thin patient into the next room and telling Haas they were ready. Haas asked Schlegel to excuse him for a moment, stood and drew a curtain across the arch after him.

What Schlegel heard told him clearly enough what was going on: a sigh of protest that became a quick squeak, a thud and a brief thrashing, the sound of a limb erratically beating the table, followed by a silence more profound than the preceding one because of the three parties one was now obviously dead.

Haas returned, again drawing the curtain. Schlegel heard the body being removed on a trolley with squeaky wheels. Haas rejoined Schlegel after washing his hands. He didn't say anything, clearly confident of his professional rights.

Schlegel said laboriously, 'Someone attacked the women you photographed. Did any say who their attackers were?'

Haas said he had been there only as a technician.

'There were similar cases before last August, but the photographs only started then.'

Haas glanced down and inspected his arm. Schlegel thought he might as well be speaking to himself.

Haas said his speciality was rabbits and cats. He had a line in novelty pictures, which he insisted on showing. They were twee beyond belief; scarily so.

'Good for kiddies. Do you have children?'

He insisted Schlegel bought a set anyway.

The next time Haas left the curtain open. Schlegel instinctively tensed as the needle was poised, with Haas flicking and slapping the area around the heart. He had put on rubber gloves and a medical apron. He drove the needle in and pushed hard on the plunger. The man, almost identical to his predecessor, froze for a second then went into spasm. His back arched and the orderly rushed forward and held him down.

Haas came back and said, 'It's no life for them by the end. A relief, you could say. It's better they don't struggle. They go more easily.'

He sat, as if to say: I have nothing to hide and all is above board and whatever you prove there is nothing you can do about it.

Schlegel persisted with his questioning, despite a growing helplessness.

'At least two cases I have come across recently happened off the books. Bock and Horn from the post office.

'Not what I am hearing.'

'Can you explain your proximity to the first incident?'

'In the same building, no crime in that.'

Stories seemed to float into place, and stick, as though by osmosis. Haas's version was that Wirths' prisoner doctor had left Bock unsupervised. Schlegel's counter was that

Bock as a garrison member was supposed to have been looked after by a staff doctor.

'In theory. On paper. It doesn't happen like that. Anyway, the doctor is Wirths' pet so he is protecting her.'

'What do you think?'

'She was negligent. She should go.'

'Where?'

Haas smirked. 'Wherever they get sent. Another camp probably. It's a merry-go-round.'

Schlegel sensed with the next exchange they were close to the centre, when Haas suggested he stop wasting his time and talk to the security police – inference, don't be bothering me and fuck off – because that department had the authority to exercise its own initiative.

'Not according to the book.'

'The book stopped making sense years ago.'

'Yes, but anyone looking at the problem must ask: If it isn't allowed, why is it still going on?'

'That person has his head in the clouds. Like it or not, the programme is one of radical housekeeping. It's not our fault Dr Wirths can't keep his books in order.'

Another patient was produced. Haas used it as an excuse to dismiss Schlegel. Schlegel felt almost as though he wasn't watching anything of consequence, because any sense of the individual had long been removed, leaving only the husk, and a repeating mechanical action, almost like watching the striking of a cuckoo clock.

Haas, whether through thoughtlessness or calculated cruelty, prolonged the wretch's life for an inconsequential minute or two, by pausing to return as Schlegel was leaving to say it was possible the deaths of Bock and Horn were ordered, as a way of closing the case.

'Why?'

'Because the commandant doesn't want it known what is going on under his watch.'

'Are you saying he is collaborating with Grabner on this?'

Haas enjoyed the confusion he sewed. That was the point, Schlegel realised: this constant derailing.

'When they are sworn enemies?' Schlegel insisted.

'Just because they are basically against each other doesn't mean they are all the time. Needs must when the devil drives.'

Schlegel ate early in the canteen, depressed by his indifference to what he had seen. Wirths had warned of the corrosive nature of the place. The canteen was crowded and the only free table was by the food counter. Meatballs or schnitzel. He spotted Ilse in the queue and waved her over. She seemed pleased to see him, which was by no means usual, Schlegel had found. He said to take the meatballs. 'This tastes like old tyre.'

She joined him and asked what he was doing. Not much, he said, thinking she might tell him what Schulze would not about fancy dresses and Tanner's lifestyle. They agreed they both felt like getting smashed.

'For a change,' said Ilse.

He said he had seen stuff that day he would rather not have. Her sympathetic look said it wasn't necessary to elaborate.

She took him to a crowded, smoky bar where records were played with dancing. They got companionably drunk, listening to the music, not needing to say much. She asked him to dance. He pulled a face and said he didn't really. She laughed and said, 'Just push and I'll pull.'

On the crowded floor he managed a passable slow shuffle, aware of her hand on his neck.

When it was time to leave she took his arm to help her

walk straight. Outside she stopped and said, 'Kiss me,' so he did. She tasted sweet and of alcohol. How could everything feel so out of kilter and yet so normal? he wondered, as she pressed against him.

They walked on and she said, 'I am not so drunk.' Schlegel wondered what he was getting into then decided to go along with whatever the night might bring.

'I want to go to Canada,' he said.

The request seemed to excite her.

'For the dare, then,' she said, slurring her words attractively. 'Not such a dare, actually. It's pretty much a free-for-all.'

Security amounted to two sleepy guards reading comic books who paid no attention, beyond acknowledging Ilse, who cheerfully said, 'Tour of inspection.'

She told him this was the original Canada. There was a much bigger depot now in the new camp where goods were pre-sorted – clothes, leather, banknotes, coins, photographs, drink and so on – before being sent over.

She said, 'The new camp is a dump and no one goes there if they can possibly avoid it.'

Schlegel thought about whether he was compromising himself. They passed the main storage area, which was fenced off, with goods stacked in aisles, on shelves reaching to the ceiling. A wire door was open and people could wander freely inside.

She took him up back stairs to a gallery which overlooked the warehouse floor. She seemed not drunk now and in thrall to all the possessions arrayed below. Despite the lateness of the hour people were still in. Schlegel saw Groenke standing with the commandant's wife inspecting rails of women's clothes. He pointed her out to Ilse who said, 'She's always in, top shopper.'

'When did this start?' he asked.

'Last summer. Everyone was amazed how much turned up. It lay around for days. On the long evenings if it was known a train was coming people used to get drunk and go down and see what they could pick up. No one had expected anything like it.'

She could see he wanted to know if she had. 'Not told, don't ask.'

Then people were banned from showing up.

'That was Dr Wirths, who complained things weren't being done properly.'

Her mood softened. She presented her face to be kissed, her hand gripping the back of his head. She smiled afterwards and said lightly, 'We skate on the thinnest of ice.'

She took him to a room off the gallery, full of furniture, and dragged him through a rack of coats into a private corner draped with rugs and cushions.

They lay down and she recited as though in the grip of an erotic reverie: 'At first it was a free-for-all. Show up and help yourself. Then there were Sunday rummage sales and after that shops opened in the garrison, run by some of the more enterprising wives, selling off stuff.'

'Where did the money go?'

She touched her throat and told him to put his hand on her breast.

'To various relief agencies, so seen as as in a good cause. That went on until one of the wives was found pocketing the money.'

'And now?'

He moved his hand down. She told him not yet and said, 'The store is run as part of the garrison and profits go towards various garrison trust funds.'

'How do you know this?'

'I went out with someone who worked in Canada.'

'Went out with *because* he worked in Canada?'

'You learn fast,' she said. 'Now you can.'

Ilse's most attractive trait was a practical, clinical efficiency which made it clear she was there only for her pleasure, and if he hadn't been available she would have found someone else, or, failing that, seen to herself. Her skin was as irresistible to the touch as he could have wanted. He knew he was in safe hands and let her guide him, making sure he was not too quick. She kept up a wry commentary, as she took him. 'I am embarrassed by how much this place turns me on. I am as randy as anything. I think I am turning into a man-eater.' She laughed a lot and treated the business less seriously than he did, taking him on her own amused terms. Towards the end she put aside the game and concentrated hard, telling him to stick three fingers in her mouth and pinch her nose. Her eyes rolled back in her head. Schlegel supposed he wasn't up to much in terms of performance but he seemed to give her what she wanted. Despite the constant and surprising itch of sexual curiosity since coming to the garrison, he hadn't felt compelled to act on it. She thanked him afterwards and said she had got what she came for. Schlegel felt grateful. She had fucked him with easy grace. He was nevertheless left confused by her blunt requests and supposed he was quite conventional in his thinking about women. He laughed at himself, as if all of a sudden he was a connoisseur. Still more wrought than relieved, all that connected in his head was Ilse's possession of him and the taking of his wristwatch, both weirdly scrambled acts of being had.

They lay there enjoying their breaking the rules. Ilse looked around and said, 'The novelty was like a drug at first. I saw two women have a catfight over a Schiaparelli. Was I one of them? Not told, don't ask.'

'I need to go again,' she said, putting her hand under her dress. 'Unless you want to help.' She told him what to do and laughed at his straight ways.

'What an upright young man!' She said she would ask around about Ingeborg Tanner. 'Stories about people always float close to the surface, especially the nasty ones . . .' She broke off to instruct him and tell him he was getting better. 'You can practise on me,' she said with a gurgling laugh. Did he like her? He couldn't say but he was captivated by her dreamy disobedience, knowing afterwards there would be the inevitable comedown and unwanted clarity of hangover, which would make him want only to go back to her.

The following morning, Schlegel took breakfast alone and did his best to tell himself if Morgen was in trouble he would know by now. He wondered whether the episode with Ilse was a one-off. Their parting had been as casual as the encounter. She mentioned another bar with music, on the other side of the railway, and said she might be there the next evening. No invitation was extended beyond the information given. Schlegel suspected that for her the circumstances counted for more than the partner.

He walked down the long road to the garrison, past Dr Wirths' house, and was surprised to hear his name being called. He turned and saw the doctor standing in his shirtsleeves.

'I was hoping you might pass. I was going to come and see you anyway.'

He invited Schlegel in and sent his Polish girl off to the shops.

Schlegel knew the doctor was having trouble getting supplies but he was still surprised how little had been managed.

It was like living in a cave with a few bits of furniture. A dog lay on the floor, too depressed to rouse itself.

Wirths waited impatiently for the girl to be gone and turned eagerly to Schlegel.

'Wait until you hear this. I have major evidence against the commandant ...'

Wirths invited him to sit on one of two wooden chairs. Schlegel supposed the doctor had something medical in mind. The commandant's wife had said how much pressure her husband was under.

'A rather unsavoury case of obsession,' Wirths went on. 'The commandant has been besotted with a female prisoner ...'

Schlegel faltered. He could only mean Sybil.

'And now he has had her executed.'

'Executed,' Schlegel repeated hollowly.

'Shot.' The doctor's lips were moist with excitement, strands of spittle stretched between his teeth as he spoke. He made a chopping motion with his hand and said the commandant would have to face a military tribunal.

Schlegel was assaulted by images of Sybil shot against the wall in the yard of the punishment block.

'What happened?' Schlegel asked, dreading what he would hear.

Wirths explained how a lot of his prisoner staff had been arrested during the recent big security crackdown.

'It was a vendetta against me because I question the security police's methods. The point is, one of my men managed to smuggle out the extraordinary story of the woman put briefly in the cell next to his.'

She had been fetched from detention, after being dismissed from her job in the commandant's house, and put in the cells in the commandant's block, where the commandant had taken to visiting her at night.

Schlegel thought already the story didn't square with his information that Sybil hadn't been held in the commandant's block. Had the commandant been responsible for her being delivered and fetched in the household car? Was he the architect of Sybil's fate? Clearly infatuated, but did that extend to sex? The man was surely too much of a stickler.

In Wirths' version the commandant, after tiring of the woman, had her transferred to the police punishment block.

'As a way of getting rid of her.'

The night before her execution, she had told Wirths' supervisor her story.

In the next morning's clear-out she was called into the corridor and taken up to the yard.

Wirths said he had checked. There was no record of any woman being on that day's execution list.

'Which means she must have been slipped in as an extra. They do it as a way of getting rid of troublemakers. Nor was there any record of her being in the cell next to my supervisor, which means it was done off the books.'

'Does this happen often?' Schlegel asked, helpless.

'It is forbidden to have sexual relations with female prisoners but many do and when they tire of them . . .'

Wirths let the sentence hang. He was too taken up with his own excitement to notice Schlegel's anguish.

'In confidence, the commandant must go, and this is the ammunition. The affair is well documented.'

So Sybil was now dead, unofficially erased from the face of the earth.

Schlegel supposed it must be true, given how little exemption existed. Haas's lethal despatches still burned in his head. Someone had done the same to Sybil, with a bullet and a gun. No cruelty, only utter indifference. No conscience involved. Human garbage. Was that what the commandant had thought, diverting her into the disposal system? What a way to die, staring at the wall, counting down. Yet part of him was incapable of believing it. He had always been certain they were destined to meet again. My God, he suddenly thought. It could have been Palitsch who pulled the trigger, or Broad. Would they have even noticed, or was one back of the neck the same as the next?

Schlegel wandered the streets in a daze, only vaguely aware that he needed to get out of the sun. He found himself standing on the doorstep of the commandant's house, not knowing what he would say.

Frau Hoess came to the door, assuming he was there for her husband. She appeared depressed, he thought. He said he had a garrison matter he wished to discuss with her.

She sighed. 'I suppose, if you must.'

She didn't offer to take him to a reception room and they stood in the hall.

'I want to ask about one of the garrison women, Ingeborg Tanner.'

He thought: No, I want to ask about Sybil.

Frau Hoess stared into the distance, apparently uncomprehending.

'Your husband,' Schlegel prompted.

'Yes. The poor woman. The men get demoralised and hit the bottle and then they hit the women.'

'Why does that happen?'

He expected no answer – it was a weak question anyway.

'You would have to ask them.' She motioned him to follow her to her husband's study where she instructed him to sit and seated herself opposite, leaning forward so their knees were almost touching, and whispered as though she were afraid of being overheard.

'There's no excuse. Even my husband has been known to raise his hand to the children. I think with the rest it's because they don't consider themselves soldiers, not in the fighting sense, and feel belittled, so take it out on us. Not my husband, of course. He's a decorated soldier. He was the youngest sergeant in the army, at the age of seventeen. Anyway, it was one of two matters I raised with the Reichsführer-SS at the time of his inspection.'

'Saying what?'

'Telling about the battering of women, of course.'

Schlegel wasn't sure what to make of what he was hearing.

'What did he say to that?'

'He said it went against the chivalric code for a man to hit a woman. He asked for evidence.'

'In what form?'

'He wanted to see photographs.'

'So you were the one who organised the pictures.'

'For forwarding copies to the Reichsführer's office. You see, I had hoped you had been sent as a result to investigate the matter.'

There seemed no point in disabusing the woman.

'And the second matter you raised with him?' he asked, curious.

'The special project.'

'And what is that?'

'I can't possibly say. It was a private matter between myself and the Reichsführer-SS.'

'Yet you are prepared to discuss the garrison women.'

'That is a garrison matter.'

Schlegel found it hard to believe the woman had a confidential relationship with Heinrich Himmler.

'Is there any news on the dismissed seamstress?'

Frau Hoess looked like she was trying to remember, to show that the subject had long since been discounted.

'No,' she said.

'I am being told your husband managed to have her shot.'

She started to laugh, stopped, and spoke in a rush. 'No, no. He may be under enormous stress but he is not going to jeopardise his position by doing that, when he can have the woman sent away, which he did.'

'Are you sure?'

'Yes, I am certain.'

Schlegel could see she wasn't. He wanted desperately to believe her.

'To go back to last summer, what was the Reichsführer-SS's response to the violence you reported?'

'To appoint a psychiatrist to the garrison.'

'Krick?'

'Yes. He came a month or so after I spoke of the matter to the Reichsführer-SS.'

'Did Krick say as much?'

'No, but it's obvious.'

Schlegel spent most of the rest of the day drinking. Up on the far edge of the commercial sector was an informal bar, known locally as a speakeasy, a rough place that stayed open during the day and was frequented by guards before night duty.

He didn't particularly feel the need to get drunk, beyond making some space in his head. Just as it was the military way to guard everything, so everyone had learned to control their thoughts. No one made the connections any more, even obvious ones. People no longer questioned. Whatever inner rebelliousness that still existed in him had no outlet. He presumed in soldiers it was channelled into the fury of the battlefield. He did not think of himself as in any way extraordinary but knew enough to know he was living through remarkable times and, thanks to poor health and family influence, he had been spared the horror of becoming cannon fodder or disgracing himself on the battlefield – which he almost certainly would because he could see no sense in violence, probably because he had no talent for it. As it was, the chances were he would survive the war, for which he supposed he ought to feel more grateful.

He left the bar, still refusing to accept what Wirths had told him about Sybil, clinging to the forlorn hope that the commandant's wife was right.

He rode out again that evening to look for Palitsch, whom he found at home in shirtsleeves and braces, drinking beer. As always he was friendly. Schlegel took a beer off him and asked about his sex parties.

Palitsch did a double take before deciding the question was harmless.

'Aw, man! They went on for about three weeks. I was out of my head at the time.'

They were both drunk. Palitsch had had the afternoon off.

'What about Ingeborg Tanner?' asked Schlegel.

Palitsch too had that habit of looking like he was trying to remember. He sniggered. 'Brief fling. She was up for it. Rode as hard as any jockey.'

He looked at Schlegel, as if to ask what more was there to say. Schlegel watched him go blank and suck reflectively on the top of his beer bottle, until he said, 'I used to have an ordinary life here, with a wife and children. My wife was tall, with lovely eyes and the nicest smile. We raised geese and I rode my motorbike. The kids are with their grand-mother now.'

He moved on seamlessly to say he'd had to let Tanner go. 'She was crazy. She started turning up with this creep who didn't fuck and liked to watch and take pictures. Tanner not only wanted an audience, she liked being photographed so she could look at herself afterwards. Then there was a fight involving the guy and he beat someone up. I had to tell her she and her friend weren't welcome. Fuck parties were one thing, photographed fuck parties quite another.'

'Is that why the men moved on to female prisoners?'

'What is it that you are investigating?'

'I will have to file a report on Tanner.'

'I hope you aren't stupid enough to come after me, or anyone else. No one takes kindly to that. And what will you say?'

'Probably that she was killed by an unknown assailant unconnected to her private life.'

'That sounds about right.'

'I hear she became a rather embittered figure.'

Palitsch appeared on guard again.

Schlegel said, 'I can only know what not to say if I have some idea of what went on.'

He related the story of Tanner's jealousy and reporting her lover to the security police.

Palitsch opened a clasp knife lying on the kitchen table. 'Do you ever do this?'

He splayed his left hand and in rapid succession stuck the point of the knife in the gaps between his thumb and fingers, until the blade was a blur. He appeared quite relaxed but Schlegel saw he was sweating from exertion.

Palitsch stopped as suddenly as he had started and held up his unblemished hand, saying he was about the only one who had never stuck a knife in his finger. Schlegel expected to be told it was his turn but instead Palitsch said, 'Ask me anything. There have been others who were told to sort this or that and none succeeded.'

'Why not?'

'Because they either got sucked in and gave up, or died.'

Schlegel repeated what he had been told about Tanner's lover being a top organiser.

Palitsch snorted. 'Who's telling you? Fritz was low-level. A reconditioned carburettor, a dodgy bicycle . . .'

'He could have paid someone to do it.'

'He probably could have afforded it, because most people can, except Fritz was too dopey.'

'What did the photographer look like?'

'Thick neck.'

'Name?'

Palitsch shook his head.

'Medical orderly?'

Palitsch shook his head again. It sounded like Haas, thought Schlegel, moving on to the question he didn't want to ask. He counted silently until he had Palitsch's attention, noting the feral shift in his eye.

'Did you shoot the commandant's seamstress?'

Palitsch went blank again, then looked up from under his eyebrows, as if to say he had cottoned on to why Schlegel was really there.

Schlegel wondered whether the man's pleasant, slightly stupid manner hid something altogether smarter and more dangerous.

Palitsch made a pistol of his finger and drew a bead on Schlegel.

'She never made it to the wall, man.'

'Meaning?'

'She must have been sent back inside.' He offered his braying laugh. 'Rescued in the nick of time.'

He grew sober and reflective.

'That is something, isn't it?' The question sounded almost pleading.

'What is?'

'You look for one thing, you often find another.'

Schlegel said he didn't follow.

'Don't you see, man? You come to talk about fuck parties and find instead this woman is alive after all.'

He sat back looking pleased with himself, as though personally responsible for Schlegel's good fortune.

'I saw her in the yard but I didn't shoot her.'

'How many of you shooting?'

'Two. Big clear-out that morning.'

'Who was the other shooter?'

'The Brazilian, Broad.'

'Maybe he shot her.'

'No. I was keeping an eye out for her. I fancied doing her myself. *Droit du seigneur.* Some jobs you do better than others. It's quite personal and totally detached at the same time. I wouldn't expect you to understand.'

'If she was brought into the yard and not shot what happened?'

'I said. Someone sent her back.'

'Who was in charge of the yard?'

'Grabner was down there that morning, when he doesn't usually bother.'

'So if Grabner recognised the commandant's seamstress and thought the commandant had sneaked her in among those to be shot . . .'

'He would pull her out, to spite the commandant.'

'No more motive than that?'

'Of course, Grabner may have plans of his own. If she now falls under his protection it is a calculated insult to the commandant.' Palitsch grew philosophical. 'I know it happens all the time, but it is not actually *that* easy to have someone killed in the case of someone like the seamstress, unless she can be inducted into a process.'

'Lethal injections are used pretty freely.'

'Don't you see what I am saying? The commandant is in the business of administration. He doesn't have access to the killing machine. He can't just turn up in the infirmary with a gaggle of people he wants rid of. There are trials, medical assessments.'

'Don't you kill for the purse?'

'I get paid but I kill as an executor of the law.'

'Why do you do it?'

'For the extra money and because I am good at it.'

'No stuff off the books?'

'Why should I? It's not worth it. I can shoot all the people I want.'

'Do others do it?'

'Ask them.'

'Did you kill Tanner?'

'No reason to, man. I'd already had her and was done.'

'You just said about Fritz how easy it is to pay to have someone killed. Why not the commandant?'

'Because he *is* the commandant! He is too isolated. The doctors aren't going to do him any favours, nor are the security police.'

'And is it a killing machine that they run?'

'Sanctioned. It's not personal or even that ideological.'

'What do you mean?'

'It's not about kikes or frogs or Polaks or Ivans in the end. Punishment block: x number of cells, y number of prisoners.

Punishment repeats and punishment grows. There is always a surplus. Old gives way to new. Thirty into twenty-five won't go, so five are surplus to requirements. What do you do with them? How do you solve the problem? That's all it is here, problem-solving, and don't let anyone tell you different.'

That night it rained. Schlegel decided to investigate the bar mentioned by Ilse, in the hope she might be there. It was about a twenty-minute walk from the garrison. The steady downpour was such a relief after the arid days that Schlegel did not bother to shelter and let himself get soaked, delighting in the rain and wet road magically reflected in the dim headlights of the occasional passing vehicle.

A long footbridge took him over the railway tracks. The bridge was up from the station and crossed the goods area, which was much larger than he was expecting. At the time of their arrival it hadn't been apparent how big the junction was.

He could just make out a train was in and being unloaded. With the arc lights blurred by the rain and the steam from the standing engine, he had little more than an impression of a shadowy crowd. Everything looked orderly, with silent queues. The only chaotic element was the suitcases and bundles being chucked anyhow into huge piles. Otherwise everything was methodical.

He supposed the contents of Tanner's locker would once have been part of similar baggage collections. Once he reached the other side of the footbridge, he realised nothing was stopping him from going over. There was no fencing. All attention was on the gathering of luggage and the procession, which took place in near silence, other than children crying. Schlegel crossed back over the tracks and passed a junction box near where the engine stood, hissing and billowing smoke. He emerged level with the head of the queue, which was being divided by a tall officer standing under an umbrella, flanked by two men in civilian rain-coats, also with umbrellas. Schlegel was surprised by how close they were. He could see the needles of rain hit their umbrellas. The tall man looked familiar and when he turned to speak to his companion Schlegel saw it was Dr Wirths. The two conferred for a moment and Wirths took the man's elbow and drew him aside, which was when he looked up. It was no more than a moment – like a snapshot for future reference, Schlegel thought – and the doctor made no acknowledgement, in fact seemed deliberately to ignore him, were it not for a change of expression from professional detachment to the look of a haunted man.

Schlegel could hear the music from outside. Inside was hot and wet and steamy and crammed with people, most in sodden clothes. The place was so packed Schlegel could not see the walls. He moved into the crowd. It was like Berlin rush hour. He found himself dancing by default in the sweaty squirm. The band was playing on a raised plat-form too low to see anything more than the top of Broad's head. The music was wild and loud: guitars, wailing violins, thumping tambourines and Broad's accordion. Everyone was drunk. If there was a beer table Schlegel couldn't see it. He struggled his way through the crowd, thinking about sex with Ilse and how he found it thrilling and unsettling. The band played on like men possessed, apart from Broad, relaxed in the middle, improvising his accompaniment. Schlegel gave himself up to the music and jigged around with a succession of women, one of whom shouted, 'Happy New Year, darling!' He sweated into his damp clothing like he was in a Turkish bath.

Only when the evening broke up did Schlegel find Ilse, who wrapped her arms around his neck and said she was drunk. They left together with a crowd, including Broad, who mopped his brow with a large handkerchief.

'Phew!' he said cheerfully. 'Hot work!'

'Is this the *Arabian Nights*?' asked Schlegel, in bemused wonder.

'More Sodom and Gomorrah.'

The rain had stopped. The air was heavy and damp. Ilse clung to Schlegel's arm. Her usual joking mood had a bitter edge. 'The men all take what they want when they want. Now so do we. You count as fresh blood. When I am done with you I will pass you on.'

She laughed weirdly.

They crossed over the bridge. The train was still in the siding, with everyone gone; the luggage in even larger piles was being loaded onto carts.

'What's going on?' Schlegel asked, curious to know what they said.

'Just a train,' said Broad.

There was talk of going on somewhere for more drink. Schlegel said he needed one.

Ilse squeezed his arm and whispered, 'Take me to Canada.'

V

Morgen arrived back at the garrison wild-eyed and smelling of drink, after travelling all night on a slow goods train. He told Schlegel, who was still in bed, to get a move on; a taxi waited.

The driver was the one who had taken Morgen around the square on their arrival. Morgen gave their destination as the new camp guardroom. He said nothing during the short journey, about his absence or anything else, yawning so much that his cigarette fell out of his mouth and he stared in disbelief until Schlegel retrieved it.

Schlegel looked out of the window and thought how sex with Ilse had become complicated in ways he found arresting and unsettling. The previous night she said she was having her period. She used a colloquial term he hadn't heard before. She changed her dress for one of the smart ones lying around and told him to rub himself against her; she showed him the spot. Against the dress, he was thinking; that was the thrill for her, contemplating the implications of soiling the borrowed clothes of an unknown woman, probably dead. Ilse had a handkerchief ready. She seemed entirely practical and guilt free. Only fools get caught, she said, changing back into her dress.

Juppe was waiting under the arch by the guardroom, grumbling about having been so summoned. Morgen announced he was there as legal prosecutor on the authority of the Reichsführer-SS. He intended a full inspection of the guardroom and a crematorium.

Juppe's Adam's apple jumped.

The guardroom was a shock. They were traditionally functional spaces but this more resembled a hotel lobby, with a huge stove and armchairs, on which soldiers sprawled drunk, uniforms in disarray, being waited on by exotic female prisoners wearing a haphazard array of fine clothing that looked like it had come from a dressing-up box. One of the women was cooking potato pancakes, which the others served to the men, who fondled them as they passed.

Morgen stared. Their arrival made no difference, other than one man raising his bottle in salute. Even the stickler Juppe appeared indifferent to this breach of protocol. Morgen told him to dismiss the women and have the men line up. Juppe sounded apologetic as he carried out the order. The men took their time, not bothering to fix their dress, making a point of insubordination.

Morgen asked a soldier why he was drunk on duty. He answered that he was not technically as they were off-duty now. Where was the present guard? asked Morgen. Late, he was told. Someone sniggered. Juppe made sideways eye contact with the men, to say it had nothing to do with him.

Morgen inspected the room, leaving the guard to stand. He turned on Juppe and asked why he shouldn't have the lot of them cashiered.

Juppe swallowed hard and said the men had been working all night on two transportations.

Morgen insisted on a locker inspection and the men grew nervous.

Their contents reminded Schlegel of Ingeborg Tanner's, except the range of goods was much wider.

Among the hoard were several jars of fleshy material floating in liquid.

Morgen asked what on earth they were.

Bulls' testicles, he was told.

An astonished Morgen asked why.

Because they were an aphrodisiac, one finally said, and the rest laughed.

Morgen's anger was evident as he turned on Juppe and demanded he summon the security police to confiscate the lot and take the guards' names.

Outside, the new camp appeared vast in its sprawl: row after row of wooden barracks, a few brick. Its flimsiness made no pretence to be anything other than the grimmest residence for those with no choice. Huge crowds gathered standing in several compounds for roll call. The stink of unwashed humanity befouled the air so much Schlegel had to wind up his window as Juppe drove them down the long main street past watchtowers like crows' nests.

Compared to the lunar appearance of the compounds, denuded of all natural growth, the top end of the camp was softer and more wooded. They stopped outside a high-security area, hidden by high brushwood, behind which stood two resting chimneys. Away to the right a column of smoke rose above the trees.

Juppe questioned the extent of his authority in what he could show them.

'Full inspection,' Morgen insisted.

Apart from the immediate guard, which let them in, the place appeared deserted. Inside, a large compound doubled as a sports field. Schlegel saw goalposts and a football pitch laid out with white lines. In the distance, two young men kicked a ball.

Even more unexpected was an elaborate formal garden, next to where they stood, with a tree at its centre and four intersecting paths. Sofas and armchairs lay scattered around outside the main entrance, another bizarre touch.

The building appeared solid compared to all the streets of sheds. Apart from its stubby chimney, it looked more collegiate than medical, Schlegel thought. He didn't know why they were there. Nor could he read the atmosphere between Morgen and Juppe. Morgen appeared both incandescent and apathetic. Where was Ingeborg Tanner in all of this? Schlegel wondered.

Juppe declared himself unfamiliar with the building and seemed uncertain what to do. Morgen lost patience and walked over to the footballers.

Schlegel was aware of Juppe standing stiffly next to him. 'What is going on?' Juppe asked. Schlegel said he didn't know.

Morgen came back with one of the men, who bounced the football as he walked. He was probably no more than twenty but had an air of spectral detachment. He wore flannels that looked like the bottom half of a suit and a canvas shirt. Morgen said he had keys. The young man spoke only when addressed. His accent was Austrian. Schlegel supposed Morgen had bribed him with cigarettes.

They went into the building, the young man still bouncing the football, and stood in a tiled corridor, with fire extinguishers and noticeboards. Morgen said he wanted to inspect the furnaces.

The man took them to a large, functional expanse with a bank of incinerators, all spotlessly clean. It was like a factory, Schlegel thought, compared to the tiny crematorium in the garrison.

Why were the furnaces resting? asked Morgen. Because

a shift had just ended, said the man. They would be fired up later that day. Morgen asked if he worked there. The man said he did. The warm room was like a slumbering giant.

Morgen asked what else was in the building. The man said just a medical section, including a dissecting room. Morgen asked what was upstairs.

It was where they slept.

There was a lift. Morgen asked where it went. To the basement. What was down there? Morgen asked. Changing room and showers.

'Why a lift?' asked Morgen.

The man said he hadn't designed the building. At Morgen's look of caution, he said he had heard the basement was once intended as a mortuary.

Morgen said nothing, then asked why changing rooms.

It was part of the doctors' delousing programme, the man said.

'What do you mean?'

Juppe interrupted. 'Dr Wirths insists everything is fumigated.'

'Show me,' said Morgen.

'We have to go back outside,' the man said.

Juppe added, 'A lot of them turn up filthy as it is.'

A wide flight of steps led down to a basement. The man switched on the lights and bounced his football. Each echoed slap sounded like a punch. Juppe gave the impression that the man's behaviour was somehow distasteful. Schlegel saw benches and pegs and signs in different languages, all orderly, but the space was oppressive with the ceiling being not much higher than he was.

Dr Wirths had made no mention of this aspect of his health programme.

'And the showers?' asked Morgen.

Down the other end, said the man.

Schlegel thought of the shame of strangers forced to stand naked. Morgen lit up and offered the young man a cigarette, excluding Juppe. 'As long as you stop bouncing that football.'

Schlegel watched them exhale. The space reminded him of an indoor rifle range: the same sort of low sealed room and distance. He had once watched a man being blasted to pieces in one.

Morgen asked, 'What's supposed to happen after this?'

The man gave him a look of incredulity and said in the same neutral way, 'They're promised a hot drink.' He bounced the football.

Morgen told them to wait and walked down towards the showers. They stood in silence until he came back after a few minutes weaving like a drunk struggling to remember how to put one foot in front of the other. He said he had seen enough.

Morgen didn't care to travel back with Juppe after the main gate and they had no transport. He asked how long to walk. Juppe had no idea, never having done it. It was still early, not yet hot. Prisoners were preparing to march to work.

The road was long and straight. The dust trail from Juppe's departed vehicle lingered. Schlegel listened to the scrape of their shoes. They squabbled about Morgen going off without telling.

'Where were you, anyway?'

They came to a large old tree. Morgen said he needed to rest. They sat under the spreading branches. Schlegel could see nothing of where they had been, only road, ditch, field, unrelenting sky.

Morgen told how he had been to investigate the scandal

of a Jewish wedding feast being allowed to take place in a camp further east. Not only did it turn out that the authorities had given permission, they had paid for it too and done nothing to stop proceedings from degenerating into an orgy with Jewish women.

He recited this in an automatic way as though it were not the point.

'I was inclined to dismiss it as far-fetched until the man in charge admitted everything. Every word true. Drink, debauchery, soldiers joining in, and the bill picked up.'

'Are there disciplinary charges?'

'There are no witnesses. The Jews are all dead.'

Schlegel supposed they had been shot.

'No. They have special camps.'

Schlegel was confused. 'Like here?'

Morgen seemed reluctant to say. 'There's no work there.'

Schlegel stared at the blank landscape. 'Do I need to be told this?'

'It won't make the slightest difference. The man in charge insisted everything is sanctioned at the highest level. His authority is the Chancellery. I saw the payslips.'

From anyone else, Schlegel would have dismissed it.

'No,' said Morgen. 'This man talks to Bormann in the Chancellery. He said there is nothing I can do. It is beyond the law.'

'Are you saying the same is going on here?'

Morgen didn't answer at first.

'It's the old euthanasia programme, re-dressed. Same crew, new rules, not just the sick now – everybody: men, women, children. All over.'

Schlegel supposed he understood. He couldn't be sure. A breeze rustled the leaves. As rare as hen's teeth, he thought. Everything was parched; the rain as though it had never happened, not even puddles after the downpour. Then he thought: I know now.

'The man I spoke to was disparaging about the commandant, called him an *arriviste* – dismissed him as the Zyklon-B boy – not one of the old gang.'

'Zyklon-B?

'A cyanide. The others use carbon monoxide. He was quite frank and drunk beyond caring.'

A gang of prisoners marched past at double time, their leader shouting the pace. The guards slouched and jogged to catch up, their weapons rattling.

Schlegel watched them go and spoke of what he had seen the night before, the train, Wirths pointing, splitting, dividing and separating.

Morgen smoked for a long time. 'Then our good doctor is not the quiet humanitarian he makes out. What did you think he was doing?'

Schlegel supposed he had been watching some kind of quarantine process.

'No. Our friend Dr Wirths is a death selector.'

The commandant saw them in his office, wanting to know what visiting the crematorium had to do with Ingeborg Tanner. They were left to stand. The reprimand was inevitable. Morgen asked if what was going on was part of the same death programme he had learned about.

The commandant said, 'It is not a legal matter, therefore no concern of yours.'

'On whose authority—' Morgen began, and the commandant shouted back it was none of his business, categorically.

Schlegel's mind turned over like an engine refusing to fire. Death was everywhere. Armies annihilated each other. The world teetered on the brink. Civilians were no longer exempt.

Roundups, towns and cities flattened, bombs falling from the sky. Who drew the line? Who said there were limits? Perhaps there were none. Perhaps it was what everything was moving towards. Remove the barriers of geography and people became cargo for export to waiting centres.

The commandant repeated that Morgen could do nothing. However, investigating the death of Tanner, they could arrest whomever they liked.

'Whatever you come up with, I would respect your authority and not question your decision.'

'And Dr Wirths?' asked Morgen.

'By all means,' said the commandant, rubbing his hands.

'He's right,' said Morgen afterwards. 'We can do nothing. It is what happened next that we can, possibly, do something about.'

Schlegel listened to the words coming out of Morgen's mouth. He hardly sounded like a man who believed what he was saying. It was like a slapstick farce where every time someone bent over and stood up they got whacked around the back of the head with a plank, the action repeated until the audience was sick with laughter.

'What did happen next?'

'Everyone grew corrupt. We weed out the corruption.'

Schlegel feared Morgen's helplessness in the face of the larger annihilation would lead them to operate outside the law.

'Of course, there is a big danger,' said Morgen.

'They will try and stop us or we'll get it wrong.'

'That and something else. This place is sick. The thinking behind it is sick, in terms of the monster it has become – no one imagined that an obscure penal colony would turn out the way it has. The place itself is physically sick – typhus, dysentery, starvation, one epidemic after another. Corruption is infectious. It is *the* epidemic. There are no moral coordinates. The danger is we ourselves become corrupt.' Morgen lit up. 'Knowing monstrous things will make us monstrous.'

Morgen spent his days half-drunk, smoked-out, in a state of myopia, trying to see the refraction between the surface and beneath. It was an absurd spectacle and a pointless labour, investigating one or two unauthorised murders in a place where thousands were being murdered daily.

Among staff the place was always referred to as the garrison. About eight hundred souls worked there: doctors, engineers, switchboard operators, nurses, clerks (huge paperwork), organisers, above all the administrators, then the guards and security police, cooks, orderlies, dog handlers, drivers, school teachers, librarians, specialist workers, from Hungary and Rumania, some from Italy, drawn by the overtime, and the local civilian workers from outside. The list went on.

He wasted hours looking at back-bulletins issued by the commandant's office, courtesy of the central archive. These were exhaustive on the official life of the garrison, with not a hint of its secret, a testament to the pall of boredom that suffocated everything. Nowhere to go. The fantasy of collective enterprise. Demoralisation. Get smashed. He read dreary lists of petty admonitions, garrison social occasions, gardening competitions, discounts on theatre and opera tickets in Kattowice, marital engagements and weekly stalls, puzzles, quizzes, an anti-litter campaign, clean up after your dog, admonitions of public drunkenness and warnings against drinking and driving. On and on.

The human being is such a selective animal, thought Morgen, and highly developed in what it chooses to consider and ignore. The place stank. Dog shit everywhere. The endless burning and pillars of smoke. The finest ash that fell all over. Sickness that verged on catastrophe. And that all-pervading stench, not how you would expect burnt flesh to smell, more reminiscent of tallow candles in a church. For all that, the appearance of the garrison remained orderly: cars and lorries came and went; corridors smelled of polish and disinfectant; barriers went up and down; the various factories on site maintained productivity. Even the risk of epidemic was barely referred to, beyond health posters issued by the medical office, and the occasional stray remark along the lines of they had dropped like flies.

Flies were the garrison's commonest enemy, along with wasps, lice, mosquitoes and a particularly vicious kind of horsefly. A frequent sight was jam jars full of dead insects attracted to their fate by some sweet sticky liquid. The weapons were extensive: sprays, swats, sticky traps, the deadly jars. It was generally agreed few sounds were more satisfactory than a fly swat hitting its target.

And there in the black hole of the middle, hiding in plain sight, the negative reverse of all that order and scurry. He must have been blind. Devastatingly simple, beyond comprehension, thought out every step of the way. They walked voluntarily into the building, took off their clothes and left by the chimney.

Knowing solved nothing, only raised questions about organisation, authority, purpose, sanity, cold logic (with a hint of glee) and folly. There was a euphoria, he suspected, at behaving like gods, and enjoying the cleverness of the trick that let tens of thousands go unprotesting, as sheep to the slaughter.

The secret became its own weight. Schlegel sided with the quietness of Schulze, partly out of cowardice, based on a realistic appraisal. Morgen's enquiry was too fantastic;

he admitted as much himself. The more Schlegel tried to direct him back to matters in hand – Tanner, corruption in the camp, searching for Sybil – the more stubbornly Morgen persisted they were inseparable.

'Even Sybil?' asked Schlegel.

'I suspect she may yet lie at the heart of the mystery.'

Schlegel couldn't see how.

Morgen snapped, 'Then ask yourself how she came to be spared.'

Rules of procedure applied even less. Investigation pre-supposed enquiry; yet what could they ask?

It marked the start of their split.

Schlegel sought refuge in the leftovers of the action parties, hard drinking and available women, in floating venues announced by word of mouth. He went with Ilse, more as a friend, as she was now keen on a spotty young man who was deep into the whole business of the camp. She introduced Schlegel to other young women and teased him for doing nothing about them.

One night she left early and he wasn't sure why he stayed. He had an intense conversation with a woman who nodded vigorously, grinned tipsily, friendly as they clinked bottles, understanding each other perfectly. Her green brooch, pinned to an enviable bosom, was jade like Tanner's. Schlegel admired it while fingering Tanner's in his pocket, thinking the sight of another was a sign. That was how it was. Superstition and chance. Working anything out seemed meaningless if the path of fate was already decided.

The woman pulled a face at her brooch. 'A bit passé. Last year's craze.'

'What happened?'

'Craze over.'

She lost interest and moved on. Schlegel used Tanner's

brooch as an excuse to approach a haughty woman with an aquiline nose that she used to look down. She asked why his hair was white.

'A fright in the night,' he said, and she didn't laugh. She was an officer's wife and 'slumming' as she put it.

He asked if she thought Tanner's brooch was worth something.

'Not as much as last year. Prices were through the roof.' She frowned. 'I don't see why. There was much more of it about last year. Now you hardly see any at all you would expect it to be worth more.'

'Because rarer?'

'Obviously. What do you do?'

New faces turned up. The laughter got too loud. Schlegel ended up maudlin. Which of these people did what exactly? Which were the knowers and which the hangers-on? He remained incapable of processing what Morgen had told him, except in the most bathetic terms.

He woke up in a ditch, staring at a grubby moon, thinking about the great harvester and how it would flatten them if they stood in the way. The machine was the beast and the beast was the machine. That was what he worked out lying in the ditch.

To Morgen's mind, the subject was difficult to broach with Schulze but he cornered her when they were alone. There was little chance of Schlegel turning up. The man seemed to be in the process of abandoning all responsibility, which he could understand; perhaps there would be method to his waywardness. Schlegel worked best on a long leash, scaring himself half to death by wandering too close to the edge.

Two aspects dominated Morgen's thinking: Why there and how?

Schulze flinched as if knowing what to expect. Distraught, she said she was not qualified to speak of such things.

'You must have known what you were building.'

She lowered her head and addressed the desk, claiming she was responsible for organising labour, which involved endless squabbles with the works office, nothing to do with planning.

She looked up, composed herself and rallied. 'I deployed workers, including many civilians, to dozens of sites. It was a matter of daily logistics and it took up all my time and more. My job had nothing to do with what they were building.'

'Give me an example. Forget about the civilians.'

'Site six might require twenty unskilled labourers and five skilled workers on one day and a different number the next, and site twelve two hundred unskilled and forty-five skilled. Most of the day was spent haggling with the works office about why these numbers were impossible. It was a desk job. We never saw the builds, during or after.'

'And what were sites six and twelve?'

'The numbers were used more than once. When a site was completed the number was reallocated to another.' She added rather helplessly, 'We dealt only in numbers. It was a numerical system. Even the prisoners were catalogued by number.'

He was surprised when she later volunteered, 'Like everybody else, I know what I chose not to know. We don't see the trains coming. We don't see what happens or where they are taken.'

'You see the smoke.'

'It's a smoky town; lots of factories, lots of chimneys.'

Morgen noticed how most talk broke off before its natural end, out of an instinctive wariness.

He asked if she was prepared to type up her own account, based on her experience, and in confidence.

'As there is no official record,' he said.

'It would be punishable if I were found out.'

'Not by me.'

Picking up women was easy, Schlegel finally worked out, for the simple reason that everyone wanted drunken sex on the edge of oblivion. Its availability was a novelty, not based on the usual codes of society and attraction but primitive urge. He decided he had been naïve about Sybil. There was no such thing as love, only gratification.

It took the shortest time before he could not live without these nights. The struggle of the morning hangover was followed by the agonising transition into a state of nervous anticipation as to what the next night might bring. Schlegel had no idea what Morgen got up to but to judge by the state of him their hangovers matched.

And all this time he was doing what – other than stumble through the job – he barely knew. The hangovers made him slower, creating a different kind of space and level of insolence. He grew less afraid. The night's reckless transgressions became the next day's storehouse. It all made sense, even the sight of a young woman throwing up and laughing about it as they fucked. They were, he supposed, in the belly of the beast, and the nightly purges were the whirling pagan feast that countered the crawling nightmare of the day.

He woke in someone's garden, stiff and aching, above the beginnings of a mackerel sky. Damp air; winter not so far away. He went to the night canteen and sopped up as much grease as he could. Afterwards, he loitered and found himself gravitating towards the commandant's house. He selected a spot over the road where he could doze under the shade of a tree and dumbly watch the comings and goings. Staff started to arrive for work. He supposed he was there because it was where Sybil had worked and he was keeping a vigil.

A garrison vehicle drew up and the driver fetched the commandant, who came out in a hurry, still eating and nearly colliding with arriving staff. He hopped around in a pantomime of apology and hurried off, looking in a good mood for once.

Schlegel supposed he ought to go back to his room and wash. He was aware of smelling the sex on him. He was about to when he saw Frau Hoess leave, smartly turned out, get in the Opel, parked beside the house, and drive off in the opposite direction to her husband. Schlegel thought. The front door was open. The staff had just walked in. He rather urgently wanted to be inside, snooping, an act of wilful penetration, leaving his spoor, haunting the same space as Sybil. He was still drunk, at the top of the slide down. His fuzzy thinking receded and he saw clearly the reason to look was because answers lay in the house.

The owners absent, only staff; he suspected the nature of the household was such that servants didn't volunteer information to their employers.

He stood up, picked the loose grass off, brushed himself down and crossed the road. The door was open. He stepped inside and shut it softly. He heard a man's laugh coming from the kitchen, then a pause before several women joined in. While the cat's away, he thought. They sounded like they were sitting with their feet up, gossiping.

Schlegel stared at the parquet in the hall, wondering what his excuse would be if discovered. He inspected the visitors' book open on the table. No guests for several days. He flicked through the pages, and saw the name of the commandant's boss on several occasions, Pohl, signed with a fat flourish and complimentary remarks. Pohl was a frequent visitor.

Schlegel supposed this list told the story of the garrison and if the reasons for the visits were understood . . .

Himmler's signature, angular and spiky compared to Pohl's plump, comfortable one.

The commandant and his wife looked like they had been big entertainers the previous year, not so much now.

Schlegel wasn't expecting the number of visits by Fegelein. He counted nine. Using the visitors' pen he noted the dates on an old receipt.

He went exploring, trying to appear casual. The hall gave on to a windowless corridor with three doors. To the right he could hear the man continuing to joke with the women. The mood was lethargic and bewitched.

The door on the left opened into a dining room dominated by a mahogany table and sideboard, with a corner cupboard displaying silver and crystal. The paintings looked good quality. It was altogether much more last century than he was expecting. Perhaps the commandant's wife was a secret antiquarian. Schlegel had the impression the room wasn't much used now.

The next one was where the commandant's wife had taken him: black leather and bespoke furniture including the giant walnut desk, its surface covered with family photographs whose loving assembly reminded him of the sterile pinning of butterflies. The drawers were leather-lined, which he presumed was Groenke's touch. He had never come across anything like it. Even his mother, who was no slouch, made do with lining paper. A large safe stood in the corner, flanked by glass-fronted cases, floor to ceiling, full of what looked like unread books.

The room smelled of the commandant, a combination of stale tobacco, cologne and something else. If rage had a smell, thought Schlegel . . .

A door between the bookcases took him into a sitting room, again black leather and a wooden floor with exotic rugs, less formal than the dining room. How settled it all seemed. He supposed the project was entirely Frau Hoess's. The house had an air of opulent secrecy, quite at odds with the woman's modest everyday appearance.

He went back into the corridor. The house was quiet apart from chattering in the kitchen. He wondered about upstairs, knowing it would be harder to talk his way out of being found there. He went up anyway, feeling his nerve was holding.

He glanced in a bathroom, then came to the master bedroom, with separate beds, his-and-her wardrobes, one with glazed doors, and boxed radiators as well as a tiled stove. A large oil painting of wild flowers above the beds. A leather chair of a sort whose name Schlegel couldn't remember, with opposite joined seats so the parties could face each other. He suspected it was a long time since the occupants had used it. The room felt sterile. The wallpaper – beige with a leaf pattern – continued next door, the children's bedroom, with brightly coloured furniture.

The room beyond seemed to be for guests, yet felt more lived in than the bedroom. Schlegel looked in a carved oak bureau and realised the wife used it as a secretaire.

In contrast to the general order, the desk was a mess. A cursory search revealed letters, statements, bills, cheque books and paperwork, interspersed with children's notes and drawings that invariably said, I love you, Mummy. In her bureaucracy, Frau Hoess was not organised. The contents looked like they hadn't been sorted in an age, beyond a rudimentary system of stuffing papers in pigeon-holes, several of which were devoted to a considerable correspondence.

He picked out a pile of letters. They seemed to be entirely gossipy notes from female friends. An exception was a formal thank you from Fegelein for her hospitality. He flicked through more: different examples of flowery handwriting, varieties of coloured writing paper. Then he saw Pohl's signature. He presumed another thank you note. It was, but more.

He read: 'My deepest appreciation and gratitude for your recent gifts of the stone of heaven. Such fine examples! If this is the product of your enterprise such bounty indeed. To think, our very own mine!'

Stone of heaven? Mine?

Schlegel heard footsteps running upstairs. He waited, listening, his mind empty of excuses. The footsteps ran on, up another flight.

He felt exhilarated, almost giddy.

He folded the letter and put it in his pocket.

More stairs led to a top floor in the eaves, with two doors off a landing. He made no effort to disguise his arrival, didn't bother knocking, calculating it would be just staff. The first room was full of women sewing, surrounded by rolls and rolls of fabric. They worked in silence, a quiet that said they had been talking away before they heard him coming. He inspected them as if searching for someone, shook his head, bade them good morning and excused himself.

He repeated the action with the second room, which showed more of the same. At least a dozen seamstresses worked up there. One would have been Sybil. The biggest shock was the astonishing array of fabrics, enough to satisfy a small factory.

He went back downstairs. As he stepped into the hall the kitchen door opened and he was confronted by a big, raw-boned man with high cheekbones, handsome in an obvious way and about the same age as him. The man was in his socks, with one hand inserted into the shoe he was cleaning, of superior quality. Schlegel smelled frying fish coming from the kitchen. The man was dressed like a dandy in an embroidered waistcoat and leather trousers. He seemed quite at ease, though from the menial task he was performing Schlegel presumed he was a prisoner and the kitchen joker.

Some sixth sense told Schlegel the man had as little right to be there as he did.

For a moment everything was normal then the man swore under his breath, ran back into the kitchen and scampered out again carrying the other shoe, winked at Schlegel and disappeared through a door. Schlegel stood blinking in surprise. He stepped forward and saw the commandant, preoccupied and muttering to himself as he approached across the lawn.

Schlegel stood paralysed between taking the front door and following the man. He could hear the commandant's boots on the steps up to house.

He stepped inside the second door. A dim bulkhead light was on. Steps led down to darkness. He heard the back door open and close and waited for the commandant, who continued talking to himself. He remembered Schulze on the habit of inappropriate laughter and had to stifle a fit of the giggles.

He heard the commandant go upstairs and trod gingerly down the flight of steps, wondering how he was supposed to get out. He could hear no sign of the other man, so supposed there must be a way. He switched on lights. One was for a laundry room. He could hear staff moving in the kitchen above.

The second space took up most of the footprint of the house. Schlegel, thinking of the bolts of fabric upstairs, decided there was a big difference between storage and hoarding. He was looking at a veritable Aladdin's cave of stashed goods: shelves of jars, tins, preserved meats, cans of Seville oranges, exotic teas, coffee beans, pharmaceuticals, bulging sacks of sugar, flour, logs and coal, and what looked like cans of gasoline or paraffin. At a time of such shortages the sight was beyond belief. And none of it locked away, presumably because the staff wouldn't dare touch it for fear of their jobs.

A whole section was given over to cartons of cigarettes. Schlegel helped himself to an armful. At least they would float him for a while. He took one of several string shopping bags, hanging on a peg, to carry them.

He looked around, wondering about the other man. On the garden side of the cellar stood a thick steel door on a latch.

Schlegel opened it and saw darkness. He could find no light switch. He was without matches as he didn't smoke; he didn't remember seeing any but went back and checked. He was right; enough candles to light up a football pitch but no matches. He told himself he wasn't afraid of the dark.

As the door shut behind him Schlegel could see nothing. It was as though his eyelids had been glued shut. He stuck his arms out, like in blind man's buff, feeling the shopping bag dangle ridiculously. He stretched his eyes wide trying to sense something and saw nothing. Was this the perpetual darkness that awaited them all? Was this the place where the dead rose up? He was assailed by primal fears, however hard he tried to exercise his reason. He badly wanted a drink and would have given anything for a torch.

He felt his way forward, hands outstretched, until his hand reached the wall, which he took for a guide. He once lost contact and spent an age trying to find it again, deprived of all spatial awareness. The wall should have been within touching distance, yet wasn't, and he supposed he must have stumbled around in panic after losing contact. After that he found it easiest to shuffle sideways, back to the wall, using both hands to guide him.

All he could hear was his wet breathing in the dank air. The tunnel seemed to go on and on. What purpose it served he had no idea. If the other man was an interloper Schlegel supposed it served as his regular exit and entrance. Perhaps he was having a romance with one of the household staff. He ransacked his head for inconsequential, ordinary thoughts to stave off panic.

At last he came to what felt like a fork and grew dimly aware of the possibility of light. This came to seem even more disturbing than total darkness, because of the fallen world it would take him back into.

Morgen was impressed by the cigarettes and immediately helped himself. They were the brand Broad smoked. Morgen pronounced them disgusting but in terms of petty cash it was a start.

'Everything is forgiven,' he said ominously.

'Where's Schulze?' asked Schlegel.

'Avoiding us. She knows I am keen to pick her brains and she is not. It must be hard living in this world without having done anything technically wrong.'

Morgen treated Schlegel's snooping around the commandant's house as though it were perfectly normal. Schlegel showed him the letter from Pohl to Frau Hoess. Morgen looked impressed and, like him, asked what was the stone of heaven and what sort of mine.

'Recent gifts, it says. Can we suppose the good lady is bribing her husband's boss?'

Morgen appeared diverted by the prospect.

Schlegel reported what he had seen in the attic and cellar storeroom.

'Acquisitive, would you say?' enquired Morgen mildly.

'Pathologically so.'

'Canada, would you say?'

'I have heard her described as a top shopper.'

'If the stone of heaven is from Canada, being passed on to Pohl in Berlin . . .'

Morgen sat with his head wreathed in smoke. Jade, thought Schlegel.

'What if you had got caught?'

'I nearly was.'

Schlegel was still puzzled by the existence of the tunnel, which had brought him out into trees and undergrowth outside the garrison, beyond the commandant's garden.

Morgen shrugged and said, 'You are a strange boy. What's your next move, if I may be so bold?'

'I thought I might join the photography club.'

Morgen looked surprised at that. 'I didn't know you were a snapper.'

'Palitsch's description of the man photographing Tanner at the sex parties matches Haas, who took the pictures of the beaten women and—'

'Was hanging around the bath morgue when Bock died,' Morgen finished for him.

Schlegel added that he had gone through Frau Hoess's visitors' book and, while Pohl was a frequent guest, Fegelein had at least nine recorded visits.

Schlegel saw Morgen became animated for the first time since his return.

'Here, let me see.'

He pored over the scribbled dates. 'Fegelein was here when Tanner was killed. The point is, was he here at the time of any of the beatings or disappearances?'

'The beatings were domestic.'

Morgen gave him a withering look. 'They say. Apropos of them, I had an interesting conversation with the commandant's wife. Not a conversation as such, more a series of loaded remarks.'

'When?'

'Probably while you were prowling around her house.'

He had run across her on the main street and was pretending he hadn't seen her when she came over and chatted about the unseasonal heatwave before suddenly asking how the investigation into Tanner and the garrison women was going.

'I told her we were in possession of photographs of some of the cases, and she gave one of her big sighs and asked, "Who do you think alerted you?"'

Schlegel reminded Morgen, 'You thought she rather than her husband might be the one behind our recall.'

'I am not sure now. I suspect Pohl, the better to keep an eye on us.'

'Did she say anything else?'

'She leaned forward – reeking of violets – and told me not to be obtuse. I had to understand she could not be seen to be directly involved.'

Schlegel hung around the photography club. An exhibition space displayed members' photographs – still lives, landscapes, animals, portraits, a lot of children, uplifting stuff.

No photographs of the garrison or the camps; not that you would want them. Most areas had 'no photography' signs, along with the plethora of other warnings. Several members were keen to share their enthusiasm. Schlegel said he was a novice. He was shown darkrooms, a small library in a separate room, a seating area with technical magazines. The equipment itself was kept under heavy lock and key.

Sad, but there it was, said the man showing him. The club was still recovering from the theft of a large part of its stock a year ago.

'Fortunately, top camera companies use us to test new equipment.'

While Schlegel waited he sat reading technical magazines and tried to look interested.

Haas, previously blasé, seemed nervous upon spotting Schlegel. Perhaps he had been told about their investigation. The man was clearly desperate to resist any overtures but soon succumbed to flattery as it was probably the first time anyone had paid his work the slightest attention. Schlegel talked enthusiastically about the pictures he had bought and asked if there were more.

Haas had albums of rabbits in hutches, goats, donkeys, and what he described as a humorous photograph: a stallion with his tool out, reaching almost to the ground. Humorous photograph number two was of mating donkeys.

Schlegel laughed loudly, as he was supposed to. He made appreciative noises for the longest time and suggested a beer. He knew a stall nearby, used by lorry drivers.

Schlegel paid. He said he was interested in a certain kind of photographs. He wanted to learn how to take them.

'I've been told you're the man to see.'

Haas's eyes said he guessed where this was going.

'Perhaps I could pay you, for a tutorial.'

Haas said nothing. Schlegel produced a packet of cigarettes. He watched Haas's greed overcome caution, until he broke off and said he wasn't the one Schlegel was looking for.

Hooked nonetheless, Schlegel saw.

'What equipment do you use?'

For what he called special work Haas used a tiny Minox camera not even on the market but sent by the company to try out.

'A spy camera. Fits in the hand.'

He demonstrated by showing his cupped palm, leaving it there.

Schlegel handed him the pack of cigarettes and counted out a further five.

'Another beer?'

He could see Haas thought him a fool for giving away so much.

They walked back to the club drinking their beer.

Haas said he was turning some of his pet pictures into greetings cards. He had even talked to the commandant's wife about perhaps letting prisoners buy them with their credit points to send to relatives.

Haas appeared quite at home in the club. Schlegel wondered about his domestic circumstances. He saw him living alone. Haas seemed in no hurry. He fiddled around with his albums while Schlegel wondered how much longer he could feign enthusiasm. Haas argued the merits of crinkled borders against straight edges and decided the former were better suited to casual photographs.

'Last year we were given the new Agfa colour stock to test, much faster, permitting shooting at lower light levels. I got some interesting results. Would you like to see?'

He took a box from a locked cabinet and suggested they

go to one of the darkrooms. The club was not crowded but people were around.

Haas switched on the light outside the door to show the room was in use. He pointed proudly to the enlarger, the latest model. He showed the developing trays and explained how they worked and why it was necessary to use a red light to protect the light-sensitive paper. There was standing room only. Schlegel was forced into closer proximity than he would have liked. Haas smelled of cheap aftershave.

He produced three contact sheets, each with 36 frames. Some had been separately enlarged.

The images shared the appearance of having been taken surreptitiously. Some ordinary party shots showed young men and women lounging with drinks.

In one he spotted Fegelein in casual clothes on a sofa with his arm around a woman. In another, he was standing with his back to the camera, holding a champagne glass. Schlegel stared at Tanner looking at the lens, with bright reckless eyes that told of more than alcohol.

'How did you know Tanner?' Schlegel asked, trying to sound casual.

'She did some modelling for me.'

Haas couldn't resist, and out of the box came a series of enlarged, crisp black-and-white nature shots: dappled sunlight, soft contours, wholesome, revealing Tanner's spec-tacular naked body, with her arms aloft to greet the light. She appeared totally at ease, the camera in love with her.

Schlegel pointed to the contact sheets, 'Were these her idea?'

'She wanted me to photograph her, to see how she looked.'

Haas said it as though it were the most obvious thing in the world. Schlegel supposed Tanner's appetite had made it seem quite natural. He was equally sure for Haas she had existed only as a demonstration for his skills, and what greater technical challenge than clandestinely photographing her having public sex at orgiastic parties.

At first Haas had thought it impossible for technical reasons.

'I couldn't just go and set up a camera and ask permission. Then the Minox came along and I was curious to see how the new Agfa stock performed.'

A further challenge was to learn to frame by not looking through the viewfinder, which would draw attention.

'I was quite pleased with the results.'

He showed Schlegel two more contact sheets, saying they were his first efforts.

'It shows you the problems with this kind of work.'

Erratic framing often missed or cropped the subject.

By the second sheet Haas had mastered the method. The camera had a lot of depth of field, he explained.

The photographs of Tanner stood out because she knew the camera was there and adjusted accordingly. Schlegel inappropriately thought how eminently fuckable she looked, consuming men for her pleasure. In one shot she appeared transfixed in ecstasy as some unseen male ploughed away behind.

Schlegel asked for a magnifying viewer. Two of the contact squares interested him. One showed Tanner face-down naked on a couch, with the man on top partly visible, face missing, still dressed, his flexed arms taking his weight. The point was what he wore. Schlegel compared it with the earlier picture of Fegelein. Same outfit.

The second frame showed Tanner still dressed and standing, with Fegelein behind, one arm around her waist, the other stuck down the front of her dress. Tanner's head was arched, showing a long white throat. Her hands were driven hard between her thighs. Fegelein was glassy-eyed. The hand fondling Tanner's breast threw into relief the brooch pinned to her dress, now in Schlegel's pocket.

Schlegel asked if Haas knew the man.

Only that he came from Berlin.

'You do realise,' Schlegel began. Haas looked expectant. 'Some of these pictures could be worth a lot of money.'

'How much?' asked Haas slowly.

'It depends. You would have to ask him.'

Schlegel said what Fegelein did and watched Haas's reaction.

'Special envoy to the Reichsführer?' Haas repeated.

Schlegel watched Haas grow carried away, a little man suddenly presented with big dreams.

'How would it be possible?'

Schlegel gave him a clap on the shoulder. 'Fegelein's always up and down. Ask Groenke, if you know Groenke; he'll know when he's next due.'

'Everyone knows Groenke. Do you really think so?'

'Speak with Fegelein. I am sure he'll see the point of you putting a value to them.'

Haas looked pleased, more important.

'As we understand each other, I have a question. Who authorises the injections?'

Haas saw no objection in answering. 'It's a medical initiative. Others decide. Senior doctors. It's a due process.'

He smiled, frighteningly plausible.

'Who selects?'

'That's easy. Hartmann, basically. He's the one who signs off on them.'

'And Wirths.'

Haas shook his head. 'He only does external selections.'

'You mean at the station.'

Haas gave a tight smile.

Schlegel pointed to the contact sheets. 'Make sure to keep them safe. You could be talking a lot of money for such specialist work.'

Schlegel was on his way back to the office when he saw one of the lobby telephone booths full of enough smoke to suggest it was on fire. He knew it was Morgen before the door was pushed open and he was waved at to wait. Schlegel watched the switchboard girls with their headsets, connecting and disconnecting calls, fluent in their actions and confident of their skills. It was like watching a mime show or an elaborate guessing game.

Morgen emerged, trailing smoke.

'That was the Kattowice traffic police. Fegelein was here at the time of that hit-and-run accident.'

'The woman no one could identify?'

'The dates match. What's more, two of the numbers in Tanner's little black book, when you add the Berlin area code, take you through to the Chancellery, with the second a direct line to Fegelein's office.'

Schlegel told him Haas's photographs put Fegelein even more clearly in the picture.

Morgen said, 'But why give a girl from the local motor pool direct access to him. One of the top men in the Chancellery, not short of girls.'

'We know he is corrupt. What did Kattowice say?'

'An old cop with bad lungs, one of the morning drinkers, he groused about how uncooperative the garrison is in cases of drunk driving on public highways, throwing up so much red tape.'

'Where are we going?' asked Schlegel.

They were walking down the main street. Schlegel's shirt was sticking to his back, his shoes full of sweat.

'Motor pool. The old cop has a civilian witness and half a car number plate, which matches no local vehicles. Any enquiry to see if it fits any in the garrison comes back access denied.'

They spoke to a female clerk in charge of vehicle leasing, who sat fanning herself, looking sticky enough to eat.

She glanced at the detail of the number plate Morgen had written down and said it almost certainly matched one of theirs.

She went off to fetch the vehicle's record.

Morgen said, 'There's a league and Kattowice are bottom of it.'

'What are you talking about? Football?'

'Drink-drive homicides. Heini oversees all such traffic offences, referring every case to his office. There is a district league table of cases solved, with Kattowice a notoriously poor performer thanks to the garrison.'

The woman returned with the file. Morgen flicked through it.

'So much for bureaucracy.'

Most of the entries were patchy and incomplete.

'But on the date in question we can see the vehicle was signed out for three days to one Hermann Fegelein.'

There were no further users after Fegelein, with no record of the vehicle being damaged, but six weeks later it was dismantled for spares, and on the last page a stamp said account closed.

Morgen left in high spirits, saying, 'The car doesn't exist but the record does, to say it doesn't. That's bureaucracy for you!'

Schlegel waited while Morgen fugged up the telephone

booth again, calling the old cop to say he should put in a formal request to the Reichsführer's office to interview his special envoy to the Chancellery about a traffic homicide.

With that, and the prospect of Haas blackmailing him, Schlegel thought it looked like Fegelein was in for a busy time.

That night Schlegel walked over to the party house where he had run across the woman with the jade brooch, on the off chance, but it was closed. He wandered around until he reached an area where the buildings were fewer. The moon cast a shadow. A party announced itself by music coming from the end of a lane. Steps took him up to a crowded kitchen. The joint looked like a thieves' den of hard drinkers and tough women, probably guards, where privileged criminal elements mixed freely with rowdy soldiers cutting deals.

In the squash Schlegel recognised the fancy waistcoat belonging to the big young brute he had seen disappearing from the commandant's house. He was in close conversation with another man. When Schlegel saw who, he beat a hasty retreat, despite an urgent need to get drunk, until a heavy hand fell on his shoulder. It was the man in the waistcoat, insisting he stay.

'Sepp wishes to be reacquainted.'

The need for drink won out. Schlegel was expected to buy. The only alcohol on offer was a clear liquid in a flat bottle. The price was exorbitant until Sepp stepped in, after which it was halved. Sepp appeared amused by Schlegel's predicament.

'An uncomfortable fraternisation, no?'

They drank out of cardboard cups. Sepp stuck to mineral water. 'Just Mattoni these days. I only meet the devil in drink. Cheers!'

The room was raucous, the underlying spirit mean.

Sepp introduced the other man as Böhner, all very formal and correct, and the more disturbing for it.

Böhner was canteen supervisor at the local Bata shoe factory.

With that, the reason for the man's presence in the commandant's household became clear to Schlegel. Shoes and leather meant the factory was almost certainly part of Groenke's empire. Böhner's job would be of value in terms of what he could supply. Schlegel remembered the smell of frying fish. He checked the man's shoes. The ones he had been cleaning. Top quality. He took a slug of drink, pleased with his observations, and asked, 'Do you provide the commandant's wife with shoes for her kiddies?'

Böhner frowned, not sure what to answer.

Schlegel went on. 'Well, they would be new, wouldn't they, whereas the ones she could get from Erich Groenke are more likely to be used. I expect she insists her children have proper new shoes or their feet might become deformed.'

Whatever rotgut he was drinking had a hell of a kick.

'Or racially infected,' he added.

'Yes, ha-ha!' Böhner said, confused. He changed the subject and asked how Schlegel and Sepp knew each other.

Sepp sniffed the air and said, 'I smell copper.'

Böhner looked disconcerted.

'Don't worry. He's out of his depth here. Our friend didn't approve of our methods.' Sepp turned to Schlegel and said sweetly, 'I am sure we can arrange a good tanning for you. You will make a pretty lamp shade.'

Schlegel looked around the noisy smoky room, throbbing with the prospect of violence.

Sepp said to Böhner, 'We carried out our orders and did

our patriotic duty but when we continued to do so on our own initiative he and his fat pal objected.'

Schlegel protested. 'You were feeding human flesh into the food chain.'

Böhner found that funny and roared with laughter.

Sepp shrugged. 'Only Jews. We were licensed bandits.'

'Called to account. Was that Baumgarten I saw riding with the posse?'

'Who's Baumgarten?' asked Böhner.

'Baumgarten could tear you in two with his bare hands – well, maybe not you, Böhner, you're a big boy – whereas I look like I wouldn't hurt a fly. Do you enjoy pain?' Sepp sniggered. 'Me, I never really understood pleasure until I discovered pain.'

Böhner looked too stupid to appreciate pain beyond dishing it out.

'Anyway, what brings you to the party?' Sepp asked Schlegel.

The drink was rough, filthy stuff. Schlegel stared at his cup, wildly drunk already, lost for an answer.

Böhner said to Sepp, 'How come you're talking to him? I would be killing him.'

'The Lord works in mysterious ways. I can't complain. This is a good billet, if you know how to work it. I still slaughter the beast. I'm clean of the demon drink. I have seen the error of my ways. I asked what brings you?'

'More of the same. Berserkers and werewolves.'

Sepp turned to Böhner. 'We were Wotan's outriders.'

'Wotan?'

'The avenging spirit of the hunter god. Storm and frenzy.' He told Schlegel, 'We will ride again and then you and your friend's number will be up.'

Schlegel could never get over how harmless Sepp looked, with a lisping voice that gave everything an air of sinister comedy, but he didn't sound so funny when he said, 'I have seen the light of the Lord retreat in haste when the devil rides out. The devil's best trick is to persuade us he doesn't exist, don't you think?'

Schlegel fell into a funk under the man's cobra stare. Sepp pulled a face and started miming sexual ecstasy with grunts and squeaks that sent Böhner into fits of laughter. Sepp leaned in and whispered under the din, 'This is the face I will pull when I terminate your sorry existence, for it is written.'

Sepp's hand gripped Schlegel's arm. 'The difference between us is you are drunk and I am not. Remember that as you stagger home through the dark night of your soul.'

Schlegel pulled free, pushing through the crowd, earning himself a punch in the back on the way out.

He hung around outside, too idiotic and far gone to go to his room, needing more drink, to write the night off.

Böhner and Sepp came out after about twenty minutes, chatted briefly under a streetlight, went their different ways. When Schlegel saw Böhner drinking from his bottle he decided to follow, in the preposterous hope of sharing the rest. All he knew was he was drunker than usual, which meant very.

Böhner was lurching, not yet staggering. Schlegel had to keep one eye closed to focus. Böhner paused, as if aware of being followed. Schlegel hung back. The night was bright and soft. The streets still had people.

Schlegel watched Böhner enter the commandant's garden via the door in the wall, using his own key. He waited and followed. The door had been left open and he slipped through and stood under a fig tree, mesmerised by the double moon reflected in the black pond. He closed one eye, making the moon slide into one.

Some grand, inebriated carelessness made him want to violate the household and be caught in the act of smothering children in their sleep.

The back door to the house was locked. The entrance under the steps was open. Böhner's way in, he supposed. Was the woman so abandoned as to receive him as her husband and children slept? It was obvious they were lovers. It explained his earlier presence and why he had disappeared before the commandant found him.

Schlegel felt around for a switch, which lit the short flight to the cellar. He listened to the blood drum in his head.

He stuffed his pockets with Ibar. His resolve hardened and he determined to mount an assault on Frau Hoess's secretaire. There was bound to be more evidence. But the door from the cellar to the house was locked. Thwarted, he relieved the shelves of more Ibar and left, remembered the string bags and took one.

He circled the house in the expectation of finding what he saw: the lit windows of the office, revealing the commandant drunk and insensible on the sofa, muttering in his sleep, naked from the waist down, trousers around his ankles.

Schlegel went back, paused in the walled garden, beguiled by the reflected moon. He heard a woman sigh, then again, and was slow to realise he was listening to the approach of her sexual climax.

His first thought was they must be in the garden, then he saw Frau Hoess, face squashed against the summerhouse window, her mouth an ecstatic circle, breath misting the glass. She seemed to be looking straight at him as he listened transfixed by the sexual grunting being dug out of her and thought of their lives as a tangle of threads.

*

'Have you heard?' asked Schulze as Morgen arrived in the office.

'What?' She looked pretty, he thought.

The garrison's jungle drums had been beating hard.

'Palitsch has been arrested for racial defilement and Dr Wirths for stealing morphine.'

Morgen found the arrest of Palitsch no surprise. He had been caught compromised with a famous beauty from the Gypsy camp.

'Is he so careless?

'The word is he was set up by a jilted lover of the woman, a prisoner supervisor. She was in on it too, and the security police.'

Morgen thought of trapped wasps struggling in sticky jam jars and said news travelled fast.

Palistch was known to be heading for a fall but the arrest of Dr Wirths was a shock. The security police had raided his house and found a quantity of morphine in the chimney of a stove.

'Nobody would have believed it of the man. He is always so righteous and indignant.'

Morgen presumed the evidence was planted, the latest move to discredit the doctor in the war going on.

'Are you so surprised?' asked Morgen.

Schulze said instead that so many security roundups were having an adverse effect on the workforce. A recent move to break up the camp underground had seen the transfer without warning of hundreds of skilled workers overnight, leaving huge shortages and departmental chaos.

Morgen hadn't heard about that and valued her knowledge.

'There's something else,' she said, hesitant.

It was obviously personal. 'Yes?' he asked.

'I am under pressure to stop working for you and return to my old job because of the mess.'

'How do feel about that? You said we weren't popular.'

'That wasn't really for me to say.'

Morgen sensed she was putting distance between them. He presumed she was reporting to Kammler, though he had no evidence. He suspected she considered him negligent towards Schlegel, and felt protective. The man was becoming a walking disaster. That said, his lack of method, beyond blind instinct, was producing results. His snoop around the commandant's house, however foolish, was inspired.

The stone of heaven was jade, Morgen had since learned. Libraries were wonderful things: a book on precious stones in the garrison's extensive children's section had told him so.

Pohl was thanking Frau Hoess for her gift of jade.

As for the meaning of the mine, plenty of regional coal pits existed, using labour from the camps, but he couldn't see Pohl or the commandant's wife getting excited about anything so dirty.

Schulze said she had typed up some notes as he had asked. It took him five minutes to read them. He was aware of her nervousness and could tell she had done it against her better judgement. He supposed they were part of the reason for her pulling back.

He burned them in his ashtray and said she didn't have to look so anxious. No one would know.

Her account told of her time there, who she had worked for, and some of the main events. As a document it was entirely innocuous, almost pathetically so, but Morgen was sure it was loaded with significance if he could read between the lines.

A key date that seemed to be emerging was the two-day inspection by the Reichsführer-SS fourteen months before, in the July of 1942.

Schulze mentioned all the panic for its preparation. Otherwise, Morgen's sole source was the wretched garrison bulletins, written up in such drearily upbeat terms that he hadn't paid much attention. The visiting cortege was welcomed by a prisoner orchestra playing the triumphal march from *Aida*, blah, blah, and two happy, fruitful days followed examining the many projects close to Reichsführer Himmler's heart, especially the herb farms and plantations, followed by a succession of splendid social entertainments.

Looked at more objectively – in terms of politics and the garrison's fate – Morgen saw that the visit had marked a change that may have been pivotal.

The following month Schulze's department was flat out building the new crematoria, which were finally green-lit after five months of what she described as dithering and tinkering with plans to little avail.

'Plans for five months?' asked Morgen.

She said there had been blueprints from the start. Blueprints for this and that, including a new crematorium from the word go. Efficiency on paper, they called it. They had got used to plans going nowhere. What got drawn up bore less and less resemblance to what was built.

'How so?'

'Drawings for brick prisoner barracks. No bricks to build them with.'

She said everyone had been caught on the hop when the crematoria were commissioned. They'd thought them just another set of drawings and were even more surprised materials were forthcoming, because it was already a time of extreme shortages.

Morgen supposed she had never discussed any of this with anyone in terms of her own life. Nobody did. He understood why Krick was popular with the wives; it was all about them.

Schulze told him the place had been a boom town at the beginning. Her arrival in February 1941 coincided with the announcement of a massive redevelopment programme. Morgen said he had read of no such plans in the garrison bulletin.

'You wouldn't. It was a civilian project, to provide a modern town for the big new petrochemical plant that was announced at the same time. The garrison was involved only as the provider of labour. It had no say in the plans.'

She said they had all gone off to lectures given by star architects and landscape gardeners, who talked about quality of life and the huge improvements in store. Everyone was impressed because the standard of living was terrible.

'My first digs were horrible.'

They had all been quite proud in the beginning. The place was a backwater. The garrison and original camp were very make-do. Things could only improve. But the mood quickly soured. Schulze remembered meetings between town and garrison where the camp was objected to as an eyesore for being in the wrong place, too close to town, an embarrassment, and needed to be moved.

Morgen wondered if his answer lay somewhere in all these bureaucratic wrangles.

'Yet the camp is still here and expanded.'

She told him the new camp had been meant as quite a grand project, with special building manuals, intended to set standards and complement the town's development. Where the town would have estates for chemists and their families, the new camp was planned as a labour colony to be built by Russian prisoners, except the national construction programme was immediately cancelled and they were all transferred elsewhere to work in weapons manufacture.

'So they went. This was when?'

'The new year of 1942. They had been here only a couple of months.'

'Which left the construction department with no one to build its camp and nobody to put in it.'

'That's what it looked like.'

'It must have been a nerve-racking time.'

She agreed. 'And we weren't popular with the commandant's office.'

'Because you answered to Kammler.'

'Yes. Endless attempts were made by the garrison to shut us down. We were told we were a waste of money. The whole project was considered redundant. We were building a ghost town.'

'But that didn't happen.'

'Everything was very tense until the end of February when Dr Kammler came for an inspection and told us the work would carry on, which was a great relief.'

'Of course. Your jobs were secure. So the purpose of the camp changed. What was it for now?'

'What they called a new civilian influx. One of the first tasks was preparing the Russian quarters in the old camp for the first women that were sent at the end of March. A wall had to be built where there was fencing before.'

Morgen thought. Five crucial months in which the garrison was transformed, without answering the vital question of how such an obscure spot became a death factory.

And perhaps we won't know, he thought, beyond understanding nature's abhorrence of a vacuum. Perhaps because it was a dump.

He still wondered what he was hoping to prove, beyond satisfying his own bloody-minded curiosity.

He went out of the stifling office and sat on the stairs by an open window, sweating into his shirt, smoking, staring at the bleached grass.

He considered Schulze's memory important in the context of a secret world and its selective official record, that overabundance of useless, unread paperwork.

He was guessing. He thought: By the time of the July inspection facilities must have existed to show the garrison was already capable of killing large numbers on site. But where and on whose initiative?

It could only mean there had been some secret temporary solution.

He went back upstairs, wondering how to ask Schulze without compromising her because he wanted to think of himself as a decent man and she had done nothing wrong other than be a creature of the system.

He said, 'I am vexed by one matter. Prior to the four new crematoria being commissioned what did they use? Just the one here in the garrison?'

'Yes, but there was a crisis because that had to be shut down for most of the spring and summer of 1942 for the chimney to be replaced.'

Morgen doubted it would have been practical anyway, trying to undertake a big secret like that in the middle of a busy working area.

'It's fair to say that you knew the building programme inside out.'

'I was familiar with it,' she said cautiously.

'Was no temporary facility built during that time?'

'There were endless meetings between the commandant's office, our office and the doctors addressing the problem.'

Morgen thought the matter would have been further complicated by the danger of epidemics and hundreds of dead Russians having to be dug up, making burial impractical on any level.

'It was one thing after another. The reluctant decision reached was to construct open-air burning pits in woods at the far end of the new camp.'

Not what he was looking for.

'And this was the work of your office?'

'As a result of agreement between the different departments.'

'A headache for everyone.'

'Of course.'

'What else do you remember?'

'Well, there was a surveyor's report on the laying of a narrow-gauge track whose work was contracted to us, and the area must have been screened because I remember an order for a considerable amount of brushwood fencing from the landscaping department for the construction office to assemble.'

'And during that time no temporary morgue or crematorium was built.'

'Some wooden barracks were put up near the pits.'

'Like the ones you see in the new camp?'

Schulze looked ashamed. 'Yes. They are converted horse stables.'

'How so?'

'We ran out of bricks and Dr Kammler did a deal with the cavalry, which had a surplus. They could be constructed with a minimum of skilled labour and just a handful of carpenters.'

Morgen thought. Such huts would be insufficiently sturdy to serve as any sort of gassing centre.

'What would these huts have been used for?'

'We weren't told. I presume for holding bodies waiting to be burned.'

To be taken there on the little railway, Morgen supposed. He contemplated the irony of Dr Kammler's vision of a brave new slave world reduced to medieval burning pits.

He found it impossible to say whether Schulze detected any ulterior motive to his questions. She seemed puzzled but unruffled. He suspected she was used to deferral, willing or not, and kept her own counsel. Maybe she was a good liar. It went with the place.

There were no lies because it was all lies. It was the kingdom of lies.

Schulze had seen what was happening to Schlegel too often, people losing themselves, not realising this so-called escape led to collapse. Garrison suicides, of which there were many more than the authorities admitted, were invariably listed as after a short illness.

She ran across him in the canteen where his late breakfast coincided with her early lunch. She noticed his dishevelment and said nothing, tried to talk normally, saying she had been tied up with a panic in the construction office.

'People off sick and extra work.'

He asked what the matter was.

She decided to answer honestly.

'I don't know how much longer I can stay with you. I don't know what I can do because I no longer know what you are doing. You have become so secretive.'

Schlegel mumbled, 'It seems to be a condition of the place.'

'Are you all right?'

'Fine.'

She placed a hand on his arm and said, 'You don't look it.'

'What concern is it of yours?'

He didn't mean to sound bitter. All he wanted was for her to leave her hand there.

'This place drives most people crazy for a while.'

He asked if it had happened to her.

'It happens to everyone,' she said, removing her hand.

Schlegel nodded. The sly side of his brain was already calculating that night's opportunities. Ilse said Canada was like a drug. He wondered if this addiction had become liberated and now floated like a contagion. Life seemed more purposeless than ever. No one had told them the charnel house was part of the bargain.

He asked her how he could meet officers' wives.

'Better avoided,' Schulze said, trying to make a joke of it.

When she saw he was serious she suggested Krick, as he treated most of them.

'He's very fashionable.'

Schlegel wondered about her and Krick as he accompanied her to a telephone booth by the switchboard. She sat and he stood. When she spoke to Krick she sounded flexible and ironic, as if she didn't quite trust him. She explained what she wanted. She put her hand over the receiver – a gesture that delighted him – and asked what it was about. He blew out his cheeks. She answered for him. 'I think he fancies moving up the social ladder.'

She pulled a face and he remained enchanted. Perhaps the answer was to treat life like a drawing-room comedy. He sensed depression lurking.

Krick called straight back to say he could see a woman now. Schlegel overheard him say most of the wives had nothing to do other than fritter their time on social activities.

Schulze said it was a bit of a walk. She was drawing a map when he asked on impulse that she accompany him.

She surprised him by agreeing. She had an errand to run

in that direction. He found himself wanting to tell her about Sybil.

Instead they walked in silence until Schulze said Krick had just been to Switzerland for a psychiatric conference.

'He was a guest speaker, so he got dispensation to travel.'

Schlegel wondered what on earth he lectured on. Counselling those taking part in mass shootings? Applied psychological thinking on how to depersonalise the process by principles of industry? The process of death took much longer than they made out, starting with being shoved into trucks, an unwitting rehearsal for the terminal chamber.

They reached a fork. Schulze said, 'I go this way,' and pointed to his direction. They had walked the last part in silence, not uncomfortable this time, thought Schlegel.

The officer's wife was smartly turned out, her house a smaller version of the commandant's, its fittings distinguished by choice items. She offered proper coffee in a smart drawing room, saying it was cooler than the conservatory. Her husband had been away and managed to bring back some beans. She didn't say what he did.

The coffee was served, tasted and appreciated. The woman had honeyed hair and a pert air. Schlegel could hear servants and children upstairs. She seemed very young. She was informal. 'Call me Kirsten,' she said after he had addressed her properly.

Schlegel made appropriate small talk. The woman struck him as not stupid but so wrapped up in herself it amounted to the same thing. He thought: As if I can talk.

She didn't ask about him. Krick's endorsement seemed enough.

'So handsome,' she sighed.

Schlegel presumed she was a client of the man and wondered what on earth she found to talk about; she gave no sign of any interior life. He watched her cross her legs. She appeared faintly libidinous. Another characteristic of the garrison was the constant possibility of sex. He supposed she was available, in principle. He admired her blouse and asked if it was silk. She wore pearls and a brooch, not jade. He noted plain expensive rings and diamond earrings, tiny studs, so discreet the overall image remained wholesome.

'I am new here, finding my feet,' he said. 'The thing is, perhaps you can advise me. I found this and was wondering what to do with it.'

He produced Tanner's jade brooch and saw the woman's eyes widen. He handed it over and watched her finger it greedily.

'I don't have a fiancée or I would give it to her. Do you think it worth anything?'

She seemed undecided and returned it, saying it was beautiful.

He asked, 'I say, do you have any drink? I know it's early but I have a terrible hangover.'

The woman giggled in a way that said she did too. She offered plum brandy.

'I don't make a habit of it but some of us girls had a get-to last night.'

Schlegel made a point of admiring the furniture. As he suspected, the curtain material was courtesy of Groenke, as were the leather covers used to hold magazines.

'Your shoes look French.'

'Belgian, in fact. Quite a good make. Not couture but not high street. I'm glad you like them.'

Schlegel stuck to surfaces and watched the woman glide expertly. Maybe she was smarter than he was. Anything remotely unpleasant she dismissed, as when he asked if the epidemic had made life difficult.

'We don't want to think about that.'

A genteel burp was followed by the offer of another brandy. The glasses were tiny and crystal. It turned out she had been at the commandant's party.

'I knew I had seen you before. Tall men are quite unusual here, and then there's your ...'.

She stopped in embarrassment. Hair, he finished for her.

A cat came in the room. 'Ah, diddums. This is Tiger.'

Schlegel took the plunge.

'You look a bit sad.'

'Do I? Not really.'

She seemed flattered by the observation.

He made a point of stroking the cat even though he was allergic. Sure enough, he started to sneeze. Sneezing, he realised, while convulsed, was the publicly acceptable version of all those private unsocial noises people made, and strangely intimate for it. The woman stood and brushed his shoulder, saying she would fetch water. She told him to drink out of the glass backwards. He said that was for hiccoughs and she replied, 'It works for this too.'

They laughed. He did as he was told and the fit passed. Their eyes met and he thought: The merciless sun beats down on her as it does on the young man bouncing his football.

She said it was a pity the children were around. The air grew thick with expectation. It had nothing to do with him or her, Schlegel knew. Fegelein said they were puppets controlled by a superior force, an absence of will almost, as they staggered unseeing towards the abyss.

He asked how long she had been there. A couple of years, she said.

'When was the best time?' he asked politely.

Her face brightened. 'Oh, last summer. Such beautiful clothes, the likes of which we had never seen.'

She went coy on him and he had to tease out the details. She wanted to be considered risqué but not easy.

The bare facts were: the officers' wives held daytime fashion parties, wearing borrowed or stolen clothes, with modelling parades, while their husbands were at work.

'I shouldn't be telling you this.'

Schlegel said he had heard jade was all the rage. That was why he was wondering about his brooch.

'Yes. Diamonds became common. Opal and topaz were fashionable but nothing like jade.'

'And now?'

'Hardly anything.'

'Why?'

The woman looked torn. Schlegel urged her to continue.

Eventually she said, 'If you want a price you need to take it to the commandant's wife.'

The answer to his next question: the commandant's wife had a monopoly.

It was a perfect evolution, starting with the girls helping themselves, then the officers' wives barging in. Accessories became an extension of fashion parades, then the whole lot was picked up by the commandant's wife, who decided to make it more commercial.

As she had cut out the other wives this became a source of jealousy.

It only required him to ask if the commandant's wife was popular to know she wasn't.

'I hear she runs a sweatshop in her attic using materials from Canada.'

The woman pulled a face. 'That's not all. She keeps open accounts with different parts of the camp for which no payment is made.'

Schlegel persuaded her to take another brandy and

listened to her run on. All Frau Hoess's daily and entertainment needs, including official functions and the formal parties which were part of the commandant's social calendar, though less so these days, were met by the prisoners' kitchen, via a shopping list given to household staff. Meat came from the slaughterhouse, milk and cheese from the dairy, five litres of milk when her family ration card entitled her to not much more than one. None of it paid for.

'Yugoslavian cigarettes,' said Schlegel.

'For so-called odd jobs.'

'Do you smoke?'

'Only socially.'

'Then take these. I don't.'

He passed her a packet from Frau Hoess's stash.

'Are you sure? I mean, a whole packet.'

She would go to bed with him for half that.

'I'm feeling generous.'

Perhaps thinking she was being bought off, she volunteered how in a desperate effort to claw back some favour the commandant's wife had established a tailoring shop in the garrison and was letting other wives in on a share of the profits.

'How recent?'

'Brand new.'

'Are you part of it?'

'I have my pride.'

She knew it fell somewhere under Erich Groenke's control but not its location. Each prisoner had to produce two outfits a week, everything from everyday to evening wear, which was collected on Saturday afternoons and rewarded with an extra ration at the discretion of the client.

How developed it had all become in its deviant ordinariness; most things could be shown to connect. Schlegel could imagine Frau Hoess, in one of those conversations held outdoors, complaining to Groenke about the huge amount of storage clothes and fabrics took up, and was wondering if he could satisfy her desire for something smaller and more manageable. Jewellery, perhaps. Jade.

'Do you know anything about the seamstress the commandant and his wife fell out over?'

'She can hardly talk.'

'What do you mean?'

'She was screwing that stud from the Bata factory long before he got his soppy crush, so it hardly seems fair to fire the woman to spite him after he found her in the greenhouse with lover boy.'

Schlegel said, 'It has been a most entertaining interlude.'

He kissed her on leaving, their lips sticky with plum brandy. The possibility of meeting later was left floating.

'You know where I live.'

They kissed again, open-mouthed.

Outside the soupy air was so still he could see all the dust particles and midges. The sky was green.

Schlegel found Morgen pacing the office, the room full of smoke. He was told he looked awful. Even Morgen, the least punctual of men, now complained about Schlegel's timekeeping.

Schlegel thought Sybil was perhaps even working for Frau Hoess's new concession, if the quarrel had been patched up. Maybe her firing had been about getting her out of the way of her husband. Schlegel had a lot to tell but Morgen seemed barely interested in Sybil these days.

'What are those?'

Morgen said they were architect's drawings from the garrison archive, which duplicated ones held in Berlin and the construction office.

'They are the closest we have to a history of the place.'

Schlegel wanted to shout there was nothing to solve. The moment would never come when anyone admitted Morgen was right and what was being done must stop. It was too late anyway.

His hangover persisted. The awful woman's plum brandy had only made him feel worse.

Morgen threw down his glasses and sat blinking at Schlegel.

'They have drawings for crematoria going back to 1941. Revision. Revision. Revision. But nothing to say what is really going on. Look. Morgue. Morgue. Morgue. No mention of changing rooms or showers. The only possible clue, 4 May 1942, annotations to plans for the new crematorium. Technical drawing 1311 proposes in-house facilities for melting gold and casting into ingots.'

Morgen growled in exasperation and said Scholz's thesis was in circulation, so the amendment was probably standard to every crematoria, death factory or not.

For a second Schlegel saw through his fog into a vast secret universe, visible only in its surface organisation, involving the continent's rail networks and all the logistics of roundup and deportation. They had witnessed the big Berlin clear-out earlier that year.

Morgen went on, 'The point is there might be a case to answer. We know corners are cut on an epic scale. The security police and doctors have their own unsanctioned programmes. What if the rest is an escalation?'

'Meaning?'

Morgen folded his arms over his stomach. Schlegel noticed he had put on weight. With his eyes closed Morgen said, 'Prophecy and improvisation.'

'Another of your riddles?'

'Quite plain, I think. If you go back over the leadership's speeches you will find what is happening was foretold, which we misread for exaggeration or metaphor. No one expected anything so literal. Our leader didn't walk among us. He left it to us. He saw into our souls and read something very dark in our psyche that sidestepped two thousand years of Christianity. And work it out we did, and the ones that did nothing were party to all those auctions from requisitioned properties in Berlin and the taking from Canada because how it got there is of no consequence to the takers. Look at this place, a temple to improvisation and corruption the result.'

Morgen deduced the garrison was intrinsically different from the death camps, which had replaced the defunct euthanasia campaign.

'No one from that programme is here. So is it a separate enterprise, an anomaly even?'

'Are you saying the killing programme here might not be technically authorised?'

'Through an oversight, perhaps, which means it may – just – not fall into the same extralegal category as the other.'

'You mean prosecutable?'

'Whether anyone will let us live to carry out those prosecutions is quite another matter.'

He stood up.

'Palitsch has agreed to talk. Not so tough now. A crybaby looking to cut a deal. Wirths will too.'

Morgen had to explain about their arrests, with a look that asked what planet was Schlegel on.

'And the security police will let them?' Schlegel asked trying to sound clued-up.

'The security police's motives are unfathomable, but that slippery little chancer Broad is saying they are looking to offload.'

'Why?'

'Probably because Grabner wants to cut a deal, giving us them in exchange for letting him off.'

'Are you all right with that?'

Morgen shrugged. 'We'll get him anyway.'

The cynicism was new. Morgen struck him as being as desperate as the rest of them.

Broad was waiting at the punishment block. They could see Palitsch sitting in the assizes room. He pulled off the difficult trick of appearing craven and cocky, with his easy slouch, knees planted wide, hands dangling. He nodded at Schlegel, his eyes betraying his need.

Broad said, 'A word first.'

He took them to another room and shut the door. He barely had a stripe to his name yet felt he could address Morgen as an equal. Morgen, never one to stand on ceremony, looked as though he wanted to snap a salute out of Broad. Instead he asked for a cigarette when it was garrison etiquette not to, and Morgen had been there long enough to know. Morgen took the cigarette and waited for Broad to light him. Round one to Morgen, Schlegel thought. Broad wouldn't forget. Schlegel considered him one of the more entertaining types but deeply untrustworthy.

Broad told them it was being said the commandant wanted dismissal and a long sentence for Palitsch, preferably with an option of capital punishment for the death of Tanner.

He was like a megaphone when it came to discretion, saying his boss Grabner was playing them off against the commandant.

'Perfect,' said Morgen. 'It's also known as falling between stools.'

Schlegel supposed it was Broad's job to convey his master's wishes even when appearing not to. He admitted Palitsch was being sacrificed, as a peace offering to the commandant, given their mutual loathing.

Broad imitated playing his squeezebox. 'That old vendetta rag.'

Schlegel wondered if Broad knew how much he irritated Morgen.

They joined Palitsch. Broad tried to stay, claiming it was part of the deal, said in his usual lazy way.

Morgen looked about to explode, said nothing, and held the door until Broad ambled out, hands raised in mock surrender.

Schlegel remembered Palitsch and Broad's drunken interruption after the round of executions. It was as well to remind himself.

Palitsch watched cautiously, waiting for them to settle.

Schlegel thought perhaps he wasn't aware of being framed. For all the pretence of a front, the man looked confused and needy, and when he spoke it came out whiny.

He said the racial defilement charge was being pressed by other parties.

Morgen said, 'We were told you wanted to speak to us.'

Palitsch, slow to cotton on, finally pretended he had.

Morgen surprised him by saying, 'Tell us what you know and, depending on how useful I find it, I will limit the number of questions we ask about you.'

Palitsch's expression shifted. Still crafty, thought Schlegel.

'Tell us about the commandant,' said Morgen.

Palitsch looked at them, not sure why he was being asked.

'Did you ever see him exercise any personal cruelty?' Morgen prompted.

'It's not really his style.'

Schlegel mentioned the whipped groom. Palitsch shrugged to say that was routine.

Schlegel supposed the commandant was as capable of killing Tanner as anyone. There was the sexual frustration and his black museum was a temple to morbidity. He could see them all lining up to take turns. Pick a suspect, any suspect, and he could be shown to be capable.

'You would exonerate him then in terms of personal conduct,' Morgen went on.

'The commandant is always very careful about being correct.'

'More facilitator than initiator?'

'It's a desk job, however much he pretends otherwise. He attends meetings, talks on the telephone and keeps regional bureaucrats happy, which I believe he does very well.'

Morgen asked, 'Is that as good as you are giving?'

Palitsch looked nervous for himself. 'Are you talking about the time he made eight hundred prisoners stand in minus-twenty-six degrees until a quarter of them died.'

'For any good reason?'

'A problem with overcrowding was how he put it.'

Palitsch looked pleased by his effort.

Morgen said, 'Tell us about gassing here.'

Schlegel held his breath.

'What gassing?' Palitsch gave a short whinny and added that a sense of humour was essential in the job. He continued to regard them uncertainly.

Morgen said, 'Off the record. Depending on what I am hearing, we could have you placed under our jurisdiction, take you back to Berlin.'

Morgen made a show of dropping the case.

He may as well have fired a starting pistol. Palitsch was

falling over himself to tell, saying it started for the same reason the commandant left eight hundred standing in the freezing cold.

'Numbers.'

'So the problem of overcrowding persists,' Morgen noted drily. 'Was it his initiative rather than Berlin's order?

'Neither, technically.'

The experiment had been thought up by one of the commandant's deputies, after a drunken idiot of a soldier had wandered into a building being fumigated and survived only because he managed to stagger outside and fall down and break his arm.

'You could see him in his splint for weeks afterwards and everyone said, ho-ho, there's the cretin who gassed himself.'

'When was this first experiment?'

'After the Russians came, towards the end of 1941.'

'I need you to be specific about the commandant's role.'

'He made sure he was away that weekend.'

'Why?'

'If it's not Berlin's order, he's not going to leave his fingerprints all over it.'

'Are you saying the commandant deliberately looked the other way?'

'Not how you are thinking. The executions were authorised. The method was new.'

'In what way?'

'It didn't need an engine, like the buses they used elsewhere. Nothing to break down. No pistol to jam.'

'You are talking about the cyanide poison used for standard block fumigations.'

'Yes.'

Morgen held up his hand. 'Just so I am sure. What was the commandant's attitude to this new method?'

'He could see what would happen and was against it.'

'Why?'

'Everyone would take advantage.'

'Tell us about the experiment.'

Palitsch looked uncertain. 'This is not about me?'

'Not if it isn't about racial defilement.'

Palitsch looked uncomfortable.

Morgen said, 'To show I have a sense of humour too.'

Palitsch laughed without conviction. He pointed to the floor.

'The first time they did it downstairs. I got a telephone call on the Sunday because they had fucked up the dose, or whatever you want to call it, and half of them hadn't died, so I had to go into the cells with a gas mask and finish them off with head jobs.'

'What was the purpose of this first test?'

'Backlog. The Gestapo from Kattowice had come and set up court – in this room – and had a big political sorting of hundreds of Russian officers.'

Purge and panic, Schlegel thought. He wondered if the local Gestapo even had Russian speakers.

'How many sorted?' asked Morgen.

'Seven, eight hundred. The doctors chucked in a bunch of sick prisoners as well.'

'Big numbers.'

Palitsch shrugged. 'Bullets are expensive. Shooting takes time and is noisy. Someone came up with a method that was dirt cheap and could get rid of loads in one go. It was only a matter of time before somebody tried it.'

'How long does it take, done properly?'

'Fifteen, twenty minutes.'

'Problem solved then, compared to a day's shooting.'

'You could say.'

Palitsch looked at Schlegel, not knowing what to make of Morgen's almost breezy tone. Morgen folded his hands and closed his eyes.

'So I can picture it properly, this new service was like a standard delousing except the building was sealed and people were left inside.'

Schlegel found it impossible to tell if Morgen was being droll.

'You could say,' Palitsch replied. 'Except you need much less of the stuff, but more than they came up with that first time.'

Palitsch treated it as a perfectly logical and normal extension of existing problems.

'So they had to do it again?' asked Morgen.

'Soon after. The punishment block was considered the wrong location. They had to drag the bodies out afterwards through the camp, not that bodies on carts are an unusual sight, so next time they used the morgue in the old crematorium.'

Morgen looked surprised. 'In the middle of the garrison? So everyone could stand and watch?'

Palitsch grinned. 'Ha-ha, no, not on a Sunday. Day off. The doctors had got interested. This was their turn and they made sure the commandant attended. Stone's throw from home. Back in time for breakfast.'

Palitsch smirked.

'The first test wasn't theirs?'

'Political sorting. I said. Grabner and the Gestapo. But the doctors knew because they chucked in a bunch of sick.'

Palitsch sat quite relaxed now.

'What do you make of the commandant's absence on that first occasion?' Morgen asked.

Palitsch shrugged. 'He didn't have to be there as his deputy was, but he was unhappy well before then.'

'How so?'

'He didn't want the petrochemical plant. He didn't want the Russians. He complained early on Berlin would turn the place into a dump. Women, he didn't like them coming. The rest of us weren't complaining.'

Palitsch gave a hee-haw laugh.

'What did he want from the place?' asked Morgen.

'He didn't want factories. He was a farmer.'

'So he was fairly passive in all of it?'

'Not at first. We worked our arses off to build the place up, no thanks from Berlin, which wanted change in ways the Old Man didn't.'

'You were there from the beginning?'

'Day one.'

'What happened after the second experiment?'

'People suddenly expected us to take care of their problems. Just as the Old Man feared.'

'Berlin?'

'I doubt if Berlin knew.'

On an officers' social occasion someone had bragged about the new method to the proprietor of a network of regional Jewish labour camps and next thing was all those considered unnecessary to his requirements were being offloaded onto the garrison.

Schlegel wondered if gossip really had been responsible. Far from any deciding programme, the whole thing seemed to have been determined by a snowball effect.

Morgen leaned forward. 'Offloaded on a legitimate basis?'

'Not me you should ask, though there was a previous clearing in the summer of '41 under a new heading – unfit for work – which let a team of doctors come and weed out those incapable of recovery.'

'And they were killed here?'

'Sent home.'

'But later these regional camps could offload, knowing the garrison had the facilities for disposal, and you were obliged to get rid of them?'

Palitsch looked amused by the idea. 'Well, they couldn't be put to work, could they? 14f13.'

'14f13?'

'Designated unfit for work. Dead weight. Not wanted. Nowhere to put them.'

'How often did this happen?'

Palitsch looked vague. 'Not much, for the reason you said.'

'Enough to prove it worked.'

Palitsch held up his palms in a strange gesture and said, 'It may not look like it but I respect the dead.'

Morgen asked what happened after the garrison crematorium was closed for repairs.

'You mean, where did they do the business?'

Morgen stared, his loathing of the man no longer disguised, and Palitsch started backtracking, saying they would have to ask the police or the doctors.

Morgen looked surprised. 'I thought you were police.'

'No. I am a roll-call leader. Freezing my balls off in winter while idiots that can't add up try to do a head count, which can leave everyone standing for hours.'

Morgen, astounded, said, 'But you execute for the police.'

'For a per capita fee. It was no skin off my nose to shoot a bunch of riffraff.'

'For a fee?' Morgen repeated blandly. 'With overtime?'

'Double on Sundays.'

Morgen shook his head, as though he had heard everything.

Schlegel asked, 'Do you have any more to add about Ingeborg Tanner?'

Palitsch stared at him with his pale eyes, unbothered.

'She behaved like one of the boys, and some men didn't like that.'

'Any in particular?'

'She gave that creep from Berlin the runaround.'

'Fegelein?'

'Is that his name? The smoothie.'

'And?'

'Showered her with gifts when she couldn't care less.'

'What sort?'

'Jewellery. Silks. Perfume. French knickers.'

'Do you know what he was doing here?'

'Hush-hush. He was always bragging he was on a secret mission.'

'Was she promiscuous?'

'She was more like a man. To her mind she could go with whoever she wanted.'

'Was she popular?'

'A terrific lay, but socially popular didn't matter to her because she couldn't care what anyone thought.'

They left him to it.

He looked at them beseechingly. Morgen waggled his hand and said, 'Interesting.'

Palitsch looked crushed. Not a man in good shape, Schlegel thought. The bully turns craven.

Outside, Morgen fumed.

'This had nothing to do with orders and everything to do with the time-honoured and haphazard tradition of suck it and see.'

None of it was policy.

Schlegel said it nevertheless belonged to a tradition of culling that had gone on for several years.

Morgen looked interested.

Schlegel said it had started in '39 with involuntary euthanasia. Next it was the turn of the Poles. Then in the summer of 1941 huge numbers of civilians were shot in the wake of the military's eastern campaign.

'And last summer it started here,' finished Morgen.

Schlegel had been in the east in 1941. Morgen knew.

There the daily refrain went: Shitty work but someone has to do it. What he most remembered was endless discussion on how to improve things: how to make it more efficient, less stressful, even for the poor bastards they were shooting. Everything was approached in a tough, practical way. Problem-solving. The job. Always how. Never why the fuck are we doing this? They were part of the grand design, left to sort it out for themselves, until the bureaucrats and the rest turned up, by when it was too late.

Only now did Schlegel see a self-regard to the process, vanity even: Look at me being tough about this shit. He was reminded of Haas admiring and flexing his muscles. Krick they had found ambiguous, probably because he reflected that vanity they could not admit.

Compared to the arduous ditch-shooting of a whole village, getting a crowd to undress willingly and step en masse into a chamber could – in terms of efficiency and time management, and herding the action off-stage – be taken for progress.

Schlegel had rarely talked of that time in the east to Morgen, and only did so because he suspected it connected to what was going on now.

Morgen asked, 'What do you think happened here?'

'The same. Moaned and got on with it.'

'And Berlin?'

'If the situation developed because of local gossip Berlin would have got to hear sooner or later.'

Morgen said, 'We're talking about what Schulze called a quiet spring, after which it all went crazy.'

Schlegel thought about how the wife had talked of their fashion parades.

'I expect a situation was being set up to create pressure – overloading being the obvious example – until the loyal apes worked out for themselves what needed to be done.'

Morgen thought. 'If you are right, they may just be legally accountable, *if* no specific order was given.'

Dr Wirths agreed to see him in his research office, next door to the punishment block. Despite charges pending, the commandant had overruled Grabner to allow the doctor to carry on with his work. Morgen said Wirths expected them to side with him, given that the charges were patently false.

Wirths made a show of being his reasonable self, if more testy, to correspond with his portrait of the important man inconvenienced.

He stood and insisted on shaking hands, as though he were in charge.

'Thank you for coming. I want to speak to you so we can clear up this mess.'

His office was on the third floor, looking towards the river. Lower levels would have a view of the prison wall. The doctor's was a tranquil one of sky and trees. Compared to most, the room was deliciously cool.

He invited them to sit.

'They're doing it to discredit me, that must be obvious.'

He wished to address the preposterousness of Grabner's charges.

Morgen said, 'Perhaps you can help us too.'

Wirths looked earnest. 'However I can.'

'It has come to our attention that corruption in the

garrison is the result of another activity, of which we have only recently learned, and to conduct our investigation we need an understanding of the whole picture, if you get my drift.'

Wirths looked less certain. 'I am not sure . . .'

'Your duties extend to that other business.'

Wirths gripped the arms of his chair. 'It is a confidential matter.'

'Then on whose authority are you acting?'

Wirths cast about uncertainly. This was not what he expected.

'It's not straightforward. I don't get instructions.'

'Then tell us how it works.'

'When I came I had no idea of what I would find – a complete absence of meaningful facilities that reduced sick prisoners to defecating in the tins they ate from. One said it was impossible to know what real hunger is until you begin to eye another up in terms of edibility. Can you imagine! In this day and age, like we are in cannibal Africa! I voiced my scruples to the commandant, including my misgivings about what you call the other business, which I consider against my Hippocratic oath. The commandant pointed out the hardness of observing orders without precedence and the need to execute them without prejudice.'

'Orders?'

Wirths faltered. 'What else would they be?'

Morgen said, 'So you represent the arrival of the plausible man, with, if not a conscience, then at least the will to be conscientious.'

Schlegel was surprised by Morgen's sneer.

Wirths massaged his temples. 'I have spoken of what I found. With no cure on offer and conditions so dreadful, wholesale clear-outs were considered the only option. I must stress this was before my time.'

'You inherited the situation,' said Morgen dryly.

Wirths said nothing.

'Spell out for us what happened to these prisoners, before your time?'

It wasn't sarcasm, quite. The flippancy shown to Palitsch was replaced by a harder, sardonic tone that paid scant respect to the doctor's opinion of himself.

'They were taken away . . .' Wirths eventually offered.

'And?'

Wirths stared, reluctant or unable to go on.

Morgen stared back. 'Yes, before your time. I am asking what happened.'

'Gassed.' The sibilance was exaggerated by his hushed delivery.

'Or dispatched by lethal injection,' Morgen added, sounding unnaturally loud.

He yawned ostentatiously, a sign for Schlegel to take over.

'Tell us about Ingeborg Tanner,' Schlegel said.

Wirths appeared thrown by her name.

'Did you know or know of her when she was alive?'

'I told you she came to my attention for medical reasons.'

'Are you familiar with the so-called action parties?'

'Now what are you talking about?'

'Orgies, more or less,' said Morgen.

Wirths looked desperate. 'What are you here to prove? I ask for your help, now you question me about orgies. I am a married man.'

'Everyone is a long way from home. Tanner was murdered. The fact that you removed and had the body destroyed before autopsy . . .'

Wirths slapped the table with the flat of his hand.

'Enough! We are not here to talk about this. Of course

I had nothing to do with this woman or her death. What I will show you are doctors who get away with murder.'

Morgen said, 'Can we get to the point?'

'This is the point.'

'You select incomers for death.'

Wirths failed to suppress his anger. 'Are you acting as your own judge now?'

'I merely said I need to know what is really going on so I can draw my conclusions.'

'Orders without precedent and the need to execute them without prejudice, the commandant said.'

'But not without scruple,' said Morgen, not withholding his sarcasm.

Wirths looked to Schlegel to say he was completely misunderstood.

Morgen asked to whom Wirths answered and whether he acted in consultation.

The doctor shook his head. 'You have no idea. My brief was to combat the typhus. Everything followed from that. My superiors in Berlin couldn't care. I was acting not on their instructions but my interpretation of a secret general directive addressed to garrison doctors.'

'Secret directive?' asked Morgen.

'Not what you think. One that reinterpreted the role of the senior doctor as actively working towards the improvement of the health of the camp.'

He threw up his hands to show he acted with only the best motives. He ploughed on, long-winded, apologising, repeating himself, saying how difficult it was for outsiders to understand. A further bulletin issued by the Reichsführer-SS confirmed the task of the garrison doctor was to improve working conditions and control the mortality rate.

'Which I did. Categorically. Even that dangerous idiot Grabner says so.'

They crossed a line when Morgen said, 'Tell us about ramp selections.'

Schlegel suspected Wirths wished to unburden, and Morgen had guessed. Wirths sat for a long time, his hands hidden between his knees, looking utterly deflated.

'It was a complete mess, you have no idea.'

Ramp selection from the start had been troubled by inconsistency, rivalry and contention.

'Did you know about them before you came?' asked Morgen.

'Of course not. I knew nothing.'

'No preparation or instruction?'

'None!'

'Chucked in at the deep end?'

'There weren't enough hours in the day to do the job in hand.'

'Of course. Curing the epidemic. How would you define ramp selection?'

'Choosing newcomers able to work.'

'So not mothers, children or the elderly.'

'More children are being taken now, as messengers,' Wirths said, on the defensive.

'I expect they are pleased about that,' said Morgen, deadpan. 'Would you say those selected for work are better off than those that aren't?'

Wirths looked at Schlegel and asked, 'How am I supposed to answer?'

Morgen went on. 'I expect we are talking of circles of hell, whichever. Where are these newcomers from?'

'All over.'

'By train?'

Again Wirths looked at Schlegel.

Morgen said, 'I don't understand why they can't just send you workers, as they do to other labour camps, do you see what I mean?'

'I am not privy to that information.'

'So ramp selection, was it something you chanced upon . . . and decided to reform?'

'Your tone is not helpful.'

'I am having trouble working my way around this.'

Wirths adopted a schoolmasterly manner. 'There is an ideology but on a practical level the considerations are quite different. After the decision to send transportations for labour in the east we were faced with the problem of those unable to work. We couldn't send them back. We couldn't send them on. It was impossible to keep them, the camp being too small despite its size. Chronic overcrowding made it a breeding ground for disease. The quarantine zones were at breaking point. It was a humanitarian crisis.'

Morgen laughed in the doctor's face. 'That's one way of describing it.'

Wirths protested. 'We would have to have protected these incomers against disease, which was why I was sent here in the first place. We lacked effective remedies as it was. It was a nightmare. It still is.'

Morgen asked, 'And you assumed responsibility for ramp selection?'

Wirths' defensiveness was making him sound pompous. 'Any selection is about fitness for work, and must be conducted on medical grounds alone, by qualified doctors. That much *is* directed by Berlin.'

Schlegel supposed it true. From the beginning, sanctioned killing had sought medical endorsement.

Schlegel wondered if Wirths was a sympathy seeker,

turning everything into the tragedy of the perpetrator faced with an impossible task.

Wirths' vocabulary was always towards reason and consideration. Humanely. Orderly.

Schlegel thought back to the night at the station and wondered whether Wirths saw himself as a man doing the job on his own terms, properly and with decency.

'Above all for the sake of those not selected,' Wirths finished.

'Those not selected,' repeated Morgen.

'Do you have any better ideas?' snapped Wirths.

Morgen leaned back, satisfied to have got a rise.

'Shall we liken the method to modern slaughterhouse practices, cool and technical as opposed to hot-blooded and arbitrary. You wouldn't want a riot on your hands.'

Schlegel watched the artery pulse in Wirths' temple.

'It was like an Arabian souk. Doctors were being excluded from supervision and selections degenerated into free-for-alls, not made easier by staff strolling down to see what they could salvage. A carnival atmosphere developed, with many drunk. They called it the big welcome.'

Wirths dry-washed his hands in disgust. Even Morgen seemed taken aback by the callousness of the spectacle.

'How was your complaint met by the commandant?'

'He argued more transports were being sent than they could handle. Rival departments were promised numbers by Berlin they didn't get, so they took to going down and recruiting their own workers. The commandant thought it best – what he called soft selection – with everyone getting a chance to take their pick.'

Wirths worked himself into a frenzy of righteousness. He banged the table again. 'But it was not by the book!'

'Is that still the case?'

'The crisis has passed but that didn't excuse poor organisation, overcrowding in quarantine sections, insufficient supplies and troops drinking on the job.' Wirths trailed off.

'Insufficient supplies of what?'

'Of the fumigant.'

They watched him struggle to decide how much to tell.

Morgen prompted. 'No one is taking notes.'

'It was a nightmare,' Wirths said, offering his favourite preface. 'Tons of the stuff was needed to combat the epidemic, but the commandant decided not to inform Berlin, so officially there was no epidemic.'

'Making it hard to justify the size of the order,' said Morgen. 'When was this?'

'July last year.'

'1942. And you came?'

'At the end of August.'

'How much fumigant is needed for gassing?'

'Almost nothing. Much less than for a block.'

Palitsch had told them the same. Schlegel thought: Floor cleaner for lethal injections, a fumigant capable of eliminating thousands; only Germans could turn a death programme into an extension of domestic science, using forms of household cleaning, leaving everything spick and span.

'Tell me again, to be quite clear,' Morgen went on. 'Any order for the fumigant has to be approved and supplied by Berlin.'

'Correct.'

'And is there a separate order for the fumigant when it is used for the other business?'

'There is only one general order.'

'So Berlin approved the order, not knowing it was to combat an epidemic that officially didn't exist, and the other business.'

'As far as I know.'

'One general order,' Morgen repeated.

Schlegel knew Morgen's methods well enough by then – the slow circling before the swoop.

'Yes,' said Wirths, looking uncomfortable.

'Then on whose authority are you making your selections?' Morgen asked innocently.

Wirths gestured, incapable of speech.

'It looks to me as though everyone makes up the rules as they go along.'

'Not at all!'

'If you weren't telling Berlin about the epidemic, what else weren't you telling?'

Wirths protested. 'They knew about it by the time they sent me. It's why I came! The other business . . .' He trailed off.

'There are places dedicated to similar ends where there is a chain of command, and the situation there is extralegal and there is nothing I can do, but here . . .'

Wirths stammered. 'I assure you . . .'

He rallied and belatedly asked if they were cleared to discuss such matters.

Morgen said, 'I have talked of it with a man whose name is almost identical to yours. Wirth. Do you know him, Dr Wirths?'

'No.'

'He answers to the Chancellery. Your near namesake told me in no uncertain terms. I saw his payslips. I am bound to ask whether you know him or answer yourself to the Chancellery?'

'No.'

'If you are not part of that machine, to which do you belong?'

Wirths again was lost for words.

Morgen leaned forward. 'Yet you and your near namesake seem to be in the same business.'

They watched Wirths squirm, a man dishonoured by any question of his integrity.

Morgen went on. 'I have to ask whether you, as a man with his hands on the controls of what we must call the death machine, is in fact authorised or whether you are a more sophisticated version of the rogue doctors you complain about.'

Wirths turned to Schlegel. 'The man is mad! No one could be more torn or conscientious about his duties than I. You have seen. I am dedicated to cure. I am on the side of life! I thought you were for us.'

'Which "us" is this?' asked Morgen.

'Reform. Getting rid of the thugs and boneheads who have been here too long and hinder progress.'

'Death selection?' asked Morgen quietly.

Wirths wailed again. Morgen asked how he accounted for himself.

Wirths eventually said, 'One holds only so many cards. It took me weeks if not months to get to the bottom of corruption in my own department.'

'We are not talking about that.'

Wirths asked why Morgen had got it in for him. Morgen said nothing. Schlegel watched a slow build of cloud on the horizon. Most of the time the sky had been a pitiless blue.

Morgen finally said, 'I agree it is difficult. Go on.'

Wirths quietened down and apologised, stressing the onerousness of his task and the inappropriateness of what he had found – no consistency, a shambles of improvisation.

'Selection must be regarded as an extension of the medical authority insisted on from the start.'

'The start?' queried Morgen.

'When the garrison took on the responsibility of removing those unfit for work it was supervised by medical staff. "Let the syringe remain in the hand of the physician." I quote. If anyone must be killed then a doctor has to witness.'

Morgen said, 'And that allowed you to put a medical gloss on selections because doctors had to be consulted on any decision regarding the ability to work.'

Wirths agreed. 'It made selections part of my medical duty to improve working conditions.'

Schlegel thought: And gave you control. It was extraordinary how logic could be applied to the most twisted situations. He wasn't sufficiently indoctrinated to believe in racial hygiene but listening to Wirths he could no longer be sure. Was it the first step towards a brave new world where such housekeeping was taken for granted? Crookedness of life would be removed to be replaced by serene pastures dedicated to health, pleasure and efficiency.

Wirths asked if they would help refute Grabner's charges.

Morgen said, 'Grabner will no doubt claim Berlin ceded him responsibility to deal with the situation as he saw fit, but he may find no one in Berlin willing to come forward. So may you find yourself exposed alone for having assumed this dreadful responsibility.'

They left Wirths crushed and walked out in silence. Schlegel wondered if the doctor's selective vision extended to acknowledging the existence of the bathhouse morgue in his basement.

They continued through the camp without talking. Morgen barked at the guard to let them through. The guard jumped to and didn't ask to see their passes.

Morgen eventually said, 'Wirths, like the rest of them, suffers from the disease of logic known as paranoia, only in a more rarefied form. His response to the untenable is to select like mad – divide up, pick sides, choose, as though this endless selection and relentless organisation can become a thing in itself.'

Schlegel took to walking past the leather factory in the hope of spotting Sybil.

Everything had begun to look older as the unseasonably hot weather persisted. Schlegel saw in people's faces they were starting to think of winter and in the shortening evenings he watched families with punnets going to pick the last of the berries.

That night a very drunk man jumped out of the bushes at him, laughing. Without thinking, Schlegel clubbed him with his fist. The drunk fell to the ground, still laughing. It didn't seem to be Schlegel's foot kicking the man, seeking out his balls, making him scream. Boredom and terror fused in a moment of electrifying clarity as he was shown the nature of the beast within.

He didn't expect the oily coagulation of exultation and disgust that followed, or how the giddiness of the moment contained within it the collapse into demoralisation. He wasn't even drunk, yet his thinking afterwards had all the bursts of clarity and incoherence he associated with drinking. He didn't need a shrink to tell him it was a projection of himself he had been kicking.

The same logic seemed to apply to what he did next. The tannery was shut. There was no obvious vantage point other than a tree on a forlorn triangle of grass, low branched and easy to climb. A broad fork provided a passable seat. He sat in the last of the light, watching the green surroundings darken and the purple sky make an incomplete jigsaw of the leaves.

He slept and woke stiff. A day of resolve, he told himself. No more backsliding.

A figure approached in the distance. That figure became a woman. He saw only her silhouette, backlit, slender, emerging out of the sun rising over the rooftops. Her walk was familiar. She slowed outside the tannery and slipped inside.

He scrambled down and hurried to the door but she had locked it and when he banged no one came.

Haas was next to be drawn into Morgen's net. They saw him in his office. Schlegel wondered how many he had dispatched already that day. The curtain to the annex was drawn.

Haas remained endlessly pleased with himself, with the deliberate lack of imagination and humour that seemed to be the indicator of dangerous men.

'Tell us about Bock the dentist,' said Morgen.

Haas folded his arms in a practised way that showed his muscles. He blamed Grabner. Morgen appeared delighted by the answer.

Haas could name the orderly that had administered the injection.

Morgen said, 'It seems to be a very well-trodden corridor between the security police and the doctors.'

He made a point of repeating whatever Haas said, giving it the formality of a statement, trying not to sound incredulous.

'You say there was an attempt to poison Bock in the cells. He complained of being ill and was making such a fuss that Grabner was telephoned. You then overheard the call come through saying to put Bock out of his misery.'

Schlegel thought: For Morgen all that matters is Haas saying it is true.

Haas was equally willing to go on record as having seen Dr Wirths remove morphine from the pharmacy.

'Wirths blames Grabner for that.'

'I say Dr Wirths. He's by no means the only one.'

'What else about Wirths?' asked Morgen.

'Are we talking inhumane experiments?'

'His cancer research?' Morgen sounded surprised.

'That's what he calls it. His brother runs a clinic in Berlin, which is all about subsidies and patents and grants and nothing about results.'

Tubo-ovarian abscesses, Schlegel remembered.

Haas nodded. 'The test is supposed to detect uterine cancer in its earliest stages. In questionable cases the cervix is removed and sent to the brother's clinic where the tissue is studied.'

'Surgically removed?' asked Morgen.

'The test is unreliable, but Wirths and his brother hold the patent for the instrument, and the operation is unnecessary. A biopsy would suffice and post-operative conditions are not conducive to recovery.'

'And the women are left sterile?' Morgen asked.

'Most are Jews.'

Haas sat back, even more pleased with himself.

'Anything else you care to tell us about the good doctor?' asked Morgen, still assessing what they had just been told.

'He thinks nothing of killing prisoners if it is in his medical interests.'

'Are we still talking about female experiments?'

'That's block ten. There's a forbidden ward upstairs here where Wirths keeps patients who are injected with typhus, and various remedies tried.'

'Yes, yes,' said Morgen. 'I came across this in Buchenwald. In among all the orgies and drinking binges' – he shot

Schlegel a look – 'there was a way of getting rid of tricky prisoners by referring them for a similar experiment. In earmarked cases a placebo was administered, giving the patient less chance of recovery. But we must distinguish between legitimate experiment, pseudo-science and downright cruelty. What is your personal assessment of Dr Wirths?'

'A man of manners but a real sadist of the worst kind.'

They moved on to Fegelein.

'He has been coming here quite a lot,' said Morgen. 'Do you know why?'

'Shopping trips, it was said.'

'Canada?'

'Ostensibly to assess and report on the situation. A lot of that went on, as an excuse to come down from Berlin and stuff their pockets. Plus he had the pick of the girls, being something of a star.'

Haas had a shameless instinct for giving Morgen what he wanted.

Fegelein had threatened and abused Tanner. Fegelein liked hurting and Tanner had told Haas it was why she stopped seeing him.

'Did Tanner tell you about Fegelein running down a woman in a car?'

From the calculation in Haas's eyes, Schlegel suspected he hadn't, but it took him no time to say, 'She was too scared to talk about it, except to say it happened and Fegelein hushed it up.'

Schlegel had to admit the man was very good. When they had last talked Haas hadn't even known Fegelein's name.

Morgen said, 'We may need a sworn statement.'

'Happy to oblige.'

Once they had left the building, Schlegel said, 'You can't do this.'

'The law won't uphold us, so we apply our own law.'

You look almost as full of yourself as Haas, Schlegel thought, but decided not to say it.

It was a half-day in the garrison. Schlegel spent the afternoon drinking with the lorry drivers at the beer stall. Joshing, pointless conversations, spent either at cross-purposes or on parallel tracks, always amiable, with bottles raised in toast. Four, five and six litres later drivers on overtime disappeared into their cabs and roared off, to be replaced by others. Schlegel sat saying little. He was rarely bothered and stayed, aware of his weight settled on the stool. The drivers sprawled on benches at tables with little straw roofs.

As it got dark Schlegel went and sat back in the tree. His wait was soon rewarded by a woman approaching from the same way as before. She paused before the door to the leather factory, seemed about to go in then changed her mind and walked on.

By the time he scrambled down he had lost her between streetlights. His last sighting was by the high wall of the slaughterhouse. When he got there she was gone.

He was ashamed of himself. He had failed, and what would she think anyway, being accosted by a drunk.

He returned on instinct to the party house where he had seen Sepp and Böhner and became deliberately horribly drunk. He was getting a persecution complex, thinking he was being followed everywhere. He behaved obnoxiously. He tried to pick a fight and was laughed at. He was told by a couple of thugs in charge to go home and sleep it off.

His first thought was where could he find another party. He took a path across a field. The area was full of such short cuts. He didn't even have time to see it coming when they jumped him. A whirl of shadows he thought were trees. The pain shooting up his shin he thought was him tripping over. Not until he saw red after being punched in the jaw did he work it out. More than two men, maybe three, perhaps even four. He knew he must look pathetic, cowered, arms raised, not because he was afraid, which he was, but because he didn't know how to respond to the battering. He thought it might be better that he was half-cut. He was in no condition to defend himself, not that he was any good at that sort of thing, and he went down easily, in a slurry of panic and resignation. The moment had been a long time coming. The men didn't talk, just grunted. Schlegel was dragged away from the path, into bushes. Brambles scratched his face. He wanted to say he had nothing worth stealing but already his mouth was too swollen and he lay listening to his screams as he had the shit kicked out of him. He fancied one of the men was the big lad Böhner, and, why he didn't know, that another was Broad. The pain was excruciating and so systematic it had to be more than random drunken violence. He was being taught a lesson. He was being made an example of. His head was swelling to the size of a melon. He grew more afraid before passing out, thinking they might not stop before they killed him, so his beaten and deformed corpse could be served as an example to Morgen, and Morgen would give his body that look of mild disappointment which he seemed to reserve only for him. He heard bone snap, followed by a last almighty kick to the head, taking him down into the black of the commandant's tunnel.

Schlegel came to in the garrison hospital in a room to which no one came. Outside was night.

His chest was strapped. The little finger of his left hand

was in a splint. It was swollen and throbbed badly. One eye he could barely see out of. He lay in a haze of painkillers.

At last a nurse came and told him he had concussion and had been given a tetanus shot.

By day the view outside was a sullen grey. He itemised his ailments, as opposed to his injuries: pain in the joints, aching muscles, backache, headache, a dry cough. The cough became a marker of time and its persistence started to drive him crazy. Had Dr Wirths come calling? Had he been injected? Had the purpose of the beating been to put him in hospital so he could be taken care of? Why not just kick him to death?

Pohl might not risk removing Morgen but make sure he got the message by beating an associate.

Stretches of sedated exhaustion left him sad for Ingeborg Tanner, pondering the grotesqueness of that kingdom of death and their absurd investigation. He doubted they would ever find out who killed her. Morgen, taxed by his own sense of dishonour, was now left in the impossible position of trying to interpret the law. It was like watching a child with a bucket against a tidal wave.

Schlegel supposed they had fallen into a pit of suffering where the mythical and primitive ruled, with old fault lines exposed, Pandora's boxes opened, in which lay the shock of institutional familiarity, an unsettling combination of the uncanny and the homely – street signs, block numbers, noticeboards, recreation, work schedules, food, drink, music, fucking, stimulants, wrought-iron mottos, scratchings on walls, flowerbeds, lawn sprinklers, the camp orchestra sending gangs off to work, the willed pretence of ordinariness, sentimentality even, in the artless numerals painted on the lanterns that hung outside each barracks' door, as though vernacular detail might persuade everyone what they were doing was either useful or normal. The familiar was what they should fear most, that was the only lesson to be drawn. The gap between the ordinary and unfathomable would always be accommodated, as history showed.

He was surprised by Schulze, hovering in his open doorway, hand raised in an imitation of knocking. She looked smart in the suit she had been wearing on the train.

'How did you know I was here?'

She didn't answer and said, 'You haven't been allowed visitors until now.'

She appeared preoccupied.

Schlegel had no interest in talking about himself and wanted to ask about her. He had read occasionally in old books about people revealing their true feelings. He didn't know what his were, beyond that lather of anxiety which marked the months and days. Perhaps life was not a progression, as they had been promised, but more chaotic and random.

Schlegel suspected Schulze, like him, didn't know where to start. They exchanged banalities. Yes, he was all right. It was his fault; he should have been more careful. Had Morgen said anything?

Schulze said, 'He pretends not to be but he is quite fond of you.'

He deflected the remark rather than accept it, losing the moment, thinking of the garrison wife he had met through Krick, and how she skated so effortlessly over things. Perhaps the great achievement of the huge social experiment they were embarked on would be the elimination of all inner life and uncertainty through a process of externalisation.

He said without thinking, 'I was in the east with Krick.'

'He said you weren't sure if he had recognised you.'

'Anti-partisan duties. Do you know what they are?'

'I can guess.'

Following that glancing encounter with Krick two years ago, he was now talking to the woman he slept with. He embarrassed himself by blushing, even more when he saw her notice. He sniffed and coughed until he wept. Acute self-consciousness swamped him as Schulze consoled him. All he could think of was the awkwardness of afterwards. Hearing footsteps in the corridor he hurriedly extricated himself. A nurse entered and told Schulze she had to leave because the patient needed to rest.

Morgen was the worst kind of hospital visitor, desperate to get out as soon as he sat down. Schlegel had apparently crawled to a road and been found there after collapsing. The doctors had reported the case to the security police.

'And sure enough, Broad is telling everyone.'

'What's his story?'

'They say you were getting out of order and asking for trouble. You beat up a man the other day, who reported it.'

There was nothing Schlegel could say to that.

Morgen lit up in defiance of the no-smoking sign and blew out of the window. He said dealing with the miasma of corruption was like trying to shovel liquid shit. Schlegel suspected Morgen felt let down by him becoming unrighteously corrupt, compared to Morgen's righteous corruption.

'We could stay months and get no further. How long are you in here for?'

'They haven't said.'

'Well, hurry up, I need you back. I fear we are running

out of time. The witness to the hit-and-run case has identified Fegelein.'

'Reliable?'

'A town councillor; don't know if that makes him reliable.
Fussy, pince-nez and wearing a Homburg in this weather. A
complainer too. Bangs on about how difficult the garrison
makes life for everyone in town. He heard rather than saw
the accident, walking his dog before work. The car raced
round the bend. The man memorised the number plate but
forgot half of it in the shock of finding the woman when he
had been expecting another car.'

He had only glimpsed the driver because the man was
accelerating and a woman was in the passenger seat, but his
description of her placed Tanner firmly in the car, which by
default put Fegelein at the wheel.

'Fegelein is apparently on his way here now.'

Schlegel knew Morgen hated being fed lines, so waited
to be told.

'He's mad at me because the old traffic cop has been on
his case, and he told him he was going to come down and
sort us all out. So I will surprise him with the councillor,
who has agreed to confirm if Fegelein was the driver.'

Schlegel thought: Bribed probably. They weren't living in
times when anyone stood up for anything.

Morgen stubbed out his cigarette in a pot plant. Although
the man was obviously itching to be gone, Schlegel suspected more was to come.

'I spoke to the commandant. He said after what had
happened to you he can no longer vouch for us.'

'Had he in the first place?'

Morgen shrugged. 'As I said, time is running out. I
told the commandant I have enough verbal evidence of
Grabner's illegal acquisitions and unauthorised killings.

The commandant got nervous at that and pointed out Grabner took his orders from security headquarters in Berlin. I told him I had investigated and could find nobody who would admit that these initiative killings had been condoned.'

'Did you?'

'Of course not, but they're not going to say anything else.'

The commandant, nervous of being implicated in Grabner's killing machine, told Morgen he would rather that was not exposed and to press the corruption charge.

'I said we couldn't trust the security police to conduct a proper search and needed outside help.'

'From?' asked Schlegel.

'Kattowice Gestapo. Not ideal, but . . .'

Schlegel had feared the answer. It would be a hornets' nest.

Morgen went on. 'The commandant is pushing for us to make a move. He told us to search Palitsch's house while we are at it, and he would rather it were our charge rather than Grabner's against Dr Wirths.'

Morgen's words hung heavy and meaningless. The room felt like the air was being sucked out of it. Irritated by his dry cough, Schlegel took in what Morgen was saying in a daze. Outside the window, aspens, leaves crisped by the sun, that infernal chemical light.

After Morgen was gone, Schlegel got up shakily and sat in a chair, too weak to do anything other than stare out of the window. Occasionally he dozed, his head snapping back in prelude to another bout of that wretched cough, and panic flooded back.

Fegelein passed down in the street, carrying a grip, like he had just arrived. He happened to look up, grinned at Schlegel and drew a bead with his pistol finger, dropping his thumb in imitation of the hammer, and blew on his finger like a crack shot.

Morgen was eating alone when Fegelein marched in to ask if he was responsible for a drunk policeman telephoning him about some traffic offence. His manner suggested the matter was no more annoying than a fly waiting to be swatted.

Fegelein was wearing a fancy concocted uniform. Morgen asked if he had designed it himself. Fegelein said it was a modification of his cavalry one.

'A staff version, approved by Heini. As a matter of fact, I have just had it made. Tailors here are much better than any-thing you find in Berlin now, apart from the ones Goebbels uses, but he monopolises them.'

One of Fegelein's assumptions was a sense of false equal-ity, as if they could both afford the same. Morgen wondered if Fegelein's new uniform was the work of Frau Hoess's sweatshop.

'Perhaps you could introduce me. I am a suit short. Moths got the last one.'

'Are you serious?' asked Fegelein.

'About the suit or the traffic accident?'

'Ha-ha. Tailoring every time.' He looked at his watch. 'Tell you what, come now. They're doing adjustments on another. They do evening fittings for the busy soldier and you need smartening up. Very reasonable rates. In fact, you decide what to pay, depending on what you think it's worth. I tip lavishly compared to some.'

Morgen said, 'I am talking about an accident in which a woman was left to die, and the woman travelling with you has also since been killed.'

Fegelein looked unruffled. 'Come on, man, there's a war on. Isn't this all a bit old hat? Admit you're a sore loser.'

He touched Morgen lightly in a gesture of commiseration.

Morgen removed his arm, noticed the man's irritation at the withdrawal, and said, 'As you are here perhaps you could find time to answer our questions.'

'With that drunken idiot I spoke to on the phone?' Fegelein paused, smooth again. 'Why not? Always a pleasure to run rings round you. Shall we say here, tomorrow morning at ten? Come now. Let's get you fitted up.'

Morgen wondered why the man was keeping him so close. Perhaps to distract, the way conmen and pickpockets did, with feints and diversions to deceive the eye.

'How long are you here?' asked Morgen as they walked out.

'Depends.'

'For horses?'

Fegelein leaned in. 'Confidential.'

One thing about Fegelein was he wanted you to know.

'Medical,' he eventually said.

'You look fit enough,' said Morgen insincerely. The man was liverish, with the beginnings of a jowl.

'Not my health,' said Fegelein.

'Whose?'

'Can't say.'

Morgen knew Fegelein was the type to share secrets to make himself appear more important and his indiscretion was that of one blessed with the ability to talk his way out of anything.

Morgen continued to engage him in the hope he might give something away. Fegelein talked about the disappointment of the stamp sale.

'Jews have been putting out a load of fakes.'

He produced a jade cigarette holder and took his time fixing a cigarette, waiting for Morgen to admire. This duly done, Morgen asked where he had got it.

'Some girl gave it to me.'

'That wouldn't be Tanner?'

Fegelein laughed. 'No, it wouldn't be, as a matter of fact. God, you are so predictable.'

They carried on. Fegelein was due to stay a couple of days and made sure Morgen knew he wasn't taking anything so vulgar as the train but flying in *Immelmann II*. Morgen had no idea what he was talking about.

Fegelein walked with the air of a man expecting to be noticed. When he thought he wasn't being observed, he assumed a spoiled, sulky expression. If he found the tables turned, Morgen was sure the man would squeal like a baby.

'*Immelmann II?*' Morgen prompted.

Part of the Führer's private fleet, said Fegelein, smug.

As Schlegel turned in bed to try and settle he was aware of Frau Hoess standing like Schulze, with her hand up to knock on an invisible door, the difference being the gesture was charming when performed by Schulze.

'Angel of mercy,' she cooed. 'Can I come in?'

What struck him immediately was the woman's glazed eyes, high on something that made her skittish. He hadn't seen her since her sexual transport and knew she was aware of that.

Beyond any superficial concern for his welfare, he was sure she was there to nullify any advantage he held concerning her compromise.

She didn't know he had the letter from Pohl.

She drew up a chair by the bed, held a perfunctory discussion about his health, then asked, 'How do we sort out this mess?'

'What mess?'

'Be frank. Tell me what you know.'

He saw no point in prevarication. 'There is an illicit trade in jade that starts here and ends up Berlin. It involves senior figures.'

The woman appeared quite unbothered.

'Does this have anything to do with Ingeborg Tanner?'

'She had a piece of jade given her by a senior Berlin official.'

'You mean Hermann Fegelein. Where does my husband stand? Are you protecting him along the lines discussed?'

Again Schlegel saw no reason for evasion. 'There is a persecution campaign against him. I have been told you are behind it.'

It wasn't so much of a wild guess. The woman was obviously a terrific schemer and admitted she was terrified her husband was about to lose his job. But if diagnosed as sick with nervous exhaustion everything would be suspended. She had already told Schlegel as much. It was really all about *her* not leaving. She had her own little empire, the likes of which she was unlikely to have again.

She appeared quite unperturbed by the accusation. 'Only to protect him, you must understand that. Is that all?'

'And the seamstress you dismissed is back working for you.'

Again the remark met with no surprise. She said lightly, 'Staff these days. She by comparison is exceptional and the problem has been worked through. I told you my husband did not have her shot.'

'Does your husband know she is back?'

'Of course not. His judgement is not of the best at the moment. Now, come on, I need your help.'

She surprised him by taking his hand, in an apparently conciliatory gesture, held it for a moment, said it was cold, rubbed it to get the circulation flowing and guided it under her skirt, saying that would warm it up. He felt flesh above the garter and suspected she wasn't wearing underwear. Her thighs gripped, making it impossible to retract. Her eyes went vacant and her mouth slack as she recited in an automatic voice, 'I wonder sometimes if I am not a split personality. On the public side the woman of the world, the prudent, reserved hostess, and on the other, a hitherto unexpected side.' She repositioned his hand higher. 'A woman of insane passion, a wild romantic, hysterical in body, nymphomaniac in soul; it's all highly improbable.'

Schlegel watched detached, thinking of the garrison's subterranean riverine sexuality, and crossing the Styx into Hades and the female sexual spirits of folklore that came and possessed the male.

She gently extracted his hand but continued to hold it.

'You are wrong about the jade. But the matter is delicate.'

'It involves both your husband's boss, Pohl, and Fegelein.'

'It involves Fegelein only in that he is keen to buy his way in, on behalf of his boss.'

'Himmler?'

'No, in the Chancellery. Bormann.'

'Is that why Bormann is keen to protect your husband? Fegelein warned us not to touch him.'

'Bormann and my husband go back to the very beginning.'

'Then why can't he be part of what you are talking about?'

'Politics, what else?'

'Is this your special project?'

Frau Hoess sighed. 'Not so special if everyone is talking about it.'

'Is the project the mine?'

It seemed worth the hunch.

She took a long time to answer. 'Here in the garrison, three of us knew about the Jordansmuhl operation. I did.

My husband, though not the details. And Erich Groenke, who had to organise the workforce and transportation, but I doubt very much that he blabbed to Fegelein because Erich knows on which side his bread is buttered.'

'On both sides, from what I have seen.'

Frau Hoess trilled her rehearsed laugh.

'Why can't Bormann be part of it?'

'If Heinrich even suspected Bormann knew he would probably close down the whole operation. You can see the trouble Fegelein, as much as I love him, has got us into.'

'How did Fegelein find out? Through Tanner?'

'She was just some bit of fluff.' Frau Hoess considered. 'Unless she heard something. Except it was all highly confidential.'

'Why would she hear something?'

Frau Hoess considered. 'You may be right. Tanner worked in transportation. She might have known about the lorries and told Fegelein.'

'Enough to get her killed?'

As with all narratives to do with the secret life of the garrison, there were gaps, omissions, a sense of stories deliberately badly told. The questions Schlegel meant to ask slithered away. He sensed Frau Hoess was proud of her authorship, whatever it was, and the best approach was to be direct.

'What is Jordansmuhl?'

'A jade mine.'

'Where?'

'Near Breslau, a few hours away.'

He presumed it was true, however bizarre and far-fetched. Jade he associated with the Far East. Frau Hoess remained in her semi-trancelike state and Schlegel wondered what made her pupils dilate so.

'How did you learn about it?'

'At a dinner party, from an otherwise dull mineralogist, who said it was one of two or three in Europe, certainly the only one in these parts and fallen into disrepair.'

Intrigued, she had asked Groenke to find someone among the prisoners to submit a paper on jade. The Reichsführer's general inspection was pending. At first she'd had in mind no more than a diverting anecdote until she started to think, what if.

'A probably impossible dream but if something came of it my husband's position would be strengthened. I was by no means sure he would survive the inspection. I knew the Reichsführer would see terrible, demoralising things while he was here. The epidemic had just broken out.' Seeing Schlegel about to interrupt, she held up her hand. 'A labour deal was going on with Speer, who had taken over armaments, and Berlin decided things here must be presented in the best light, in order not to jeopardise negotiations.'

So neither the Reichsführer nor Speer was informed of the epidemic. Schlegel recalled both Wirths and the commandant more or less admitting the same.

Frau Hoess's concern was if the truth about the epidemic and generally dire conditions got out it might destroy her husband's career.

'I also wanted to raise with the Reichsführer the matter of violence being done to garrison women because I knew no one else would. But it was one bad thing after another, and the Reichsführer is nothing if not positive. So I thought some good news and an intriguing prospect might distract him from how awful everything else was.'

The first day of the Reichsführer's inspection was noteworthy for his foul temper. He showed no interest in anyone's problems, shouting at her husband, 'Over the *how*, *you* blow your brains out, not I!'

'Imagine that! His mood improved only at a lavish reception when I took charge of showing him plans for his apartment for when the town becomes one of his official sites. He fussed over the fabric samples, courtesy of Erich Groenke, who was allowed to meet him. The Reichsführer insisted I attend the private party to which he was adjourning, where he was at last on excellent form, relaxed with wine and an uncharacteristic cigar.'

Frau Hoess brought up the subject of the mine and the Reichsführer, intrigued, arranged to continue the conversation the following morning at her home, for which he expressed his unbounded enthusiasm. He talked at length with the children then spoke alone with her.

'I told him of the riches of Jordansmuhl jade, known as the warrior's stone and stone of heaven.'

Irresistible but impossible, said the delighted Reichsführer, forbidding her to entice him further with such tantalising tales. Such a venture was impossible, given the times.

'But I could see from the twinkle in his eye he wanted nothing more than to condone such a wild and romantic project. I impressed on him how the ancient Hissarlik nephrite axes, found in the Dardanelles by the archaeologist Schliemann, were in fact from Jordansmuhl rather than from the mountains of Xinjiang, as thought. The white jade of the axes was far rarer than the green stone – which could also be found in Jordansmuhl. This white stone I told him was known as the hardened sperm of the gods.'

The Reichsführer, seduced, applauded and told her the project had his quiet blessing but he must know nothing officially.

Before he left he promoted her husband, who never forgave her, thinking her beguilement was responsible for his promotion.

Frau Hoess composed her features into a mournful expression.

'Poor Rudi. My husband is crushed by his job.'

'Has he spoken to you of his difficulties?'

'Of course not. I wish he would love me as he does his white mare. He fears God, I know that.'

Schlegel said nothing.

She switched effortlessly, saying. 'I have told you what you need to know in exchange for you forgetting anything you may have seen.' She slipped her hand under the bedclothes onto his leg. Schlegel looked at her, thinking God forbid he should ever feel the slightest attracted.

'You're tired now. Let's take this further when you are better.'

Sybil was waiting in the shop, which stood in an alley at the back of Groenke's leather factory. Inside resembled a normal tailor's, with fabrics on display and fitting rooms. Fegelein was unction itself, apologising for their lateness, flattering at every opportunity.

Sybil made a point of deference, even offering small talk about the weather and whatever, but she barely glanced at Fegelein and didn't look at Morgen at all, so didn't recognise him. He supposed this disregard was part of a selective survival process.

Fegelein enjoyed her working close. He produced the jade cigarette holder for her to admire and, being in the business of showing off, revealed he was there on behalf of the Führer's doctor whose latest medical prescriptions were being tested by the garrison's pharmacy. Fegelein said the man was a wizard and his booster shots were available to Chancellery staff. These let one go for days without tiring, with none of the usual debilitating aftereffects.

Looking down at Sybil, on her knees, attending to his hems, Fegelein said in a soft voice, 'It also increases sexual performance, in quantity and quality.'

He made a gesture of almost touching her head, turned and smirked at Morgen, making a circle of his forefinger and thumb and pushing the cigarette holder in and out.

He looked back at Sybil.

'You're wasted here. What can we do to get you out? This is Morgen, by the way. An old friend and sparring partner.'

Being introduced as an old friend left Morgen even more compromised. Sybil glanced up and he saw the tremor of recognition before she ducked back down, terrified of being denounced. He was desperate to indicate otherwise but could see suspicion had become second nature to her.

Fegelein was too caught up in his seduction to notice, fussing over her as she attended to his alterations.

Morgen watched as she became more flirtatious with Fegelein. He presumed it was a way of rejecting his presence. He grew admiring and disdainful watching her play, knowing his own motives were clouded by cheap envy of the man's charm and ability to transcend the law.

'It is a handsome uniform,' Fegelein said. 'I couldn't be more admiring of your skills.'

Sybil was adjusting the trouser hem, with pins in her mouth.

'Too modest. You can be saucy with me.'

Morgen cringed.

Sybil said, 'It's hard with a mouthful of pins.'

'Here, let me relieve you.' Fegelein took the pins from her mouth. 'I'll hold them.'

He handed her them as needed, his fingers brushing hers.

Morgen thought, what if he insists on fucking her?

He wanted to leave, but decided to stay to spoil Fegelein's fun.

'I do prefer being tailored by a woman. Morgen, you must make an appointment.'

Watching Fegelein's odious charm and Sybil's calculated submission started Morgen thinking.

What he had in mind was probably dangerous and not kind to her at all. She caught his eye and looked away, leaving him shocked by his hardness towards everything.

Fegelein's verdict afterwards was, 'She's cute.'

On the whole he found prison girls nervous fucks, he said, and not worth the bother, except in special cases.

'Anyway, it's not allowed,' he added insincerely.

They came to a junction. 'Parting of the ways. Till ten in the morning then. You will find I wasn't driving the car. I was in bed all that weekend.'

Morgen waited until Fegelein was gone and walked back.

Sybil was sitting smoking a roll-up, staring in distaste at Fegelein's uniform on its dummy.

Seeing him, she said, 'I thought it was you.'

Her mistrust was evident.

He said, 'I suppose you learn not to see here.'

She seemed to dismiss the observation as meaningless and asked why he was there.

'To investigate corruption in the camp but we are running out of time.'

Sybil said nothing, her expression sceptical, as if to say where to start.

Without knowing why Morgen said, 'Most of the time I think I know who I am but not really, because there are moments like passing clouds when I believe there is no real or fixed self, beyond an accumulation of random reactions to any given situation.'

'You talk of luxuries. Events unfold around me with the least of my knowledge.'

Morgen detected the slightest lowering of her guard. He lit up and smoked in silence, trying to get her used to his presence.

'What do you know?' he eventually asked.

She looked away with a distracted gaze.

'I work for the commandant's wife supervising her seam-stresses' evening shift. Some days I spend sorting in Canada for Groenke, and once a week I get dressed up to meet the commandant's wife to show her jewels, and without fail she reminds me how fortunate I am to have her blessing. Otherwise there are no bearings, no choice and no identity beyond being at the behest of this woman.'

'By jewels you mean jade?'

'Jade in particular.'

'How come you are protected?'

'I have no idea.'

Morgen held the end of his cigarette to Fegelein's jacket until it burned a neat hole.

'Tell him I did this, except he won't be around much longer to ask.'

He watched her assess the possible consequences of his action for her and could not tell what she was thinking.

'There may be an end to all this,' he said.

He explained what he had in mind.

She sat for a long time, stood up and said, 'Schlegel will never forgive us.'

Schlegel woke unable to breathe, with something pressing hard against his face and on his chest. He saw black, shot with red. He thought it was panic, causing a huge convulsion, and his unconscious body was being invaded by the terror his waking mind refused to process. He could not tell if his eyes were open. Explosions detonated in his head. He worked out he was being smothered. A dry drowning. He had no idea who his would-be killer was; not a doctor, who would have just stuck a needle in. The weight on his chest grew heavier as his lungs used up the last of their air. He attempted to struggle. His legs started to thrash. His brain was shutting down. Useless fury coursed through him. Then suddenly he could breathe again, huge gasping lungfuls.

The room spun and Schlegel saw stars. The sight that greeted him made no sense. Fegelein, jade cigarette holder in his mouth but cigaretteless, was talking to a pretty nurse, who looked more charmed than bothered. It was like finding normal service resumed after a massive signal failure. Fegelein showed no sign of exertion. A pillow lay on the floor. Fegelein looked at Schlegel while saying to the nurse, 'I was passing in the corridor and this man was having some kind of fit. I tried to steady him. It seems to have worked. Good to see you're feeling better.'

The man's nerve was such that the nurse would think Schlegel mad if he announced Fegelein had just tried to kill him. Or perhaps he hadn't; a sense of indolent play suggested it didn't matter whether Schlegel lived or died. Looking at the man smiling, Schlegel decided he wouldn't bother to try again because the message would get to Morgen.

More disconcerting was the notion of Fegelein as Frau Hoess's emissary, she his angel of death, and all the rigmarole of placing his hand up her skirt was a prelude to the smothering, the inference being Fegelein was acting for her.

Fegelein strolled out with the pretty nurse without so much as a backward glance.

*

Schlegel was woken by Morgen the next morning, telling him to get dressed, he was needed, they had a busy day ahead. He had with him Schlegel's other suit, a change of clothes and his gun, which had been left in his room.

'Are you up to it?' Morgen asked.

It wasn't really a question. Besides, Schlegel was bored of lying in bed.

He dressed with agonising slowness and told about Fegelein.

Morgen grunted, not even surprised, and said, 'Your word against his. First off, you can watch him get his comeuppance. A taxi's waiting.'

Schlegel gave an edited version of his encounter with Frau Hoess.

Morgen exclaimed, 'A jade mine near Breslau! And she's running the show to keep everyone sweet?'

He paced the room in wonder, lit up, blew out a plume of smoke. 'It sounds exactly the sort of crackpot scheme they would all fall for, a grown-up version of kids sticking their hands in the sweet jar.'

Schlegel moved with a slow deliberation that he could see already annoyed Morgen who, by contrast, ran downstairs and called back up, 'First we sort out Fegelein. Then we have the Kattowice Gestapo coming to turn the place upside down. I will spare no one, not even the commandant and his wife. As for Fegelein, who agreed to present himself at ten o'clock, he has a driver booked for Kattowice airport at eight.'

Morgen had his usual taxi waiting. They picked up their witness, the local councillor, who used the journey to bombard them with complaints about garrison behaviour.

Schlegel tuned the man out. Another deadly bright day. His beating may have left him a mess and turned his brain to mud, but it let him see more clearly the filth beneath.

He broke the unwritten code, asking the fussy councillor if he knew what went on in the garrison.

It was obvious now they all did, even the taxi driver.

The councillor hummed and hawed then said, 'Thousands upon thousands are sent but the numbers always remain the same.'

'Yes, an enormous feat of management,' said Morgen sourly.

They arrived early at the airport – little more than a field and a few huts – and waited for Fegelein, whose plane was turning over on the runway.

There were no other passengers. Schlegel stared at the flaccid windsock and thought it must be important if Fegelein had the plane to himself.

Fegelein strolled in alone, ten minutes later, toting his valise, light of footstep, like a man whose business was successfully completed.

Schlegel saw the recoil of horror, followed by a second of collapse before the lie slid easily into place.

Fegelein announced he had been called away early. Morgen turned to the councillor and asked if this was the man he had seen. Fegelein rocked like a boxer taking a punch then grinned and held out his hands, inviting Morgen to handcuff him.

Morgen said he was taking him in for questioning.

Fegelein showed his teeth. 'Stop wasting my time. I am here conducting personal business on behalf of the Führer.'

With a dramatic flourish he produced an impressively embossed document that said in unequivocal terms the bearer must be allowed to proceed unhindered by all parties.

'All parties,' said Fegelein, with a self-satisfied air.

Morgen stepped aside. 'A postponement, then. I will see you in Berlin with a formal summons.'

He pointed to Schlegel and said, 'You can add attempted homicide to the list and trading in stolen property.'

For a second the man's aplomb deserted him. Schlegel suspected the loss of face lay in recognising Morgen's relentlessness, which would not stop until one of them was destroyed.

The moment was followed by a flare of hatred before the man's equilibrium was restored.

'I can recommend the seamstress,' Fegelein said as he sauntered off.

Schlegel asked Morgen what was meant by that. Morgen had no answer and Schlegel saw something he had never expected to see in Morgen, the look of a guilty man.

He asked again. The question was brushed aside. Morgen said trucks from Kattowice were due at nine hundred hours.

'Time to roll up the carpet.'

The garrison went about the start of its day unawares. Kattowice provided a good turnout of men and dogs. Their leader was a rotund man, quick to laugh, who reminded Schlegel of old-school cops with their amiable veneer hiding a mean spirit and casual expertise in the infliction of pain. Schlegel's beaten-up appearance provoked no comment.

The man cast around with a knowing eye and said to Morgen, 'Ready to go?'

Grabner was first. They passed him on his morning run, kitted out in a tracksuit, puffing away, running with high knees and sharp elbows.

By the time he came home a tidy pile of unaccountable goods had been assembled and his wife was hysterical. Grabner hissed like a tyre deflating and looked so little-boy-lost Schlegel thought he might ask for his mother.

Dr Wirths was still at home. They went in with dogs, one

of which attacked the doctor's runt. Wirths, visibly upset, telephoned the vet as men moved through the house. There was nothing to look in apart from the stove, which yielded another cache of morphine. Wirths protested to Morgen that it was a crude fit-up.

A call came from upstairs that cash had been found. The Gestapo man came down waving French francs.

Morgen, implacable, stared at the doctor with controlled aggression and stroked the injured dog until a knock on the door revealed a surprised vet, introducing a level of unreality to the proceedings. Wirths seemed almost tearful, in terms of all his good work being undone. In some ways, he struck Schlegel as the worst of the lot in terms of bargains made with himself.

The day's noises shaped themselves: the clang of a lorry's dropped tailgate, banging of doors, slamming of lockers, dogs straining their leashes, all fangs, drool and mad eyes. Schlegel sensed panicky telephone calls going on all over.

Schlegel was sure the Gestapo man was planting evidence, with Morgen's knowledge. He didn't even bother to ask himself if he cared. It was wrong but not as wrong as everything else.

Palitsch's shed produced its expected haul. They had a locksmith with them by then.

Schlegel felt rotten. His cough persisted, irritating everyone.

The location of the contraband store where all confiscated goods were taken afforded Morgen a certain amusement. It was in the offices of the security police, whose staff were taking the heaviest hits. Schlegel escorted several consignments and signed them in with Broad, in charge of the desk, with teams behind already cataloguing and storing the goods in the barred area known as the cage.

At the rate they were going the garrison would have to shut down. As for Morgen giving the Gestapo man carte blanche, carelessness was not a quality Schlegel associated with him.

The Gestapo broke for lunch, after agreeing with Morgen the bulk of the work was done. Schlegel wondered how much they had all been helping themselves.

Morgen accompanied Schlegel to the cage to survey the morning's haul. What lay before them was both pathetic, for the rubbish people bothered to steal, and astonishing in its sheer volume. Who hadn't been at it? Schlegel asked himself.

They were joined by Broad, who was quick to take them aside.

'You had better come and see. It has only just been reported.'

He led them to the adjoining main security building and up to its attic where the smell of death was palpable.

The huge space ran the length of the building and was piled high with junk, except for a cleared space the size of a boxing ring. The floor looked like someone had thrown paint all over it. Dried blood, Schlegel presumed. Haas's naked body hung by its knees and wrists from a horizontal pole suspended between two trestles. The exposed scrotum and buttocks were a livid, bloody mess.

Morgen inspected the body and said, 'Haas was a victim of his own medicine. Someone stuck a syringe in his neck. It's still there.'

He flicked it idly and addressed Broad.

'How come he has only just been found?'

'The boys up here work irregular hours. Besides, they're probably all clearing their lockers before you lot can come and turn them upside down.'

He laughed.

Haas had died an agonising death. Pearls of white lay on the floor: his smashed teeth. Morgen told Broad he was going to need a photographer with a flash gun. Broad left them to it. Schlegel thought Haas's last photograph, with him the subject, would make a pretty picture.

So this was where they did it, he thought. He associated torture more with cellars and basements.

He asked whether Morgen believed the security police were behind it.

'From the state of him, it looks like knowledge was extracted, but I doubt if the police would report a job it was responsible for.'

'Motive?'

'I expect Haas got greedy and tried to blackmail Fegelein.'

Which was only what Schlegel had suggested. He couldn't decide if he felt bad about that.

Morgen said, 'You can buy death for pocket money.'

Irked by his conscience, Schlegel found himself saying loudly that he supposed Fegelein went to Groenke, that was how things worked, but at no point could the chain be linked.

'There's one way to find out,' he finished.

He took Morgen to the photography club where Haas's negatives, contact sheets and copies were gone from his locker, a crude break-in involving a crowbar.

Morgen left the Gestapo to get on with it after lunch and told Schlegel they had an appointment with the commandant.

Schlegel saw a repeat of the furtive look he had noticed at the airport.

'Well?'

Morgen, reluctant, said, 'You won't like it. I can only ask you to trust me.'

He refused to elaborate other than they needed to get a move on.

The commandant thought the meeting was a report on the morning's proceedings and the Tanner case.

Instead Morgen said they had uncovered a trail of corruption that reached Berlin and the main suspect was responsible for the hit-and-run accident. Tanner, also in the car, was involved in the illegal acquisition of goods from Canada and passing them on to Berlin. She had also participated in sex parties, a feature of the previous summer.

'What!' exclaimed the commandant.

'A combination of an unexpected influx of goods and the enforced confinement of the epidemic led to a breakdown in morals.'

The commandant clutched his head. 'Sex parties?'

'Palitsch organised them,' Morgen said.

'No surprise there.'

The commandant blamed a lack of brothels. Before quarantine the men had used local military ones.

'The biological urge.' He gestured helplessly.

Schlegel thought if prisoners had a brothel why didn't garrison men.

Morgen said they had questioned Palitsch about Tanner's death and thought him not guilty.

'Is the other Fegelein?'

Morgen nodded.

The commandant added, 'The man is an unprincipled womaniser.'

Morgen said, 'I will go to Berlin to deal with him.'

Schlegel found the clarity of Morgen's account very different from his own. He saw only overlapping ambiguities. He still couldn't picture Tanner's death. Fegelein, Krick, the commandant, all appeared in his mind's eye as possible wielders of the hammer.

He was in a daze after the morning's events. His dry cough annoyed him as much as it did everyone else and he cursed every tickle that prefaced it. He ought really to be in hospital still. He wondered about checking back in after they were done. He must look a mess yet no one said.

Morgen gave Schlegel the same ambiguous glance as before, with something extra that appeared like regret.

The commandant made to stand, thinking they were done.

Morgen went to the door. Schlegel was unprepared for what happened next. The commandant struggled too and had to use the table to steady himself.

Schlegel, his mind in turmoil, realised the commandant would think he was seeing a ghost because as far as he knew the woman was dead.

Sybil stood, head downcast, hands clasped, an unwilling object of inspection.

Schlegel was no less surprised than the commandant. Anger followed shock, directed at Morgen for exposing Sybil.

He could read nothing from her expression and feared she was being used with no thought for her safety.

'Tell us,' Morgen ordered Sybil.

In a voice barely audible she said, 'The commandant forced me to have sex with him.'

Again the commandant had to steady himself.

'Tell us,' Morgen prompted again.

Sybil whispered, 'I am Jewish.'

'Fuck,' said Schlegel.

The commandant rounded on him, telling him not to use such language in front of a woman.

He shouted at Morgen, 'She can't be Jewish. My wife won't have them in the house.'

His face quivered. His arms flailed and he looked about to attack her. Morgen hustled Sybil from the room. Schlegel caught a glimpse of Broad in the background. Sybil had ignored him throughout.

The commandant raved on at Schlegel about his inappropriate language under the circumstances, then demanded of Morgen, 'Are you the destroyer of the temple?'

'You brought it on yourself.'

The commandant shouted in a cracked voice, 'I remain faithful to my leader and my wife. You are the traitor. I will address the Reichsführer on this matter.'

He saluted, insisted Morgen salute him back, and marched out.

Morgen stood smoking, nervous and shifty.

Schlegel, almost as unhinged as the commandant, asked, 'Do I get an explanation?'

'Don't worry. I will protect her.'

'I presume it is a frame.'

Morgen appeared desperate. 'We hold bad cards.'

'And now?'

'We go and talk to Groenke.'

'Groenke!'

Groenke was in the leather factory where it looked like it had been a flustered morning. He wanted to take them upstairs to his office until Morgen said he would prefer outside.

Groenke looked uncertain.

They stood in the street. Morgen composed himself and said to Schlegel, 'Your turn.'

Schlegel's head spun with dizziness as he said, 'I want only to know about the seamstress. Tell us about her and we will overlook the rest, the short cuts, the scrounging, the stealing, provision of stolen goods to the commandant's house.'

Morgen nodded. Groenke paled.

They watched him calculate the odds.

'I speak to a man in Berlin who calls himself only Werther.'

'Call him now.'

'I have no way of returning his calls.'

'No guess as to who Werther is?'

'All I know is he holds my call-up papers and failure to comply would mean the Eastern Front line.'

Groenke looked stricken at the thought.

'And Werther spoke to you about the seamstress?'

'He said when she came she was to be found immediate employment in the commandant's household. When I pointed out she was ineligible on racial grounds I was told the central record would be altered and to make sure her camp work card conformed.'

What a train wreck, Schlegel thought. He was disgusted with Morgen. Wild, out-of-control images assaulted him, of Sybil forced into sex with the commandant. Was that part of the plot or had the plot caught up? Until then Schlegel had presumed Morgen insisted she lie. Either way, the man had grown diabolical.

Morgen walked away without a word. When Schlegel caught up Morgen did his best to make everything appear normal.

'However unclear the specific reason, we know Kammler sent us. Sybil's presence is probably connected to that, which means she is part of Kammler's plan. Groenke acts for Kammler, though I suspect not entirely, and Werther is either Kammler or a close associate.'

'Is any of this justified?' Schlegel wondered aloud.

'To deal with the devil one has to become like the devil or even the devil himself.'

Schlegel asked if Sybil had been lying on Morgen's behalf, meaning had she or had she not had sex with the commandant.

Morgen dismissed the question as naïve. 'With me she has a choice, that is the point.'

He would arrange for her to keep her present identity and transfer to a camp near Munich, which had a VIP section, for diplomatic prisoners, prior to moving her to a nunnery in Bavaria.

Schlegel thought: A Jewish seamstress in a nunnery! He was under the impression most church institutions had been shut down and, anyway, she probably would not be welcome.

'There is a military hospital attached, so this one is allowed to continue. She can train as a nurse. She will be safe. Her identity will be protected. Not a bad deal, considering.'

Distasteful nevertheless, thought Schlegel.

Morgen said there were only two reactions to what they had learned: horror, which precluded any action – the route Schlegel had taken – or cynicism, which at least allowed for the possibility of action.

'Better than nothing,' said Morgen, wearily. 'We must use all methods at our disposal.'

The commandant sat in the summerhouse and slugged back half a bottle of brandy. He could smell his wife in there. As if he didn't know. He would return to the marriage bed and insist.

The speed of the drink pitched him back to his profoundest collapse: Brandenburg penitentiary, 1924 to 1928.

He kept a Bible hidden, to remain acquainted with the enemy. His father had wanted him to be a priest; so he had in his way; the shepherd guiding his flock through a cruel world. He lived among the downcast and condemned. If he was hard it was because he wished they learn from him. Low as he had fallen, he had climbed from the pit to walk the narrow path above the eternal void.

He read from his Bible: 'For the whole house of Ahab shall perish: and I will cut off from Ahab him that pisseth against the wall, and him that is shut up and left in Israel.'

Yea, he thought, I shall slay seventy persons, put their heads in baskets and send them to Jezreel.

He had arrived at his Gethsemane, that drowning dissolving into nothingness, and always the terror: that the love that called him was not blessed but the anti-word of the serpent. He despaired as one not loved, his lovelessness a measure of his journey from God. He had worshipped false idols, set his tent in a cold and empty place, far from God's mystery, surrounded by death, in flight from dying, in a land where all lost meaning and meant nothing. He was but a distant sinner. Goodness impossible. Evil irrevocable. But God was eternal forgiveness.

He told the two grooms: three horses, his western saddle, both to ride out with him, two canvas bags and two male corpses to put in them, for one shall be king of the Jews; he the forgiven thief.

They scurried like ants while he contemplated the helplessness of his charge, seen as master by all save himself. For the damned there was only one way: that of the prodigal son – a return to the father.

The grooms returned trundling a cart, four bare legs sticking out the back. If they were curious they dared not show it.

'The servant does not love the master,' he told them. 'The servant lives in the reflection of his master's dignity and in return the master grants him freedom to exist in the state of non-dying.'

The boys stared.

'How can we not be afraid of death?' he asked.

He laughed at their fear and said he wasn't going to shoot them.

They rode out through the troubled evening, canvas bags slung over the grooms' horses. He ordered them to ride ahead. The mare settled his mood. He drank from the bottle and measured the grooms' backs and thought perhaps to shoot them after all. He undid the flap of his holster. The third bullet for the mare, the last for him. Temple, mouth or under the chin?

In Dachau he had taken charge of the firing squad, usually men too trembling to shoot straight, leaving him to walk among the dead and pick off the botched jobs: pistol behind the ear, *coup de grace*, the jolt of the passing bullet, the last register of the eye of the now dead man. He imagined the moment his, curious not afraid. Each shooting was a step back from the abyss, knowing any moment the ground could open before him. He had subscribed, loyal, unloved and loveless servant, serving his masters as the grooms now served him. He confided to no man that secret world of interior puzzle, which led to the destructive impulse and breakdown. The empty terrain of his life a forsaking of God. Fencing. Borders. Rota. Serried ranks.

He stopped, not understanding where he was or whom he addressed. The grooms had dismounted, dragging the bodies down.

'And gave them for the potter's field, as the Lord appointed me,' he recited. Sin was a free deed. There were no extenuating circumstances. Temptation was the pleasure of abandon, release from the bonds to wallow like a pig in shit, in the guilt he had grown to love through fear. Daily horrors brought no consolation compared to the thrill of that within, to be visited sparingly. The field of blood, unto this day.

The grooms looked at him, waiting. He was still mounted. Now they had come to Golgotha he saw what he had in mind was not possible. The poles were too far apart. He could have sworn there was a section where they were more grouped. A train passed in the distance. A plane went by overhead. 'Why is it all a fucking mess?' he asked. They had no answer; sensible boys. Any would see them shot. They hung their heads; that's right, eyes down.

'Where are the nails?'

There were none. He could see both boys calculating whether to speak up.

'Dumb animals get shot too,' he said.

No nails. No hammer either.

'And where are the fucking crosspieces?'

The grooms cast around in consternation.

'Then answered all the people,' he told them, 'and said, His blood be on us and on our children.'

He directed them to place the two bodies on either side of the pole. It was obvious what they were meant to do but they had not a clue.

'Facing up, at more of an angle to the pole. Not that much! Now with their arms outstretched, feet folded.'

He saw he had got it wrong and told them to place the body on the right before the pole, then that was wrong. He told them to leave them as they were. It didn't matter. The unholy mess was in his head.

He told them to go. They hesitated.

'Get out or I will chase you with my whip!' As they made

to mount he said, 'The love of the master imprisons, it does not set free. The master who holds the slave does not grant him dignity. That dignity must be given away in order to increase the dignity of the master. Now go.'

The grooms mounted and hesitated again, too stupid, their brains addled.

'You are free to leave, by which I mean free. I absolve you of all duties. Go where the wind listeth and if anyone asks, you ride with my blessing.'

They rode past uncertainly, in the direction of the camp. The commandant watched their backs, calling after, 'Verily I say unto thee, today shalt thou be with me in paradise.'

By the end of the afternoon the contraband cage was full, with a backlog. Wirths and Grabner were being held in cells in the commandant's office along with other major cases. Lesser offenders had their identity papers confiscated and replaced with temporary passes. Most of the Gestapo men looked comfortably drunk. Their leader regaled them with stories of how unpopular Wirths was, his bleeding heart causing more trouble for everyone than it was worth.

They were standing around drinking and smoking, waiting for the last strays.

The Gestapo man was saying it was more or less official sport to be invited by the security police to come and make rogue selections where it hurt the doctor most, particularly carting off nearly-well prisoners from recovery sections.

He said he had spoken earlier to Grabner, who was so incandescent with rage at his arrest he could barely speak.

'And it's not as though he finds it easy putting one word in front of another at the best of times. He wishes – and I interpret loosely – one last raid be carried out, which both kicks Wirths in the nuts and raids the jewel in his crown.'

'Which is?' asked Morgen.

'His cancer treatment ward. So you know.'

The man looked like he was testing the water.

Morgen said, 'Your decision,' as though inviting him to step into trouble.

'We have one final task this afternoon,' he said. 'The commandant's wife.'

Schlegel thought the cupboard was probably already bare. The woman would have had a day's due warning. Now Morgen had the commandant cornered, he suspected the raid was for show. He sensed deals going on all around him. Having turned over everyone else, including all staff lockers – where the most bizarre trophy turned out to be a stuffed elephant's foot – they could hardly not inspect the commandant's house.

Frau Hoess and Morgen seemed almost rehearsed in the procedure. She said, 'If you must.'

Morgen went down to inspect the cellar, came back up a moment later and told her he had been misinformed.

'Of course,' she said. 'No harm done.'

'Really nothing?' asked Schlegel, incredulous.

He insisted on looking himself and found an empty cellar. It was all stacked in the tunnel, he was sure, but the steel door was locked. He went upstairs intending to demand the key to make a proper inspection, even if he did make a fool of himself. When the doorbell rang Frau Hoess was quick to answer and exclaimed, 'You came!'

She embraced the newcomer, a big man, resplendent in uniform, its lapels decorated with oak leaves.

Such a senior officer could only be Pohl, and not there by chance. Schlegel presumed whatever Morgen's bargain with the commandant's wife, it hadn't included her summoning Pohl.

Morgen's thunderous expression seemed to confirm that. He and the newcomer stared at each other with open hostility.

'Your house is corrupt, sir,' Morgen said.

Frau Hoess contributed a strategic bout of weeping.

Pohl said, 'You have no proper brief here. It's all subterfuge. Who are these men?'

The Gestapo man gave his name and rank. Schlegel didn't bother to answer. Morgen said, 'My assistant,' and Pohl turned away.

'Suspend the operation as of this minute. Morgen and your bruised and lanky friend, follow me. The rest of you out.'

He marched from the house and took them across the garden to the summerhouse.

Pohl had the overbearing manner of a graceless upstart. Schlegel knew his type from social functions hosted by his mother before her downfall, men inflated into loud braggarts by the fanciness of their uniforms. Pohl could claim to be more physically impressive than most, with an aggressive Roman profile of the sort seen on ancient coins.

'Well?' he asked. 'Let me remind you that you are on my territory, without my permission.'

Morgen said, 'You would have only refused it. I am here on a point of law.'

'Take the commandant off your list for a start. His tenure is my business.'

Morgen said he had already prosecuted the former commandant of Buchenwald for corruption, implying Pohl's authority counted for nothing.

Pohl pushed his face into Morgen's. 'After which I set up our own internal review of all camp commandants. Many are in the process of being replaced. The case here is pending.'

Morgen stood staring at a chair leg, kicking it with the toe of his shoe. He said it had come to his attention that the commandant and his wife were part of a smuggling ring which went all the way to Berlin.

'Particularly jade,' he said as he stopped kicking the chair.

Schlegel spoke up. 'There is a mine too, probably operating illegally.'

'What good little detectives you are,' said Pohl with overplayed sarcasm. 'What do you know of the Reichsführer's affairs? Does he give you the time of day?'

Morgen said he was operating to a brief when Schlegel thought he probably wasn't.

'Yes, but how well do you know the Reichsführer?'

'He asked me to act as his conscience.'

Morgen had a hard job sounding like he believed it. Pohl looked doubtful. Schlegel thought Heini wouldn't lift a finger if Pohl locked them up.

'Listen, boys,' said Pohl, downshifting, treating them to the largesse of his confidence. 'The Reichsführer has his fancies. Herbal medicine one year, and all the camps had to grow acres of the stuff, reflector lights on bicycles, mineral water. We indulge him, as we do with jade.'

Morgen looked like a man outplayed.

Pohl went on. 'He wishes to create a market by making it more valuable. He wants it adopted as the official stone of the organisation, except the white jade he craves is proving hard to find.' Pohl made a show of his empty hand. 'I have no personal interest in jade other than it concerns the Reichsführer . . .'

He let the sentence trail. Suddenly it was all man-to-man, the rueful confession, all splendidly insincere for being so blatant. It was also clever. For a big man Pohl was a graceful mover; a good dancer, Schlegel suspected, on the floor and in the office.

Pohl addressed Morgen. 'Take Wirths and Grabner and whatever small fry, but you know their cases will take months to come to trial. There are more urgent matters to attend to. Yes, yes, the law, you will tell me.' Pohl stuck his hands in his trouser pockets and asked, 'Has either of you a cigarette?'

Morgen was obliged to offer. Pohl leaned into the light held. He waved away his first exhalation and said, 'You would make life a lot easier for everyone if you got down off your high horse. I know what goes on here. People help themselves. There are grey areas. The rewards are few. The pay is lousy. Stuff goes missing.'

'There is a difference between pilfering and looting on a grand scale.'

'I will deal with that. Now direct me to a telephone.'

Morgen said the nearest was in the commandant's house.

They trooped back. Pohl flicked the butt of his cigarette into the pond. The telephone was in the hall. Pohl ordered Morgen to call the adjutant's office and request an armed escort immediately. Morgen, seeing what Pohl intended, refused until Pohl produced a silver-plated pistol from his holster.

Frau Hoess came from the kitchen, wearing an apron. Pohl said they were just waiting to clear up some business. She asked if he would be staying for supper.

'I might. They won't,' said Pohl.

Juppe came, accompanied by two guards with rifles.

Pohl told him, 'Escort Morgen from the premises. Hold him under guard and put him on the night train. If he turns up again shoot him and I will happily sign any release to say he was resisting arrest.'

It threatened to be an inconsequential ending until Frau Hoess rounded on Morgen like a harpy, beating his chest with her fists, shouting over, 'Why did you come?'

Her eyes glittered the way they had in the hospital. Schlegel was unconvinced by her outburst. He had been watching throughout. Her previous expression had been one of complete relief.

She stopped as suddenly as she had started.

Schlegel had no opportunity to speak to Morgen, who nodded curtly and was gone.

Pohl turned to Schlegel. 'Twenty-four hours to wind up your affairs, then out. Any unfinished business you hand over to Kattowice.'

Schlegel gave his most lackadaisical salute and slouched off like a beaten dog.

He stumbled around with no clue what to do. No one would let him near Morgen. He had no idea what the man's plans were for getting Sybil out. He presumed some arrangement had been made with Broad, but her safety looked precarious with the latest turn of events.

Broad wasn't at the contraband cage. The stashed goods reminded Schlegel that money was the one language they all understood, and the only way was somehow to buy Sybil out.

He tried talking his way into the cage, in the hope of pilfering whatever he could, only to find himself undone by Morgen's instructions, which demanded all pockets be emptied before entering, and searched on leaving.

He went to the office looking for Schulze, who wasn't there. He considered her more level-headed than he was. He sat down trying to think, his brain racing uselessly until it gave up and he fell into a stupor.

He was woken by Schulze, who asked if he was all right.

'Not really.'

She said it was all over the garrison how Pohl had chucked Morgen out.

Schlegel said, 'They are putting him on the night train.'

'What are you doing now?'

He said he didn't know, other than run around like a headless chicken.

She asked if he would go with her.

'Where to?'

'I will show you my allotment.'

He looked at her, confused.

She said, 'I want to talk to you. It won't take long.'

They walked through the garrison towards the river. Everything felt briefly normal to Schlegel. There was nothing he could do for the moment. He would think of something. He couldn't tell if he was sick or in some heightened state of anxiety, which amounted to the same thing.

They crossed into countryside. Schulze said the allotments were about a ten-minute walk.

'Have you the time?'

'I need time to think,' he said.

She struck him as preoccupied, the way she had in the hospital.

She said, 'I am looking for a father for a child.'

Not sure he had heard correctly, he asked whose.

'Mine. The one I mean to have. Then I can leave. I've had enough.'

'What about Krick?'

'The man's far too vain to contemplate one. He would refuse to acknowledge it was his, and you need the father to sign off proof of paternity.'

Schlegel thought back to their first encounter and his impression of paths crossing. Was this what was meant by

325

his premonition? He didn't ask whether she had in fact come to his room that night because knowing would spoil it. He had no idea what to think. She wasn't part of the easy crew he frequented and he had considered her accounted for.

'I want a tall child,' she said, and he realised she was serious.

She repeated that Krick wasn't around.

'I am not sure I want any offspring of mine to inherit his untrustworthiness.'

Schlegel said his genes were not of the best. 'Indecisive, backsliding, cowardly.'

'Better that than what they teach here.'

It was the right time of the month, she said.

They reached the allotments, plots of tamed earth with their own little sheds, some converted into summer huts. She said the gardening craze had started the year before, with everyone confined to camp. A lot was an excuse to bury treasure.

Schulze struck Schlegel as easy and far-sighted. He asked if she was serious about getting out.

'Yes. If there is an afterwards, we will all be held guilty. I don't know if there will be but I want to start building a life far from here. I have put in for transfers but they are reluctant to move administrative staff. Some are starting to say soon no one will be allowed to leave. For the moment, having a child is the only loophole. That is why everyone is being so careless about birth control. You will have to vouch for it but that is all. Everything afterwards is taken care of by the state.'

'I can't promise anything. I am a mess since hospital.'

They sat in Schulze's shed, a wooden hut not much bigger than a cell. She said she liked it there. It was about the only place she did.

Sunflowers were popular. They sat surrounded by the

tall stalks of that summer's crop. Most people had stopped growing vegetables because they got stolen.

Schulze sat with her hands clasped around her knees. Schlegel knew he should be getting on but it was his first relaxed time since being there. The hut's boards were warm from the day. Trying to feel useful, he went in search of something to lie on. Most huts were open because they were empty. Under a water barrel he found some dry sacking, dusty but clean, and wondered about a child he had never thought of having.

Later, Schulze said, 'We should have done this a long time ago.' Schlegel agreed. She was one of very few he wanted to know better. His head wasn't giving him trouble for once. He even stopped coughing. Given the impossibility of everything else, there was only the moment, a sense of connection, a future perhaps, and curiosity, when it had otherwise been eradicated, and plain lust, as though he had been hot-wired. They were all over each other, laughing. This had better be good, she said, because it will be the only time. It was easy. Everything worked without thinking, when usually he found sex questionable in its physical negotiation and what was left unsaid.

He fell asleep and when he awoke she was gone, and as with the time in the inn he was left wondering if he had dreamed it all.

Schlegel went back to the office. He was down to his last four packets of cigarettes. He went in search of Broad and this time found him standing around in the contraband store, as lackadaisical as ever.

'I hear your pal is on his way home, and I am asking why didn't the big man chuck out the pair of you while he was at it? How long have you got?'

'Twenty-four hours.'

'For what?' asked Broad enigmatically.

Schlegel ignored the troubling question and said Morgen had subpoenaed the seamstress and he understood Broad had her safe.

'I need you to hand her over as I will be taking her out this evening.'

Broad gave him an incredulous look and suggested they step outside. A back door took them into a grass arena.

'I am continuing to bet very long odds on you.'

'What do you mean?'

Schlegel was back to feeling like he was swimming through treacle.

'It's too late to talk to me. Your seamstress is no longer in the block.'

Schlegel sensed Pohl closing everything down. He supposed the conversation was about Broad being willing to trade.

'Can I find out where she is?'

'A little birdie is saying.'

It took 35 cigarettes for the birdie to tell. Schlegel suspected he was being robbed blind.

Sybil had been transferred to Dr Wirths' cancer treatment ward, across from the punishment block. The inference was obvious. Bock the dentist had made the same move just before his death. Schlegel had a flash of Sybil already laid out in a morgue bath.

Wheels were starting to turn as the machine cranked into action. The Gestapo man had said the ward would be cleared as a final act of spite against Wirths. Fuck, thought Schlegel. Had Pohl not turned up and were Morgen still there, he suspected the Gestapo would have held off. He asked Broad if Pohl was now in control.

Broad hummed and hawed. Five more cigarettes and he said, 'Word is the woman causing all the trouble has to go.'

Two packs of cigarettes left.

Schlegel ran to the medical block, in as much as his enfeebled state let him.

If the in-fighting at the top was Pohl against Kammler, then Morgen, he and Sybil could all be counted as Kammler's agents and, after letting them dance a while, Pohl was now making his sweep.

Two idling trucks stood outside the medical block. Women were already milling around, downcast and resigned. The first truck was being loaded, supervised by a couple of guards. The Gestapo men were all inside.

Schlegel checked the first truck: a dozen or so women sitting on opposite benches; none was Sybil.

Another batch was brought out. Two Gestapo men handed them over and rushed back into the building. About thirty women were waiting, with one guard splitting them, making some stay for the second truck while the first was filled. Schlegel was surprised by the lack of urgency, even with lives hanging in the balance. No one protested or cried. It had all the inevitably of a transport going to market.

Schlegel spotted Sybil at the back of the group. He ordered her to come over, shouting brusquely like she was in trouble. She stood opposite him, looking nervous and uncertain. He muttered, 'Stay with me and say nothing.'

He walked over to the guard that looked more amenable. The comparison was meaningless; both appeared as shifty and unpleasant as the other. The guard, indifferent, said, 'Once they are for the truck they are for the truck.'

He wasn't putting himself out for anyone.

Schlegel tried the other soldier, who said, 'The numbers

have to match. We can't let people be taken off or we get into trouble.'

Schlegel was desperate to avoid bargaining with the Gestapo, who had no doubt been told to clear the lot.

He took the guard aside, out of Sybil's hearing, and showed him a packet of cigarettes, saying the prisoner was his woman and he wasn't done with her yet. Gambling everything, he produced his last packet of cigarettes and said, 'For your friend,' knowing the creep would pocket both packs.

The guard nodded as if to say it was a lot to pay for a woman and he hoped she was worth it. He jerked his head and told them to make themselves scarce before the Gestapo came out again.

Schlegel sensed some of the other women starting to stare at Sybil and for a terrible moment he thought they might turn on her. He roughly grabbed her arm and dragged her off, trying to make it look as though her fate was as unquestionable as theirs. He frogmarched her fast until they were out of sight, let go of her arm and said they had to get out that night, somehow, and Morgen was no longer there to help.

Morgen sat in the station waiting room under armed escort, watching Juppe strut. Someone had at least packed his case, which was waiting. Because of his guard, people stared, as much as they dared.

Morgen thought: piles of bodies, piles of money. He could broadcast it as much as he liked, no one would listen, even if he commandeered the station's loudspeaker system. Truth eradicated all hope.

He worked out he had three moves left and the third would probably cost him his life.

He feared for Schlegel's safety; the boy probably should not even be up. Sybil he had given his word to, now as good as useless. He supposed she would be auctioned off to the highest bidder, if matters got as far as that.

Once more unto the wilderness.

Morgen's attention was caught by a woman walking into the waiting room. He couldn't see properly because he was cleaning his spectacles. There were almost no women waiting that weren't passengers but this one had no luggage. She was also casting around anxiously.

Morgen put his spectacles back on and saw Schulze, sitting down now on the other side of the room. Juppe didn't recognise her and Morgen supposed he didn't know her. He was slow to realise she might be looking for him; at first he had thought it chance. When Juppe's attention was elsewhere she gestured that she would see him on the train, stood up and left. Morgen could see her through the waiting-room window, pacing the platform. He supposed she could only be the bringer of bad news.

The train arrived half an hour late. Juppe said no sleeping berth was available but the compartment for garrison use was empty with no other passengers expected. Juppe gave a sarcastic wave, said, 'Bye-bye,' and repeated Pohl's warning that he would be shot on sight if he came back.

Morgen pulled the blinds down, having no wish to watch his departure.

He was joined by Schulze as the train left.

She said, 'I think I have worked out how it was done.'

The missing piece: the secret chamber of which there was no trace.

Morgen had no doubt of its existence. Palitsch said all business came down to housekeeping, and the one thing of which there was always a surfeit: the unwanted. And in the background always the bureaucratic machine sorting and justifying the reason for existence. Somewhere must have served to demonstrate what the garrison was capable of *before* the commission of the death factories; to enable them. Cost and economics. Such a huge new build could only be justified if shown to be worth it. Its temporary predecessor would have had to continue operating through that winter until the first of the new builds opened in the spring.

Morgen was in no hurry to know the answer. In some ways he would rather not. The problem with a secret of that magnitude was there was nowhere to take it. As an accessory, such knowledge became contagious. Now he had in effect been cashiered there was nothing he could do except let it fester in his head.

He asked Schulze what she remembered of the mood at the time. She said the same questions were being asked in the bar every night. What were they supposed to do with all these newcomers turning up in droves? They remembered how the Old Man had begged from the start they stop sending more prisoners and got turned down flat, and now they had to take everyone sent, and the Ministry of Food sent fewer supplies.

'There must have been stories.'

'Yes, but knowing not to ask was something we had all learned by then.'

She confirmed that the construction of any temporary disposal site would have required carpenters, masons, plasterers, surveyors and draughtsmen. She had checked again and said, 'Nothing was built or worked on near the burning pits that the record shows, apart from the prefabricated huts we discussed.'

Morgen thought: The record always shows, one way or another.

Schulze said, 'However, there are some clues. I told you about the surveyor's report on narrow-gauge tracks, which we laid, and brushwood fencing from the landscaping department, which we were contracted to assemble. What I didn't know was the exact same order was repeated later that summer.'

'Would you not have known?'

'Not necessarily. The department had expanded and several of us were dealing with labour allocation.'

'Then you are saying there were *two* sites not one.'

It confirmed his theory of demonstrating capability.

'What have you worked out?' he asked reluctantly.

'Kammler.'

She had no proof but it was the only possible explanation for what she was about to say.

'What would a second site add?'

The answer was obvious, but that was not what he meant. The time-consuming part of the job would be clearing up and disposal. Unless extractor fans were used, the gas would have to disperse naturally before bodies were removed, a lengthy process before everything could be cleaned and prepared for the next unsuspecting batch. A single site would by default spend time idle.

Morgen suspected the revolutionary moment was realising the addition of a second chamber would enable work to continue around the clock. He presumed such a structure had only two requirements: being airtight and an unthreatening appearance to deceive those about to enter.

'Tell me what you know.'

Schulze said the key was how Kammler had transformed all camp bureaucracy through technology. This particularly related to the workforce, with the introduction of a new central register, which let him control everything from Berlin.

'How?' asked Morgen. The logistics would be mind-boggling.

'It's an automated system. It's what I did my course on in Berlin.'

'Then why were you working with us if you are trained to do that?'

'I suspect I offended my immediate boss. He was not happy about me doing the course in the first place. There is so much in-fighting.'

'How did you get chosen?'

Schulze looked away. 'Dr Kammler recommended me.'

He still wondered if she was Kammler's spy. One thing he had learned was most of the time you didn't find the answer.

'What are the advantages of an automated system?'

'Centralisation. It's the same numerical system they used for the census. It lets you see exactly how many workers are deployed where, throughout the whole camp network, and if there is a shortage or surplus then transfers can be made immediately.'

'But how does it work?'

'A punch-card system allows individual data to be sorted automatically.'

Morgen had never heard of such a thing.

'And before Kammler?'

'Most camps hardly knew what its workforce was. The record-keeping was appalling.'

'How does this have a bearing on what you are talking about?'

'Immediately after Kammler's February 1942 inspection there was one other significant change.'

In a move no one foresaw, all prison labour was transferred to Kammler's command.

'Once he had control, he could siphon off the cream, for

what became known as mobile brigades, which answered directly to him. We lost our best people. Kammler just took them.'

'How did they work?'

'Outside the camp system. He was interested in the private sector. Specialist teams to be moved around as he saw fit.'

Morgen saw what she was saying.

Creating his own independent workforce made complete sense if Kammler's immediate business involved the secret future of the garrison. With his own people to hand as early as March, he would have brought them in to live and work on site, bypassing the construction office and the garrison, and nobody would have known they were there.

It also placed Kammler, like Wirths, with his hands firmly on the death machine.

Morgen thanked Schulze and asked why had she told him.

She said she didn't know, other than prove to herself she hadn't known. Morgen said she needn't speak of it again.

The garrison war now took on another dimension, as part of Kammler's modernising revolution. Nevertheless, Morgen's instinct told him that Wirths' denunciation of the crematoria as follies wasn't altogether wrong. Any interim sites probably disposed of many more than their replacements. By then the bulk of the job was already done and they were white elephants.

The journey to Kattowice took little more than an hour. Schulze said she would take the milk train back and be in time for work. She asked what he would do.

'Go to Breslau, I think, and try and look at a mine.'

He wondered whether to tell her. The confounded business of secrets. There was no beast worse than man.

If he were an ox he would be wailing from the burden he carried.

Schulze surprised him by asking if he would be a good father.

'Certainly not. Why ever do you ask?'

'Can you see yourself as one?'

'I have no wish to add to the misery of existence.'

He couldn't tell if he meant it. Personal questions made him uncomfortable. From most people he would have dismissed Schulze's asking as sentimental but sensed with her it was not.

He told her about the mine instead. She said it sounded like another of those stories.

He said even the most grandiose dreams came down to little more than the grubby reflections of the beholders.

He asked if she knew anything of Schlegel.

'He's not in great shape.'

Morgen tried to make light of that, saying, 'It's often when he does his best work.'

After a silence she said, 'He may have helped me get out of the place too.'

'How?' Morgen didn't understand.

'It's too early to say yet.'

'I haven't got a clue what you are talking about.'

Schulze's laugh was so carefree that Morgen felt forced to laugh too.

He slept after that in the pit of exhaustion and was briefly aware of her departure at Kattowice, kissing him on the cheek and wishing him good luck.

Schlegel's only thought was to find a safe place for Sybil. He was thinking of the tunnel from the commandant's house whose exit lay outside the garrison, close to the road and hidden by trees. Sybil seemed barely aware of him explaining. Why should she believe him any more than all the rest?

Where he felt like he was on a collapsing bridge over a raging torrent, she seemed like marble. Only when he stumbled and unthinkingly put his hand on her shoulder did she flinch, and after that he dared not touch her. They crossed the main street and went down the path through the glade that led to the door to the commandant's garden. It was locked, the wall too high to climb. He asked if she knew how to get in. Her face was ethereally pale, almost featureless, in the gathering night. Would they just stand there spellbound?

A breeze came up, rustling the trees, after a day of heat and humidity like a wet flannel.

He kicked the lock to the gate. On the third attempt it gave.

He led them across the lawn to the house. The entrance under the stairs was open as before.

A siren came from the direction of the camp, wavering until it got up to speed. He slipped them inside.

In the cellar some contraband had been reinstated. Schlegel helped himself. Food. Water. Chocolate. A sack to put it in, and a couple more to act as blankets should they need them. His mind went blank; he stared, seeing a sea of nothing. Then everything went black.

For a moment he couldn't say what had happened. The siren droned on. He heard distant gunshots and presumed another escape. He could hear Sybil breathing and experienced an absurd leap of hope, believing it marked the start of her return. He said, 'It must be a power cut.'

He told her to wait. He would be back soon. He promised she was as safe there as anywhere. No one would be poking around down there in the dark. He couldn't think of anything to say that didn't sound cheap or corny.

He felt his way out. After the black cellar the night appeared preternaturally bright. The siren came in waves. All lights were out, including the big camp arc lamps. The whole garrison was down. He heard horses riding out. Gunshots, sirens, horses – the posse, he hoped, chasing an escape; distraction to add to the confusion.

He crossed the commandant's garden, left by the gate and walked to the front door. He saw candles on upstairs. The bell didn't work. He banged on the door.

Eventually Frau Hoess answered herself, carrying a candle, which she held up to light his face. She wore a housecoat and raised her free arm to her brow, saying she had been upstairs resting. She seemed neither surprised nor interested to see him, yet he was aware of a sexual current. Her skin was flushed, her eyes bright and unfocused. He said he needed to talk of a matter of urgency.

'You'd better come in, though why I should welcome you after the way you behaved . . .'

She took him into the sitting room where she lay on the sofa and he sat opposite, elbows on his knees, wondering what to say. He threw his hands in the air and gave up.

Whatever else, Frau Hoess was a woman of intuition.

'Tell me about her,' she said softly.

Schlegel wondered about her narcotic state.

He told a pack of lies, thinking all that counted was the conviction with which it was told.

He gambled everything on the woman being a frustrated romantic. He knew he must pour his heart out to her – as she would have it – telling of his impossible love. He was delirious enough as it was.

The wail of the siren gave urgency to the telling. The

intimacy of candlelight lent his garbled account a conviction it would not otherwise have had.

She listened entranced as the words cartwheeled out of him and he gave her the tear-jerking star-crossed tripe she obviously craved – his seamstress lover's lowly background and troubled past, driven into prostitution by a drunken wastrel, who used her earnings to feed his gambling habit, beatings . . .

Frau Hoess sat up, putting her hand to her mouth as he went on – his mother's disapproval . . . more tragedy when a corrupt policeman tried to force his attentions and when she refused had her arrested for soliciting, just as they were planning to elope.

'My God, what a story! This is why you are here!'

'To see if I can get her out.'

He was starting to believe himself. What a pair they made: he feverishly hysterical; she lost in doped reverie. She patted the seat next to her. They went through the hand-holding routine. Schlegel thought: Patently undesirable yet fatally attractive.

'How enchanting,' she said. 'I will cast you as Orfeo and her as Euridice, thrown into the underworld and you come down to rescue her. So marvellous!'

She told him of her recent opera visit to Kattowice.

'A rapturous production. And now that very story unfolds in front of my eyes. My husband is the least romantic of men. You must not look back as Orfeo did or you will lose her.'

She looked at him in wondrous excitement.

'Of course! The River Sola is the Styx. I see now. It makes perfect sense. What will you do?'

'I can only throw myself at your mercy. All other avenues are closed. I fear her situation has become imperilled.'

He saw the rapture as he held her eye and said, 'I need desperately to pay the ferryman.'

Frau Hoess clapped her hands, thrilled.

'A secret getaway! What do you need?'

'Funds, not to put too fine a point on it.'

He watched consideration turn to calculation.

'No, impossible!'

'Perhaps I can perform some labour in return.'

Calculation turned to something harder.

'Perhaps. No, still impossible.'

After further cajoling she declared her hand.

'Yes, I will give you a task. I appoint you my secret emissary. Take jade to Fegelein. It will extend my influence. It will remind Bormann of the debt he owes my husband.'

'Debt?'

'My husband once prevented him from going to prison for a very long time, so the obligation is considerable.'

Schlegel almost lost his nerve as he leaned in and said, 'They will call you the queen of jade.'

The woman chirruped with delight.

'Wait here.'

She went away and came back in the hooded cloak she had worn at the party and waving a torch, which spoiled the effect.

'Come.'

He followed her through the darkened garrison, down streets full of strange commotion, with more people out than he would have expected, the atmosphere heightened by the lack of light. He was surprised by the absence of an emergency generator. He could smell burning. No smoke from the chimney; the refuse incinerators, he supposed. He feared that the woman would come to her senses before the business could be completed. He wasn't sure how much longer he could keep up his pretence, like an actor about to dry on stage.

Their destination was the tailoring shop, in an alley behind Groenke's factory. Frau Hoess let them in, stooping to use a key she wore around her neck. In a small room immediately by the front door stood a safe. She tumbled the dial until the numbers clicked and the door swung open to reveal tray upon tray of jewels, with several devoted to jade. Frau Hoess pulled them out and spilled them on the table. She pointed out the best stones to show Fegelein, and the lesser ones, which he could sell. She veered between girlish excitement and beady control. Schlegel suspected it would excite her more to betray them. She would of course accuse him of stealing the jewels.

'The gemstone of nobility,' she murmured. 'It relieves anxiety and takes away fear. You look calmer already. Jade is the perfect stone for those disappointed in love. I can see you have been and I know you can tell I have.'

She pressed a stone into his hand and said there was a price.

Schlegel pointed out it was getting late.

'My commission. Pay now. It won't take long.'

Seeing what she had in mind, he said he feared it might break the spell of his love for Euridice.

'Don't be silly. That's just a story.'

She lifted her skirt and pulled down her underwear – silk, Schlegel noticed – and leaning across the table exposed her buttocks, saying, 'Take me like a beast.'

Schlegel flicked through the limited lexicon of erotic imagery in his head, in desperate search of enough to perform the task in hand, trying to think of it as no more than the conclusion of a financial transaction.

The commandant arrived to find the garrison plunged into darkness, let himself in by the backdoor and paused, listening to the house; quite often it spoke to him at night. He avoided the children upstairs and went straight to his study. He sensed his wife was not at home and entertaining her stud. He drank deep from a bottle of brandy and gargled, using it for mouthwash. The alcohol went straight to his head. He took a torch and went to the cellar, certain his wife and her vile lover had been there. The space was empty but he detected a recent human presence. They would be in the summerhouse. The commandant recited aloud that in the realm of matrimony he was the decider and the time had come to settle the hash of his wife and her friend. He pictured her hysterical, the lover craven and shaking, and he within his rights to shoot the pair of them. He savoured the prospect of intense melodrama. He made shooting noises, pointing his finger, paused, looking around, saw a hammer and nails and even some planking that could have served for the crosspieces he had needed earlier. All there. He was distracted by an open sack of flour, pure as driven snow. He bathed his face in it and picked up the hammer and a nail, telling himself he would not cry out.

Tomorrow would be taken up with the prisoner escape. He had heard the sirens and gunshots. Lockdown. No work. Prisoners confined to barracks or out for a daylong roll call in the blistering heat.

To hammer a nail one had to hold it. To hammer a nail into his own hand presented a problem. He found a rag to cushion the top and pushed down until it had enough purchase to stand in his palm. He then banged down hard with the hammer. The pain was blinding, intense yet ecstatic, and in the moment of not crying out he reconfirmed his vows to the leadership, thinking how could he ever have doubted.

Using the rag, he grasped the top of the nail and yanked

it out, which hurt far more than the shock of driving it in. Through force of will he stopped the cry bursting from his lungs.

He stared at the puckered hole that winked at him, weeping water and blood. He dribbled brandy and felt its clean sting travel through the wound and thought of the lanced body of Christ.

He heard soft, frightened breathing, little gasps, and realised someone was down there in the dark with him.

Sybil stared at the ghastly illuminated mask hovering over her. She knew it must be the commandant because she had heard him talking to himself, doing what she could not tell. He was shining a torch up into his face, which appeared unnaturally white and distorted. He whispered not to be afraid.

'I am alone. No one knows I am here. You are quite safe.'

He continued to shine the torch upwards.

'I mistook you for my wife.'

He seemed excited and confused.

She thought: If not one monster another. Perhaps the apparition before her was a dream, or there by magic, or a projection of her own sick fantasies. For a long time now her mind had been in danger of collapsing.

Even if the commandant were real, he was not himself, as if he too had taken leave of his senses. His face, deadly white, looked like it had been powdered. He showed no curiosity about why she was there and kept inspecting his hand. He asked if he could sit next to her.

'No funny business,' he said.

He continued to hold the torch to his face. For the first time she saw him as human and pathetic. He insisted on showing her his hand. It wasn't until he shone the light on it that she saw the tight hole in the palm. He splashed brandy over it, saying that would stop it from becoming infected.

He asked, 'Why would the Holy Elect choose a non-believer to transmit his message?'

He repeated that she was safe, which had the opposite effect. She had been more physically threatened but never felt in more danger. She realised what he had just done to his hand, and if he was prepared to do that to himself what wouldn't he do to her? Even with the selection in the hospital ward only an hour before, it had been clear what was at stake. Here she had no idea. In terms of her own fate, she suspected that whatever black hole existed in the commandant's head, night and furtiveness were essential to his method.

She decided she must be dreaming after all.

He wanted to know why she was so reserved and she realised it was the same old business of favour for favour.

As coldly as she could manage she said, 'For the obvious reasons of your position and being married.'

With tears in his eyes, still holding the torch, he tried to kiss her. She reminded him of her pariah status.

'If you were Jewish you would be down as Jewish. I know Morgen forced you to say what you did. I have always treated you with the utmost respect. Morgen is contemptible.'

After asking permission, he smoked.

'You're right. We should wait. I can arrange your release and fix you up with a nice room in a beautiful house where perhaps you will let me visit. We can get Erich to furnish it in whatever style you wish.'

Morgen had offered her freedom, then Schlegel, now the commandant. None on her own terms. A nunnery or boudoir. Schlegel had never made it plain what he had in mind, something clumsy and confused no doubt. Not that she believed any of them.

Yet another siren went off, different from the rest. He stood and said, 'You must come. Tomorrow we can move you to your room. It has French doors into an orchard garden.'

The night was orange, with a crowd of people hurrying towards the main street. As Schlegel got closer he stopped, stunned.

The building which held the contraband was ablaze, already running out of control. Their evidence was going up in smoke and no one was making any effort to stop it. Never in his wildest dreams had Schlegel anticipated anything so blatant.

Pohl's grand finale!

A rapt crowd applauded every whoosh and crack. The fire cast long, flickering shadows. People leaned out of high windows. Part of the roof went with a crash that raised a cheer. The pillar of smoke spiralled away into black night.

Someone said the fire engine had been vandalised and they were having trouble getting water.

Schlegel stood transfixed, knowing he must hurry, still queasy at the memory of Frau Hoess bucking beneath him, ordering him to slap her until he was more excited than he wished by her wild convulsions, saying afterwards how awful she had been, but such operatic digression was permissible, and by possessing him she was releasing him to be free with his true love.

She asked why he had a Jewish cock. 'Not because, surely?'

Schlegel said an English mother; it was not uncommon there.

'Next time hit me harder, beat the bad out of me.'

It was hard not to laugh but he was ashamed how lost he had become in her.

She insisted they leave separately.

The price of transgression was revealed upon Schlegel's return to the commandant's house. The cellar was empty. He called out as much as he dared, thrashed around in the dark, feeling the floor, in the unlikely event of Sybil falling asleep or passing out.

He had lost her and he had run out of time.

It hit him, with mounting panic, that the fire was why Pohl had let him stay: planned for that night and he the scapegoat. They were probably after him now.

No Sybil, no way out of the garrison, a pocket full of precious gems, which they would accuse him of helping himself to . . . They wouldn't leave him a leg to stand on.

He crashed through the dark, back outside, and paused a moment by the garden gate, stunned by the spectacle of a tree catching fire, its leaves gone in seconds.

He worked his way round the back of the crowd, failing to get a grip on his disintegrating thoughts. Whooping children contributed to an atmosphere of deranged fiesta. A man ran forward and chucked an empty beer bottle that caught the light as it flew towards the flames. The fire engine was finally being got to work and a hose turned on. The children started to dance around the leaky hydrant, getting soaked. The plume of water, hesitant at first, was lit silver by the glow of the backdrop. What sounded like fireworks started going off. The crowd stilled, then panic spread as it was realised they were gunshots. Someone asked, 'Are we under attack?' No, it was ammunition in the building, it was said. Bullets cracked. Some threw themselves on the ground, to general laughter.

Schlegel pushed deeper into the crowd, checking for Sybil in vain, sensing they would have him under lock and key before the end of the night. He couldn't tell if he was sweating from the fire, terror or sickness. Screams went up when an army of rats fled the building. Some burned as they ran. A huge crack rang out as more roof collapsed, to an enormous roar. The joke was well and truly on him. He was probably the only one in the crowd with pockets of contraband.

He saw Groenke, in his cart, trying to make his way through the squash. He moved away, working another direction. He thought he glimpsed Sybil but the next moment she was gone. The darkness and flames made everything hard to read.

Sparks leapt into the sky, tarmac bubbled itself back to pitch, grass smouldered. Another crack, another beam gone, another cheer. Someone blew a bugle for fun, to applause.

The fire showed no signs of abating. Schlegel abandoned any pretence of method and chased this way and that.

The mounted troop returned from its sortie, rifles cradled, hooves ringing, pushing through the crowd, the horses dancing sideways, disturbed by the flames, ears pricked, eyes wide. In an empty circle a group of children played a skipping game. Schlegel saw Pohl in consultation with the commandant, looking weirdly pale. He hadn't realised Pohl was still there.

Everything took on the appearance of choreographed moves: one wrong step and that would be it.

A second fire engine arrived, more hose laid. Schlegel saw Broad, loitering in the recess of the hospital block entrance. He was drinking and drunk. A beer stand set up nearby was doing a brisk trade. Broad saluted him with his bottle, and confirmed the worst.

'I wouldn't hang around. They already have you down for this.'

'And you think I did it?'

'Not for me to say.'

'What would you do?'

Broad, amused by Schlegel's predicament, gave a magnanimous shrug and nodded towards the river. 'Hide out in the zone. Give it a couple of days. Patrols and the posse will be out looking for you and whoever else escaped tonight. By the third day they will lose interest and you can make your move.'

'That easy?'

'They can't fine-comb twenty-five square kilometres.'

'There's still getting out.'

'For a contribution to a charity fund of your choice . . . ' Broad whistled, feigning innocence.

Schlegel showed two cheaper pieces of jade.

'Not bad.'

Schlegel produced what turned out to be Tanner's brooch. He started to say it wasn't available but Broad relieved him of it and said that was the one he wanted.

'I could always arrest you for being in possession of stolen goods, earn myself big kudos.'

For a moment Schlegel thought Broad only had in mind to cheat him.

Broad laughed at his discomfort and said, 'I started as a guard on the perimeter fence, so I know this. Follow the railway south to the outer fence. Count five watchtowers from the railway line. There is a mined strip in front of the fence, with warnings, but between the fifth and six towers isn't mined. The fence is lit at night but you will see a dark corridor where the lights don't reach and you can cross to the fence and crawl under. The strip on the other side isn't mined either.'

'Why not?'

'The guard got drunk and shot up the mines and then it became a way of bunking off.'

'How long ago was this?'

'It'll still be there. Nothing down there gets checked and the guard's asleep half the time.'

Schlegel asked, 'And getting out of the garrison?'

'That's the difficult part. Your problem not mine. Head down and *bonne chance*.' He pointed to the conflagration. 'Plenty of distraction.'

He clapped Schlegel on the shoulder and skipped down the steps.

The fire had peaked. People were starting to drift away. Still no Sybil.

In terms of that night's orchestration, Frau Hoess did not have in mind the sight of her husband in the company of her seamstress. She had been enjoying the fire in a way that thrilled her. It put an end to a lot of embarrassing problems. Pohl had swaggered around like a grandee, delighted with how things were turning out, and slipped off to be driven back to Kattowice to catch his aeroplane, pausing to kiss her hand and confirm her future was secure.

Her euphoria at Pohl's news that she could stay – regardless of what was otherwise decided – lasted until she spotted her husband edging shiftily through the crowd, his face preternaturally pale. Then she saw it was some sort of mask, like actor's pancake. What on earth did he think he was playing at? He would ruin everything.

She saw the seamstress being prodded ahead of him. She wasn't being forced but she didn't look willing either, which could only mean her husband was up to his old tricks. How furtive he looked, glancing around to check they weren't followed. No danger of that. All eyes on the fire.

She was watching from an upstairs window of the

administration block where a crowd of wives had gathered and fortifiers were being taken. Despite the drama outside, the mood was light-hearted, though Frau Hoess was aware of some stopping to stare as she swept out glaring. She was downstairs in time to see a basement light switched on in her husband's block. His and the woman's legs were visible through the angle of the window.

She didn't blame the woman; she wouldn't have any choice.

Frau Hoess stamped her foot, not liking what she was seeing after the beguiling diversion of Schlegel's romantic alternative.

Her silly lovers' dream was already spoiled because Pohl blamed Schlegel for the fire, which – as a possible provider of his alibi – she knew he had not started. Nevertheless, she would have to be careful to get her gemstones back before light fingers went to work.

She suspected Schlegel's story was a pack of lies but so highly attractive because it was a version of her own; except she was Orfeo and her then husband-to-be the downcast, after all those years in prison. Toughened but spiritually broken; a virgin too. How many months of coaxing had it taken to make him upstanding? More than she cared to remember. She suspected while in prison he had succumbed to carnal acts with men, for want of choice. She had asked, being curious, and he denied. She told him it didn't matter, she would forgive him anyway, and made it her secret mission to take him in hand and save him from himself. The truth was, he wasn't much interested in the physical. Too highly strung, always rushing, couldn't see how a woman needed time. He made excuses. He was busy. He had to work. He wasn't in the mood. Excuses for his inability to perform. The crushes were a pathetic imitation of the way other men made free with garrison women.

There was no question of letting him make a fool of himself with the seamstress. Besides, he didn't deserve the woman. He would turn it into something trite, and she would be cast in the role of the vindictive, jealous wife.

He would fling Böhner at her. Accusations would fly. Others would get to hear, and snigger. She was the one staying. A reputation to consider. First wife of the garrison. Queen of Nephrite.

There were good artists among those in the camp. The painter who came to make running repairs because the children scribbled on the walls was supposed to have been quite famous. What she had in mind was something like Klimt's portrait of the Bloch-Bauer woman, so deliciously decadent, but not officially degenerate. Those brazen women, swimming in primeval ooze. Dare she have herself done in the nude? She was starved of love. It was out of the question she avail herself of another officer. She had wondered about Krick but decided to keep their relationship professional. She needed him as an ally. When it came to slumming, Böhner was adequate but there was nothing operatic about him, to be rated no higher than a swain.

In her romantic heart of hearts she wanted to be the one fleeing through the night, her lover's hand in hers. But if the seamstress was her surrogate – released by her generosity, thereby thwarting her fool of a husband – she would become the enabler, helping to release the lovebirds into the sky.

Part of her cared nothing for their fate, and anyway, she reminded herself, the original had turned out badly; she didn't believe that tacked-on happy ending for a minute. Her real motive was to spite her husband; the rest was dressing.

The show was over, the place strewn with rubbish and empty beer bottles. Already a litter patrol had been hauled out of the camp and put to work. Apart from the odd flare, the flames were reduced to an angry glow. There would be ash everywhere in the garden. They would have to brush every leaf. What she needed was someone to invent a vacuum cleaner for outdoors.

She found Schlegel wandering in a daze. She told him and he looked in disbelief towards the commandant's office.

Ten minutes later they were all in her Opel, with Frau Hoess driving, Sybil in the boot, which was too small for two, leaving Schlegel folded up on the floor behind the front seats, covered with a blanket. The car was waved through the gate. She took them over the river. Broad's plan was the only serviceable one Schlegel had. He was in no fit state to travel. A sickness of fear, he thought, as much as contamination.

They stood in the road and watched the car leave. The sky was still stained from the fire and away in the distance the chimneys blazed. A big moon cast spectral light. Schlegel said they must leave the road and make for the railway. He hoped to move them quickly south before daylight to the lakes where it would be easier to lose any pursuers.

VI

Morgen spent the day waiting at Breslau station for his brother. Theodore was a Tibetan scholar working for the Ahnenerbe, a cultural body of research and fellowship, so-called, staffed with frauds keen to sell their crackpot ideas to its gullible founder, Himmler. If jade was the Reichsführer's latest craze, then the Ahnenerbe would be involved.

Morgen and his brother famously didn't get along. Theodore considered himself the cleverer. Sometimes Morgen wondered if they in fact had the same mother.

When Theodore was willing it was done with mandarin condescension, such as agreeing to drive from Berlin to collect him.

Morgen was thankful to find himself back in a real world, however grim, surrounded by familiar sounds and smells. Cigarettes already tasted better and he felt relief at his deliverance and guilty about Sybil and Schlegel, who he hoped would pull himself together enough to work something out.

Theodore swept in late in the afternoon, with a septuagenarian driver wearing jodhpurs and a chauffeur's cap.

The weather had finally broken. Sheeting rain drummed on the car's canvas roof and the unreliable sweep of ancient wiper blades revealed a smeared, drowned landscape. Bad roads, empty villages, closed churches, their priests gone. Theodore was vague about their destination.

The road went into woods and they started to climb.

At the top of the hill their destination, shrouded in mist, revealed a huge baroque castle. Servants came with umbrellas to usher them inside. Morgen wondered what such a palace had to do with Tibetan scholarship.

If the castle's exterior was high baroque, the room they were shown into was as plain as a monastery, stripped of all historical artifice, leaving it uglily modified and austere. Outside, statues stood in the rain, presiding over drained ponds, idle fountains, long expanses of wet lawn and empty formal walkways.

Theodore finally revealed his hand, saying the place was being prepared as the leadership's eastern bastion.

That made sense, Morgen supposed, and still wondered what it had to do with Tibet.

'Is Adolf here?' he asked irreverently, knowing it would irritate his formal brother. He realised he had no idea what Theodore thought about anything behind all the correctness and irritation.

As for the mine, which was about half an hour to the south, Theodore confirmed the project had been talked up to Himmler. Scholarly research on jade was being conducted and the usual opportunists were putting in for exotic Far East research trips, almost out of the question by then, but not entirely. That said, the project remained cloaked in mystery, with no paperwork from what Theodore could see.

'How did you find out?'

Morgen said it came down to a woman and a dinner-party conversation. Theodore recoiled, having no time for women or social intercourse.

Theodore, sounding important, said, 'There is someone you should meet.'

'Here?' asked Morgen, surprised.

Indicating that he should follow, Theodore led the way

down long corridors, some formal, some back passages. They passed a gang working on the installation of an elevator. The men were prisoners and looked efficient and knowledgeable.

They emerged in another part of the castle yet to be renovated. Morgen had quite lost all sense of direction. At a set of huge double doors, three times their height, Theodore knocked. A man's voice called for them to come.

Morgen's first impression was of mirrors reflecting a riot of rococo. A man in a suit at the far end of the palatial room, behind an elaborate desk, stood to greet them while putting a telephone down with the confident air of a communications expert. Theodore hung back, bowed and retreated. Morgen was confused, never having reckoned his brother to be a broker in the power game.

Morgen was invited to a chair with carved woodwork and embroidered upholstery. In the tall mirror behind the desk he could see the back of the man's head and his own reflection looking dishevelled and insignificant.

'Dr Kammler,' said Morgen.

Everything felt overexposed, with the night as clear as a photographic negative. Sybil saw Schlegel stagger and thought him ill.

She heard the lorry before he did, pulled him down into a shallow drainage ditch. Schlegel held on to his gun and berated himself for not having left the road sooner. Dry grass threatened to make him sneeze. The lorry stopped just ahead. Schlegel's body convulsed twice as he held his nose. He supposed they must have been spotted. The engine continued to turn over. A door slammed. Schlegel waited for the guard to jump down. Every sound seemed magnified. Schlegel clenched his nose, waiting for the next convulsion.

A coarse remark was met with sarcastic laughter. Only two men, by the sound of it, both drunk. The one who had stopped to relieve himself said as he got back in the cab that he was in no fit state to drive.

Schlegel didn't know how much darkness they had left. They needed a resting place before daylight, preferably in shade as they had no water or food. It was not a landscape for hiding, being flat and open. Buildings would be searched. The labour gangs and their guards would come and there was no telling where they would work. And the posse would be out. Any sweep over exposed land would flush them out.

Ditches and rough terrain made the going harder. Schlegel grew unsure of their direction. He seemed to be walking off his illness although it left him terribly weak. He choked his cough with his sleeve, fearing the sound would carry.

Deep in the zone, they found their way blocked by a high bank and ditch whose channel gleamed dark and sullen. Forced to follow it, they found no crossing. Schlegel feared the detour was taking them off course.

When at last they came to a bridge they had to decide whether extra sentries had been posted. Schlegel told Sybil to wait and crawled forward using the bank for cover. He lay listening, on the verge of passing out from tiredness. Berating himself for wasting time, he got up, started to cross and froze at the smell of cigarette smoke. As he inched his way back two guards began chatting lazily.

They trudged disconsolately on. When Schlegel noticed Sybil starting to lag he felt obliged to keep turning to check and in the process put his foot in a hole and went over on his ankle, with a sharp cry.

He lay there, foot throbbing, waiting for the first sounds of alarm.

When nothing happened, he sat up feeling foolish, cursing the pain, aware of Sybil's silence. The sprain reduced him to a hobble. He didn't point out it considerably reduced their chances of getting away.

'We find it more productive these days to lease camp labour to private companies,' Kammler said. 'Auschwitz was always too improvised but it was deemed the regional site most suited to expansion because of its transport links.'

'Has the whole operation been a business takeover?' asked Morgen, astonished. Everything the man was talking about suggested as much.

Kammler seemed pleased with Morgen's analysis.

'Slave labour per se is inefficient. About a quarter as productive as a regular workforce. However, if you specialise and break it down into technical units . . .'

Morgen pictured the man's career as a traceless rise through a succession of offices, a master of the bureaucratic process, a new language of jargon and strategic alliances based on acute readings of any shift in the standing and influence of his patrons, moving up and on, making sure not to burn bridges.

'Put thugs in charge as Pohl did, you know you are relatively secure. But huge concentrations of prisoners, as was the fashion, increases security problems. And anyway, business and industry were not keen to have us as competition, so they stood off. I have always favoured fruitful cooperation but you have to offer a proper service beyond making promises you can't keep. Fortunately, we are now able to reverse that.'

Morgen felt like he was being hypnotised and it took all his will to resist. He was sure now the lot of them were in it up to their necks. The only hope he clung to was that the commandant – and Wirths – remained liable. It was infernally complex. Such was the command structure that it could be held they had exceeded orders. With nothing written down, those orders could always be turned into a deadly game of pass the parcel. Perhaps the commandant had been considered expendable from the start. Perhaps he and Schlegel had too.

Kammler was saying, 'There is no profit to be made from human hair, which has to be laboriously collected, dried, packaged, and shipped, only to be sold off for next to nothing.'

Taking the plunge, Morgen asked about the crematoria.

It earned him an admonitory look. 'You are straying.'

Morgen said while he understood certain areas were beyond the law others existed where he believed it had been broken.

Kammler said, 'Problems of interpretation are always difficult. Order versus initiative.'

'I believe the commandant took the law into his own hands.'

'Are you so desperate to see the back of the man?'

Kammler smoothed the table as if clearing a path. 'A decision was made to turn his into the premier camp. Because of the projected size it was decided by the doctors and the commandant to build more crematoria. One was planned from the beginning and it quickly went to four, on the insistence of the doctors.'

'You had no say in this?'

'I am not a local expert. I defer to those on the ground.'

'Gas chambers?'

'Cooked up between the doctors and the commandant.'

'You knew nothing?'

'We provided a service. We are technically contracted by the garrison.'

'To build crematoria not gas chambers?'

'Look at the plans. They show what we provided. Any subsequent adjustments were agreed between the commandant's office and the civil engineer responsible for the furnaces.'

Kammler stared at him with unreadable eyes. He looked scrawnier, more under pressure, not getting enough sleep, as were they all. Morgen was slow to recognise the man's amphetamine habit. Whatever he was on seemed very good.

Without sounding boastful Kammler said he had an empire to run and needed to be constantly on the move. While Auschwitz was an important component he had to delegate.

'Our concern was deadlines and getting the job done over any purpose others had in mind. I am a technocrat.'

Morgen edged Kammler forward, asking about the commandant, who seemed to lie at the heart of everything.

Kammler took his time deciding. 'It depends on whether someone advised him what was about to happen.'

'What do you mean?'

'Hoess demonstrated through tests what the garrison was capable of ... You may say he was merely reacting to an already dire internal situation, or perhaps he was auditioning for the job, about which he had been tipped off. He is a total fanatic, of course. Others were competing for the post too.'

'I am told he distanced himself from the process.'

'He was bound to cover his tracks in such a radical area.'

Morgen asked instead, 'What about the two temporary gas chambers?'

Kammler seemed surprised he knew. He shrugged, as if they were no concern, and said, 'From what I recall, a deal was done to take in a large number of skilled Slovak Jewish workers. Unfortunately the Slovak government reneged at the last minute, unless it included the workers' dependents. Do you see what I am saying?'

'They insisted on getting rid of the chaff.'

Morgen remembered the commandant describing the Slovak deal as Kammler's. Maybe it was. That didn't make him responsible for the Slovaks changing their terms.

'The onus fell on the commandant. He exploited an existing medical category.'

'14f13. Unfit for work.'

'You have done your homework. The commandant had a site in mind, which he required me to inspect. We rode out, early one morning, accompanied by Fegelein.'

'Fegelein!'

'I told you I trained at the man's riding academy and knew him slightly. I was surprised by his presence, then decided it had to do with his position in the Chancellery.'

Kammler was clever at painting himself as along for the ride. The commandant had earmarked a remote abandoned farmhouse for conversion. According to Kammler, all subsequent discussion was between the commandant and Fegelein.

Morgen asked its location. Kammler's answer put it in the vicinity of the burning pits; so Schulze had been right.

'And your role?' asked Morgen.

'Insurance, I suspect. I was the ranking officer. If called to account, the commandant could always point to me as the senior man, therefore responsible for the initiative.'

'What were you told?'

'The commandant required the job to be done under wraps. He asked me to provide a secret workforce for it.' Kammler gave a disarming laugh. 'It allowed me to push for something I otherwise would not have got. To comply, I needed my own private technicians, which I didn't have.'

Schulze had said it happened very fast, with Kammler being given control of all slave labour, from which he created his mobile brigades, leaving the commandant outmanoeuvred and ceding his entire workforce to Kammler's central command.

Morgen still found it impossible to apportion blame. He supposed Kammler had an equally convincing alternative, when it suited, in which he took executive control, with the commandant seen as scared of what history had in mind for him.

Had it all been a waste of time? Morgen asked himself. Whatever Kammler had required of them probably no longer applied. In terms of his own contribution, he was sure it lay beyond any ripple effect, and was of no point or consequence.

Kammler enquired blandly, 'What are your plans now?'

Morgen said he didn't know.

'Come and work for me.'

'As what?' he asked, thinking, out of the frying pan ...

'Security. A lot of the work I oversee is at the forefront of technology. Exciting stuff. Think about it. The camps have been bypassed. The real work is much less centralised. It takes place in satellites and is far more entrepreneurial. It will be the post-war model. In the meantime we need new and advanced forms of security. With the enemy bombing we enter our Jules Verne phase. We are going deep underground. The world is on the point of being transformed. Technology will win us the war. Rockets to the moon!'

Kammler looked drunk on power.

And thus, Morgen supposed, the case of Ingeborg Tanner was closed, without getting even close to a solution.

Fegelein would no doubt talk his way out of the homicidal driving charge, as he always did. Pohl was right: the cases of Grabner and Wirths would take years to reach court. And the commandant would be protected by being shifted sideways or up. They had achieved nothing.

The sun was already high when Schlegel awoke, immediately aware something was wrong. He looked around and couldn't see Sybil. Not in the empty stretch of field ahead nor in the surrounding trees.

He supposed her gone after seeing how much starker everything was by day – their lack of option, his curtailed mobility, their vulnerability, the slim chance of him bringing her to safety.

The best they had managed for hiding was a clump of silver birches, more grove than wood, with no undergrowth, which anyone passing would search.

Until twisting his ankle Schlegel had felt cautiously optimistic, despite his sickness, or perhaps because it left him so light-headed. Luck appeared to be with them and he had dared to believe in their deliverance.

He scanned in vain for any sign of Sybil's return, knowing she wouldn't be back. He would have to wait out the day before attempting to move. Whether any of the sparse ground growth or tree bark was edible he had no idea. A few spindly mushrooms growing by trees he feared were poisonous. Dehydration worried him more. All he could do was preserve what little energy he had. He marked the edge of the trees as his boundary. If no one encroached on it he would be safe at the end of the day.

He sweated and shivered, coughed into the ground, passed out and woke, noting the sun's numb climb. He slept again, with one eye open, or so he thought until he found a hand pressed to his mouth and Sybil's face close to his. She put a warning finger to her lips.

Schlegel, confused, was aware of singing. A passing work gang was belting out its marching song. He was surprised they could sing the chorus: 'Have you up there forgotten about us?'

When it had gone Sybil said, 'They have patrols out looking, motorbikes on the roads and men on horseback searching the land.'

She had gone to a low hill in the distance. She thought they were safer staying where they were. The hillock had no shelter and they would burn.

Schlegel sensed no connection from her, yet was pathetically grateful for her return.

She produced two small raw beetroot and a curly green-leafed vegetable, which she thought was cattle feed. The stalk needed a lot of chewing and the first taste of the leaf was bitter but it became quite sweet. Schlegel's beetroot tasted earthy. He told her as a child he hadn't liked them. She looked at him as though the remark was meaningless. He realised she considered memories useless, and words too, unless essential. Nothing was embellished. Schlegel still saw their plight as a shared experience where he suspected she didn't, which made her return with food the more surprising, until he realised he was the one with the escape route.

The posse used whistles to communicate. They saw them about a kilometre off, approaching in a flat line, taking their time. Schlegel counted fifteen riders.

It was too late to run. Schlegel whispered to Sybil she should slip away while she could. He said he would shoot to give her more time. She shook her head. Schlegel supposed he would take out the men nearest, then her; they would rape her otherwise before killing her. Then he would shoot himself.

He slid the safety catch off. He was about to raise his head when a distant gunshot sounded, then another, followed by a blast on the whistle and the commotion of riders moving off at speed. Schlegel watched them go, doubting whether his nerve would have held.

Afterwards, they sat hunched in silence. He watched the shadow of leaves play on her unreadable face and had never felt more alone.

Time dragged ever more slowly. Schlegel feared they would not be as lucky next time but the day passed. They rested as much as possible and set off at last light. Sybil led. Schlegel struggled to find a rhythm, using something between a hop and a limp. Another bright night, with a moon and high cloud. They heard a train pass on its slow way south.

When they reached the railway Schlegel stood mesmerised by the sight of the hard metal gleaming into the distance, all the way to Prague and Vienna. With everything so still they may as well have been the only living creatures. In that deceptive idyll, the moon caught Sybil's face and its beauty caused him to catch his breath.

He was dogged by faintness. His body shook. His mouth was as dry as sandpaper. A splitting headache left him wanting only to give up. His greatest fear remained that he had been contaminated, making escape pointless as death was already waiting.

The ground gave way to meadows and clumps of trees. It grew cooler. Schlegel sensed the change of atmosphere but the lakes were a long time coming; then suddenly he saw the silver sheet, sinister and otherworldly.

They found the water surrounded by a complex network of reedy creeks. Schlegel reasoned the more lost the harder to find they were. It was not the sort of terrain that lent itself to mounted searches. Someone could stay there days without anyone knowing.

Sometimes they had no way forward and were forced to retrace their steps. A spit of land took them down another channel, its water green in the first of the light. The air grew tainted with marsh gas. They found an abandoned canoe, dragged into the reeds. The scum on the water lay undisturbed, showing it hadn't been used recently. The creek widened and they came to a tiny wooden jetty, from which a path led through high grass to a small clearing in which stood a low wedge-shaped hut, like an upturned flat-bottomed boat. They approached cautiously. The structure was only waist-high, with one end higher and a hatch for an entrance. What its purpose was Schlegel had no idea. The ground inside was dry and sandy, the material woven from long thin branches; willow, he thought; as good as anywhere for a refuge.

Despite staying in a palace, Morgen was given a simple bedroom with a cot and a basin, in what felt like servants' quarters. He had plenty to think about but soon fell asleep, the only welcome part of the day.

He turned up for breakfast with a large and ungainly scrap of lavatory paper stuck to his face after cutting himself shaving. There was no sign of his brother.

When Morgen realised who the only other diner was the situation grew even more unreal. It was the shrink, Krick.

Morgen presumed the man's presence was no more coincidence than Kammler's, and again he wondered what his brother's real business was.

Krick greeted him as though it were perfectly normal they should run across each other in the leadership's secret lair. He invited Morgen to join him.

It was a proper breakfast too. White tablecloth, linen napkins, plates with a crest, silverware, fresh bread rolls, cold meats, cheese, jams and real coffee.

Trying to sound casual, Morgen asked Krick what brought him there.

Krick said he was on his way back from Switzerland.

'Psychiatric conference. Carl Jung was the principal speaker.'

There was little Morgen could say to that.

'Are you on your way back to the garrison?'

'Alas. Not the most salubrious posting. They neither know what to do with me nor where to put me. I am stuck in the commercial sector in an office by a delivery yard where they whistle and crash about all day.'

He produced a pipe and asked if it was all right while Morgen was eating.

Morgen found the man a bit too polished, with his cool, modern demeanour, as if to say psychiatry was over its fusty Jewish connotations.

Krick surprised him by bringing up the subject of Ingeborg Tanner.

'Your colleague asked and I said I had spoken to her on the telephone when she made an appointment, which she didn't keep.'

Now he remembered they had met after all.

'Under what circumstances?'

'A party.'

'What makes you remember now?'

'I happen to be treating one of the garrison wives, just had a baby and is depressed. It happens quite a lot and I was reminded of talking to this other woman at a party about her wanting a child and being upset it wasn't happening.'

'Tanner, you think now?'

'I am pretty sure.'

'Pretty sure?'

'We were drunk.' Krick gave a worldly smile. 'The unusual part of the conversation I recall was she asked me to give her the baby.'

Morgen wondered why Krick was telling. Had Tanner been pregnant when she died?

'Anyway, I didn't take her up.'

Morgen thought: Really, such a catch?

'A lot of young women are trying,' Krick went on, in a way that suggested he wasn't short of choice. 'Perhaps because so many young men are being killed.'

Krick stared at the smoke from his pipe and said, 'Wouldn't you say the world divides now between men who have killed and those that haven't?'

Given the question, Morgen felt bound to ask if he had.

Krick answered evenly. 'I remain a curious observer.'

'Tempted?'

'On a professional level, one is bound to wonder about experiencing extremes as told by others.'

Morgen was tiring of the man, suspecting it was all mind games. He reminded Krick that he technically remained a suspect in the Tanner case as he grumpily attacked his roll, thinking his breakfast was being spoiled.

'Of course. I found her body and my name was in her book. Does that make me a suspect?'

'The coincidence of you finding her made us wonder.'

Krick warmed to the game. 'Aha, you mean my arrogance is such that having committed the crime I could not bear it going unreported because the fuss is half the fun. And I have a low opinion of investigators, knowing you are too stupid to make the connection between the person who found the body being the murderer.'

Morgen wondered about the man's superior tone. Had he killed Tanner he would know they could prove nothing.

'Anyway, it's not so much of a coincidence as I cycle that way every day. What is your best theory?'

Morgen ignored that he was being patronised.

'An act of retaliation by an ex-lover, carried out by a proxy, which I am sure can be arranged for a pittance.'

'For sure. Everyone is bored enough to kill.'

Krick remained intrigued by the prospect of his own guilt. Morgen wished the man would shut up.

'Well, I suppose I could have done it, like the tempted priest who hears too many confessions and is drawn to experience the sin, in a theological way.'

Morgen spread an unhealthy amount of butter on his roll, not knowing when he would see any again.

Krick went on. 'We live in a time where the usual constraints no longer apply, so I am surprised more of the likes of her haven't been done in.'

Morgen grunted. 'Quite understandable. Men generally loathe women. There is a history of violence in the garrison towards them.'

Krick rewarded Morgen with what looked like his practised secretive smile.

'Of course I didn't kill Tanner.'

Morgen asked brusquely, 'Then what are you saying?'

'That killing has become so commonplace it has lost its taboo. The few men who do consult me worry they have become inured. Medical history has been a process of advance. Perhaps with ethics it works the other way around.'

'You mean what was once considered forbidden has been transcended. The more advanced, the less ethical.'

'Sophistication is a process of adaption. Everything becomes technical not moral. Do you wonder what it's like to kill someone?'

Morgen saw the man was trying to get a rise out of him and obliged by saying, 'Present circumstances apart, no, not really.'

Krick chose to treat the remark as a joke, which annoyed Morgen more.

'In fact, I have news of Tanner. I should have told you before. It may look like I have been dallying when I show you this.'

He had a briefcase, from which he produced a letter. He made the most of his pause. 'A confession.'

'Whose?'

'Not mine.' Again the deflecting laugh. 'The matter seems to have resolved itself quite easily in the end, almost disappointingly so. I should not really be showing you.'

'Why not?'

'Because it is confidential to my investigation.'

Morgen wasn't sure he had heard correctly.

Krick handed the letter over. Written in a shaky hand and black ink, Morgen read: *Since I killed that woman I cannot go on.*

'Short and to the point.'

The letter was dated and signed, with the name spelled out in capitals.

Morgen said, 'I am no connoisseur of suicide notes, but it strikes me as not at all the last words anyone would write. It doesn't specify Tanner.'

'Perhaps he didn't know her name. A random attack. I can't see it being anyone else.'

'Confidential to your investigation, you said.'

'Yes. The powers that be take suicide seriously. I have been asked to write a report.'

Morgen looked at the name under the signature. 'Who was Hertz?'

'Security police. One of the torturers. I presume he became demoralised and coarsened. Many in that department do.'

Morgen remembered the attic where they had found Haas's body. So Hertz was part of the torture machine, part of the system.

Krick went on, with an air of academic authority. 'I believe it makes sense. It is psychologically stressful work, this business of breaking bodies. They're always in and out of the staff infirmary, nerves shot. The droll thing is, they are thinking of stopping torture of prisoners because of the adverse effect it has on the practitioners.'

Krick refired his pipe. 'Dishing it out comes at price. Panic attacks, nervous cramps, loss of weight, anxiety and persecution complexes.'

'In the case of this man Hertz, what do we suppose?'

Morgen chided himself for the 'we'.

Krick raised his hands in what appeared a benediction.

'A man who holds life and death in his hands, and practises it every day. Perhaps he did know Tanner and she wouldn't sleep with him. Perhaps the back of her head was too tempting to resist . . . crack goes the skull, like an eggshell. If you break people's spirits for a living it must be hard to be refused. We have become lovers of the dead.'

The anticlimax of solution, Morgen thought. He could still picture Krick the likelier perpetrator.

Theodore came in and nodded at Krick in such a way that Morgen couldn't tell if they knew each other or it was the polite acquaintance of two strangers. Nor could Morgen make out the point of Krick's presence. Perhaps he answered to Kammler too, but why would Kammler want Morgen to be aware of that, unless some new scheme was being hatched.

Theodore ate in silence, ruminating. Krick looked like he was about to make his excuses when Theodore said, 'Tell my brother about your recent trip.'

Krick looked surprised by the fraternal reference. Morgen wondered what his professional assessment would be. A pathological case of sibling rivalry, no doubt.

'Interesting if apostate,' said Krick. 'Do you know anything about Carl Jung?'

Morgen gestured reluctantly, unwilling to concede a point in front of his brother.

'Carl Gustav Jung,' Theodore recited. 'Probably one of the finest minds we possess. He took psychoanalysis away from the Jewish influence of Freud, to huge opprobrium.'

Krick said he had attended Jung's seminars and held discussions with the man when studying in Zurich ten years earlier.

Morgen presumed Krick was implying he was a protégé. Sure enough, with great false modesty, he went on, 'I was privileged to be presented with a draft of Jung's 1936 Wotan lecture.'

'Are you familiar?' Theodore asked.

Morgen snapped, 'Not my field of expertise.'

Theodore flashed him a look to ask: What is?

Krick composed himself to look suitably humbled and grave.

'I quote: "A hurricane has broken loose in Germany while we still believe it is fine weather." Our leader as god of storm, god of secret musings, wind of change, German weather, the soul snatcher who is also seized. It is not an unsympathetic portrait.'

Morgen supposed Krick wished to boast and looked at Theodore, who indicated to be patient. Krick continued to sing the great man's praises in terms of his work on meaningful significance and the transpersonal unconscious.

Morgen nodded, bored, and only paid attention when Krick said, 'Last summer one of the Führer's physicians telephoned Jung in Zurich and asked him to come to Bavaria to make a mental assessment of the Führer.'

'This summer or the summer of 1942?' Morgen asked.

'1942.'

Adolf was a virtual recluse, with speculation on his health and ability to direct the army, but that was recent, with no such rumours the year before. The story sounded interestingly far-fetched, which meant it was probably true.

'Why?'

'Concern among high-ranking officers about the Führer's increasingly erratic behaviour. He was drinking heavily.'

Theodore interrupted. 'The teetotal, vegetarian image is Goebbels' manufacture. The man likes nothing more than a bratwurst and beer. Anyway, Jung turned down the offer.'

Krick nodded. Morgen wondered why he was being told.

Krick went on. 'The fact is, since Stalingrad, Hitler is no longer a prophet. His religion has crumbled. Even the average German is overwhelmed by the symbolic implications of the defeat. Goebbels, who remains fanatically loyal, stated that an entire conception of the universe has been defeated, spiritual forces will be crushed, and the hour of judgement is at hand.'

Morgen wondered who was behind the move to approach Jung. He had been aware at the end of the butchers case of political scenery being shifted: Himmler arranging a secret

Jewish ransom train, as a way of opening back channels, with the war turning.

Krick said, 'It started to go wrong long before Stalingrad. The Führer believed in Hörbiger's fire and ice theory and wherever he advanced the cold would retreat before him. Hörbigerians claimed they could predict weather months and years in advance, and announced the Russian winter of 1941 would be mild.'

It was all madness, thought Morgen. It was one thing for Frau Hoess to spout on about Hörbiger; quite another to commit an entire military campaign to the man's theories.

Krick looked mysterious and said his most recent visit to Zurich was as a personal envoy to make Jung reconsider.

Morgen thought it unlikely that an eminent neutral would consort with a tainted leadership.

'He refused, of course. It was obvious he would.'

'Then what was the point?'

'Jung's assessment would have been damning.'

Krick left it at that. Morgen asked if the overture was bound to be rejected then what was the purpose of the feint.

'Ha-ha,' said Krick. 'Let's say I was the messenger in the hope Jung would become one too.'

'To whom?'

'The Americans.'

One in particular, Krick went on, an extrovert and wealthy woman, named Bancroft, who lived in Zurich and was unusual for the openness of her marriage. She had become part of Jung's circle and was the lover of the local head of US intelligence, for whom she worked.

Morgen guessed Krick's mission was to alert Jung to growing discontent surrounding the leadership, hoping he would pass it on to the Bancroft woman and she would tell her lover, and thus the Americans would be secretly appraised.

'Why tell me?' Morgen asked.

Theodore took over. 'Schlegel's stepfather would wish that you knew, I suspect.'

'Do you know him?'

'I didn't say that. But I presume the arrest of Schlegel's mother was carried out to keep his stepfather in line, because he is suspected of too many side deals with the Swiss and the Americans. He is ill now, which makes the situation more delicate.'

Morgen could not tell if this was an overture and Krick and his brother were trying to recruit him to their cause.

Schlegel lay chased by fevered hallucinations and shallow dreams. Tanner's death became part of the great pagan sacrifice; Morgen told him he should admit killing her, and starting the fire, while he was about it. Morgen made him repeat: The radical stance of the regime is that it has done away with the pretence of God, the master in whose name so many atrocities could be committed.

Schlegel was told he must stand responsible for his own actions. He saw Sepp in an MC's hat, shouting, 'Step this way!' Evidence was produced in the shape of a butcher's hammer with Schlegel's fingerprints and the commandant interrupted to say he would be taken out and shot by Palitsch, who had requested the job. When Schlegel protested that Palitsch was already under arrest everyone cheered as though he had made the wildest joke. The room with its steep benches could have been an old lecture hall but the atmosphere was more that of a courtroom. The main exhibit was Tanner's disembowelled body with its open ribcage, and Dr Wirths explained the finer points of his autopsy, including evidence of photographic imprints in her brain showing her final attacker. A blowup of Schlegel, hammer raised above his head, was pinned on the board. Broad stepped forward to denounce him as a Soviet agent.

Then he was standing staring at the wall, lungs pumping like rusty bellows, aware of breathing his last as Palitsch stuck the barrel into the back of his neck and twisted it. But instead of shooting, Palitsch delivered a breathless little monologue into Schlegel's ear. 'Fanaticism, and its counterpart lethargy, lacks true awareness. It represents an untrue existence, even though one's entire strength is used up in the longing for infinite leadership.' Then he was watching Sybil as she sewed with her back to him. When he called her name, his voice wasn't his, and her face when she turned wasn't altogether hers. Some of it belonged to Schulze and the rest to the bruised woman at the commandant's garden party.

In more coherent moments it still seemed to him that Tanner had been killed as a sacrifice, to distract from the corruption, and, yes, he could see Krick doing it – out of forensic curiosity and an eagerness to know. Without his discovery, Tanner's body otherwise might have lain unnoticed for days. As it was, it brought them back and deeper into the garden of evil. Then again, all was mirage. Anyone could have done it. Theoretical guilt. Men lined up, like they were waiting outside a brothel, to take a swing at Tanner as though she were a fairground machine. Practically every man in the garrison had murdered or been responsible for murder, facile as it was to say. All were stained with the original sin, in which none believed, all fallen, the crime as movable as the carousel of stolen goods that went round and round. If the detective was as liable as the criminal what justice? How could one serve, except in a self-serving way, without inviting despair? And in the middle of it all, the posturing commandant who, as his world fell apart, saw it only in terms of tragic destiny.

Sybil sat outside, knees clasped. Schlegel was delirious and the place wasn't as perfect as it looked. Dead stuff floated in the water.

Sometimes the commandant stank so much of death that his uniform had to be sent to the dry-cleaners and the girl who cleaned his boots did so with a handkerchief over her face.

Sybil went down to the shore and stared at the placid lake: how easy to walk in until it covered her. She stood in the shallows, mud oozing under her feet. Sun starred the water. She moved forward, marking where she thought it would cover her head.

The commandant came home for lunch. Because the radio was on she didn't hear him enter the room where she was allowed to work alone. She was wearing her hair up. Had he stared at her neck as she sat quietly stitching? He would have seen a thin, dark, watchful women, she supposed, transformed by his masculine gaze into something she no longer considered herself, a creature of desire.

The commandant kissed her, clumsily, tasting of tobacco. She fled and locked herself in the lavatory, and afterwards pretended to be ill, knowing the kiss broke the spell and marked the start of her fall.

She looked back at the shore, already far off, the water still only up to her waist. She heard the lazy drone of an aeroplane. The noise persisted. She saw nothing. The sky stayed empty, everything frozen. The great orb of the sun hurt her eyes. She stared, fixated by a dark blemish in its halo that became the plane, flying at her, the whine of its engine drowning everything as it dipped low to skim the surface. She ducked and leaned back to let the water cover her, feeling the shadow pass over.

With everything tranquil again she returned to the shore.

Schlegel seemed not to make the connection that they were now conducting air searches. Later she heard the plane's buzzing, always far away.

Apart from the beetroot and green leaves, they had eaten and drunk nothing. Water everywhere, which they dared not risk for fear of pollution. Sybil was warned off by the sight of three dead floating toads. She made forays into the reeds. The canoe had a hole. She stood on the jetty, staring at the scummy water, trying to put foolish thoughts from her head. A long waving tendril she thought a plant unfurled into a water snake. The aeroplane droned in the distance.

She studied the shoreline growth. Red berries she dismissed as too risky. The bullrushes looked harmless and she supposed their stems might provide sustenance; likewise a form of seaweed. She braved the water and disturbed a shoal of eels, fast and slick, coming out of the reeds. It took all her resolve to gather her meagre crop.

They chewed the stems of the rushes, harsh tasting, as was the seaweed.

Schlegel, still fragile, became more lucid. He spoke of his mother's failing memory and his stepfather's sickness. It would make more sense if the illnesses were the other way round: his mother had never been known to tax herself mentally and his stepfather had always seemed physically at ease. He saw Sybil wasn't listening and stopped but she asked him to go on. It reassured her to hear a voice talking normally.

She said she was like his mother; her past was lost too. She had trouble remembering what anyone looked like.

She got up wordlessly and lay down in the shelter. Schlegel sat thinking about their crushed world and the impossible gulf between them.

He went and lay next to her. Her hand was by her side. He touched her fingertips and she didn't respond. He held her hand and she didn't respond, though he was certain she was awake. He spoke and she didn't answer. He woke to find his hand empty and Sybil with her back to him. He lay listening to her breathing.

Morgen found it galling to be offered the prospect of an explanation by one so irritating as his brother. The mine was about half an hour away. The rain persisted. Theodore dispensed with his driver, saying he would take the wheel. Morgen dreaded the prospect.

Theodore said, 'There are things we must talk about.'

'Let me drive then.'

'You are a worse driver than I.'

They squabbled, tossed a coin.

'Gives you more time to think,' Morgen said condescendingly.

No traffic other than the occasional horse and cart. Everything dirt-poor. Morgen asked about the mine.

It wasn't much of one, Theodore said. Of course they were tunnelling.

'We're a nation of mad tunnellers, in case you hadn't noticed.'

Morgen had. Kammler's mobile squads had created an elaborate secret network under the castle. Kammler had proudly shown him, a virtual city of passageways, going deeper and deeper. Madness.

Theodore said, 'Someone obviously talked up the mine

to Heini and it is being done off the books. What Heini doesn't know is nothing of value is produced.'

That was a surprise. 'Nothing at all?'

'The seams are flawed. Someone is pulling the wool over his eyes.'

Morgen supposed Frau Hoess must be pretending Canada's jade was the product of the mine, which made it as useless an enterprise as all the rest.

Morgen asked Theodore if he knew the place.

'Yes. I was curious to see for myself.'

'What did you find?'

'Thirty prisoners transferred from Silesian coal pits and crucifixion as a form of punishment.'

'What?'

'The guard is bored, stuck in the middle of nowhere. They got tired of stringing up prisoners by their arms behind their backs. It tends to dislocate the shoulders, meaning they can't work, so they rope them to a beam. The prisoner must use his arms to force himself up to breathe. It results in agonising contractions.'

Morgen looked at his brother and said, 'I thought you lived in an ivory tower.'

'Scholarship doesn't preclude knowledge of cruelty,' Theodore replied enigmatically.

'What is the point of the mine in terms of its symbolic purpose?'

Theodore sighed. 'Heini's big interest is with the three great sciences of the Middle Ages – mysticism, astrology and alchemy. It makes him susceptible to the wiles of crackpots and charlatans, possibly even myself included.'

Morgen stared at his brother. Had he made a joke?

Theodore ignored him and went on. 'Heini's jade obsession stems from an equally silly one for a Welsh mystic writer named Machen, because of his tenuous connection to another of Heini's great infatuations, the Holy Grail.'

'Does the man really believe any of this?' Morgen asked.

'Enough to take himself off on a secret wartime mission to an abbey near Barcelona, where he believed he would find the very pot Christ used to consecrate the Last Supper.'

'Thinking it would win us the war?'

'Heini isn't alone in believing Christ is descended from Aryan stock.'

Himmler's attraction to Machen was his birthplace, believed to have been the seat of King Arthur's court, from which the knights departed to seek the grail.

'Machen was an initiate too, a member of the society of the Golden Dawn,' Theodore explained. 'When the commandant's wife raised the question of a defunct jade mine, Himmler was stirred to say, "For those with eyes to see, coincidences are clad in shining light."'

'How do you know this?'

'Walls have ears. It gets worse. The basis of giving her the go-ahead was because Machen once wrote a book called *Ornaments in Jade*.'

Morgen stopped and turned the car around.

'I've had enough of perdition,' he said, reduced to slack-jawed disbelief at Heini's vanity.

'It is a pointless exercise,' said Theodore. 'No need to bother, I agree.'

He paused. 'There is something you should know.'

Theodore's silence filled the car. Morgen asked if he had added the pregnant pause to his repertoire.

Theodore tutted. 'This is serious. Our leader is not a well man.'

'Heini?'

'Adolf.'

'How ill?'

'Some form of palsy. There is a race on to cure him. Bormann is using Fegelein to liaise with doctors in the place where you have just been.'

'He more or less admitted as much.'

'Adolf is in the hands of quacks. Did Fegelein tell you he serves more than one master?'

'Bormann and Heini too?'

Theodore nodded. 'Given his craze for soothsayers and the occult, Heini is using Fegelein in necromancy and magic practices to cure the Führer, perhaps even involving the sacrifice of animals and children ...'

So the man was accountable after all, and not only of the crime Morgen had thought him guilty.

The lake no longer looked so threatening or inviting. Sybil risked bathing in one of the cleaner creeks but still dared not drink the water.

She made a longer solitary foray because she now considered the reeds her friend. She was surprised she had any imagination left to create a fantasy out of the place. Her confusion over Schlegel holding her hand had abated. No motive beyond reassurance, she told herself, and how often in the past months had she craved that.

At the edge of the reeds open land stretched ahead, and, beckoning like a shimmering mirage, or miracle, a squat water tower and a field of cabbage. The surroundings lay empty, the way clear. Fortune favoured the brave, she told herself, and in platitude lay hope. She was almost happy. Food. Water. The place to herself. She scuffed the dirt with her toes, remembered fallen leaves. She watched her feet, not because she had to as one did in the camp, where the first lesson was never look up, but because she wanted to.

The plane came out of nowhere, from behind, so close that Sybil glimpsed the goggled pilot's gaze. A singing and whistling in her ears was followed by the report of the shot; no mistaking that. Someone was firing at her. There, on the horizon, blurred by the heat haze, she saw the line of riders starting forward.

She ran back and tore blind through the reeds, lungs bursting, panic leaping, trusting instinct. She passed the canoe and the jetty.

She paused long enough to grab Schlegel and drag him away, ignoring his grunts of pain.

She worked their way deeper into the channels. When the land gave up she splashed on, hoping the water was shallow enough to wade. They ran themselves to a standstill and stood bent double, hands on knees, sucking air. Schlegel caught his breath enough to say the plane flew over so low it had seemed about to crash. He didn't add that he had stood paralysed at the thought of them being picked off separately, certain only that he did not want to die alone.

He realised he had left the gun, which he had put aside to prevent it from digging into him when lying down.

They listened. No sounds of pursuit. They followed the next creek until it became little wider than a trench. The reeds grew higher, leaving only a slit of sky. Schlegel found the water easier on his foot. They moved silently, listening. The plane circled high above.

The water grew shallower until it barely covered their ankles and the channel disgorged into a delta of marshy grassland, a stretch of a hundred metres, beyond which more reeds. Sybil said it was too dangerous to walk but the ground was broken up enough to crawl across.

They crossed without incident. Schlegel thought by then there was nothing to distinguish them from the primeval landscape. The channel opposite was deeper and more choked, sometimes so dense they had to clear a path.

The increasingly foul water reached to Sybil's shoulders and Schlegel's chest. They passed a sodden dead wading bird floating stickily, one orange pencil-like leg snapped off. Schlegel feared that soon neither the water nor land would be negotiable. He was about to say they should turn back when Sybil held up her hand and lowered herself until only her head was visible, pressing back into the side of the bank.

Schlegel heard the scrape of reeds against the boat and casual swearing as he sank down in the water.

One voice cursing to himself, bored more than annoyed.

Schlegel saw the canoe's emerging prow and submerged himself. The sludgy water left him unable to see anything of the surface. He counted until he could hold his breath no longer and rose to find the canoe still there, drifting and apparently empty until a man with a half-smoked cigarette sat up. Schlegel saw forage cap, spectacles and a kid in uniform.

The canoe tipped easily. Schlegel saw the big circle of surprise made by the boy's mouth, heard the hiss of cigarette hitting the water, felt the squirm of flesh and held down hard, meeting little resistance, other than weak, involuntary thrashing. The bubbles of the boy's last gasp broke the surface in a thin stream, followed by angrier gassy belches. Schlegel continued to hold down until he was sure the lungs were flooded.

He stopped, opened his eyes, shut tight from the exertion, only for the water to explode in front of him. Hands clamped his throat, cutting off his air supply, pressing until the inside of his eyes felt they were bleeding. He went under. Water poured in through his nose. As the grip intensified a tiny undimmed part of his brain wondered inconsequentially if he would die from strangulation before he drowned. He thought: A life struggle and still distracted by all the wrong details – how the boy still had his glasses on; the way his own fingertips had puckered from being too long in the water. His throat felt like it was swallowing coals, then something gave.

Schlegel broke the surface with a roar. The boy's body floated on its back, blood in the water from where Sybil had whacked his head with the canoe paddle. He lay dazed and blinking and looked about to cry as Schlegel pushed him back under.

This time Schlegel waited until Sybil said, 'That's enough now. Stop.'

The cigarette floated on the surface, shedding tobacco.

They turned back, in case the canoeist was scouting for a patrol. From the angle of the sun Schlegel calculated it was late afternoon. Clouds were building, signalling a change after such unseasonable heat.

Hope was no longer part of the equation, but their luck had held.

With the lakes behind them, they decided better the partial shelter of woods than the open. But in the trees they wandered aimlessly, finding no way out. Tempers frayed. Sybil said one way. Schlegel didn't have the strength to argue. Lack of concentration made him careless. He wondered if it was possible to eat raw acorns.

As it was, they dined sumptuously on blackberries until their mouths and hands were stained purple. Sybil had been right: the trees ended and there were the watchtowers, half a kilometre ahead, with the railway in the distance and surrounding them huge hedges of blackberries, past their best but enough to gorge on.

They counted the towers away from the railway line until

they came to the fifth. A thorny hedge offered the best shelter until nightfall. Schlegel lay on his back and used his feet to clear the brambles. He emerged scratched and bleeding as the first splashes of rain hit the ground, kicking up puffs of dust, then falling hard and heavy, soaking them, and they lay on their backs, half out of the shelter, mouths open, drinking it in.

They moved forward through the dark curtain of rain. Fifteen or twenty minutes of muddy progress to reach the strip. The wet smear of the arc lights barely penetrated the night. The only sound was the relentless downpour. Sybil's heart was in her mouth and she feared she would vomit it up, along with a purple stream of blackberries.

At the edge of the strip Schlegel was about to set off when he saw the tripwire, a metre off the ground, visible only because of its silvery glisten. He pointed it out then gestured to say he was making his move, and reached out to touch her hand for luck.

The rain blunted the range of the lights. He could not see the watchtowers at all as he crawled forward.

Sybil followed, timing her arms to follow his movement, as though bound by a cord.

As Schlegel reached the fence the rain stopped as abruptly as it had started. The sound turned to dripping leaves. The dark corridor was reduced to a meagre strip as the lights achieved full penetration. He could see the towers and reasoned if he could see them . . . A man coughed.

Schlegel inched under the fence. He paused and waited. Sybil seemed to have fallen behind. He couldn't see her. He pressed on, trusting her to catch up. The edge of the outer strip grew visible. A guard in the tower hawked phlegm.

He was about to move forward when he saw three metal

rods sticking out of the ground next to where his hand had come to rest. A mine. The slightest contact would detonate it. Schlegel stared in disbelief. Broad had promised the ground was clear. When it came to her turn Sybil wouldn't know it was there. Schlegel had no choice but to turn back and warn her. The situation suddenly appeared beyond hopeless. He was starting to make his way back when the area burst into light, exposing the towers, the fence, the strip, down to the rods of the mine. The light came from ahead, some sort of mounted searchlight, Schlegel supposed, waiting for them, smaller than the big arc lights, but blinding.

He was on his feet and running, throwing himself down, rolling under the wire, dragging Sybil with him. No one fired. He saw the mounted riders silhouetted ahead.

Two men on foot ran to intercept them. Schlegel tugged Sybil on, refusing to let go. He used her weight to swing himself into the man running at him, sending him spinning away into the strip where he flew apart, the blast of a mine freezing his shape for a moment before it disintegrated, which was the last thing Schlegel remembered.

He came to upside down, slung across a horse, tied and with a bag over his head. He heard the heavy Berlin growl of Baumgarten, addressing Sybil as princess.

Sepp lisped, 'Come and live with us. We'll teach you to skin a pig.'

Baumgarten said, 'Say goodbye to Romeo. He will look very different when you see him next.'

Schlegel passed out and came to in what sounded like a cobbled courtyard. He was hauled down, untied and pushed around until he was reeling. The hood was torn off and he stood dizzy as Baumgarten slapped him hard, then patted him like a trainer geeing his boxer for the next round's battering. Schlegel was unashamed to ask not to be hit again.

Baumgarten had something else in mind: a bottle whose contents Schlegel was forced to swallow; sharp, bitter-tasting and toxic. His brain immediately fogged. They laughed at his drunken staggering as he saw them all double, thinking they would lead him like an animal to slaughter. He shoved his hand down his throat, disgorging foul bile, stained with blackberry.

He came to upside down again, with the hood back on, otherwise naked. From the pressure on the back of his knees and wrists he could tell he was suspended from the pole which had been Haas's final destination. He tried to concentrate on points of pain to prevent his imagination running out of control. The hinges of his knees felt like they had been soldered to the metal. His arms were being pulled from their sockets. His breathing was constricted by the hood. The bag smelled of vomit.

He regained consciousness to find himself being stared at by Sepp from upside down. Baumgarten untied him from the pole and let him fall to the floor, where he lay cramping and wailing, his knees locked. They kicked him until he adopted an ungainly crawl. Like a monkey with its arse stuck in the air, said Sepp.

They made him make chimpanzee noises, bark and oink. Sepp insisted on sitting on him. Schlegel smelled the liquor coming off him in waves. Sepp was back in killing mode.

Sepp recited, 'And Jesus, when he had found a young ass, sat thereon; as it is written.'

Baumgarten watched, all the while doing a shuffling dance and beating out an invisible rhythm with his hands.

Sepp, bored of riding, looked at Baumgarten and announced with simple glee, 'Jesus was a carpenter.'

Baumgarten guffawed. 'No mention in the Bible whether he could hammer a straight nail.'

They lugged him carelessly, still naked, knees locked, down to the slaughterhouse, past bellowing cattle panicked by the thick smell of blood. A party was going on in the far corner of the hall, the space dressed like a drawing-room theatre set, with hanging drapes, cushions, sofas and chaises longues lit by a dozen standing candelabra. Women lounged in states of undress. Schlegel was paraded like a guest of honour. A plump nude reclining on a sofa inspected him and asked if he was Jewish. Someone strummed drunkenly on an out-of-tune guitar.

Schlegel was crushed by the terrible obviousness of his debasement, the debauched killers, the women so lazily comfortable. The nude said, 'Birthday suit.' Another laughed and asked, 'What's wrong with your legs, dearie?'

'A bit of cramp,' Sepp answered.

The most unsettling item was a set of splintered doors, angled up against the wall, used for target practice.

Sepp said to Baumgarten, 'Let's get some drink down ourselves. It's wasted on him.'

They gave Schlegel a milkmaid's stool to sit on. He asked for something to cover himself. Sepp went off and returned with a sack and bayonet he used to cut a hole for Schlegel's head and two for his arms. When Schlegel had it on Sepp struck a pose.

Some soldiers wandered in and a table of cards was set up. The women attached themselves to the men and were idly pawed.

Schlegel saw the scene as a pathetic example of the kind of corruption they had been sent to expose. Worse, he was watching a version of himself, smashed, chasing easy women.

Sepp produced another lethal giggle, looked at Schlegel's crooked knees and said, 'It looks like he needs to stretch his legs.'

The only comfort Schlegel could take was if they were going to kill him they would have done so already.

Even when he saw the hammer and nails, and Sepp and Baumgarten manipulating the doors onto the floor, he did not believe what they were going to do.

Sepp drove the nails through Schlegel's wrists. Big, black masonry ones, banged through the gap between artery and bone. Sepp grunted with satisfaction. When Schlegel screamed the room barely bothered to look up.

The agony of the second nail was even more excruciating. Sepp boasted he'd got the medial nerve as Schlegel's hand contracted and locked.

They levered the doors back against the wall and gave Schlegel the stool for his bent legs.

Squabbles broke out and a fight over a woman ensued when one man insisted on taking over from another, saying it was his turn. Bolts of agony travelled down Schlegel's arm from the nerve Sepp had trapped. At least he found he could gradually stretch his legs, which relieved the pressure on his arms.

Sepp used paraffin to light a large portable stove for a haunch of beef which he skewered for roasting.

Pain consumed Schlegel, leaving only the sensation of his body reduced to meat as surely as the turning haunch.

The set was completed with the introduction of Sybil in a ghastly parody of triumphal procession, carried on a chair by Baumgarten and Sepp, blindfolded, hands tied to the arms. She looked around sightless, her head twisting this way and that. Schlegel called her name. It made no difference. She sat like a marionette with its strings cut, only her head continuing its jerky movement, this way and that.

Someone put on a scratchy windup gramophone. An aria. *'Mon coeur s'ouvre à ta voix'*.

*

Berlin lay under a dirty blanket of cloud, occasionally relieved by a liverish sun. The city looked older, ageing badly, buildings reduced, endless grey, more shut than open. People wandered listlessly; there was talk of coming raids. Young men were conspicuous by their absence, apart from foreign workers – that cosmopolitan stew they were so afraid of – plus the bureaucrats, women and children.

Morgen had spent several days telephoning Bormann's office for an appointment, pulling every string he could think of, always being told the man was interested and to call back the next day. Morgen suspected he was being given the brush-off but after persisting he was given a time to present himself the following morning.

Otherwise he did nothing but lie low at a cheap hotel, in a faded chintzy room, very uncertain of his position regarding the various authorities.

The visitors' entrance to the Chancellery involved the rigmarole of signing in and being issued a pass, after which he passed down great, empty, endless hallways and upon reporting to the secretarial room was made to wait.

After an insolently long delay he was called into a grand office with a big desk. Bormann was overweight and jowly. His neck bulged over his collar. One of the desk thugs, Morgen thought, as he watched the man fiddle with his wedding ring. Bormann stood to go through the saluting business, then roared to ask what sort of mischief Morgen was up to.

Morgen stood his ground, pointing out he was a judge sworn to law.

'Ultimately, we live in a nation of laws, and there are limits that even the Party must respect.'

That was too much for Bormann, who shouted, 'How can you permit yourself to speak to me that way? You have no understanding of state matters. You're nothing. Get out!'

Morgen lasted less than a minute. Yet, even as it happened, such an obvious show of bad temper seemed staged, down to Bormann physically hustling him from the room. Morgen stood blinking at the secretaries, who looked as if it wasn't the first time this had happened. Morgen bowed at them and left.

Only outside did he realise Bormann probably never intended an audience. He was a captive of the building: to get out he had to surrender his pass. He was sure the guard had already been told to stop him leaving.

Desperate to think, Morgen went to the canteen where the coffee was as bad as everywhere else.

If people were animals then Bormann would be a pig, except pigs were more prepossessing and social. However difficult, Morgen knew he had to go back and at all costs change Bormann's mind. Better that and get thrown out trying rather than meek surrender.

He returned to the secretaries' room and said he had one more important message to give.

To Morgen's surprise, the door was opened and Bormann stood there calmer, with an almost cheeky grin as if to say Morgen had passed a test to weed out time-wasters.

Morgen said, 'In fact, I have come to ask your advice and instructions for continuing investigations.'

Bormann became transformed. 'Please, I am at your service. Have a seat.'

Bormann gestured with a cigarette to ask if it was all right to smoke, saying the Führer disapproved. Both men lit up.

Morgen thought: It comes down to a man in a room behind a desk. Bormann was the spider of power. No splendid uniform. No medals. One who stayed back, watching, calculating. Morgen felt no more confident of his chances of getting out.

He took a deep breath and said, 'Party Secretary, is it not true that in the personnel file of every camp commandant, chief of security and so on there is a copy of a declaration, signed by him, saying that the Führer decides about the life of an enemy of the state?'

Bormann fiddled with his wedding band. 'Yes, that is correct.'

'Is it also correct that this power had been delegated to you and no one else?'

'Also correct.'

'What would you think then, if someone far beneath you killed prisoners on his own initiative, at his own discretion?'

'That's impossible, it doesn't happen.'

'You see, that's how people disregard your authority in this particular camp. That's why I have arrested them.'

Bormann said, 'But that's a different matter. I hadn't seen it that way.'

'A challenge to your authority.'

Morgen watched the numbers turning in Bormann's head until he said, 'What exactly is it that you want to put on the table?'

'Commandant Hoess. Fegelein.'

Bormann gave a thin smile. 'Let's not start at the bottom!'

Morgen said Fegelein faced a charge of homicidal driving. There was a witness.

Bormann consulted a paper on his desk. 'Sadly died.'

Morgen looked at Bormann, shocked.

Bormann returned his gaze, with a hint of a smile. 'After a short illness.'

Morgen felt himself slipping. 'Nevertheless, I wish to interview Fegelein.'

'He is away. File me a request and I will deal with it in due course. The commandant?'

'He is among those who operated outside the law.'

'That is Pohl's business to settle. The matter is in hand.'

'Hoess also had an affair with a woman.'

'What of it?'

'She is Jewish.'

Bormann considered and said, 'You are wrong. She is not.'

The look he gave Morgen said he knew she was. The deadly game had gone up a level. Bormann had blocked his move.

Morgen countered by saying, 'Perhaps I could have that in writing. To avoid any further confusion.'

Bormann laughed. 'What would I write?'

'That the woman is not Jewish.'

Bormann went along with the game, producing an expensive fountain pen. He scratched a couple of lines on Chancellery paper, stamped it and handed it to Morgen saying, 'Have your pawn.'

Morgen carefully folded the paper and placed it in his wallet, feeling less guilty about using Sybil now he had acquired her exemption, providing Bormann let him out of the building after all.

He knew he should leave.

Bormann regarded him expectantly.

'I have a personal question, if that is not impertinent.'

'We are in my office, not a bar,' Bormann said coldly.

Morgen could see the man was curious nevertheless. He took another deep breath and said, 'I received a message from you through Fegelein to say the commandant was not to be investigated. As I am here I thought I would ask why.'

'I could say it is no business of yours but the answer is old loyalties.'

'I merely wish to understand how the commandant came to deserve your allegiance.'

Morgen waited, realising Bormann was pleased to have an excuse to relate his story.

'In the early days before the Party there were among the idealists who wished to do something for the Fatherland many confidence men, adventurers and scoundrels. These included a fraud named Kadow, who passed himself off as a war veteran, wore medals he hadn't won and swindled the organisation of which I was treasurer. He was warned not to show his face again, and when he did, being a fool, a group of men got him drunk and found in his pockets a membership card of the Communist youth group and roubles. I had ordered only for him to be taught a lesson, but Kadow died. Hoess was one of those convicted and he was sentenced to ten years. He knew of my instruction yet never squealed to get himself a better deal, so I only served a year. They were tough times. Since no court would have sentenced Kadow, we passed our own judgement. Feme.'

Morgen was familiar. Feme was an improvised justice based on a medieval system of secret tribunal.

'When was this?'

'Twenty years ago.' Bormann gave Morgen a mirthless smile. 'Headstrong young boys.'

He stood and said, 'There is something I should like you to consider.'

Morgen realised he had probably already walked into the trap. Not worth the paper it was written on, he thought of the signed declaration in his pocket. It was probably his death warrant.

Bormann stood behind Morgen and placed a hand on his shoulder.

'There is an embarrassment concerning your young

associate. He has managed to get himself arrested for arson.'

'Arson?'

Bormann said Schlegel had been caught stealing and set fire to the evidence. Morgen knew such a preposterous story was all too likely in Pohl's world.

He immediately asked himself where Bormann fitted in this intrigue.

'There will be a trial. You need to attend as his ranking officer.'

'I have already been warned I will be shot on sight if I return.'

'I will issue a personal warrant in my authority.'

Morgen suspected that, like Sybil's exemption, it would be worthless.

The obvious answer was that Bormann had done a deal with Pohl to have Morgen returned so he could be taken care of too.

'There's a train tonight. You will be back tomorrow. I will give you an escort, so no one gets up to any monkey business. I lost a good ally once who mysteriously fell from the window of his sleeping compartment. Suicide was the given verdict but he was in good spirits when I last saw him. We wouldn't want the same to happen to you.'

Bormann's hand rested on Morgen's neck. He said, 'I am glad we had this little talk.'

He shook hands this time rather than saluted. The handshake was moist and lacklustre.

Morgen had just enough time to go to the newspaper library and look up the Kadow case. One of the anomalies of life was that while the press was muzzled back issues of old publications were still available for inspection in all their messy glory.

The case was as Bormann had told.

Without its political context, the shortest reports read as nothing more than a fight between drinking companions, in which a death had occurred. It took one of the more sensational newspapers to report the gory details. Kadow, drunk to start with, was plied with more alcohol and at closing time taken off in a cart on the promise of a coffeehouse with women. When the blows came it was six against one. Fists. Sticks. Rubber truncheons. Kadow was dragged down from the cart and beaten in a meadow. The 22-year-old Hoess was named as breaking off a sapling maple and bringing it down full force on Kadow's head until his skull fractured. The man's teeth were kicked out. His throat was cut, two bullets fired into his head and the corpse buried in the forest, to be dug up later by the police.

The ferocity of the violence was like a presage of things to come, as if everything had been foretold in that squalid drunken murder.

All the accounts spoke of six assailants, except one, which mentioned a seventh.

Bormann had claimed not to have been involved. Morgen was sure he was, in with the rest, battering and kicking and gouging, then absenting himself, already a master of disappearance, the unaccountable man who was never there.

When Morgen left Berlin rain was hammering on the station roof. The platform was crowded, the train late, like the last time. The only difference, apart from Schlegel's absence, was the unmistakeable sight of two thugs, loitering in the crowd, men in raincoats with hats worn low, laughable in their obviousness. Morgen, careless and a little drunk, had taken no precautions. The men boarded the train after him.

*

The trial took place after how long Schlegel had no idea. Time had ceased to exist outside an infernal present. At some twilight point, Broad had strolled into the slaughterhouse, so relaxed he didn't look twice, and said, 'That's enough, boys. He has a trial to face.'

A suit was found for him, double-breasted, jacket too big, trousers too short. No tie and laceless shoes.

The process took place in the usual room in the punishment block.

Everything became speeded up. Scrape of chairs as all stood. The travelling assizes judge positioned centre. A couple of bored makeweights. Stenographer. A legal clerk. On the wall behind the judge, a portrait of the leader, stern and messianic. Schlegel was spared the salute because handcuffed. To the right of the judge, the man whose presence Schlegel blanked. The nerve of him, showing up like that!

Charges. A sublime cameo from Frau Hoess, dressy and sombre in hat and veil. What an outfit! Speaking of what he had stolen. Evidence produced. Yes, she said. Next, no witness but a report on the man he had drowned: homicide. Next, no witness: charge of aiding a prisoner to escape.

Words made individual sense; joined up, none.

Schlegel offered nothing in his defence. The witnesses were radiant in their certainty of his depravity. He had spoken up once to say Frau Hoess had taken sexual advantage. An audible gasp. Frau Hoess's *froideur* allowed for no interpretation other than that such a liaison beggared belief, adding, 'You can see he is quite mad.' They nodded.

He hoped in vain Sybil would be introduced so he could see her again. At least she had survived without violation, with Baumgarten saying: Just a bit of innocent fun, come back another time and we will really show you how to shove it.

Schlegel thought he might as well be watching a

projection in his head. His mind now seemed to occupy its own lonely, floating auditorium, above everything. He had looked back when Frau Hoess had warned him not to. He should have listened to her.

Ten minutes, twenty minutes? No clock in the room. The whole thing unceremonious for its speed. Everyone beyond care; get it over with. Schlegel's wrists were bandaged. He was doped up on something that wrapped him in a cocoon – the word shaped itself and died in his mouth – making him docile and stupid, a spectator of someone else's fate.

He continued with all his might to resist Morgen's presence, sitting there as part of the presiding body. He could only suppose the man had done his deals, made his peace and part of the price was he attend this charade. That was the most charitable explanation Schlegel could come up with, given that Morgen should have been shot on sight.

Outside the weather had broken for good. Fog and drizzle. Berlin weather.

Did Schlegel have any last words? He wished he could rally enough to denounce the lot of them, especially Morgen. He made a point of staring and Morgen steadfastly refused to look back.

No, he said. The charges were technically correct and entirely false. The best he managed was to mumble that he did not recognise the authority of the court, and to address the judge to say, 'Let their blood be on your head.'

The judge banged his hammer and shouted order.

He pronounced the death sentence. Thirteen charges in all, including setting the fire that had destroyed the evidence. A witness to that too, a man he had never seen before, produced to be asked: 'Did you see this man standing before you set fire to the building?' He recited the sentence back like a bad actor trying not to forget his lines.

A show trial, ha-ha, thought Schlegel, starting to come down. What did Morgen make of it? He could see the old Morgen shrug and say: Justice is seen to take its course. The new Morgen, he had no idea.

A last choice, offered with insolent politeness. Death by hanging or firing squad. His decision.

The judge informed him that the cost of his execution would be deducted from his final pay packet.

Schlegel's cell door was banged. Visitor!

His hope was Sybil, however unlikely.

Instead it was the one person he never would have guessed.

He had to look twice, thinking why had they sent him an old woman. His mother had aged – a gaunt figure, confused, her pride extinguished. Dressed neatly but shabbily. She wept on seeing him, asking what had they done to him, what had he done to himself? They clung to each other, for the first time in as long as Schlegel could remember. He felt sticklike bones. He could tell she was privately disappointed by her errant, wayward son, undone by dishonour. He would have preferred she had not seen him this way. He watched her lose her words, saw a flash of her former self when she said her memory was shot. Weakness was not something she had ever admitted to. Had she been told it was a last visit?

Schlegel thought: One leaves knowing no more of the world than when one came in.

Nothing connected, other than a few rotten memories that could just as well have been borrowed or appropriated.

In a while his mother would still be there and he wouldn't; that was all. Did it even matter if he went out with dignity or was dragged to the wall in a screeching funk? He might almost prefer the latter because it suggested life was still worth clinging to when all evidence stated the contrary.

As for his mother being there, he knew it was unlikely to be a mercy visit.

Her explanation had the illogic of another bad dream.

News of her transfer had filled her with trepidation, she said. She had remained secure where she was and had influential people on the outside working on her behalf. She had been advised of a camp for VIPs and her name was down for that. When told she was being sent there instead she had wept in despair.

She whispered, 'People say this a place from which you don't return.'

How had she known he was there? he asked.

'Oh, Frau Hoess told me. I work for her now,' she said brightly. 'She asked for me because of you. Thank you, darling!'

Morgen tried to remember his trigonometry. He presumed he was dealing with a triangle consisting of Bormann, Pohl and Himmler and it was a matter of calculating the correct angles. It was evident Bormann was making a play sending him back; it would be political because Bormann was not one to act on a whim. Morgen had presumed as a gesture to Pohl; now he wasn't sure. Bormann's dubious magic pass seemed to be doing its job, leaving him at least shunned, as though he were contagious.

Himmler's role was hardest to decipher, having been absent throughout, or operating on a deeper level than Morgen was aware of, for which he would probably need Heini's alchemists to decipher.

These calculations didn't even get him as far as

Kammler's stratagems or the role of his increasingly enigmatic brother.

Bormann had scotched Morgen's pursuit of Hoess by contradicting Sybil's Jewishness, thereby protecting his old friend.

Krick reappeared and made no mention of their previous meeting or discussion.

Sybil remained missing in that Morgen didn't know where she was and his enquiries yielded nothing, especially from Groenke. Morgen had no idea whether she was safe or in jeopardy.

He didn't know what to do about Schlegel. He knew he should go and see him yet didn't.

His failure to discern Bormann's motive for sending him back started to drive him crazy.

News came through that the commandant was being kicked upstairs, into the camp inspectorate, a straight job swap with the garrison's new commandant. Morgen supposed Kammler had achieved his aim by ushering in a new regime more attuned to his methods. Pohl had done his job, protecting his man, and the cold-hearted Bormann had shown a rare example of loyalty in that Morgen supposed it was he who had told Pohl how to sort out the mess.

What his own moves were, Morgen had no idea. He suspected his magic pass could become invalid at any moment.

The other big news was that Frau Hoess would be staying and not even moving house to make way for the new commandant, who was said to be a bachelor.

The commandant left the garrison a frail imitation of his former self, a man lost. He spent his last days riding the field. Winter almost.

Schulze found herself travelling on the same train, sharing a compartment reserved for staff, which they had to themselves, prior to adjourning to their separate sleeping berths. The commandant seemed not to recognise her, then only distantly and asked to be reminded.

'The construction department?' he said vaguely.

He offered her a sandwich, made by his wife. She declined, out of politeness.

Before leaving she had gone to Broad to say she needed a name for the father to be eligible for the pregnancy care programme. Krick had refused, believing the child not to be his, and Schlegel was disqualified. Broad's agreeing didn't surprise her. That he asked for nothing in exchange did, only joking to say if he was the father he should get to know the mother better, then stopping to add, 'There's a new word going around. Called hope.'

The commandant wiped sandwich crumbs off his trousers. He stared at Schulze but addressed himself. 'Until the daybreak, and the shadows flee away, so the litanies of lust rise amid the filthy stench of the abattoir, but thou art all fair, my love; there is no spot in thee. Yea, the evil one cheats all those that give themselves up.'

The odd thing was, she thought, he sounded quite normal. He turned away and she saw his tears.

The train passed the new camp. The security lights were coming on though it was not yet dark. Schulze was stunned by the endless enormity of what they had built. It went on and on. She had managed to avoid going there after its first days. Her life since had been contained entirely by the garrison. The chimneys blazed and she remembered how the early work shifts ran round the clock, night generators powering temporary arc lamps, the distinctive knock of their diesel engines broken by the scream of a prisoner as he trod on a live wire and short-circuited the system, the incident registering out of no more than the corner of her eye. She did a lot of bicycling that winter down to the surveyor's hut which doubled as the site office. It had no telephone, requiring messages to be taken by hand. When the road was icy or after a snowfall she had to walk or cadge a lift. The Russians stared at a woman alone. Walking home in the dark she thought about them eating each other.

When the camp finally disappeared the commandant said, 'It is not what I had in mind.'

Morgen sought out Broad, that astute reader of which way the wind was blowing. The main victim of the internal war was his own department. The story was no more tough punishment. Cooperation was being encouraged, with the prison hierarchy's loyalty being bought through rewards and incentives.

'There will still be a day of reckoning,' Morgen said.

'They're talking about it already,' said Broad.

Morgen suddenly thought: Bormann and Kammler. In tandem?

Kammler possessed what looked like close to genius when it came to seeking those with the most power. He had attached himself to Himmler and Speer, both of whose stars could be said to be waning, which was not the case with Bormann.

He thought of Krick's Swiss moves and supposed Kammler had knowledge of them, if not actively involved. Cultivating Bormann as well meant he must have a foot in both camps.

The day of reckoning. Morgen suddenly had a glimmer of what Bormann had in mind.

He had inadvertently played into Bormann and Kammler's hands by arguing that the whole Auschwitz death operation was a rogue enterprise.

Morgen now suspected Bormann was sending him back precisely to distance the top level from the perpetrators, to prove the opposite of the truth, which was they'd had their hands all over the thing from the start. He had been naïve to believe otherwise.

Bormann saw what no one else had: Morgen would no longer be a problem if he became part of the solution. Broad was right: someone would come one day and start taking names, for they all knew too much. Bormann clearly intended that he, Morgen, be the inquisitor, the one who erased all trace of the record, so the top could deny such things had happened with its knowledge.

It was an exquisite move.

Morgen made his own moves, flimsy as they were. Whatever else others had in mind he would continue to weed out corruption. To that end he recruited Broad, saying he could not afford not to throw in his lot. Broad, amused by any level of game playing, was amenable. He seemed grateful for being able to start distancing himself. Morgen recruited Palitsch with a view to sending him back into the garrison later as his investigator, setting a fox to catch a fox. Morgen was sure they hadn't even started to scratch the surface. He backtracked with Dr Wirths, saying he would value his strategic alliance. He apologised and said he'd had to run Grabner on a long lead to bring about his downfall.

Having lined up his ducks, Morgen was still left with a sense of utter defeat. Sybil's whereabouts remained unknown. As for Schlegel, he was at his wits' end trying to come up with a way of sorting out the boy.

Morgen drank alone at night. The space around him, if

not polite, was at least unobtrusive. He used the drink to try looking at things in a different way. What if the answer lay not in geometry and calculation but in leverage. He had been trying to work out everything by himself. He asked himself where he had leverage. The answer was obvious.

The commandant's wife was, Morgen was pleased to see, so astonished at the sight of him he thought she might faint.

'This will only take five minutes,' he said.

It took seven.

Schlegel got his execution. In the yard against the wall. He was the only one. Broad was the shooter. Unceremonious. He wouldn't want to do it again.

It was Morgen's idea. 'Otherwise they will keep you locked up here for months with all the red tape. I need you on the outside. Are you up for it?'

'Do you trust Broad that much?' was all Schlegel could think to ask. It was an astonishing proposal.

'Give him an extra packet of cigarettes to be sure.'

Not funny, thought Schlegel.

Meanwhile, Sybil was being brought back within Groenke's orbit.

Frau Hoess had been quick to see the sense of his proposal. Unless she acted on his behalf to find Sybil he would be forced to reveal to the Reichsführer-SS the worthlessness of her jade mine and that she had been hoodwinking him. There was also the small matter of Schlegel's courtroom accusation, which suggested she was with him when he was supposed to have been setting the fire.

Morgen sighed. 'Both would involve considerable dishonour. There would be no question of you being able to stay.'

She carried it off well, he thought, with grudging

admiration. Monstrous as she was, the woman was a terrific horse trader.

Schlegel left the punishment block technically as a dead man, in a cart of his own, with Broad driving.

Right up until the last second he could not be sure if he wasn't the victim of the ultimate practical joke and instead of firing wide the bullet would drill his brain and that would be that. It was done at night. Broad seemed sheepish almost as he slouched up the steps behind Schlegel. Schlegel addressed the wall.

'Any last words?' asked Broad, a joker to the last.

Schlegel felt the barrel against his neck, shut his eyes like he had been told, to stop brick dust getting in them, heard the bang in his ear, which vibrated from the report, and stood there in shock until Broad said, 'Now you have to fall over.'

After that they stopped pretending. No one was around. Broad stuck a cigarette in Schlegel's mouth and said, 'A new life.' The cigarette tasted foul but he persisted. He got up in the back of the cart of his own accord and lay down. Broad rode them through the camp gate into the garrison. Instead of going to the morgue he stopped by the remains of the burned-out building to let Schlegel down and tip an imaginary hat in farewell. Everything else was as Schlegel had been told, except there were no matches. The commandant's garden gate was still broken from when he had kicked it in. The door to the cellar was open, as was the steel door into the tunnel. It had been his idea to use it as his escape from the garrison, on the condition there was a torch or matches to light his way. As it was, he had to go through the whole business of scaring himself stupid in the dark, far more unsettling than the business in the yard. More than once he thought perhaps he was already dead.

He felt his way down the tunnel with agonising slowness until he reached the split and ran the rest of the way, stumbling in blind panic. After the dank oppression of the tunnel the night air was cool and sweet. He was to stay there, in the undergrowth by the road, for Morgen to collect him with Sybil and a car. That was the plan, except he waited and they didn't come, leaving him standing like a fool, paperless, without money, technically dead, wondering what on earth to do next.

The commandant's wife ate alone, thinking: I have my happy ending, staying on in my beautiful house with its fabulous garden. The only thing that spoiled her mood was that horrible little man Morgen with his insufferable moral superiority, which was why she had arranged for Juppe to be waiting for them at the gate, 'to check everything is in order'. Let them stew! Anyway, she had taken the precaution of telling the Reichsführer how she had been deceived by a Jewish conspiracy to discredit her and what she had been led to believe was the product of the mine was nothing of the sort. She had taken the necessary steps and those responsible had been punished.

She went upstairs, content, to join her younger children for their bedtime story. Her only remaining concern was that she was pregnant from before taking the precautionary measure of inviting her husband back into her bed.

She listened to Schlegel's mother read to the children. She had a beautiful voice but the children laughed at her because she couldn't remember her words, sometimes even the simplest.